Large Print Boc
Bockoven, Georgia.
A marriage of convenience

A MARRIAGE OF CONVENIENCE

Georgia Bockoven

A MARRIAGE OF CONVENIENCE

WHEELER
PUBLISHING, INC.
ROCKLAND, MA

★ AN AMERICAN COMPANY ★

Published in Large Print by arrangement with HarperPaperbacks, a
division of HarperCollins*Publishers*, in the United States and Canada

Wheeler Large Print Book Series.

Set in 16 pt Plantin.

Library of Congress Cataloging-in-Publication Data

Bockoven, Georgia.
    A marriage of convenience / Georgia Bockoven.
        p. (large print) cm.(Wheeler large print book series)
    ISBN 1-58724-007-6 (softcover)
    1. Custody of children—Fiction. 2. Birthfathers—Fiction. 3. Aunts—
Fiction. 4. Large type books.
    I. Title. II. Series

[PS3552.O282 M37   2001]
813'.54—dc21   2001017758
                                                          CIP

This book is dedicated with heartfelt love and appreciation to the nurses of the neonatal intensive care unit at Kaiser Permanente Hospital in Sacramento, California. A special thank-you goes to five incredible women who gave their compassion and friendship as well as their skills—Penny Conroy, Judy Gates, Denise Hirshfelt, Donna Lomax and Patti Read, and to Myra Pierce, M.D. and Stephen Greenholz, M.D. for going that extra mile and for caring.

Most especially, this story is a love letter to John Murdoch Bockoven, born October 18, 1989 at 2 pounds 2 ounces.

1

No one should have to die in August—not at twenty-six—and most especially not Diane Taylor.

The words echoed in Christine Taylor's mind, forming a litany of fear and despair.

Not Diane. Please God, not my beautiful little sister. Don't let this be happening. Let it be my worst nightmare.

Chris unzipped the overnight bag she'd brought into the house less than a half-hour earlier and dumped its contents in the middle of the bed. With shaking hands she sorted through the jumble, replacing the toiletries. She then went over to the Queen Anne dresser, yanked open the top drawer, and blindly grabbed a handful of silk and satin. Next, she stripped the three nearest hangers in the closet, grabbed a pair of flat-heeled shoes, and tossed it all into the suitcase.

Of course it was a nightmare, she insisted to herself as she poked stray pieces of clothing out of the path of the zipper. After the weekend she'd just put in, she was due for a few bad dreams.

But not this one. This hurt too badly. It was time to wake up.

She glanced at the clock on the nightstand. Her flight to Sacramento would leave in less than an hour and a half. She cursed her shortsightedness at buying a condominium on the opposite side of Denver from the airport. If she missed this plane, she would either have to wait until morning or fly to San Francisco and try to pick up a connecting flight. Either way, if her mother's message was to be believed, it would be too late.

How could Diane be dying on such an ordinary day?

How could Chris have so easily decided to switch her Sunday evening flight from Kansas City to Monday morning so that she could get a full night's sleep? It had seemed so logical, the perfect solution, but going to work directly from the airport meant she had been away from her answering machine at home for five days instead of four.

Chris shuddered when she thought how close she had come to postponing listening to her messages yet one more day. She'd come home exhausted, depleted of even the energy it took to make a peanut butter sandwich. Three successive out-of-state weekend conferences had translated into twenty-two straight days of work with no end in sight. As product manager for the new light beer Wainswright Brewing Company was introducing in two months, she felt its success or failure would be the result of the work that went into it at this preliminary stage. While the taste of the product was important, it was nothing compared to the image the product conveyed. Wine coolers had taught everyone in the industry an important lesson about marketing, one that none of them were likely to forget.

She was on her way to the front door when a compelling urge to try reaching her mother one more time came over her. She'd tried three times already, but no one had answered. Dropping the suitcase on the tile entranceway, she went into the living room and picked up the phone. As she waited for the connection to go through, the scene of only an hour ago played again in her mind.

Five minutes of ignoring the flashing red beacon on the answering machine was all she'd managed before letting out a resigned sigh and going over to rewind the tape.

A familiar beep had sounded, followed by an equally familiar voice: "Christine, this is your mother. You have no idea how much I despise these damnable machines. I want you to know, if it wasn't important, I would hang up."

How like her mother to greet and threaten in the same breath. Chris had moved to Colorado ten years ago, thinking distance might salvage what little remained of their mother-daughter relationship. But then everything had seemed possible at twenty-two.

"Your sister asked me to call you. For some reason, she thought you would be interested in knowing she's in the hospital here. I reminded her how busy you are with that job of yours and how hard it is for you to tear yourself away, but she insisted you would want to know.

"Anyway, according to the doctors, it doesn't look promising for the baby...or for Diane for that matter. She'd like you to come, but I told her not to count on it. You do what you want. You always do."

Doctors? Baby? Sacramento? What in the hell was going on? Chris had talked to her sister just a short time ago. Scanning her memory, Chris tried to pinpoint precisely when she'd last talked to Diane. Her heart sank. Could it really have been last May? Three and a half months ago?

Diane had telephoned the day before her own birthday knowing Chris always made a point of remembering the day with phone calls and a big bouquet of spring flowers. She said she was going to be out of town and didn't want to miss Chris's call or have her flowers decorating the front step while she was gone. To make up for the missed bouquet this year, she'd made Chris promise to send one twice as big the next.

Before Diane hung up she'd gone into a complicated explanation about having phone trouble. She ended by telling Chris not to worry if she couldn't get through, but to drop a note in the mail; as soon as it arrived, Diane would call her.

Which all made a perverse kind of sense now, but had seemed a little odd at the time—certainly not alarming or even noteworthy, except in hindsight. Chris had had no reason not to believe Diane; they had never lied to each other.

Until now.

The rest of the conversation had consisted of Diane going on and on about the man in her life, about how good it felt to finally be out on her own, and how much she loved living in Los Angeles. There hadn't been

4

word one about any baby or, God forbid, moving back to Sacramento.

Chris had tried calling a couple of times after that and reached a recorded message saying Diane's phone had been disconnected and that there was no new number. Because she'd had nothing important to say, Chris had decided to skip the note and try again later.

What in the hell was "It doesn't look promising for Diane or the baby" supposed to mean? How typical of her mother to be cryptic when there was something important, protracted when instilling guilt.

A message from a friend had followed, and then her mother's voice had come on the machine again: "For God's sake, Christine, where are you? Your sister needs you. Now!"

The edge of fear in her mother's anger had sent a chill down Chris's spine. She glanced at the regulator clock over the television. Eight-thirty. Her stomach knotted as she got up and crossed the room. How many hours ago had her mother called? How many days?

Chris had turned off the answering machine then, picked up the telephone, and punched the series of numbers that had belonged to Harriet Taylor longer than Chris had been alive.

But there hadn't been any answer. For what seemed like an eternity but couldn't have been more than a minute, Chris had stood frozen with indecision. What if her mother was exaggerating? What if she wasn't? Chris couldn't take the chance. She had started calling the airlines.

Now Chris glanced at the clock and then

at her suitcase, waiting by the front door. She waited for the sixth ring and had started to hang up when a breathless voice answered, "Taylor residence." It was Madeline Davalos, her mother's live-in companion.

"Madeline, it's Chris. My mother left a message—"

"Oh, Chris," she exclaimed. "I'm so glad you finally got back to us. Your mother has been frantic with worry. She'll be so glad you're here. Where are you? At the airport? Do you need someone to pick you up?"

"I'm at home, Madeline. I just got my mother's message and I wanted to call to find out what's—"

Her voice heavy with disappointment, Madeline said, "You've got to get here right away, Chris. The doctor told us there isn't much time. Your mother's at the hospital now. We've been there day and night. I just came back to pick up a fresh supply of her pills."

"What doctor?" Chris demanded, trying to anchor the incomprehensible in details.

"Monroe. He's the onco...onco...the cancer doctor who's been taking care of Diane."

"Diane has cancer?" Chris breathed.

"They found it when she first went in about the baby." Madeline's voice broke. There was silence and then a choked sob. "She wants to see you, Chris. She keeps asking if you're there yet."

"Which hospital?"

"The same one they took your father to when he had his heart attack."

"Do you have the number?"

6

Madeline paused. "Christine, you've got time to fight on the phone with your mother, or you've got time to see your sister before she dies. You don't have both."

"Tell her I'm coming," Chris said, relenting at last. She started to hang up. "Madeline?"

"Yes?"

"Tell Diane I love her...and that I'm sorry I wasn't there for her."

"She understands. Just hurry."

"I'm on my way." For an instant she considered telling Madeline which flight she would be on and to ask that someone be there to meet her, but then reconsidered. Madeline would have her hands full with Harriet. If Chris got to the airport in time, she could arrange to have a rental car waiting for her in Sacramento. If not, she would take a cab.

A mixed bag of memories nudged their way past desperate worry to serve as a cushion to Chris's frantic concern as she turned off the freeway and made her way toward the hospital down dark, tree-lined streets. Chris not only welcomed the memories, she clung to them, using them to keep her from thinking about what she would find when she saw Diane again.

Chris hadn't just left Sacramento ten years ago—she'd escaped. The half dozen times she'd returned since then had done nothing to heal the wounds. Each trip, she'd only needed to step through the front door of her mother's house to realize that the reasons she'd left would never be eased by something as benign as time. Finally, four years ago, after a particularly acrimonious visit, she'd given up and ceded California to her mother.

Somehow, it now seemed, she'd also managed to abandon Diane in the process. She'd never meant for that to happen. Chris had believed every word of the promise she'd made to her sister the day she'd left: distance would only separate them physically; in heart, mind, and spirit they would forever be as they were then—closer even, when the then sixteen-year-old Diane turned eighteen and came to live with Chris.

Only they hadn't counted on boyfriends and college and jobs interfering in their dream. They never lived together again after the day Chris left Sacramento. Then, somewhere along the way, they must have subconsciously bought into the belief that they would have each other forever or, if not forever, at the very least for another forty or fifty years. Believing in all of those tomorrows had made them complacent.

But could they have become so distanced from each other emotionally that Diane had felt she could no longer call on her sister? Was that possible? The thought sickened Chris.

She was almost past the hospital before she caught sight of a familiar landmark and slammed on the brakes. What had once been a single unit was now a multi-building complex, more evidence of the city's recent explosive growth. She parked and headed for the entrance, her heart in her throat.

Please, God, she prayed silently. Please, please, please let her still be alive. There is so much I have to say to her. I'm not asking for a miracle, just enough time to tell her I love her. Please, God.

The dimly lit lobby was empty. Her footsteps echoed loudly on the tile floor as she approached the registration desk.

A typewriter sounded somewhere in the labyrinth of offices behind the desk. Chris tapped the silver bell on the counter and waited. Several seconds passed. She rang the bell again. "Hello?" she called, leaning across the counter.

"Christine?" a voice called out behind her. "Is that you?"

Chris turned. A dark-haired woman stood across the lobby from her. "Madeline?"

"I've been keeping an eye out for you."

"How is she?" Chris asked. "Never mind. Just tell me where she is. You can fill me in on everything else later."

"I'll take you to your mother." Madeline spoke so softly Chris had to strain to hear her.

"I didn't come here to see..." Chris caught sight of Madeline's swollen eyes and swallowed hard against the sudden lump in her throat.

"Come with me," Madeline said, holding out her hand to Chris.

"Tell me."

"It's not for me to be the one."

"Please, Madeline," she begged. "Don't make me hear this from my mother."

The older woman stared at Chris for several seconds, her eyes glistening with unshed tears. She shrugged. Finally she simply said, "She's gone."

"What do you mean, she's gone?" Chris said, keeping her voice steady with great effort, clinging to the belief that the unthinkable could be held at bay with reason. Her sister couldn't be dead. Things like that happened to other people. People you read about in newspaper fillers, tragedies that saddened you until you turned the page and discovered the television you'd been thinking about buying was on sale.

"She died...ten minutes ago."

"Ten minutes?" Chris repeated numbly. What was that? Less time than it had taken for the runway to clear, or for the passengers in front of her to disembark from the plane, or to arrange for a rental car to be waiting for her when she arrived in Sacramento. "I didn't believe you," she said, her defenses crumbling. She leaned heavily against the wall. "I couldn't let myself believe you."

Madeline put her arms around Chris. "I know," she said. "I wanted to call you sooner, but Diane wouldn't let me. She was so sure everything would be all right. She didn't want to worry you. You know how she is...how she was."

Chris pulled away. She wasn't so naive as to think there weren't things in life that could knock her sister down, but to believe that there was something strong enough to keep her from getting back up again suddenly seemed like a betrayal. "Are you sure she's dead? She's a fighter," Chris insisted. "She's been a fighter since the day she was born."

"I know," Madeline said. "But it wasn't enough this time."

Chris's shoulders sagged in defeat. "Why didn't she tell anyone what she was going through?"

"She knew we would have tried to talk her into having an abortion. Diane was just being Diane. She really believed she was invincible. She thought her cancer could be put on hold while she incubated her baby. But seven months was all she had in her." Madeline fished a handkerchief from the pocket of her skirt and wiped her eyes. "Your mother didn't even find out Diane was back in town until last week."

"Of all the places she could have gone, why come here? She hated this city as much as I do."

"She couldn't find a doctor who would take care of her where she was, so she called Dr. Linden. He told her if she came to Sacramento he would take care of her himself. But then he decided Dr. Monroe should be called in because her cancer was spreading so fast. They tried everything, Chris—" She stopped to wipe her eyes again. "I'm rambling. That's not what you asked at all. As far as why she didn't call on you to help her, I'm sure it was because she didn't want to worry you, not because she felt you wouldn't support her."

"Worry me...worry me?" Chris shouted, flinging herself away from Madeline. Somehow, in the telling, the messenger had become tied to the message, giving blame a target. "I refuse to believe she checked herself into

11

this goddamned hospital to die with only you and mother at her bedside just because she didn't want to worry me. It doesn't make sense. There has to be more."

Madeline shook her head sadly. "I don't know what to say to you. If there was some way I could make it easier…"

Chris's anger disappeared as quickly as it had struck. "Tell me it isn't true," she pleaded.

"God knows I wish I could. She was like one of my own."

Several minutes passed in silence. Gradually Chris became aware of her surroundings again. The typewriter sounds had stopped; a woman stood at the counter, a concerned look on her face. "I want to see her," Chris said.

Madeline nodded. "I'll take you."

Chris pushed against the heavy wooden door and stood rooted as it silently swung open. Her gaze immediately fixed on the bed and the still figure lying under a neatly folded yellow bedspread. Not even in the dim light could she convince herself her sister was simply sleeping. She let the door swing closed behind her and waited for the soft click that would tell her she was alone, closed off from the prying eyes of a world that still believed the sun would come up in the morning, a world that still knew right from wrong.

There were no flowers, no cards, no balloons—nothing wishing the patient a speedy recovery. Plainly those who knew Diane had come to the hospital also knew she had come to die.

Chris moved to the bed and looked into her sister's face. Pain had etched deep lines around her eyes and mouth, making her look closer to fifty than twenty-six. Twenty-six. The only people who died of cancer at twenty-six were in those movie-of-the-week things. It didn't happen in real life. Not in Chris's life. Not in Diane's.

But it did. It had.

Chris tried to smooth the wrinkles around Diane's eyes. She kissed her and reached for her hand. "Damn it, Di," she said, her voice a choked whisper. "You held on all that time; couldn't you have waited ten more minutes? Didn't you know how much it would hurt if you left and I never got to say good-bye?" She closed her eyes, desperately willing her mind not to imprint this image of her sister. She didn't want to remember her this way. She wanted to remember the smile, the dancing eyes, the dimpled cheeks. "I would have waited for you."

A tear spilled from her eye, falling noiselessly to the taut yellow bedspread, forming a lopsided circle. "I would have done anything for you...all you had to do was ask."

The soft whir of a motor sounded behind Chris.

She stiffened. After four long years, the sound of her mother's wheelchair was as familiar as it had ever been.

"She did ask," Harriet said, moving from the shadow to the light. "With her last breath."

How like her mother to take even this from her.

Chris turned, prepared for battle. The words died in her throat. Harriet Taylor had aged a lifetime since their last meeting. While her back was as straight and unbending as ever, the rheumatoid arthritis had continued to work on the rest of her body. She seemed half her former size, frail and vulnerable. There was a sadness in her eyes that diffused the last of Chris's outrage over the intrusion.

"I assume you meant what you just told your sister," Harriet went on. "About doing anything she asked?"

"Of course I did."

"Good. That will make things much easier."

A warning sounded in Chris. "Why don't you just tell me what Diane said?"

Harriet stared at her dead daughter for a long time before acknowledging the one who was still living. When she looked up at Chris again, her eyes held a trace of their old fire. "She asked that you take her son and raise him as your own."

2

"The baby lived?" Chris asked, incredulous. "I thought Madeline said—"

"According to the doctor, seven months is all it takes anymore." Harriet turned her wheelchair so that Diane was no longer in her direct line of vision. She put her hand to the side of her face to shield her eyes when she looked at Chris. "He's not much to look at, but then, I didn't expect he would be."

"Still behaving true to form, I see, Mother. Never expect too much and you'll never be disappointed."

"I had hoped age would help modify that self-centered ego of yours, Christine. His looks have nothing to do with his heritage. Diane's cancer kept him from growing as he should have."

"What does that mean?" Chris tried to keep her voice steady, but even she could hear the fear.

"Don't worry, he's all there. He's small, that's all. Two pounds, I think they said."

"Two pounds!" she gasped, trying to imagine something so small—her purse weighed more, her neighbor's new kitten was bigger. Chris looked down at her sister. "Did she know?"

"Of course she did."

Anger flashed through Chris—at the waste, at the irretrievable loss. "I don't understand why she went through with it. Why sacrifice her life for a baby like that?"

"Ah, the maternal instincts of the feminist. How touching."

Chris gave her mother a venomous look. "You want to do battle over maternal instincts, Mother? If I'm not mistaken, you just lost a daughter." She left the rest unsaid.

"Touché," Harriet said softly.

Chris felt a swell of triumph that humiliated her. Diane deserved better. "Have you made any arrangements?"

"No." All strength left her voice. "She asked me to...but I just couldn't."

Don't you dare make me feel sorry for you, Chris inwardly raged. I need my anger to get through this. But it was no good. Her anger was spent, leaving only an overwhelming sadness. "I'll do it," she said, releasing her sister's unresponsive hand.

Chris followed her mother's van down Freeport Boulevard to Thirteenth Avenue. The two-story Federal style house had not been painted since Chris had last seen it. The fading green trim gave mute testimony to how long ago that had been.

She'd grown up here, played in the park across the street, named the ducks that lived in the pond, gone to the high school around the corner. She hadn't, however, gone to the college less than a quarter of a mile away. It was a community college, not nearly good enough for one of Harriet and Howard's children. Their friends might think they'd raised a dullard or, worse yet, that the family wasn't as wealthy as it appeared. In a neighborhood where status depended on such things—and status was all her mother had—one was nearly as bad as the other.

After two years at Mills College, the school Harriet had attended, Chris had quietly transferred to Berkeley, a modest enough rebellion that had ended in an explosion

16

when Harriet found out what she'd done and threatened to cut off all further support. Chris countered by declaring her emancipation. Paying her own way through school delayed her degree a year and a half, but the feeling of satisfaction was worth every hour she'd spent waiting on tables.

There were times when Chris was growing up when she wondered if it was possible for people to be allergic to each other. If so, she and her mother qualified. They had never seen eye to eye on anything. What looked red to Chris was orange to Harriet. Her mother was a staunch Republican; as soon as Chris was old enough to vote, she'd registered as a Democrat. If Chris loved a movie, her mother thought it was trash.

No matter how hard Chris had worked to please her mother, it was never enough—the dress was wrong for the party, her carefully brushed hair looked stringy, her conversation was dull and uninspired. Eventually Chris stopped trying, and the wedge between them grew wider with each passing year.

Chris pulled into the driveway behind her mother's car. As soon as she had helped Madeline operate the lift that unloaded the heavy wheelchair from the van and had seen her mother inside and settled with her customary evening snifter of brandy, she took a piece of paper from the telephone table and asked if there were any special instructions she should remember to tell the funeral director.

"I want 'Amazing Grace' played just before

17

the eulogy and 'Just a Closer Walk with Thee' right after," Harriet said.

Even though they were the same hymns that Harriet had insisted be played at her own mother's and father's funerals, as well as that of her husband, Chris wrote them down, because it was the way Harriet liked things done, nice and tidy, relying on notes rather than memory, having evidence to fall back on and someone to blame in case anything went wrong.

"And of course we'll have Reverend Cottle do the service, and...and..."

Chris glanced up from the paper. Tears were streaming down her mother's cheeks. She was rocking from side to side, shaking her head in denial.

"A mother shouldn't have to bury her children," Harriet said. "It's not right. It's not natural."

Kneeling beside her mother, Chris gently took one gnarled hand into her own. "Why don't we just have a small memorial service? It would be so much easier that way."

"Easier for whom?"

"For everyone," Chris said with a sigh.

"This is one time you can't take the easy way out."

Chris stood back up. Unless she did something to stop it, they would be at each other all night. "All right, Mother. We'll do it your way."

"I want a blanket of white roses covering the casket."

White roses were her mother's favorite

flowers, not Diane's. Diane had been a tulip and daffodil and lilac kind of person. Vibrant colors, undisciplined form, the kind of flowers you plunked in a vase and let find their own order.

God, could she really be doing this? It was her sister they were talking about. Gentle, sweet Diane. How could this awful thing have happened to her? Why had she chosen to die alone?

And where was the bastard who'd given her the child? Why wasn't he there, helping with the arrangements?

"Don't you mean a spray of white roses?" Chris asked. "After all, there won't be a casket."

"What are you talking about? Of course there will."

"Not when you cremate someone."

Harriet pulled her hand from Chris's. "Are you out of your mind?"

"It's what Diane would have wanted. You know that as well as I do. She tried to talk you into having Daddy cremated."

"I will not have my daughter put in some vase."

"She won't be. We can scatter her ashes in the ocean." The instant the idea came to her, it became the answer. "She loved the ocean, Mother. She doesn't belong in a casket. Let's set her free. Please think about it."

"I could think about it from now until the day they lay me out in my own casket, and the answer would be the same. I won't do it. It's heathen."

19

"No, it isn't. It's—"

Harriet reached for the control on the wheelchair and backed away from Chris. "I'll hear no more about it. Either do it the way I tell you or I'll go down there and do it myself. Is that what you're really after? If it is, just, tell me. Don't make me go through your game-playing."

They had picked up precisely where they'd left off four years ago. "I'm not playing any games with you," Chris said. "I never have."

"You think you can get what you want by—"

"Stop right there. The last thing either of us needs is to get into a fight. Tell me what you want and I'll make sure it's done."

Harriet eyed her suspiciously. "I'm not one to forget how the wolf got the sheep's clothing."

"What a charming comparison."

Several seconds passed before Harriet spoke again. "Tell them I want a closed casket...and only one day of viewing and..."

Chris continued to write, but stopped listening. She had found a way to tell her sister good-bye and nothing, no one, would stop her.

The funeral director was courteous and solicitous and eager to do whatever he could to accommodate Chris. She told him she would stay until the cremation could be performed. Although she jumped at every phone call, the day went more smoothly than she had imagined possible. Somehow the joining with Diane in one last rebellion took some of the sharp edges off the pain and allowed her to

20

function with a normality that reassured everyone around her. It bothered her that her mother would not have the chance to say a final good-bye, but she'd been unable to come up with a way to arrange it. In the quiet of the waiting room, she tried to convince herself her mother would someday understand and forgive her, but the thought was gone as quickly as it came.

Because Chris insisted everything be done as quickly as possible, she had only a few minutes alone with her sister. What had been Diane, the essence of her—the smile, the quick wit, the gentle temperament—was gone. Only the shell that had housed the indomitable soul remained.

It didn't matter. Chris loved the shell as she had loved the soul. Those were the arms that had reached for her a thousand times, in joy and in sorrow; the legs that had run behind and then alongside an older sister always eager to get somewhere in a hurry; the wondrously thick and shiny hair Chris had cut and combed and permed and wished a hundred times was her own.

Chris knew she would miss who Diane was the most, but never to see her sister again, never to know how she would have looked at thirty, at forty, as a grandmother, or as a tottering old lady leading an exercise class at her retirement home was a loss of something she had taken for granted. Eventually the loss would steal their closeness. Diane would forever be twenty-six. Chris would not. She would go on without her little sister, alone. What would they have in common if and when they ever saw each other again?

It wasn't fair. There were drug pushers and murderers and rapists walking around, being warmed by sunshine, breathing air sweetened by roses, hearing wind whispering through pines and not seeing or feeling or hearing any of it. Where was the sense to it?

Why?

Why?

Why? The word echoed unmercifully in her mind.

Brushing a strand of hair from Diane's forehead, Chris wondered if she would ever be able to forgive herself that there weren't more memories. How could she have let herself get so busy?

Grief overwhelmed her, stealing the last bit of strength she had held in reserve. She put her hands over her face to close out what she could no longer bear to see.

Her quiet tears had subsided when a door opened behind her and a man in a tan coat softly told her they were ready.

"Thank you," Chris told him. She kissed Diane goodbye, waited fifteen minutes to be sure nothing untoward would happen before her instructions could be carried out, and then headed for her mother's house.

Halfway there, she remembered the baby.

3

Chris stood outside the neonatal intensive care unit for ten minutes, walking the hallway, reaching for the door handle and then turning away, trying to figure out why she was reluctant to go inside. It wasn't like her to shy away from anything. She prided herself on being the kind of person who faced her problems head-on.

Opposite the nursery entrance was a bulletin board filled with pictures, a before and after gallery of premature babies. Wondering if her hesitancy was actually fear of what she would find inside, Chris stopped her pacing and gave the photographs a more thorough perusal. She found herself coming back, over and over again, to a picture of a man and woman with three stair-step children. The baby, small but plainly thriving, sat on the woman's lap. The man held two toddlers on his knees.

Slowly Chris began to recognize the emotion the photograph created in her. She was angry. The woman in the picture could have, should have, been Diane—if not for the two-pound infant lying in the other room. She knew it was irrational, but she couldn't help thinking that if only Diane had ended the pregnancy and treated the cancer more aggressively, she could have gone on to have other babies. But instead, Diane had traded her life, a life filled with infinite promise, to bring this one into the world.

Identifying her problem, feeling shame at her unreasoning anger, did nothing to make it go away. In her mind she knew the baby was innocent. He hadn't asked his mother to sacrifice her life for his. But Chris's heart wasn't listening. No matter how she rationalized, she kept coming back to the bottom line: if he had never been conceived, Diane would be alive. She would have had the needed surgery, taken the radiation therapy or chemotherapy, done whatever else was necessary, and gone on to be the mother of other children—perhaps not babies she had given birth to herself, but what difference did that make?

Chris turned to leave, deciding her dread of what she had to face when she got back to her mother's house was as much emotional baggage as she wanted to carry around with her that day. The baby could wait awhile. He wasn't going anywhere.

Just as she reached the end of the hallway, the blinds opened at one of the nursery windows for normal newborns. Opposite the window, the door that led to the labor and delivery area swung open. A man, obviously the father, still in surgical gown, paper boots and hat, came through the door, beaming. He was quickly followed by five other people, calling their congratulations, tripping over one another in their excitement.

They crowded around the window, eagerly peering inside. Involuntarily, Chris looked, too. A nurse dressed in maroon pants and a flowered top held a baby up for inspection.

In the hallway there we're sighs and exclamations, followed by hugs and kisses.

The strangers' joy compounded Chris's sorrow, but it did something else, too, something totally unexpected. The protective instinct that had flared in her and wrapped itself around her sister shifted so that it now included her sister's baby. By God, there might not be joy and celebration over his birth, but she would see to it that he was not ignored.

She returned to the door with the cartoon mouse in the window holding a sign that said NICU. Taking a deep breath, she went inside. After Chris had established who she was, scrubbed her hands with disinfectant soap, and put on a gown, a nurse took her to see baby Taylor.

He was lying on a waist-high three-by-three-foot table. For long seconds, all Chris could do was stare. The bulletin board she'd studied outside had done nothing to prepare her for this fragile scrap of humanity. There was flesh and bone but little else. The cheeks were hollow, the eyes sunken.

"You can touch him," a voice said softly.

Chris looked up at the nurse standing on the other side of the table. The woman's smoky blue eyes bespoke compassion and understanding. The name tag on her maroon top said Alex Stoddart. "Are you sure?" Chris asked, realizing she was afraid of the baby.

"Actually, he's doing very well. He's breathing on his own, and so far everything seems to be working. We're going to try feeding him later on today."

Chris was only half listening as she stared intently at Diane's baby. The sign above his bed said he was fourteen inches long. She thought about it—fourteen inches was only two more than a ruler. Lying on his back with his knees brought up to each side, he seemed small enough to fit in her cupped hands with room left over.

"He looks like he's been starved," she said.

"He has. There was a tumor pressing against the placenta, that kept it from providing all the nourishment the baby needed."

Chris thought for a minute. "Then that must mean he's even smaller than he should be at seven months."

"A thirty-two-week baby normally weighs three and a half to four pounds."

"My God," Chris said. "He's half the size he should be?" The nurse didn't answer. There was no need to. A new fear swept through Chris. During her junior year in college, she had worked on a program to educate inner city women on the importance of prenatal nutrition. She knew what could happen to babies who were born smaller than they should have been—everything from mental retardation to deformity. "What are the long-term effects of this starvation likely to be?" she asked, not wanting to hear the answer but not able to let it go. She was like a bloodhound when she latched on to something, compelled to follow the scent even if she knew she wasn't going to like where it led her.

"There may not be any."

Fear became anger. "Don't try to coddle me. I don't have the time or energy to research this for myself." She had no right to take her frustration out on the nurse. An apology was on the tip of her tongue when she glanced up and saw that it was neither expected nor necessary.

"I wouldn't do that," the nurse said evenly. "In this baby's case, nature plainly did its job." She reached down and turned the baby toward Chris. "See how out of proportion his head is to his body?"

"I thought that's the way it was supposed to be."

"It is, but this baby's head is fully one-third of its total length. Which means that while his body was being deprived, his brain wasn't."

Slowly, hesitantly, Chris gathered her courage and reached over the eight-inch glass side of the table to press the tip of her finger to the baby's outstretched hand.

Whether by reflex or intent, the hand closed around her finger.

Eyelids opened, revealing sad-looking blue-gray eyes. Squinting at the light, the baby blinked, frowned, and then, as he turned his head, blinked again. When he discovered Chris, the frown disappeared. For long seconds he stared at her, as if imprinting her image in his mind. Logic told her it was impossible, that he was too young even to focus his eyes on her, let alone remember her, but logic had no place in a moment filled with magic.

In a look, in a touch, a wizened little

two-pound baby had managed something Chris would have sworn was impossible: he had reached out with a hand the size of a nickel and captured her heart.

4

The sky was a brilliant orange when Chris left the hospital. Another half-hour and it would be a blanket of stars. Time had slipped away at the baby's bedside. After getting over the hurdle of the first few hesitant questions, Chris had been insatiable. She'd wanted to know everything: How fast would he grow? How long would he be in the hospital? Could he hear? Would he always be small? Would he need special care when he went home? Basically, it boiled down to the same question in a hundred different guises: Would he live?

Alex Stoddart had answered the last question with as much patience and understanding as the first. After six hours, Chris was able to walk away feeling hopeful. She accepted that she and the baby were going to travel a long road and that there would likely be some rough detours along the way, but she was convinced that there was nothing the two of them wouldn't be able to handle.

The first smile in days tugged at her mouth. The two of them—it had a nice ring to it.

No sooner was the thought out than the bubble burst. What was she thinking about?

How was she ever going to fit a baby into her life? She was on the road as much as she was home. Her job as product manager for the light beer division of Wainswright depended on her ability to take off at a moment's notice, to stay late and arrive early, to glad-hand at social gatherings, and to take work home when she couldn't fit it in at the office. Although no one had ever come right out and said it, one of the primary reasons she'd gotten the job in the first place, and most certainly the reason she'd been promoted, was that she was single and had made it clear that she intended to stay that way.

She loved her job. But, more than that, she needed it. At least she did if she wanted a roof over her head and food on her table. She was a long way away from the vacation home in Aspen and the winters in Mexico that her mother assumed she'd already attained, and the car in her driveway was a Toyota, not a BMW.

Chris shoved her doubts to the back of her mind as she hurried across the heat-softened asphalt parking lot to her rental car. It wasn't as if every question had to be answered that minute. She still had time to work things through.

While she'd been in with the baby, a delta breeze had come up and dropped the temperature out of the hundreds. Most people who lived through the blast-furnace Sacramento Valley summers couldn't tell the difference between ninety-nine and a hundred and nine; sweat came as readily with one as the other.

But in a quirk of nature, Chris had been born with a built-in thermostat that unerringly kicked in at the century mark. After all the years she'd been away from Sacramento, she was surprised to see that it still worked.

Instead of turning on the air conditioner, she rolled down the car windows and let the dry, hot air wash over her as she drove to her mother's house. It had an oddly soothing effect, bringing back feelings more than memories, bits of sharp emotions that painted pictures in her mind's eye. She could see herself and Diane stretched out on towels in the backyard, slick with layers of suntan lotion, ready to pass out from the heat but prepared to go to any length to banish winter-white legs. Faces and arms were never a worry. Those they had kept tanned on ski slopes.

Six years' difference should have been an insurmountable age barrier when they were growing up, but somehow it had rarely gotten in their way. Almost from the day she was born, Diane had acted old for her age; she was reserved where Chris was volatile, leaned toward romantic novels where Chris preferred mystery and science fiction, and was meandering in her pursuit of something whereas Chris was pertinacious. They enjoyed their differences and gloried in their similarities.

So what had gone wrong?

Why hadn't Diane told her about the pregnancy?

And why had she let so much time pass between her own calls to Diane?

The easy, obvious answer was also the most painful. She'd simply allowed herself to become so busy that every letter, every phone call had been postponed to a "better time." Only, as it invariably turned out, something else would crop up, and that better time would never come.

It had been the same for Diane. There was never a conversation between them that didn't start with an apology for not calling sooner. Even the vacation they kept talking about one day taking together had never gone beyond the exchange of travel brochures.

Now Chris would have traded a year of tomorrows for just one yesterday.

But no one was offering her the chance.

A mind-numbing exhaustion stole over Chris as she slowed the car and turned into her mother's driveway. At least she'd have the night to recoup some of her energy. She'd need every ounce for the explosion that was sure to take place tomorrow when her mother found out what she'd done at the funeral home. Chris didn't try to fool herself that there would be any way she could smooth things over.

A lion with a thorn in its paw was no more than an ill-tempered kitten compared to Harriet when her authority had been challenged.

Chris sat behind the wheel for several seconds, fighting an exhaustion that made getting out of the car seem tantamount to climbing Everest. Finally she managed to drag herself from the front seat and up the back porch steps.

The first thing she heard when she opened

the door was the soft hum of the wheelchair motor as her mother came down the hall toward her. Glancing up, Chris immediately saw that it was going to be another sleepless night.

"How could you?" Harriet seethed, her rage almost palpable. "I felt like a fool when I called over there to make sure you'd arranged for a closed casket. That idiot secretary thought I was so beset with grief I couldn't comprehend what had happened. I'll never forgive you for this, Christine. It wasn't just me you trampled on this time. Did you stop for one minute to consider what our friends will think?"

"No, I didn't," Chris answered simply. "I did what I thought was right."

"I'm not surprised. You've never thought of anyone but yourself. Well, you've gone too far this time. You've dishonored our family, and I won't have it."

Chris wearily laid her purse on the chair beside her. "Come off of it, Mother. You sound like a poor imitation of Don Corleone."

"What sin could I have committed so heinous that I gave birth to you as punishment?" Harriet asked.

It was an old line, one her mother used when all else had failed. Usually Chris ignored it. But not tonight. "You know as well as I do, Mother—you were screwing around with Daddy before you married him."

Harriet sat back in her wheelchair as if she'd been struck. "How dare you."

"It isn't any big secret that I was born seven months after the wedding."

"You were premature."

"If I was, it was by eight minutes, not eight weeks. I got a good look at what real premature babies look like today. It's a long way from the way I look in my baby pictures."

The heat of anger in Harriet's eyes cooled to an icy, calculating calm. "Someday—and I promise you this, Christine—your child will cause you as much pain as you have caused me."

"You didn't tell me you'd gotten into telling fortunes. How nice you found something to keep you busy after your loving daughters left you." Even as she was saying the words, Chris regretted them. Unable to stand up any longer, she moved her purse and collapsed into the chair.

"What is it with us, Mother?" she asked softly. "Why do we always have to do this? All we have left is each other. Can't we find some way to make it work?"

"Now that you have what you want, you're making peace overtures. How like you."

Chris couldn't be baited anymore. The last of her fight had left her. "I'd trade it all, everything I have or ever hope to have, for just one hour with Diane."

Harriet turned her face away. "How are we going to go on without her?" she asked, opening a window to her soul, at last inviting the comfort she so desperately needed.

Chris dropped to her knees and gently laid her head in her mother's lap. "I don't know,

Mama," she said in a choked whisper. "I don't know."

In order to keep the fragile peace she and her mother had established, Chris decided it was best if she didn't stay the night. She was on the phone arranging for a hotel room when Madeline quietly slipped her a key.

"It's to Diane's apartment," she said. "Stay there. She would want you to."

Chris told the woman on the other end of the line that she would call back later and hung up. She turned to Madeline. "I don't know if that's such a good idea."

"I understand how you feel, but you'll have to go there to take care of Diane's things sooner or later. Your mother spent one afternoon there by herself, and she was so exhausted when I picked her up that it scared me. I really don't think she's up to doing it again." She shrugged. "I would go over there myself, but it really isn't my place."

Chris looked down at the key. She was drawn to the idea and repelled at the same time. She had passed her capacity for pain, and instinct told her that, in order to do all that still needed to be done, she had to protect herself. At the same time, she ached for anything that had been a part of her sister.

Her hand closed around the key. "How do I get there?" she asked.

Madeline reached up to wipe a tear from Chris's cheek. "Come with me," she said gently. "I'll draw you a map."

The instant Chris opened the door to Diane's apartment, she was glad she'd come. It was strange, considering her mother's compulsive tidiness, that there was no sign she or anyone else had been there. With the empty glass of milk and half-eaten cookie on the coffee table and the bathrobe carelessly tossed on the bed, it was possible to believe Diane had only stepped out for a moment and would be right back.

Chris wandered from room to room in the tiny apartment, looking at her sister's belongings, touching them, smiling at those she remembered and wondering over those she'd never seen. She disturbed nothing, opened no drawers or closets, in no way disrupted the delicate fantasy that Diane would somehow return.

There would be time enough for that tomorrow.

When she could no longer keep herself upright, Chris went into the bedroom and lay down on the bed. She drew her sister's robe over her, breathing in the faint trace of the wildly floral Joy perfume that still lingered. She tried to hold her breath, to keep even the smallest part of what her sister had been inside her, but eventually sleep stole even that.

5

The rest of the week was sometimes a dream, sometimes a nightmare. Chris found a strange, unexpected peace in her trip to Monterey to scatter Diane's ashes. She left Sacramento in the middle of the night to be sure she was three miles at sea by sunrise. Alone on the back of the chartered boat, she counted waves, waiting for the seventh one, the one that would rise higher than all the others, meet her out-stretched hand and carry her sister on journeys she had not been able to make during her lifetime.

The wave approached and Chris opened the urn, letting the gentle morning breeze take Diane. The ashes settled on the water and then slowly merged with it. She watched the process, mesmerized with grief as the beautiful young woman with the laughing eyes became less and yet, in an ethereal way, more than she had ever been.

Finally came the flowers, one of every kind Chris had been able to find in Sacramento.

She stayed on the back of the boat until the last bloom had been swept from her sight, imagining a stranger, perhaps a fisherman, who might later happen across one of them and wonder, and in his curiosity be touched, this last time, by a kindhearted, loving woman who was no more.

When the boat brought Chris back to Monterey, she went down the coast, instead of heading home right away, past Carmel to Point Lobos State Park. There she spent the rest of the morning and most of the afternoon on a hillside, watching for otters and sea lions, listening to the shore birds and saying her final solitary good-bye.

On her way back to Sacramento that night, she pulled into a Burger King for a cup of coffee. Walking back to her car she spotted a telephone and put in a call to Paul Michaels, an old family friend.

"Christine," he said, his baritone voice warm and welcoming, filled with sympathy. "I'm sorry we didn't get a chance to talk at the service. I wanted to tell you..."

She let the words slip past her, tuning out the expressions of sorrow, the condolences, protecting herself. The depth of her own grief had left her momentarily unable to hear and respond to the grief of others. What strength she had left, she jealously guarded for the little boy she'd learned from Madeline that Diane had planned to call Kevin.

"And if there's anything I can do, anything at all, please let me know," Paul went on.

"As a matter of fact there is," Chris said. "I'd like you to handle the adoption." In addition to being an old family friend, Paul Michaels was a senior partner in one of the largest and most prestigious law firms in northern California.

"Adoption?" he repeated. "I was under the impression...uh, I just assumed the father..."

Chris drew in a deep breath, struggling with

her anger, forcing it aside by trying to concentrate on something constructive. She'd been raised by a woman filled with impotent rage, someone who railed at grocery store clerks and the defense budget with equal fury and effect. Anger was as natural to Harriet Taylor as cotton was to sheets. It was a legacy she had passed on to her older daughter, one that Chris was determined not to accept. "The father doesn't want anything to do with the baby."

"I didn't know that," he said, stating the obvious.

"I know how busy you are, Paul, and under normal circumstances I wouldn't think of imposing—"

"I have to be in court in the morning, but the rest of the day is yours."

"Thank you," she said simply, knowing how difficult it would be for him to clear his schedule and how vehemently he would deny having to do so. "You're a special friend."

"Don't go getting sloppy on me, young lady," he said gently. "We have a lot of hard work ahead of us."

" I know."

"Chris..."

"Yes?"

"I assume you've given all of this some thought?"

She reached up to rub the back of her neck. "What's to think about?"

"Somehow that sounds a little like you think you don't have any choice in the matter."

She moved her hand to her forehead. "It's not that way at all," she protested feebly.

"We'll talk about it tomorrow."

"There's nothing to talk about. Diane wanted me to take Kevin, and I want to have him. I just need you to make sure it's done legally."

The next morning Chris stopped by her mother's house on her way to the hospital, hoping that by sharing an account of the day she'd spent on the coast she might begin to bridge the gap that had grown even wider between them.

Harriet refused to come out of her room, saying she had a migraine and that her doctor had told her to avoid anything or anyone who caused her stress. So instead, Chris told Madeline about the boat and the flowers and the sea otters she'd seen, realizing as she did so that she'd come as much for herself as for her mother. She'd needed to talk to someone who had loved Diane, someone who would care that there had been a rainbow in a cloudless sky that afternoon and that the captain of the charter boat, a grizzled old man who looked as tough as a barnacle, had given her a hug when she left.

The remainder of the morning she spent with Kevin, marveling over his size, the miracle of his birth, and how inept she felt when she tried to change his miniature diaper. Everything he did fascinated and frightened her at the same time.

Before meeting Paul Michaels, she stopped back at Diane's apartment and called her office. What was supposed to be a check-in call turned into a crisis meeting. The new ad campaign the company had settled on for the Midwest had met with fierce and unanticipated resistance from a national anti-drinking organization. They were claiming the commercials were aimed directly at eighteen to twenty-five-year-olds, something the company was having trouble denying because of a leaked report showing that a large percentage of the advertising budget had been allocated for college campuses.

The philosophy behind flooding the college market with advertising was simple and time-honored: build identification and loyalty to a product early and the customer was unlikely to stray later on in life. It wasn't as if Wainswright Brewing Company had originated the idea. Anything that took place on a college campus anywhere in the country that could be sponsored by a brewery had the beer companies standing in line. Should athletics be involved, the brewers would be knocking each other out of the way for the privilege of spending their money. It just happened that this time it was Wainswright's misfortune to be in the right place at the wrong time.

While everyone she spoke to at work that day was sympathetic and understanding, no one tried to hide the fact that she was needed back in Denver as soon as she could get there. As one of her assistants so succinctly put it, "The ship is listing and the lifeboats are filling fast. Either you hop on or you drown."

By the time she arrived at Paul Michaels's office, Chris's mind was going in a dozen directions. His secretary showed her into a mahogany-paneled room that overlooked the state capitol. Paul got up from his desk and came around to greet her.

"You look exhausted," he said, leading her to a glove-soft leather sofa. "But that doesn't surprise me. With Harriet's health the way it is, I imagine it fell to you to see that everything was done."

"It wasn't the doing that wore me out," she said, letting the overstuffed sofa close in around her in a luxurious embrace. "Mother doesn't give over the reins easily."

Paul nodded in sage agreement. "Her strength of will is phenomenal. I'm convinced it's what has kept her alive all these years."

One of the reasons Chris had decided to have Paul Michaels handle the adoption was his closeness to the family. No time would be wasted trying to describe the dynamics of a dysfunctional family or clarifying motivations. It would be straightforward. Clear-cut.

She leaned forward. "I would love to spend the afternoon visiting, Paul, but I found out this morning that I'm not going to have as much time to wrap things up here in Sacramento as I thought. All hell is breaking loose at Wainswright and they want me back in the office as soon as possible."

He studied her, a questioning look on his face. "I think we need to talk about this adoption before we put anything on paper."

"There's nothing to talk about."

"Bear with me. Maybe I'm a bit more cautious than I should be because family law isn't my specialty, or maybe what I'm feeling is simply an outgrowth of our friendship." He shrugged. "Whatever it is, there is no way I'm going to put a rush on an adoption. This thing is going to be done right, both for you and for the baby. As much as you'd like to believe that becoming Kevin's mother is simply a matter of signing on the dotted line, you're wrong."

"It was Diane's last wish, and since she didn't leave a will that contradicted her deathbed statement, I don't see how there can be any question. There's even a witness. What could possibly—"

"As I told you yesterday, the father has to be considered."

"And as I told you, he doesn't want anything to do with Kevin."

"But you didn't convince me. I need to know more."

"The circumstances speak for themselves, Paul. If the father had cared one whit about Diane or the baby, he would have been with her." When he didn't immediately answer, she added, "Don't you agree?"

"It would seem that way."

"I didn't want to believe it either," she admitted. "But it's the only explanation. I've gone through all of Diane's things, and there isn't a trace of him—not a picture, not a letter, nothing. He must have hurt her terribly for her to have destroyed everything."

"She never mentioned him to you or to Harriet?"

It pained Chris to admit out loud how little communication she'd had with her sister during the past year. "All I know for sure is that she was deliriously happy over some guy last Christmas and alone and pregnant eight months later. It doesn't take a genius to figure that one out."

"On the surface, it would seem that either he was married or he wanted her to have an abortion."

"Precisely."

"Things aren't always so simple," he said.

"It doesn't matter. All we can do is work with what we've got. Diane left Kevin in my care. I'm here, the father isn't."

"Just because you're here doesn't necessarily mean you're the best person to raise Kevin," Paul said, the softness of his voice belying the explosive thought.

"What's that supposed to mean?" Chris demanded.

"I'm sorry, Chris," he told her. "But it had to be said. You're not thinking as clearly as you would under less emotional circumstances." He leaned forward in his chair. "Look, I'm sure you have it in you to be a wonderful mother, but something like this rarely works out when it's thrust upon a person. There has to be a reason you've stayed single as long as you have. I assume it was a conscious choice?"

Chris stood up, walked over to the window, and stared outside. "I like my job. I'm good at it," she said defensively.

"And you feel marriage would take that away?"

"There's a lot of traveling involved in what I do—conventions, out-of-state business meetings," she said. "I've met a lot of men, but never one who was willing to put up with that kind of thing in a wife. At least not one who was interested in me."

"Do you think a child would be more understanding?"

She spun around. "What do you want from me? Am I supposed to quit my job and go on welfare to prove what a good mother I'll be? Well, I can't, Paul. It just isn't in me to do that."

His voice became gently coaxing. "And while you're back in Colorado earning money, who is going to be with Kevin while he's in the hospital?"

She blinked in surprise. How could something so important have escaped her? "With everything else that's been going on, I guess I forgot about that."

"Didn't you tell me it will be several months before he can go home?"

"I can fly out on weekends. And I have vacation coming." She sounded as desperate as she did impractical.

"I don't want to make this harder for you than it already is, Christine. All I'm asking is that you forget about Diane and even yourself for a minute and concentrate on Kevin."

"How can you be so sure I'm not?"

"I can't. I'm simply playing devil's advocate and giving voice to your own fears. If you had wanted children, you would have had them by now. A child should be a joy to its parents, not an obligation. You can't take Kevin out of a sense of duty, Chris. It isn't right for you, and it sure as hell isn't fair to him."

She crossed her arms, cupping her elbows with her hands, holding herself tightly as if afraid she was about to come apart. "But how can I give him up? I love him, Paul. And how could I ever forgive myself if I let Diane down?"

"Let the love you feel for Kevin guide you. Diane wouldn't ask for more." He got up from his desk and went to her, taking her into his arms as if trying to protect her from the blow he'd just delivered. "Don't make up your mind now," he said. "Give it a few days. I'll be here for you, whatever you decide."

She didn't have a couple of days. She'd promised to be back to work by then. "All right," she said, torn by the decision. "I owe Kevin that much."

She spent the rest of the afternoon and evening at the hospital. The night she spent holed up in Diane's apartment with a bottle of rum, which early morning found her throwing back up. It wasn't until late morning that her tears were spent and she was finally able to sink into an exhausted sleep.

She woke at noon, showered, and returned to the hospital. When she left that night, she'd reached her decision. While every fiber of her being cried out to keep Kevin, in the end it had been the depth of her love for him that made her realize she had to let him go.

The decision was the hardest she'd ever made, and it was also the most selfless. It didn't matter that giving him up hurt beyond reason. The only thing that mattered was that it was the best thing she could do for him.

Every child deserved two parents. In the beginning she'd maneuvered her way past that seemingly out-of-date ideal with statistics. There were just too many children living in single-parent households to let her own situation stop her. But then she remembered all the newspaper and magazine articles and all the television programs she'd seen about the breakdown of the family and the devastating effect it was having on the children, and she was no longer so sure of herself.

She couldn't sidestep knowing that, if there weren't two parents, the one remaining had better be damn special. In the middle of the night when there had been no place to hide and the truth taunted her like a neighborhood bully, she had been forced to admit she would never be special enough to raise the child Diane had died to bring into the world. If ever someone deserved the best, it was Kevin.

Chris faced the business world with supreme confidence. It wasn't ego; it was the sure knowledge that she excelled at her job. What she did wasn't life-giving or worth a moment's notice in the grand scheme of things, but every day that she went to work she accomplished something that helped keep a company going. It was the one place in this world where she was needed and where she made a difference.

Still, despite the passion she felt for her job and the need she had for the sense of worth it gave her, she'd give it up without a backward glance if in the giving up she became the parent Kevin needed. But nothing could do that. All she had to offer Diane's child was love, and no matter how hard she tried, she couldn't convince herself that it was enough.

When she felt herself vacillating, she simply looked at her own mother. In her peculiar way, Harriet Taylor had loved her daughters. All she had ever wanted for them was the best—at least, Harriet's idea of what was best. Through Harriet, Chris had learned that love was not always benign; sometimes it suffocated and destroyed and hurt, and in the end it could even make you afraid of it.

She would not do that to Kevin.

He deserved the best life could offer, not baby-sitters and snatches of time from a working woman who had no idea how to be a mother. He was less than two weeks old and already life had dealt him some terrible cards. Now it was up to her to see he got an ace or two.

She called Paul Michaels at home, wanting to reach him before she could change her mind. It wasn't until he'd heard her out and agreed with her reasoning that she realized, underneath it all, that she'd called hoping he'd convince her she was wrong about putting Kevin up for adoption.

"I'm sorry, Chris," he said. "I know how hard this is for you. I've always been impressed with your grit and determination and your sense

47

of fair play, but I've never admired you more than I do this very minute."

She pressed her fingers to her temples as the headache that had been threatening all day finally surfaced. "I keep looking for reasons to change my mind."

"That's because you've accepted what you have to do intellectually but not emotionally."

"I can't get over feeling that I'm letting Diane down."

"In time that will pass. Why do you think she left the baby's future in your hands to begin with? Because she knew, no matter how difficult it was for you, you'd always put Kevin first."

A lump formed in Chris's throat. "But she thought I'd be doing it as his mother."

"What does Harriet have to say about all this?" Paul asked.

She hedged. "I know she regrets telling me in front of so many witnesses that Diane's last wish was that I take full responsibility for Kevin."

"I'm sure she does. It isn't like her to give up control. But then, I'm sure she realizes there isn't a judge in this county who would let her have him with her health the way it is. So in this case, the truth served her purposes. At least it did until you chose this course of action." He paused. "Not that it would make any real difference, but I think I should know what she had to say about the adoption."

"Not much, really." Chris punctuated the sentence with a mirthless laugh. "Other than that she will never forgive me or speak to me again as long as she lives."

"She'll come around."

"I don't think I'll hold my breath on that one."

Paul Michaels called Chris back at noon of the following day to tell her that, through an attorney friend of his, he had found what he believed to be the perfect couple and that they were anxious to talk to her about the adoption. She told him to set up an appointment for the next day.

Even though all hell was breaking loose at Wainswright Brewing Company and the pressure for her to return was fierce, Chris refused to let herself be rushed. She owed Kevin that much.

It took three interviews to convince Chris that Barbara and Tom Crowell were the right parents for Kevin, and for her to agree to the adoption. It wasn't that she saw anything wrong with them in the first two meetings, only that more questions kept occurring to her. They were patient and understanding and managed to come up with all the correct answers which, perversely, made her both happy and sad.

The more time she spent with the Crowells, the more she liked them. They were in their early thirties, owned their own home in the suburbs, and were financially secure. Most important, it had been love at first sight when she took them in to see Kevin.

Although he had gained five ounces in two weeks, he was still an ounce shy of two and a half pounds. Minute, pea-sized pockets of fat were forming on his cheeks, but he was a long way from looking anything like the Gerber baby.

For the past week, Chris had spent the better part of each day at the hospital and was secretly convinced Kevin was starting to recognize her. When he'd become jaundiced and was moved from the table he'd been on to an isolette and masked to protect his eyes from the intense lights used to treat his condition, he responded to her voice by turning his head toward her when she spoke. She didn't talk to anyone about her feelings; they were too special and fragile to share.

Sitting beside the isolette, watching Kevin sleep, she would tell him over and over again how much she loved him, sometimes saying the words aloud, sometimes sending the message in her mind. She knew the love she felt would never be reciprocated, that he not only wouldn't remember her, he most likely wouldn't even know that she had existed, but it didn't matter. For this small moment she would give him all that she was, and if in return he smiled one day earlier than he might have otherwise, that would be reward enough.

Chris spent the morning of her last day in Sacramento at the hospital. She'd been there less than fifteen minutes when she looked up to see Brittany, Kevin's day nurse, coming across the room pushing a rocking chair in front of her.

"Sit," she commanded.

Chris eyed her suspiciously but did as she was told. The twenty-year veteran of the neonatal intensive care unit was not someone to be argued with. With confidence born of experience and intuitive intelligence, she was the person the other day-shift nurses turned to for help. Whether by divine intervention or poignant need, extraordinary nurses had attached themselves to Kevin on each of the three shifts. Chris was leaving Sacramento confident he was in good hands.

Without saying another word, Brittany opened the side of the isolette, put a blue stocking cap on Kevin, and bundled him in a white blanket. After checking his monitor cables to see that they were still working, she handed him to Chris.

"Are you sure it's all right?" Chris asked, her arms cradling the almost weightless bundle.

"For a few minutes. He needs to be kept warm, though, so hold him close to your body."

"This is the best present anyone has ever given me," Chris said.

"I couldn't let you leave without holding him at least once."

"Thank you." She didn't trust herself to say more.

"If you need something, holler. I won't be far."

As if on cue, Kevin opened his eyes and peered into Chris's face. She felt her heart melt and break at the same time.

An echo of her father's voice sounded in her mind. "How much do you love me, Crissy?" he would ask in the game they played as he put her to bed each night. And she would answer, "I love you heaps and bunches and piles, Daddy." He would make a surprised face and say, "And how much is that?" It was her cue to throw her arms around him and squeeze as hard as she could. "It's this much," she'd say, giggling. He never laughed back. When he said, "Then I'm the luckiest man in the world," it was always in a voice that made her feel as if she'd given him a present.

"I love you, Kevin," she said in a choked whisper, "heaps and bunches and piles."

6

Chris easily slipped back into her routine when she returned to Denver. She got up, went to work, stayed late trying to catch up on everything she had missed, went home, and went to bed. She even went out to dinner with an old boyfriend one night and made arrangements to go shopping with another friend the following Saturday. Those who knew her said she seemed a little under the weather. She just nodded and went on her way. How did you tell someone that the joy was missing from your life?

Every night she promised herself it would be better in the morning. When morning came, she invariably found herself reaching for the phone to call the hospital to see how Kevin was doing.

But she always came to her senses and hung up before the call was completed. To falter in her resolve to stay out of his life would be to admit she'd been wrong, and that was unthinkable. The only way she could survive was with the sure, clear knowledge that she had done what was best for Kevin.

She'd been back in Denver three weeks and was entering her condominium after work one evening when she heard the phone start to ring inside. She got the door unlocked, made a mad dash across the living room, and grabbed the receiver before her answering machine picked up the call.

"Hello," she said, a little breathless.

"Chris, this is Paul Michaels."

Paul was not the kind of man who called to chat. Her heart leaped to her throat. "What's wrong?" she asked, skipping the amenities.

"I'm afraid I have some bad news. The Crowells have decided not to take Kevin after all."

"I don't understand. Why would they back out now, after all this time?"

"They said they just aren't emotionally or financially able to deal with such a sick baby."

"Kevin isn't sick, he's premature," she said, confused. "And they've known that all along. Why—"

"Oh, my God," he said. "You don't know."

The hair on the back of her neck stood on end. "Don't know what?"

"I'm so sorry, Chris. I would never have called you like this, but I thought you knew. I was sure the hospital had called."

"Just tell me what happened." She fought to keep her voice steady.

"They had to operate on Kevin this morning."

She leaned heavily against the wall. "Why?" she demanded.

"Something to do with his stomach—no, not his stomach, his intestines. They had to take part of them out."

Everything was coming too fast. A dozen questions flashed through her mind, medical questions she realized Paul would not be able to answer. She settled on the one he could. "How is he now?"

"Not good, I'm afraid."

She felt as if he'd hit her. "What in the hell is that supposed to mean?" she managed to say.

"The nurse I talked to told me the infection has spread to his blood and that he's critical."

This couldn't be happening. Not again. "I'll be there as soon as I can."

"There's nothing you can do, Chris."

"I can be there for him," she snapped.

"Let me know if there's something I can do to help."

"I will." She started to hang up, then stopped. "Paul?"

"Yes?"

"Tell the Crowells they'd be wise to stay out of my way."

This time when Chris arrived in Sacramento, she didn't bother with a rental car but took a cab directly to the hospital. It was four in the morning. The long meandering hallways she passed through on her way to neonatal intensive care were deserted. Even the family waiting room for women in labor and delivery was empty.

Always before, in her eagerness to see Kevin, she had peeked past the blinds that covered the nursery as she passed, hoping to catch a glimpse of him, knowing that to do so would make her step lighter, her heartbeat quicken in happy anticipation. This time, she kept her eyes downcast, giving herself twenty more seconds of hope.

Once she was inside the long narrow room that separated the nursery with the intensive care babies from the nursery with those who were in intermediate care, she had no place to hide. She peered through the window, her gaze automatically sweeping the area where the sickest babies were always placed on the Ohio tables. Her search ended in the far corner. There was too much equipment around the table for Chris to see the baby lying there, but she could see the nurse taking care of him. It was Trudy Walker, a woman who had attached herself to Kevin from the day he was born. She was soft-spoken and unassuming, a Mother Earth kind of woman whom it would have been easy to underestimate—until you saw the glint of steel in her eyes. Chris felt a swell of relief in seeing her.

Chris's hands were shaking so badly she couldn't open the packet that contained the brush and soap she had to use before entering the nursery. She finally had to ask a nurse to help her. Never had a minute dragged by more slowly as she stood at the sink and scrubbed. At last she was through and could slip into a hospital gown and go inside.

The rhythmic hiss of ventilators punctuated the stillness as Chris made her way to Kevin. Trudy looked up. She registered surprise at seeing Chris, but offered her no smile of reassurance. Somewhere a monitor sounded, its high-pitched insistent tone telling the nurses that a baby was in trouble.

Chris was almost to the bed before she caught a glimpse of Kevin. During the interminable hours it had taken her to get there, she had tried to prepare herself for what she would find.

Her worst imaginings hadn't come close.

He was lying on his side, his head tilted back to accommodate the ventilator tube. One arm had a blood pressure cuff wrapped around it; the other contained an I.V. setup. Monitor wires were attached to his back, chest, and right foot. The soft mat of hair that had covered his head had been shaved. Five puncture wounds gave mute testimony to veins that had blown before the second I.V. line could be started on his head. A rectangle of gauze covered his stomach. Otherwise, he was naked.

"What happened?" Chris said, hanging on to the side of the bed for support. "He was doing so well."

"We were as surprised as you are," Trudy told her. "When I left work he was fine. When

I came back on shift that night, the infection had already spread to his blood. By the time they got him into surgery he was…terribly sick."

Chris had been around the intensive care unit long enough to know that "terribly sick" was a euphemism for "near death." She put the tip of her finger into Kevin's hand. There was no response. "What did the surgeon say?"

"It would probably be better if you talked to him yourself."

"Please," Chris said. "Don't make me wait."

From somewhere across the room, one of the other nurses softly called out "I.V.'s." Trudy checked the numbers on the machines in front of Kevin, wrote them in his chart, and turned back to Chris. "He said there was good news and bad news. The good news was that he took out only two small sections of Kevin's bowel."

"And the bad news?" Chris asked.

"The entire bowel was infected."

"What does that mean?"

"We won't know how much more was destroyed until the second surgery."

Chris looked from Trudy to Kevin and then back again as understanding dawned. "But he can't live without…" She couldn't finish.

"Where are his new parents?" Trudy asked gently.

"They decided they don't want him."

"Oh, I see."

"That's all right," Chris said. "We don't need them, do we, Kevin?" Tears blurred her vision, giving softness to a harsh reality as she leaned over the side of the table to press a kiss to his temple. "It's me, Kevin," she whispered. In response to her voice, his hand closed gently around her finger. "It's Chr— No, Kevin," she said, feeling her world right itself at last. "It's Mama."

7

Chris slipped the fifth birthday candle into the LifeSaver porthole of the sailboat-shaped cake she'd made for Kevin that morning. She'd taken him with her on a business trip to San Francisco the previous week, and he'd been fascinated with all the boats on the bay, especially the ones with the "big white tops." Glancing out the kitchen window to the backyard, she saw that the garden hoses were no longer being used to fill the two large wading pools. Almost predictably, the party had turned into a free-for-all water fight with Kevin and Tracy paired off against everyone else. Two against four. Formidable odds by anyone's standards. Chris smiled. She hoped Kevin and Tracy showed mercy to their opponents.

An unchildlike scream filled the air. "That's it!" a woman's voice shouted. "No more Ms. Nice Guy."

Her threat was answered with squeals of laughter.

Chris went back to the cake. She didn't have

to look to know what had happened. As usual, Mary Hendrickson had jumped into the fray with both feet.

Mary was one of a kind. She had the social graces of a woman who'd been brought up in a governor's mansion, which she had been; the self-assurance to walk into a firehouse filled with men she'd never met before and feel completely at ease, which she did whenever her fire captain husband switched stations; and the ability to regress twenty-five years, drop on her knees, and play a game of hide-and-seek with the nearest child.

She was only a couple of inches over five feet, had long black hair that she wore in a ponytail most of the time, and carried herself with the litheness of a runner. A natural optimism had seen her through some hard times, at one of which Chris had been present—the death of her two-month-old daughter, the twin to Kevin's best friend, Tracy.

In a way, the celebration of Kevin's birthday was also a celebration of Chris and Mary's friendship. After a week of passing each other entering and leaving the neonatal intensive care unit five years earlier, Mary had stopped Chris one day and asked her if she'd like to go out for a cup of coffee, saying she needed someone to talk to, someone who was going through what she was going through and who could understand what it was really like. Chris had gone along, thinking she was lending a helping hand. It wasn't until much later that she realized she hadn't been the giver, but the receiver.

Mary had been a godsend during the seemingly endless months Kevin had stayed in the hospital, offering encouragement when Chris lost sight of the end of the tunnel, insisting she come for home-cooked meals when her clothes began to hang on her, even finding a furnished apartment for Chris when it became evident she would not be returning to her home and her job in Denver and that the rift between her and Harriet would never heal.

The back door slammed, startling Chris out of her daydreaming. "How long does it take to put five candles on a cake?" Mary demanded, toweling her hair.

"Calling for reinforcements so soon?"

"Not in your wildest dreams. I just don't want you to miss out on all the fun."

"Thanks, but I think I'll pass. Someone has to play grown-up around here."

Mary opened the freezer and took out the ice cream. "Thank God it isn't me," she said and grinned. The front doorbell sounded in the living room. "Are you expecting someone else?"

Chris shook her head. "Patty Gotwalt was invited, but she woke up with a fever this morning and couldn't come."

"Do you want me to get it?"

"If you don't mind." She started to pick up the cake. "No, wait. I just remembered Linda said if she received the information on the new client she's turning over to me she would send it here by courier this afternoon. That's probably him." She put the cake back on the counter. "Why don't you pass out towels and get everyone gathered around the table? I want lots of appreciative oohs and aahs when I bring the cake out."

"Always the showman."

Chris let out an elaborate sigh. "What can I say? It's in the blood."

"Some blood—a great-grandmother who did the cancan for a bunch of horny miners."

Chris headed for the living room. "Not everyone can be a Mayflower descendant." Laughing, she added, "Although God knows they try." She reached the door just as the chime sounded again.

Expecting someone wearing a smile and a uniform, she was taken aback to see a sober-looking, vaguely familiar man wearing an expensively tailored suit. Even though her own shorts and halter top made more sense in the stifling heat, she felt embarrassingly underdressed. In the fraction of a second it took her to regain her composure, she identified and classified the man who was now openly studying her.

With the number of times Mason Winter's picture had hit the front page of the *Sacramento Bee's* business section in the past three years, Chris was a little surprised she hadn't instantly recognized him. But then she had to admit, even if it stuck in her throat to do so, that his pictures didn't do him justice. Too bad, but typical. Mother Nature couldn't seem to get her act together when it came to producing good-looking men. Inevitably, exponentially, the more handsome they were, the more unprincipled.

61

Chris slipped her hands into her pockets and leaned against the door frame. "Can I help you?" she asked.

"I'm looking for Christine Taylor."

So he wasn't lost after all. Could this be the new client Linda had mentioned? Chris thought about it a minute. No way. The Chapman and Jones Public Relations Agency was moving up in the world, but it was still too small-time to handle an account like Winter Construction Company. Even more preposterous was the idea that they would send such a job out of house to a free-lancer like her.

While she liked her job, she had no illusions about her position with the company. Working for Chapman and Jones had been the perfect solution to what, at the time, had seemed to be an overwhelming problem, allowing her to pay the bills and still stay home with Kevin. She'd never be rich, nor would she ever see CEO written behind her name, but in exchange she had seen Kevin take his first step and heard him say his first word, and that was worth every promotion she had missed out on and every extra cent she might have earned.

"I'm Christine Taylor." She modified her tone, if not her stance. On the off chance that he really was the new client, it seemed prudent to at least make a show of meeting him halfway.

"Mason Winter." His eyes narrowed in contemplation as he took her outstretched hand. "You're nothing like I expected," he said.

"Look, I don't blame you for being hesitant."

She felt like strangling Linda for not warning her that he was coming. "Under the circumstances, I probably would be, too." She wasn't getting the reaction she wanted. "Why don't you come inside and let me show you some of the work I've done for other clients? Then, if you're still uncomfortable about me handling your account, the agency will assign someone else."

He hesitated, started to say something, then apparently changed his mind. "All right," he finally told her.

Chris stepped aside to let him enter. She looked up as he passed, intending to offer a reassuring smile, but the smile never reached her lips. There was something eerily familiar about him, something that went beyond having seen his photograph. It made her uneasy. At first she thought it was his eyes, then decided it was the way he moved. When he was inside and had turned to see if she was following, she changed her mind again and decided it was the way he carried himself that made her feel as if she'd met him before.

"Make yourself comfortable," she said, indicating a chair. "I'll be right—" A loud shriek cut her off in midsentence. She glanced toward the back of the house. Quickly deciding the outcry was from indignation, not pain, she glanced back at Mason and shrugged. "I'm afraid with what's happening in my backyard today, it's going to be extremely difficult for me to conduct business in anything remotely resembling a businesslike manner. I apologize, Mr. Winter, but for my sake as well as yours, I think it would be better if we rescheduled this meeting."

She'd recognized the look he gave her and couldn't see any sense in wasting what was left of Kevin's party on a lost cause. As soon as he left, she would call Linda and let her know what had happened. With any luck, she'd be able to pacify him when he got back to the office and the account wouldn't be lost. Then, someday soon, she and Linda were going to have a long talk about sending clients unannounced.

"Just what is going on in your backyard?" he asked.

"A birthday party. My son's. He's five years old today." She pointedly moved toward the front door. "Now if you'll excuse me, I think it's time I got back."

He stood his ground. "You don't look anything like Diane," he said evenly.

She caught her breath in surprise. The heat left her body. "Who are you?"

"I told you—Mason Winter." He waited.

"Is that supposed to have some special meaning to me?"

His eyes narrowed. "You're either damn good or you really don't know who I am. Which is it?"

"Why would I—"

The kitchen door slammed. "Mom, where are you?" a child's voice demanded.

Fear shot through her, unreasoning, inexplicable, insistent. For some reason she didn't understand, it was critically important that she keep Kevin away. "Go back outside, Kevin. Now."

Not surprisingly he stepped into the doorway instead. "Why?"

"Never mind why," she said firmly. "Just do as I say." They were words her mother had used. Words she had sworn she would never repeat. She glanced back at Mason Winter and caught him staring at Kevin, an intense, enigmatic look in his eyes. It was as if suddenly she no longer existed, as if the world had been reduced to just the man and the boy.

"But everybody's waiting for the cake," Kevin protested, tugging to adjust the neck on the T-shirt he'd put on backwards and inside out. He gave up and pulled the shirt off.

"Then take the cake with you. Tell Aunt Mary to go ahead and cut it and that I'll be out as soon as I can." When Kevin was safely outside again, she faced Mason Winter. "I don't care why you came here today. I want you to leave. *Now.*"

"That's not going to work on me any more than it did on him," he said evenly. His gaze bored into her. "You aren't the one who sent me the letter, are you?"

His question brought her up short. "I don't know what you're talking about. What letter?"

"The one from Diane."

Her peripheral vision faded until all she saw was the man who threatened to destroy her peaceful existence. "How do you know about Diane?"

"My God," he said. "Is it possible you really don't know about the letter?"

"What *letter?*" she almost shouted.

He reached into the breast pocket of his jacket, took out an envelope, and held it out to Chris.

She stared at the paper, noting the uncancelled twenty-five cent stamp but focusing on the handwriting. She looked at the graceful loops and swirls that had marked Diane's unique style of penmanship and felt a stab of pain as sharp as any she had felt five years ago. "Where did you get this?"

"It was sent to me."

She started to reach for the envelope, then drew back. Something told her she really didn't want to see what was inside. "Why bring it to me now, after all this time?"

"I was hoping you could answer that for me." He lifted her hand and forced her to take the letter.

She swallowed. "I don't know what makes you think—"

"Read it," he insisted.

Every instinct screamed at Chris to throw both Mason Winter and the letter out. Whatever Diane had written was from another time. It had no meaning now. Half a decade had passed. A new President had been elected. The space shuttle was flying again. Songs had been written, hit the top of the chart, and disappeared from the radio. What could a five-year-old letter contain that could possibly make any difference now?

Reason did nothing to ease her fear. She lifted the flap and took out a single sheet of paper. In the upper right-hand corner was the date—a week before Diane died. A memory jolted Chris. The coffee table that had held the half-eaten cookies had also held a box of stationery—yellow stationery with a spray of daffodils in the corner, like the sheet she held in her hand. Her gaze slid across the page.

My dearest Mason,

There's so much to say and so little time. I tried to reach you at work, but your secretary said you were out of the country and wouldn't be back for two weeks. I'm afraid I don't have that long, my darling. It's hard for me to accept that I was wrong, especially about this, but I can't hide from the truth any longer. I'm dying. The happy ending I had planned isn't going to happen. I'll never stand at your doorway, baby in hand, free of cancer, and tell you that I never stopped loving you for a minute.

My leaving was a lie. I'm so sorry it happened—for both of us. It hurts so much to think of the precious time that's been wasted, time we could have been together. But when I left, I couldn't see any other way. I thought I was Wonder Woman, but I'm not. I'm ordinary. And I'm mortal. My prayers are for you and the baby now. The longer I can stay alive, the better chance he has.

Instead of saving you pain, I've doubled it by abandoning you twice. But I knew that if I stayed, you would never have let me go through with the pregnancy. So you see, I never really had a choice. How could I end our child's life to save my own, especially when I believed with all my heart that it wasn't necessary? Even though I ache to tell you how much I love you and to erase the bitter memory you have of my leaving, I wouldn't be writing to you now, if it weren't for our baby.

You will make a wonderful father...

Chris couldn't go on. Her stomach knotted. It suddenly seemed there was no longer any room for the hot dogs and Coke and chips she'd consumed only an hour before. She put her hand to her mouth as she looked up to find Mason watching her.

"You already knew what was in the letter, didn't you?" he said.

"No," she answered, not even convincing herself.

"You saw it as soon as you opened the door."

"No," she repeated, her voice growing stronger.

"I'm Kevin's father."

"No..." This time there was anger, but it was countered by the determination in Mason Winter's reply.

"I've come for my son."

8

Mason saw the agony on Chris's face and realized he would probably have felt sorry for her if he didn't hate her so much. What she had taken from him was irreplaceable—five years of his son's life. Because of this woman, he and Kevin were strangers. All that connected them was the fact that they happened to look alike.

After the initial shock of receiving Diane's letter had worn off, Mason had hired a detective to find his son. The task had proven surprisingly easy. Within a week, Mason had a report on his desk. Included was a photograph taken with a telephoto lens of a dark-haired little boy in front of a yellow clapboard house. He was standing in the middle of a well-tended lawn, calling out to someone or something to his left. The photograph was blurry, but the resemblance between father and son was unmistakable.

Mason had studied the picture for days, taking it everywhere with him, looking at it between meetings, propping it up on his nightstand before he went to bed at night so that it would be the first thing he saw in the morning, reliving his months with Diane, experiencing over and over again the joy they had known together and the pain and confusion he had felt at her leaving. At last there were answers to the questions that had plagued him for nearly six years. He finally understood why she had left.

If only the understanding made it easier.

She'd been right, of course. Had he known about the cancer, he would have insisted she do whatever was necessary to save herself. He'd already traveled that road once with someone he loved. He could not have gone through it again. The child would have been his last consideration.

But now, seeing the bright-eyed, healthy boy Kevin had become, the lines weren't so clearly drawn anymore.

He mentally shook himself, leaving the memories behind, where they belonged. "I shouldn't have come here like this today," he said to Chris.

"I understand your curiosity about Kevin," she said, still wary but relaxing her rigid posture slightly. "I suppose that, under the circumstances, it's only reasonable to expect that you would want to see him. But now that you have, I'm sure you can also see that, after all this time, you have no place in his life. He has a secure, orderly existence, which is exactly what every five-year-old needs. If I were to allow you to come into his life after all this time, you would take that away from him and turn his world upside down. I can't let that happen. I won't."

His anger flared anew. "You're a real piece, lady. Do you honestly believe you can dismiss me that easily? Wave your hand and I'll be gone?"

"Well, if not a wave of the hand, then what? Whatever it takes, I'll do." Chris was noticeably shaking when she reached for the telephone sitting on the table beside the sofa.

Mason wondered whether she was afraid of him or angry at his sudden appearance in her life.

"The police?" she went on. "Is that what it will take to get you to leave? Don't think for a second that I won't call them. Get this straight, Mr. Winter—Kevin is mine." Now it was her voice that was shaking. "I don't care how valid your claim is, I'm not about to relinquish the smallest part of him to a man who has the social conscience of a Donald Trump and the morals of a Leona Helmsley."

He took the telephone receiver from her and put it back in its cradle. "So now we've established that you've read about me in the papers. I just wish the report I have on you was as thorough. Somehow the detective failed to mention your flair for histrionics."

"You have a report on me?" she asked with righteous indignation. "What gives you the right—"

"You stole my child. What better right could I have?" God damn it, she was treating him like some drifter who'd wandered in off the streets. Didn't she realize it was his son she had been raising for the past five years?

"You think I have a flair for histrionics?" she shot back at him. "I didn't steal your son, Mr. Winter. Diane asked me to take him."

"Oh? And when was that? It's my understanding she died before you got to the hospital."

She stepped back, her mouth open in surprise. "How could you know that? Did your detective find out what I said to Diane when I scattered her ashes too? Never mind. I don't want to know. It doesn't matter. I don't owe you any explanations. Time is on my side. If you really cared about Kevin, you would have shown up long before now. What have you been doing for the past five years—waiting to make sure Kevin was healthy enough to play football?"

For an instant, in the flash of anger in her eyes, in the way she held her head when she was yelling at him, and in her determined stance, he saw a resemblance between Chris and Diane, but it was gone as quickly as it had come, leaving him questioning whether he had seen anything at all. "The letter wasn't mailed until two months ago," he told her, wondering why he was bothering. "It took five weeks to catch up with me."

Her eyes narrowed, questioning. "I don't understand. Where has it been all this time?"

"In Harriet Taylor's papers at her attorney's office. The new secretary was going through some old files and found an unmailed letter in one of them. The cover letter she wrote to me was most apologetic about the delay." He let out a humorless laugh. "She even said she hoped the holdup hadn't caused any problems. The attorneys couldn't imagine how something like this could have been waylaid for five years." He fixed her with his gaze. "Any ideas how that might have happened?"

Chris didn't immediately answer. "I already told you I didn't know anything about it."

Mason sensed a change in her. He didn't try to fool himself that she was in retreat; she had simply fallen back to regroup. His earlier assessment of her had been a dangerous lapse into stereotyping, but one easily accounted for. Beautiful women of no real ambition rarely made noteworthy adversaries. He had put Chris in that category. Now it seemed that what she apparently lacked in ambition she more than made up for in maternal instinct.

A trickle of sweat slipped down the back of his neck, attesting to the ungodly heat in the unair-conditioned house. He had to fight the urge to take off his coat and loosen his collar, sensing that she might construe even that small gesture as a victory for her in this, their first skirmish. If she could stand the heat, so could he. "I assume you'll want a blood test," he said.

"It's going to take a hell of a lot more than a blood test to make me..." She didn't finish.

"Make you what?" he prodded.

"To make me let you see Kevin."

He stepped closer and looked down at her. "Somehow you've gotten the impression you have a choice," he said softly. "You don't."

She stayed where she was, meeting his gaze unflinchingly. "Why did you come here today? What are you really after?"

After learning where she lived, he'd looked her up, and had even driven by a couple of times hoping to catch a glimpse of his son—all of which his attorney had strongly advised against. That afternoon he'd been on his way to a construction site in Carmichael, one of the dozens of suburbs surrounding Sacramento where he had buildings in progress, and had swung by on impulse. Seeing the activity in the backyard through the open gate, he had stopped the car. Before he realized what he was doing, he'd been out of the car and walking up to the front door. "I only want what any father would want under the circumstances—joint custody."

She gasped and took a step backward. "You can't...I won't—" she stammered. Gaining control over herself again, she said, "Over my dead body."

He shrugged. "You can fight me if you want, but you know as well as I do that eventually, I'll win. I'm the wronged party in this thing. You've denied me a major part of my child's life. In the end, you'll be lucky if they let you see him at all." His sense of timing told him he should leave. Strategically, it would be wrong to let her see it was anger, not a calculated calm, that drove him. Let her continue to think he was a dispassionate son of a bitch. The image had served him well everywhere else. There was no reason to believe it wouldn't go right on serving him. "Think it over. Figure out how much you can afford to lose. My attorney will be in touch."

He started to leave, stopped, and came back. "Why does he have that scar on his stomach? What happened to him?"

"Why don't you ask your investigator?"

He'd been foolish to think it was possible to get a civil answer out of her. They were light-years beyond that. He nodded and turned to go. Walking away took every ounce of willpower when what he really wanted was to take at least one last look at his son, the son Diane had died to give him. But the stakes were too high to chance a scene. His time would come and when it did, he would find a way to make up to Kevin all they had lost.

Chris watched Mason Winter cross the street and get into a yellow pickup with the Winter Construction logo on the door. In less time than it took her to walk around the block with Kevin each night, her world had been shattered, not as it had been when Diane died, in pieces she could pick up and glue back together, but in fragments too small to be salvaged.

A part of her mind insisted she hide behind the possibility that he could be lying, that his coming here was part of some elaborate scheme to get something out of her. But what possible reason would a man like Mason Winter have for creating such an elaborate ruse?

Dear God, what was she going to do? Panic constricted her windpipe. She felt as if she were suffocating. Kevin was her child, her baby. Mothers didn't give their babies to strangers no matter what they called themselves. What made him think he could just walk in and lay claim to a child he'd never set eyes on, never visited in the hospital, never cried with?

If only Mason Winter was someone she could talk to, someone who could be reasoned with. What kind of man appeared out of the blue and tried to bully a woman into giving up her child? The kind of man who thought of a child as a possession, a terrified inner voice answered.

Kevin was her life. She could no more let Mason Winter take him from her than she could stand motionless on the sidewalk if she knew Kevin was about to be hit by a car.

But, dear God, what was she going to do about it?

In the four years he had been in Sacramento, Mason Winter had become one of the most powerful and influential men in the city. Winter Construction Company hadn't silently slipped into town, it had burst on the scene with a bang, coming in on a Monday and outbidding every other builder for a major site in the downtown area by the end of the week. It had managed to secure options on choice parcels of land in the northern part of the county long after everyone else had thought the land was off the market. Every light industrial site had been flooded with tilt-up warehouses bearing the Winter Construction logo.

Mason Winter had been the first out-of-town builder to recognize that a land and housing boom was about to take place in Sacramento. Only months after his arrival, investors from Los Angeles and San Francisco began to realize there were still bargains to be had in California. When the new gold rush began, Mason Winter was ready. He had done everything he could to corner the market on picks and shovels. After that, it was simply a matter of counting the money that came rolling in.

Chris had seen examples of his work everywhere, from the ultramodern high-rise office buildings that had changed the skyline of the state capital almost overnight, to the rows and rows of warehouses, their concrete walls and endlessly repetitive architecture a blight on even the industrial sections of town. Mason Winter was at odds with every conservation group in the area. He was reputed to try to intimidate politicians who got in his way and noted for making his presence felt at major charity functions in the county. He had made all of the Most Eligible Bachelor lists, and his name appeared in the Metro or Business section of the newspaper at least once a week.

There wasn't one thing about him Chris liked. The thought of turning Kevin over to him, even for five minutes, made her sick to her stomach.

She waited at the front window until she saw him reach the end of the block and turn the corner, and then she went into the kitchen. Laughter, wonderfully free and spontaneous, came to her as she stood, unnoticed, at the screen door.

Just inches away, everything seemed so ordinary, so normal, that she almost believed all she had to do was step across the threshold and the nightmare would be over. Her focus narrowed on Kevin. In its purest form, cleanly and simply put, the child she had come to think of as her own was the air she breathed. To ask her to share him was tantamount to asking her to give up a piece of herself. She could no more function without her son than she could without her arms and legs.

Right and wrong had nothing to do with it. She didn't give a damn how legitimate Mason Winter's claim was; Kevin was hers.

How her mother must have hated her to seek her revenge from the grave, to want the last word so desperately she was willing to miss out on the moment of victory.

"Chris, what's wrong?" Mary said, concern evident in her voice as she came toward the house.

"Nothing," Chris told her, instinctively trying to shelter herself and her friend at the same time.

"Don't give me that crap," she said. "You look like I felt when I had food poisoning."

"I can't talk about it now. Not yet. I have to think."

Mary opened the screen door and stepped inside. She peered into Chris's face. "How about if I move the party to my house? John is home. He'd be happy to take over."

"No. I don't want Kevin to leave the yard."

"Then I'll call John and have him come over here."

Realizing she was scaring her friend, Chris tried to smile. "Do I look that bad?"

Mary didn't bother answering. She picked up the phone, talked for a few seconds, turned to Chris, and said, "He's on his way."

Still staring at the child who had become her reason for living, Chris asked, "Who gave Kevin the Bert and Ernie puppets?"

"Tracy—who else? She picked them out a week ago." Mary leaned against the tile counter, her gaze locked on Chris. "I'll never do that again. Keeping a secret that long was almost more than she could stand."

"Where did you find them?" she asked, grounding herself in the mindlessness of their conversation. "I looked all over town last Christmas, but nobody had any."

There was a quick knock on the front door, a squeak as it opened, and then a male voice calling out, "I'm here."

"We're in the kitchen," Mary said. She reached for Chris's arm. "Come on. Let's go to my house. It's quiet there."

Chris looked up as John entered. "Keep an eye on Kevin," she said. "Don't let him go anywhere."

John nodded. "What time do you want me to send everybody home?"

"Play it by ear," Mary answered for Chris. "Let them stay as long as you can stand them and they can stand each other."

On his way out, John stopped to put his arm around Chris. "You look like hell, Crissy," he said. "Go put your feet up and let Mary pour you a stiff drink."

Chris looked on as John gathered the half dozen five-year-olds around him. Kevin immediately latched on to one leg, Tracy the other. A profound feeling of injustice came over Chris. After all that had already happened to Kevin, why couldn't he have had a father like John? It just wasn't fair.

9

The forty-foot elm tree in Mary Hendrickson's front yard sheltered the living room from the piercing afternoon sun, providing a cool, dark refuge for Chris. It wasn't quite the same as crawling into a cave to lick her wounds, but it was the next best thing.

Not giving Chris a chance to decline the offer, Mary went to the kitchen, took down a bottle of Grand Marnier, and poured generous splashes into two brandy snifters. When she returned, she handed one to Chris. "We don't have to talk," she offered. "But it might help. I know it always does me good."

Chris raised the snifter to her nose to breathe in the fragrant orange liqueur. Her hands were trembling, making the liquid climb the sides of the glass. The fumes created by the turbulent alcohol made her eyes burn. She blinked and realized she was near tears. "Damn," she swore softly, determined that she would not cry. The last thing she needed was a runny nose and bloodshot eyes.

"I'm going to take back the option and insist we talk." Mary put her arm around Chris and guided her to the sofa. "You look as if you'd just lost your best friend," she teased gently. "But that's impossible. I'm right here.

"It's not my best friend I have to worry about losing," Chris said, sinking into the chintz-covered sofa. "It's my son."

Mary stopped in mid-stride. "Kevin?"

"That wasn't a courier at the front door. It was Kevin's father."

"But I thought..." Stunned, Mary dropped into the chair opposite Chris. "How?" she asked. "Better yet, why? Especially after all this time."

Chris put the Grand Mariner on the end table and leaned forward, her elbows on her knees. "I'm still trying to sort the whole thing out myself. It seems Diane wrote a letter to him, telling him she was going to have his baby, but the letter didn't get mailed until very recently. He didn't know anything about Kevin, not even that he existed, until a few weeks ago."

"Why the delay?"

"Knowing my mother, I'd say it was because the information in the letter didn't fit in with her plans."

"Whoa—back up a little bit. What has your mother got to do with this?"

"The letter was in her file at the attorney's office." She shrugged helplessly. "They were doing some spring housecleaning and thought it was an oversight that it had never been mailed."

Mary let out a groan. "Why didn't the secretary call you first? I thought your attorney was an old family friend."

"This was a new attorney, one I never met. Mother severed her contact with Paul Michaels when she discovered he was helping me find someone to adopt Kevin."

"I still don't understand what the letter was

doing in the file in the first place," Mary said, frustration heavy in her voice.

"I'm only guessing, but I'd say Diane was already too sick to mail it herself, so she gave it to Mother to mail, telling her what was inside to be sure she was aware of its importance. Then, when Diane died before I got to the hospital, Mother saw her opportunity to manipulate things to her advantage." Unable to sit still any longer, Chris stood up and began pacing the room. "It's so logical. Losing Diane was devastating for Mother."

"So when she saw an opportunity to hold on to what little remained of her daughter, she jumped at it," Mary said.

"She knew that in her physical condition she would never be awarded custody..."

"So she told you it was Diane's dying wish that you take Kevin."

Chris stopped her pacing, picked up the snifter, and took a swallow of the amber liquid. "Boy, what I would give for five minutes with my mother. Not that it would change a thing, but I'd sure like to know why she really hung on to that letter." She gave Mary an embarrassed smile. "It absolutely amazes me how paranoid I can be at times. Can you believe my first reaction to this was that it was something she'd planned all along, that it had actually been her intention to one day send Kevin's father to turn my world upside down? Thank God the thought was transitory. Mother might have hated me, but she worshiped Kevin. She could never have done this to him."

"Maybe she simply forgot about the letter," Mary offered.

"Or couldn't bring herself to throw away something Diane had written."

"Or maybe she planned to give it to Kevin when he was older so that he could find his father if he wanted to."

Slowly, thoughtfully, Chris put the snifter back on the table. "Whatever her reason, I'm sure she never planned this."

"Maybe Madeline could shed some light on your mother's reasoning."

Chris shook her head. "When Mother did things like this, she did them in secret."

Mary noticed her glass had left a ring on the table. She wiped it off and reached for a coaster. "What's he like?" she said, at last asking the question that hung heavy between them.

Chris drew in a deep breath. "He's a sleaze, the kind of guy who would run over a dog and complain because the road was bumpy. As far as I know, about the only good thing that can be said about him is that he's never been in jail."

"How do you know? You just met the guy."

Chris reached up to rub the back of her neck. "Obviously I've left out one important detail. His name is Mason Winter."

Mary gasped. *The* Mason Winter?" She hesitated, the look on her face indicating the speed at which the wheels were turning in her mind. "My God, Chris," she said, her eyes wide. "Now that I think about it, Kevin looks just like him."

"I can't imagine how Diane ever got hooked up with that guy. They're nothing alike. Diane was gentle and sensitive. She didn't have a hard edge on her. She wouldn't have known what to do with someone like Mason Winter."

"You sound like you've made a study of him."

"In a way I have. He started making the Business sections of the papers about the same time I started combing them every day to keep up with my job." She stopped, let out a choking sound, and wrapped her arms tightly around herself, as if trying to hold in the pain. "He supports everything I'm against. What am I going to do, Mary? I can't stand the thought of turning Kevin over to him for a minute, let alone a weekend."

Mary got up and put her arms around her friend. "Maybe you won't have to. You can fight him."

"He would win," she said flatly. "I can just imagine the headlines—Desperate Father Seeks Custody of Child Denied Him by Manipulative Grandmother. Every fathers' rights group in the country would hop on the bandwagon. Between that and Winter's influence in this town, I wouldn't stand a chance."

Mary grew quiet, thoughtful. Her expression changed from bewilderment to anger. Finally there was an explosive "That was really a chickenshit thing to do—to show up the way he did, without a word of warning, as if you were some hired baby-sitter instead of Kevin's mother. What did he expect you to do, apologize for the misunderstanding and step aside so he could take his long-lost son? Jesus, how could anyone be that insensitive? I don't blame you for being scared."

"I'm more than scared," Chris admitted. "I'm terrified. My God, Mary, this stranger just walks in off the street and expects me to give him my child."

"Did he give the smallest hint that he recognized what it might do to you and Kevin to have something like this shoved down your throats?"

Chris shook her head. "From the way he acted, I'd be surprised if it's even crossed his mind."

"It looks to me as if you and Kevin are secondary to the fact that he thinks he's been cheated out of something that's rightfully his."

Chris covered her face with her hands. "My God, Mary, what am I going to do? I can't let a man like that have anything to do with Kevin."

"I don't know what to tell you," Mary said. "I'm sorry."

Chris looked up again. "Winter is a good name for him. Coldfish would even be better. It's a hundred and ten today, and he's out running around in a suit and tie, looking like he's sitting on the North Pole."

Mary leaned back, a puzzled look on her face. "What has that got to do with anything?"

"I know it seems ridiculous, but the whole time he was in the house—and you know how hot it was in there after I'd had the oven on all morning baking Kevin's cake—he didn't have a drop of sweat on him. I was a basket case, and he acted as cold and calculating as if we were conducting a business deal.

Can you imagine how he would react if Kevin cried because he got stung by a bee or stubbed his toe? I shudder to think what he would do if he found out Kevin's best friend is a girl and that they play house together."

"Are you going to tell Kevin?"

Chris flinched. "No. At least not yet."

"Whatever you decide, you know John and I are behind you."

Chris smiled her thanks. There might be a time she would have to call on her friends, but she hoped not. She had a feeling Mason Winter could be a dangerous enemy; the fewer targets he had, the better.

Sleep eluded Chris that night. She knew it was irrational, but she couldn't stop listening for cars. There weren't many, just enough to keep her awake.

After wandering around the house for a half hour and then taking a couple of aspirin for a threatening headache, she tried reading a mystery that had put her to sleep twice before, but even that didn't work. Finally she put the book aside and went into Kevin's room.

Watching him sleep was familiar, something she'd done since he was born and something she never tired of doing. Even after five years, she was still in awe of the magic he had brought to her life. She had never imagined it possible to love someone the way she loved her son, completely, unselfishly, joyfully. He gave meaning to each day.

She sat on the edge of his bed, careful not

to disturb him, content just to be near and to listen to his soft, rhythmic breathing, remembering the times his chest had risen and fallen to the cadence of a machine. The hissing mechanical sounds of an infant respirator were locked in her memory, as was the image of Kevin when he'd been hooked up to one. When awake, he had sometimes cried, but because the tube that fed oxygen to his lungs was pressing against his vocal cords, the cries had been silent. Day after day, Chris had watched the heartbreaking process, torn apart by her desperate need to help and her utter impotence. Even knowing the respirator was keeping him alive had done nothing to ease her hatred of the machine.

Kevin had been on the respirator twice, once after each surgery. She'd thought the second time would be easier because she knew what to expect. Instead, she discovered something every parent eventually learned: knowledge gave no reprieve from anguish when your own child was involved.

Luckily that time in the hospital was a nightmare only she relived. Kevin remembered nothing of the five and a half months he'd been in the neonatal intensive care unit, even though it was then that he had learned to smile and laugh and to coo and throw temper tantrums. He'd had to go back to the hospital three times since then, but he'd taken the visits in stride, reacting with a calm acceptance that Chris tried to emulate for his sake as well as her own.

The six hours a day she had spent by his bedside when he was first born became twenty after she returned from Denver. She lost twenty pounds. The nurses brought her food, and John and Mary insisted Chris give up her motel room, which she hardly ever used, and sleep at their house until Mary could find Chris a furnished apartment.

Wainswright had held her job for over two months, anxiously calling and sending work for her to do at the hospital. Finally, when it became obvious there would be no easy or quick solutions to Kevin's problems, she had mailed in her resignation. Another month went by before she acknowledged she would never return to Denver and had her condominium put up for sale. It was obvious Kevin would need years of ongoing medical care and the skill of the doctors who had been taking care of him and who were familiar with his case. That realization had effectively eliminated any thought of her leaving Sacramento in the foreseeable future.

The decision to let go of all she had worked for wasn't nearly as traumatic as she would have once believed. Being in an intensive care unit every day where life-and-death situations were a way of life, Chris found it impossible to think of her career in the same end-all-be-all terms. Promotions and successful campaigns and moments of celebration over a job well done paled when compared to the way she felt when Kevin looked at her and smiled for the first time. Not one of her triumphs had been as profound or as hard earned as the day he came home from the hospital at six months, weighing barely a pound for every month he had been alive.

Harriet and Madeline came to the hospital several times a week but never stayed more than a half-hour. Chris was so intently focused on Kevin that she had missed seeing how rapidly her mother's health was failing. It was three days before Thanksgiving when Chris, realizing she hadn't seen her mother in over a week, tried to call her.

Madeline answered the phone and told Chris that Harriet had been admitted to the hospital the week before in severe pain. X rays showed that she had three broken vertebrae, a result of degenerating bone mass from the progressively worsening rheumatoid arthritis. She'd instructed Madeline not to tell Chris what had happened until absolutely necessary. Chris hadn't been able to decide whether that was an act of generosity or spite and was as saddened by one possibility as the other.

She tried visiting her mother every day, but the time they spent together was agony for them both. In a rare moment of candor, they admitted their discomfort and agreed it was best to limit the visits to once a week, with daily phone calls for updates on Kevin. Chris always made a point of hanging up before the conversation had a chance to disintegrate, leaving them both with the illusion that they were getting along better.

Harriet had died in tiny increments over the next two years, transferring herself out of one convalescent hospital and into another until her money finally gave out. In her desperate battle to hang on to life, she grew increasingly more difficult for even the doctors and nurses to deal with. In the end she alienated everyone who tried to help her, including the ever-faithful Madeline, driving them away with her anger and frustration. In death she managed what she could not in life—the gathering of nearly a hundred friends to pay their respects. It was the first time in years they had been able to approach Harriet without fear of receiving a sharp rebuke for their efforts.

With the exception of a small bequest to Madeline, Harriet left her entire estate to Kevin, set up in a trust fund that would allow him to withdraw money for college but would not be his in its entirety until he reached thirty-five. The intention had been loving and generous, but as it turned out, it had also been almost meaningless. By the time all of Harriet's bills were paid, less than seven hundred dollars remained.

After the funeral, Madeline had moved to Michigan to be near her brother. She and Chris had stayed in touch, never missing a birthday or Christmas. There were times when Chris wished Madeline had never left, but the reasons were selfish and the requests for her to return were never passed on, beyond an open invitation to visit and stay as long as she wanted.

Headlights flashed across the window, snapping Chris out of her reverie. She held her breath as she listened for the sounds that would indicate the car was stopping. Not until she heard it drive away did she realize how hard her heart was beating.

Looking at Kevin, a delicate silhouette against Sesame Street sheets, she put her hand lightly on his back, letting his warmth flow into her, reassuring herself with the contact.

Without him there would be no reason to get up in the morning; there would be no laughter or sunshine. She slipped her hand through his silken hair, smoothing the cowlick above his left temple. Less than twenty-four hours ago, her life had been everything she wanted it to be. Well, close to it, anyway. There were times when she looked at John and Mary and felt a twinge of envy at their closeness. Knowing that what they shared was as hard to find as an honest politician kept her from dwelling on missing it herself.

She dated once in a while, but had allowed only one man, Tom Miller, to get to know Kevin. Tom had asked her to marry him, and for a time she'd considered it. He and Kevin got along all right, but after six months there was still a reserve between them. When Chris broke off the relationship, she'd explained to Tom that, in order for her to marry anyone, he would have to love Kevin as much as he loved her; until she could find that person, she would go it alone.

She'd since given up on the idea that she would ever find anyone who would fit her ideal. But that was okay. She'd never planned on marrying anyway. Having Kevin to share her life was a miracle in itself, one she'd never imagined possible. It was more than enough.

She got up and walked over to the window to look outside. Street lamps on ornate metal posts illuminated the deserted street. She had come to love her house and its location. The traffic was light and yet they were still close to downtown. Located in a quiet part of East Sacramento, the rambling California cottage had been added on to by succeeding owners over the fifty years of its existence, sometimes more successfully than others, but each addition had its own peculiar charm. There were three bedrooms, one and a half baths, a spacious country kitchen, and almost no closets.

Mary and John had found the house for Chris, convincing her it was a bargain, even at ten times the age and twice the price of her Denver condominium. It had been hard at first to trade "almost new" for "nearly ancient," but she'd come to appreciate the charm of double-hung windows, crown moldings, and hardwood floors.

The payments had been a struggle in the beginning, but increasing assignments and salary steps had more than kept her up with inflation. In four and a half years, the house had tripled in value, giving her a built-in nest egg for Kevin's education.

The first year Chris had been in Sacramento, taking care of Kevin had been all she could manage. Her pension plan, savings, and accumulated vacation and sick leave had been enough to see her through that time. By the time the funds were getting uncomfortably low, Kevin had reached the age and state of health that he no longer needed her constant care, which allowed her to begin looking for a job. She'd wanted something that would allow her to work out of her house, and free-lance public relations had been the logical choice. Not only did it fit in with her background, but it allowed her to work as little or as much as she needed or wanted.

At first the assignments had consisted of simple press releases, company newsletters, and the setups for new housing developments, whatever she could do at home. Gradually, as Kevin grew older and started nursery school, which freed Chris for set blocks of time, she had started taking on more interesting and challenging jobs—working directly with the media, going on troubleshooting ventures where she actually went into the company offices to figure out why a campaign wasn't working, and setting up publicity events featuring celebrities who had come to town for a variety of reasons, some of them as mundane as the opening of a grocery store.

She liked her job primarily for the freedom it afforded her, but the variety kept it interesting. Someday, when Kevin was older, she envisioned herself opening her own agency. Until then she would continue adding to her list of contacts and glorying in the time she had to spend with her son.

Most surprising for her about her move to Sacramento was that, after a life of fiercely protecting her privacy, she'd come to love the small-town feel of the neighborhood almost as much as she loved the house. She'd found she liked the idea that all of her neighbors knew and watched out for one another, almost as if they were one big family. Losing that would be hard, but it was Kevin losing Tracy and Mary and John that Chris was the most concerned about. The thought of taking them away from him was the only thing that had given her pause in her decision about what she had to do.

The solution had come to her as she was reading Kevin his bedtime story. It was so obvious that she was amazed it had taken her so long. Obvious but painful. Yet another reason for hating Mason Winter.

10

Mason Winter flipped through the stack of résumés on the desk in front of him, trying to concentrate on something that had been urgent the week before but which, compared to seeing his son for the first time, had now fallen far down the list of his priorities. What drove him to get the business at hand out of the way was knowing that, in order to do justice to one, he would have to take care of the other.

Winter Construction Company now had too many tentacles for him personally to oversee them all. He was driving himself and everyone around him crazy by trying to be in too many places at the same time. Projects were getting short shrift when they needed personal attention, he was regularly missing board meetings for the charities he sponsored, and his private life was almost nonexistent. His only dates in the past six months had been to the "see and be seen" functions he attended as a matter of course; the only sex he'd had was with a reporter who'd shown up to get a story one afternoon and stayed until the next morning.

The major problem Mason faced in hiring someone to oversee the mid- and high-rise division of the company was the idea of relinquishing the intimate involvement he was convinced had put Winter Construction where it was. He'd come to Sacramento with something to prove—that he could play ball with the big boys and keep batting in the home runs he'd been hitting in Los Angeles with less ambitious projects. He'd accomplished that and more in half the time he'd figured it would take.

Only two people had earned his unguarded trust during the fourteen years he'd owned his own business. One of them was his assistant, Rebecca Kirkpatrick; the other, Travis Millikin, who more and more was responsible for overseeing all the fieldwork of Winter Construction. He'd reached the point where he needed another—someone who was honest, trustworthy, and loyal, who could detect a lie before the sentence was finished, spot shoddy work by a subcontractor, and hold his own in a shouting match with his boss. He wasn't asking for much—a Boy Scout with the tenacity and ferocity of a hungry shark and the cynicism of an IRS agent would be fine, at least for starters.

Knowing there was no way he was going to give the decision-making process the attention it needed right then, Mason gathered the résumés together and set them aside. He glanced out the window at the cloudless sky. Because of the unobstructed view, he'd purposely put his office on the twenty-seventh floor of this, his first major building in Sacramento. The hours he spent behind his desk were designed to give him shelter from the niggling awareness of competition that struck whenever he saw someone else's building. It had been a noble, but failed, experiment.

Everyone from his architect to the city planner had warned him that he'd never sell the upper-floor condominiums he'd insisted be incorporated into the design of this building. He was told over and over again that the city core was a residential wasteland inhabited by transients and indigents: no one who could afford one of his high-rise homes would ever want to live there. Three weeks after the start of construction, he'd signed the papers on the last unit, saving the penthouse for himself.

His one regret was that, in order to show community loyalty and interest and to get the local media's attention, he'd hired a Sacramento designer to furnish his office and penthouse. The results were straight out of the pages of *Architectural Digest*, sterile and pretentious. While the themes were different in his office and apartment, he felt as uncomfortable in one as he did the other. He was quietly looking around for someone to redo both places as soon as it could be arranged without irreparably damaging fragile egos.

He was lost in thought, his unfocused gaze locked on a John Baldessari on the far wall, when Rebecca Kirkpatrick came in and grounded him again. Rebecca was thirty-eight, tall, and thin with brown hair that had once been blond and amber eyes that were almost hidden behind thick horn-rimmed glasses. "Did you get hold of Tony on those cost overruns?" he questioned.

She tossed a manila folder on his desk. "He said you approved them three days ago."

"The hell I did." He reached for the intercom button. "Janet, get Tony Avalon on the phone."

Rebecca held her hand up. "Wait a minute, Mason. You and I need to talk about this before you jump all over Tony. There have been a number of things you've told people this past week that you forgot you told them."

He gave Rebecca a look that said, "You better know what you're doing," pressed the intercom again, and barked, "Hold that call."

Several seconds passed while Rebecca studied her boss, obviously puzzled by what she saw. "What's with you, Mason?"

"I thought you came in here to talk about Tony." He leaned back in his chair, his hands cupped behind his head. "If that's what you're here for, get on with it. If it isn't, get out. I've got a meeting in a half hour and I want to read over some notes before I go."

97

"My, my, does the big bad bear have a thorn in his paw?"

"If I happen to be in a less than wonderful mood, it's nobody's business but my own."

"Being a little self-indulgent, aren't we?"

Mason stared at her, momentarily speechless. Rebecca never cut him any slack, but she had sense enough to give him distance when he needed it. "Give me one good reason I shouldn't fire you," he said, letting her know she was pushing too hard.

"That's easy—you're not a masochist. I'm the keystone of this organization, and you know it as well as I do."

A reluctant smile reached his lips. He sat forward in his chair. "Where did I find you?"

"It doesn't matter. You can't replace me. I'm one of a kind."

He groaned. "Something we should all be thankful for."

"Now, you want to tell me what's eating you?"

"No."

"But you're going to anyway."

"Not this time, Rebecca," he said, his voice low, the anger gone.

"All right. Just remember I'm here if you ever—" She stopped; her eyes grew wide in sudden understanding. "You've seen him, haven't you?" she said.

Mason thought about denying it but knew that it was useless. In the fourteen years Rebecca had been with him he'd never been able to hide the truth from her. She'd seen him at his best and at his worst and had stood by him when everyone else was running for the door. She was his confidante, someone he trusted implicitly. She was the perfect assistant in a male-dominated world. With her chameleon looks and nondescript business suits she was able to fade into the background at meetings, ignored by men who had no idea she was watching and analyzing their every move.

"Three days ago," he said, admitting something he'd just as soon have kept to himself.

She sat down on the corner of his desk. "I thought that hot-shot new attorney you hired told you to stay away until he had some answers."

"He did."

"But, as usual, you decided not to listen."

"It's a little more complicated than that."

Excitement replaced the concern in her eyes. "The hell with the attorney. Tell me, what does he look like?"

Mason smiled. "A lot like the picture, actually—only different somehow. The strangest feeling came over me when I saw him. It was a little like seeing myself thirty-five years ago. He has the Winters' build—narrow hips, short legs, and a long waist."

"Whose eyes does he have?"

"Diane's."

She crossed her legs and leaned back, bracing herself with her hands. "That must have been hard on you."

"Not as hard as I thought it would be. There's a lot of me and Diane in him, but there's also a lot that's just Kevin."

"I like the name."

"It was my grandfather's."

"So, what did you think of *her?*"

He got up and went over to the sideboard to get them each a cup of coffee. "I'm still working on that," he said. "The opinion I went in with changed by the time I left."

"Oh?" she said, her interest piqued. "Why was that?"

"She said she didn't know about the letter."

"And you believed her?"

"In hindsight I do. There was a lot of fear and hostility in the way she reacted, but I didn't pick up on any guilt." He handed Rebecca her cup and sat back down.

"What does she look like?"

"Medium height, not as thin as Diane, but just as long-legged and lanky-looking."

Rebecca laughed. "Try saying that fast five times."

Mason took a long drink of his coffee, hardly noticing when it burned the roof of his mouth. "She has deadly eyes, the kind that look right through you. I have a feeling Kevin doesn't put much over on her."

"Is she going to let you see him?"

"Not willingly." He grinned. "For some reason she doesn't like me."

Rebecca feigned an unbelieving look. "Imagine that." Several seconds passed before Mason spoke again. When he did, he was quiet, thoughtful. "I didn't realize how much I was counting on being able to walk away from all this and pretend it never happened until I saw him and got pulled in. Now I could no more walk away than I could fly."

"I told you," she said.

"Yeah, you did, but I didn't believe you. I never thought fatherhood would be my thing."

"It's more than being a father," she said softly. "Kevin gave you back Diane."

Mason's private line rang, interrupting them. He picked up the receiver. "Yes?" He listened carefully, then pushed his chair back and stood up. "I'll be right there."

"What's wrong?" Rebecca asked, instantly alerted.

"Nothing I wasn't expecting," he answered, grabbing his coat and heading for the door. "Christine Taylor is only doing what I would have done under the circumstances. Now it's up to me to convince her she isn't going to get away with it."

"Good luck," Rebecca said.

"Thanks, but I don't need it."

"Maybe not, but I'd still watch my backside if I were you," she said, following him into the hallway. "It isn't just bears that are protective of their young."

"Christine Taylor is the least of my worries."

11

Chris readjusted Kevin on her lap and nuzzled her nose against the back of his head, breathing in the just-washed fragrance of his hair. After bombarding her with questions on their way to the airport, now that they were there, he had grown strangely quiet, as if trying to sort out in the privacy of his own mind all that she had told him.

She had expected, at least initially, that he would react with greater enthusiasm. He loved airplanes and often asked to be taken to the airport to watch them take off and land. Now that he was actually going to fly on one, however, it didn't seem to impress him. Instead of showing excitement over what she had told him would be an adventure, he kept asking, in one form and then another, when they would be coming home again. He couldn't seem to grasp that they were moving and that they weren't ever coming back.

She thought about and then discarded the idea that he didn't understand. There was little that Kevin didn't understand. More likely he was looking for a way to get her to change her mind.

He leaned his head against her shoulder. "Could Tracy and Uncle John and Aunt Mary come, too?" he asked, breaking the silence.

"Maybe someday they can come for a visit."

"Why can't they come now?"

"Because we don't have a place for them to stay yet."

"Is our new house going to be yellow, too?"

"If it isn't, we can paint it ourselves."

"Could Tracy help?"

"If she's visiting then she could."

"How come I couldn't take all of my toys?"

"Because there isn't room on the airplane."

"Could the mailman bring them?"

"Maybe later. We'll see." Chris let out a sigh of relief when he lapsed into silence again. Feeling his pain as intensely as her own, she reminded herself that she was doing what was best for both of them. She hoped he would one day understand that she'd had to do what she could while she still had the chance.

She knew that basically it was wrong to deny a child his father. It was even possible that Kevin would someday question her decision. But she was willing to take that risk. There was too much at stake to quibble about what Kevin might or might not think in the future. Perhaps when he was older and better able to ward off the influence of a man like Mason Winter, she would tell him about his father and let him decide for himself whether or not he wanted someone like that in his life.

She'd told no one about her decision to leave town, not even Mary. Keeping a secret from someone she told everything to had been hard, but Mary would have wanted her to stay and fight, and Chris just couldn't take the chance of losing. As much as it stuck in her throat to admit it, Mason's claim was legitimate. She saw it; the courts would see it, too. In the end, there was only one thing left for her to do. If she was going to succeed in protecting Kevin, she had to leave town while she still had every legal right to do so.

The details of successfully disappearing had seemed daunting at first. Always in the back of her mind was the detective Mason had hired. If he had found them once, he could do it again. She would not only have to stay one step ahead, but make sure she left nothing behind that could be traced. Subterfuge didn't come naturally or easily to her; Chris's mind didn't work that way. She was a straightforward person who'd always faced her problems head-on. But this was different. She had never had so much at stake before.

Just when she thought she had something figured out, a reason for failure would pop into her mind. It didn't even occur to her to use a false name for the airline tickets until she was on the phone making the reservations. She still hadn't decided on their final destination, figuring it would be too easy to leave clues behind if she knew where they were going.

Calling Mary from Dallas was as far ahead as she had planned. As long as it could be done safely for all of them, she would stay in touch with the Hendricksons. But if Mason pushed his rights through the courts, she would have to disappear yet again or put John and Mary in the untenable position of having to betray their friends or lie under oath. With any luck, she could arrange for the sale of the house before that happened. Stripping her bank accounts and selling off what little stock she'd managed to accumulate would see her and Kevin through a year, perhaps a little longer if they were careful, but after that they would be totally dependent on what she could earn.

Deciding what to take and what to leave behind had been far easier than she had expected, thanks to a chance remark by John Hendrickson. During their semiweekly trek to Original Pete's Pizza the night before, he had been telling her and Mary about a house fire he'd gone to during his last shift and the things the fire fighters had tried to save for the owners. She imagined herself in the same position and questioned what she would take if she had only five minutes to make her choices. It was amazing how easy it became after that. Only things that couldn't be replaced—photographs and heirlooms—became important enough to bother about.

Those she spent that night packing, and the next morning she put the boxes into storage, intending to send for them when she and Kevin were settled and she was sure Mason was no longer looking for them.

She had driven her car to the airport and left it in long-term parking to prevent anyone from seeing her and Kevin getting into a taxi with their luggage. Once she and Kevin were settled, she would send the parking ticket and keys and pink slip to Mary with instructions to sell the car and apply the money to her storage bill.

Glancing up at the television monitor to check the arrival time of the plane that would take them to Dallas, her gaze slipped over a tall man in a pin-striped suit coming toward them. Even as her eyes focused on the screen, her mind blanked it out.

What in the hell was Mason Winter doing there? Had some maniacal god of coincidence put them in the same airport at the same time? More important, had he seen her, or did she still have time to fade into the crowd?

Her heart in her throat, she chanced a glance in his direction. All thought of a clean escape vanished. He was looking right at her.

Kevin squirmed restlessly on her lap, seeking a more comfortable position. He caught the worried expression on her face. "What's wrong, Mama?"

"Nothing," she managed to say. "I just thought I saw someone I know."

"Who?"

She tried to give him a reassuring smile. "He's gone," she said. She started to get up but before she could stand, she felt a hand on her shoulder. He hadn't disappeared; he'd come up behind her.

"Please stay," Mason said evenly, almost cordially. "I'd like to talk to you."

Kevin twisted around to see who had spoken. "Hey, I know you," he said, animated for the first time that day. "You came to my house."

"On your birthday," Mason added.

"Yeah," Kevin agreed, obviously pleased that he wasn't the only one who remembered.

"Perhaps this time your mother would like to introduce us," Mason said, pointedly looking from Kevin to Chris.

The son of a bitch had cornered her. There was no way out except to do as he suggested. "Kevin, this is Mason Winter..." The natural and honest conclusion to the sentence hung heavy in the air.

Mason let the opportunity slide by, ignoring Chris entirely as his hand closed gently around his son's. "I'm very happy to meet you, Kevin."

"Are you a friend of my mom's or one of her business people?" he asked.

"Right now I'm not either. But I hope that doesn't stop you and me from being friends."

Kevin glanced up at Chris as if seeking her approval. Before she could answer him, a United Airlines plane taxied by the window, drawing his attention. "Is that our plane, Mama?"

Mason fixed Chris with a stare. "Going someplace?" he asked softly.

"This isn't a chance meeting, is it?" she countered as softly. "You had me followed."

"I had a hunch you might try something like this."

"How clever of you. Now—"

"Ow," Kevin said. "Let go of my arm, Mama. You're hurting me."

Mason directed his attention to Kevin. "If you watch from the window over there, you'll be able to see a man on the ground telling the people in the airplane what to do."

"Can I, Mom?" Kevin asked, already halfway off her lap.

It galled her to agree to anything Mason might suggest, but it was more important Kevin not be privy to the conversation that was about to take place. "All right. But don't go anywhere else." When he was gone, she turned to Mason. "How dare you?"

The smile he gave her never made it to his eyes. "It's a father's prerogative to show his son new things."

"You bastard. Why are you trying so hard to make me think you give a damn about Kevin when the entire city knows all you really care about is building ugly warehouses and adding another name to your list of conquests? This is just some game you're playing."

"Now, why would I do that?"

"I don't know, but I'll find out."

"Am I to take it that means you're staying after all?"

She glared at him. "You can't stop me from leaving."

"If you want a court order, I can get one. There are several judges in town who would be happy to accommodate me. All I have to do is ask. And don't think I can't keep you here while the papers are being drawn up. As you just pointed out, I'm well known in this town. All I'd have to do is tell security that you were trying to make off with my son and they would haul you out of here before you could open your mouth to protest." His eyes narrowed. "You really should stop and think a minute about pushing me that far, though. How is attempted kidnapping going to look on your record when this thing gets into the courts?"

"You're bluffing."

"You obviously don't know me as well as you think you do."

"You'll never win," Chris said with more conviction than she felt.

He chuckled. "If you really believed that, you wouldn't be here."

Desperation nudged bravado. She decided

to try another direction. "Why are you doing this? What can you possibly hope to gain?"

He shot her a look of disbelief. "God damn it, Ms. Taylor, I think it's about time you got it through your head that, no matter how much you wish it weren't so, that kid standing over there is mine. Do you think you've cornered the market on parenthood? Hasn't it occurred to you yet that there's a possibility I might have a few of those feelings myself, that by right of birth and any other right you want to bring in, I might want what you so blithely assume is yours alone?" He took a deep breath and stood up. "Now, would you like me to escort you to your car?"

"I'd like you to go to hell."

"Someday, perhaps, but certainly not at your convenience." When she made no attempt to get up, he added, "I'm not leaving here until you do, so you might as well get your ass out of that chair and get moving."

"My luggage—"

"It's already on its way back to your house."

"How—" She stopped, not wanting to give him the satisfaction of knowing she cared how he accomplished what for most people would have been impossible. "Never mind," she said, slipping her purse strap over her shoulder as she rose from of the chair.

"Shall I get Kevin?"

"Stay away from him."

"You know you're going to have to tell him about me sooner or later." He paused. His voice took on a softer, gentler edge. "Or would you rather I told him?"

109

"No. If he's to find out about you at all, it has to come from me."

"You can't really believe you have a choice about telling him." He took her arm and forced her to look at him. "I'm not some bad dream you're having. You aren't going to wake up tomorrow morning and find me gone. The only choice you have left is under which circumstances you tell Kevin he has a father."

"If you cared as much as you say you do, you wouldn't do this to him."

He let go of her arm. "What? Love him? Take care of him? Expand his world a little? What is it you think I'm going to do to him that's so harmful?"

"You're going to turn his world inside out."

"Is it his world or yours that you're worried about?"

"They're one and the same," she said, barely above a whisper.

Mason looked over at Kevin. For long seconds he stared at his son. "What have you told him about me?"

"I didn't know who you were. How could I tell him anything?"

"You must have said something when he asked why all the other kids had fathers and he didn't."

"I said you were a secret his mama Diane never told me about. That all I knew about you—" She hesitated, unsure whether or not to tell him the rest.

"Go on."

She watched him staring at Kevin and was

struck anew at how much alike they looked. She tried to picture Mason and her sister together, loving each other, smiling, sharing intimacies. What had Diane seen in him that Chris could not? "I told him all I knew about you was that his mama Diane had loved you very much."

Mason's eyes narrowed as he studied her. "I guess I have to thank you for that much at least."

"It's all you're getting."

He shook his head. "Why make this harder than it has to be?"

"If you had one shred of what it takes to be a parent, you'd understand why I intend to fight you every step of the way. Depositing a seed and then showing up six years later to see how it's grown is meaningless. Time spent on the job is what really counts in a child's life. And since I'm the one who's spent that time with Kevin, I'm the one who decides what's best for him. You're not it, Mr. Winter, not by a long shot."

"A most convincing speech, Ms. Taylor. But there's one small flaw in your reasoning. Had I known about Kevin, I would have been the one putting in the time."

"That's easy for you to say now."

"Not only easy, indisputable. Who would question what I would have done back then, when I responded the way I did the minute I received Diane's letter?"

Diane felt as though the ground was being pulled out from under her. "You can say whatever you want to whomever you want, but you'll never convince me you're sincere. If you really cared about Kevin, you'd leave him alone."

"We've come full circle. I can see there's no sense in going on. I have work to get back to, and I'm sure there are things you have that need doing." He motioned toward the exit. "Shall we leave?"

"Go ahead. I'll wait until Kevin has his fill of planes. There's no sense in wasting our trip out here."

He chuckled. "Nice try."

"What's the matter? Can't trust your spy to keep an eye on us?"

"This is something I'd rather handle myself. Now, if you're ready?"

"I need time to explain to Kevin."

"You'll have plenty of time to tell him while you're driving him home."

"It's amazing. Just when I think I dislike you as much as I could possibly dislike another human being, you say something that ups the ante."

He ignored her attempt to bait him. "Do you want me to get Kevin?"

Instead of answering, she went over to the window. After standing at Kevin's side for several seconds, she lowered herself on her haunches. "Guess what?" she said.

"What?" he answered, his attention still focused on the plane.

"I've decided that maybe we should stay in Sacramento after all."

He looked at her, his eyes shining with excitement. "Really?"

She nodded, not trusting her voice.

The excitement left as quickly as it had come. "Does that mean we don't get to fly on an airplane?"

She felt like laughing and crying at the same time. How like Kevin to want something the minute it was taken away. "Not today," she said. "But someday we will."

"Promise?"

"Cross my heart." She stood up and took his hand.

"Can I tell Tracy?"

She purposely led Kevin past Mason Winter and on out of the building without looking back at him. "Of course."

"Can she come, too?" Kevin asked.

"It all depends on where we're going." Each step she took, she felt more weighted down.

"I'm going to tell her as soon as we get home."

She surreptitiously wiped a tear from the corner of her eye. "Remember," she said, "you have to be careful of promises. Sometimes they can hurt people."

He looked up at her. "You promised we would have a new place to live."

"I know," she said.

"It's all right, Mama," he said. "It wasn't a good promise anyway."

She ruffled his hair. "Maybe not, but it seemed like one at the time."

Chris and Kevin stopped at Safeway on the way home to pick up groceries and a loaf of

113

day-old bread to feed the ducks in McKinley Park. When they got to the park, Chris sat on the grass and watched Kevin carefully dole out the bread, making sure even the most timid birds got their share.

She did everything she could to encourage the generosity and gentleness she saw developing in Kevin. The world he would someday inherit was going to need men able to find caring solutions to desperate problems whether on a wide-scale political level or simply in the way they went about their day-to-day lives.

What had once been meaningless abstractions to Chris—peace and brotherhood and understanding between countries, saving the earth's resources by recycling, protecting endangered species because one loss was felt by all—had become a way of life since Kevin. She wanted to do everything she could to make sure the earth he and his generation would one day inherit was better than the one she had known. The idea was simple but profound. And her actions were the best way she knew to tell Kevin how much she loved him.

When the bread was all gone, they walked through the rose garden and then over to the tennis courts to watch two middle-aged women who missed the ball more often than they hit it.

Finally, when Chris could delay their homecoming no longer, she and Kevin climbed back into the car and drove the few blocks to Forty-second Street. Once inside, she called Mary and asked if Kevin could spend the afternoon at her house.

If she wanted to have any hope of winning her battle with Mason Winter, she had to do whatever she could to improve her odds. She walked Kevin to the Hendricksons' and waited until he was safely inside. Promising Mary she would explain what was going on when she returned to get Kevin, she went back home and made an appointment to see Paul Michaels the next day. Even though he was sure to insist he wasn't the one to handle the case because family practice wasn't his specialty, as far as Chris was concerned the passion and caring he would bring to her fight against Mason were more important than experience in similar cases. Just because Mason Winter had the law on his side, didn't mean what he was doing was right.

She spent the rest of the afternoon unpacking.

12

Mason stepped off of the construction elevator and onto what would eventually be the top floor of the Capitol Court Hotel. The project was three weeks behind schedule. Considering the delays in deliveries and inspections, that wasn't too bad, but it sure as hell wasn't anything to celebrate, either.

He'd decided it would be prudent to talk to the foreman personally to encourage him to do whatever he could to push things along.

He'd found it useful, even when things were on schedule, to give gentle and sometimes not so gentle reminders to those in charge. As a result, in its fourteen years of existence, Winter Construction had never missed a scheduled opening. Even if every man on every other project had to be pulled in to work on the hotel, it would open on time. But should that be necessary, heads would roll.

"Hey, Mr. Winter, how are ya?" came a voice from somewhere overhead.

Mason clamped his hand over his hard hat and looked up. He smiled at the construction worker peering at him through steel beams. "How are the twins, Calvin?"

"Great, 'specially since they started sleeping nights. I been meaning to thank you for the cribs you sent. They're real nice. Look real good in the room, too."

"Your wife already thanked me."

"She said she was going to, but I wanted to be sure to say something myself."

Mason's ability to show an interest in his employees' personal lives was made possible in large part by Rebecca. She kept him up to date on the births, deaths, and other occasions important to the people who worked for him, and she always made it look as though the response had been his idea alone. "They told me downstairs that Howard was up here. Have you seen him?"

"Howard's at lunch. But Travis is here," Calvin added as an afterthought.

"Send him down, would you?"

"Sure will, Mr. Winter."

"I'm on my way," a deeper, louder voice added.

Mason walked over to the makeshift stairs and waited. Travis Millikin appeared seconds later. Although he would have had to stretch to make five-six, Travis's fireplug build and weather-etched face cowed burly construction workers and dandified city planners with equal ease. Backing up his appearance was an encyclopedic knowledge of the building industry. There had never been a question asked to which Travis had to look up the answer. He was somewhere on the high side of fifty, twice divorced, now married for the third time, and as generous as he was short-fused.

"Did the plumbing pass?" Mason asked without preamble.

"The inspectors haven't gotten here yet."

"Goddammit. Didn't anybody tell them what kind of schedule we're operating under?" he asked rhetorically.

Travis wiped his hands on his jeans. "They know, and they don't give a rat's ass. Why should they?"

The building boom had caught everyone in the city off guard. Every department was understaffed, overworked, and about as tolerant of complaints as a bordello manager. Mason did whatever he could to stay in their good graces for the most selfish of reasons. Sometimes it earned him extra consideration, sometimes it didn't. "Do what you can," he said. "And keep me posted."

Travis nudged a loose fragment of con-

117

crete with his toe, picked it up, and put it in his pocket. "By the way, I like the new guy you hired. He was a little hard to get a fix on at first, kinda quiet, but I think he's going to work into things pretty quick." He cast Mason a sideways glance. "Don't take this wrong, but he reminds me a little of your brother."

Mason thought about that a minute. "Good God, you're right."

"You shouldn't let it color your feelings. I only brought it up because I knew it would occur to you sooner or later, and in this case, sooner seemed better."

"How in the hell could I have missed something like that?" Mason said absently. Travis's comment triggered bitter memories, as fresh as if they had happened fourteen days ago instead of fourteen years.

"From what I hear, you've had your mind on more important things lately," Travis said, his usually gruff voice taking on an uncharacteristic softness.

"How did you know about that? I haven't seen you since you got back from Los Angeles." Travis still made periodic trips south to tie up the loose ends they had left behind when they moved the main offices of Winter Construction to Sacramento.

"You should know by now there's not a whole lot that goes on around here I don't hear about." He spotted and picked up another piece of concrete.

"Son of a bitch," Mason grumbled. "That must mean everyone knows."

Travis shrugged. "Well, they didn't hear it

from me. I might take it all in, but I don't pass it along."

"For Christ's sake, Travis, I know that. It doesn't make any difference who knows and who doesn't, anyway. It'll be public record any day now. I just wanted to tell you myself, that's all."

"So when you going to bring the little guy around?"

Mason loosened his tie. They were in the middle of yet another record-breaking heat wave, the second since he'd moved to Sacramento. Even twenty-two stories up, there wasn't enough breeze to dry sweat. "There are a couple of stumbling blocks I have to get past first. Diane's sister wasn't exactly thrilled to have me show up on her doorstep. It's going to take some time to work things out between us."

"Do your folks know?"

Travis was the only man Mason knew who had the nerve and the background to ask him about his family. No doubt there were others on the crew just as curious, but only Travis had earned the right to comment.

Fourteen years earlier, when Mason was squeezed out of the family partnership in Southwest Construction by his father and brother and had to sue just to be paid for the portion of the company he had built with his own money, Travis had been outraged at the injustice. As the top man in the field office for Southwest, he'd had a lot to lose by siding with Mason, but that hadn't deterred him. He'd been the first to throw his lot in with the fledgling Winter Construction Company, joining up before there was even a business license or an office.

In the beginning, when, in order to save on payroll, Mason had been putting in eighteen-hour days, seven days a week, working up the bids, running the office, trying to fit in the requisite glad-handing, and keeping tabs on the work going on in the field, Travis had agreed to take a percentage of the profits in lieu of pay. At the time, when even a case of pencils had been an extravagance, the arrangement had been a godsend. Travis's gesture not only helped to provide the operating capital they needed but also gave an emotional boost to the other employees. It took less than five years for the arrangement to become embarrassingly profitable for Travis and for him to ask to go back to being a salaried employee. Mason had refused.

In the beginning, Mason had toyed with the idea of calling the company Phoenix Construction. It was Travis who suggested that using the Winter name on a business that would one day put Southwest Construction in its shadow might be a more appropriate and satisfying thorn in the side of Mason's family.

Rebecca Kirkpatrick had arrived the day they were putting the new name on the construction trailer, which at the time was doing double duty as company headquarters and Mason's apartment. She walked into the office unannounced, laid her one-page résumé on the desk, and proclaimed she was looking for an up-and-coming business to throw in her lot with and that she figured she'd just found it.

After that, it was the three of them, united in pursuit of a common goal, far closer than the family Mason had left behind. Rebecca and Travis had been there to celebrate his happiness when he and Susan were married, and they had stood by his side at her funeral five years later. During the black days that followed, when everything seemed to be falling down around him, they had been the pillars that kept him upright. They had rejoiced when Diane came into his life and felt almost as betrayed as he had when she left. They would be the only members of Mason's family Kevin would ever meet.

"No," Mason said, finally answering Travis's question. "I haven't told them, and I won't."

"What about your mother?" Travis persisted.

Anger, so deeply entwined with hurt that he couldn't tell one from the other, shot through Mason. "What about her?" he snapped.

"Don't you think—"

"Not about her, if I can help it," he finished. "After what happened, she doesn't rate grandmother privileges in my book."

"I just thought you might want to consider it. I can't help thinking she was caught in the middle of what went on, damned no matter which way she went."

"So she went neither way, becoming conspicuous by her silence."

"Maybe now that you've got a kid of your own, you'll understand some things better."

"You're getting soft in your old age, Travis."

"You know damn well that's got nothing to do with it."

Mason turned and looked toward the river. As always, his gaze fixed on the individual parcels of land he'd been trying to gather into one large tract for almost as long as he'd been in Sacramento. He considered making a comment to Travis about the progress Rebecca was making with one of the farmers they'd about given up on ever bringing around, but decided against it. While the farmer flatly refused to sign a note saying he would promise to sell his land to Winter Construction if and when Mason could pull the rest of the project together, he was at least beginning to make noises that for the right incentives, he would consider giving Mason first right of refusal. Travis still considered the enterprise foolhardy—no, more than foolhardy; he was convinced a project that size and that speculative would be Winter Construction's downfall. But in this one instance, even Travis's disapproval had not been enough to dissuade Mason.

He was determined to leave his signature on that land for future generations. Two months ago he'd wanted it for himself. Now it would be a gift to his son.

He let out a derisive snort as he took off his hard hat and wiped the sweat from his forehead. It wasn't Travis who was getting soft in his old age, it was him. "I don't know about you," he said, turning back to his friend, "but I don't have time to stand around chewing the fat. I've got places to go and people to see."

"If one of them is Tony Avalon, tell him I want his ass back on that warehouse by morning."

Mason was grateful Travis was willing to drop the subject of Mason's newfound son even when it was obvious he had more to say. "I'll have Rebecca pass on the message. If I talk to him in the mood I'm in now, he'll never do business with us again."

"I don't know that it would be any big loss."

"Maybe we should talk about that. He's getting a bid ready for the Watt Avenue project. If we're going to dump him, I want to be sure we get some other people in there we can count on." Mason walked to the side of the building and waved for the elevator.

"I'll meet you at Pava's for breakfast."

"My treat, no doubt."

Travis laughed. "You're a cheap bastard, Mason."

"And you're a rich one, Travis."

The laugh deepened. "I'll leave the tip."

Mason swung the elevator door open, stepped inside, and turned back to Travis. "Better wear something old. As I recall, the last time you left the tip, the waitress spilled coffee on you."

Mason quit work early that night to don his tuxedo for the Gala Celebration of the Arts at the Hyatt Hotel. He had intended to send a car for his date, Kelly Whitefield, but changed his mind at the last minute and decided to pick her up himself.

The dinner dance was another obligatory evening, but this time there was an interesting twist. As it was now, the Hyatt provided the only upscale accommodations in the core of the city. As soon as Winter Construction put the finishing touches on the Capitol Court Hotel, that would change. There would be some heavy-duty hustling between the two establishments to draw customers for a while—three or four years by Mason's estimation. After that, business should have increased enough to occupy two luxury hotels. In the meantime, Mason was counting on the newness of the Capitol Court to draw enough people away from the Hyatt to keep him at least comfortably, if not deeply, in the black.

It would be a tactical error for him to stay away from the evening's function. His absence would be noted and speculated upon. His presence would be ignored. Besides, he was due a night out, and there was no one better to take his mind off of work than Kelly Whitefield.

Because he was early, he decided to take surface streets rather than the freeway to Kelly's duplex. A delta breeze had finally broken through the straits, dropping the valley's temperature by fifteen degrees, making the air breathable again and an open sunroof on his car something besides an insanity.

The Porsche 911 slipped through what remained of Friday evening traffic with a fluid grace that made it a pure joy to drive. In the eight years Mason had owned the car, he'd put only thirty-nine thousand miles on it, most of them in winter when business slowed enough to allow him to load up his skis and head for the mountains. Living in northern California and not skiing was a lot like planting a garden and not eating the vegetables.

He wondered if Kevin would like skiing. The idea brought a smile. He'd spent years watching kids no taller than his knee barreling down slopes with breathtaking abandon, executing stem christies as if their legs were made of rubber, refusing to go indoors until their lips turned blue from the cold. The thought of looking up to the top of a ski slope and knowing that one of the kids hell-bent on making it to the bottom first was his son created a flood of complex and compelling emotions.

Without conscious thought, Mason reached for the turn signal behind the steering wheel as he neared Forty-second Street. It wasn't until he had actually pulled to a stop across from Chris and Kevin's house, and gotten out of the car that he realized what he was doing—precisely what he had done before and precisely what his lawyer had told him never to do again. He couldn't rouse the sensibilities to care. It appeared that the calm and calculating mind which served him so well in business turned to mush when it came to his son.

Glancing through the window as he

approached the front door, he saw Chris standing in the kitchen talking to someone. At least she wouldn't be able to pretend she wasn't home. He stepped onto the porch and rang the bell.

"I'll get it, Mom," Kevin shouted.

"Never mind, Kevin, I'll—"

Chris either wasn't loud enough or wasn't fast enough to catch him before he flung open the door. "Hi," he said, instantly recognizing Mason.

"Hi," Mason answered, taken aback by the intensity of the swell of pleasure that came over him.

"Want me to get my mom?" Kevin asked.

It was the last thing Mason wanted, but he knew he had no real choice. If there was the slimmest possibility he and Chris could work things out between them without going to court, he didn't want to jeopardize that chance by making her angry before they even talked. He was well aware, and was sure she was, too, that with anything close to a decent lawyer, she could stall his bid for joint custody for years. "If she's not busy," he said reluctantly.

Another head popped up beside Kevin's. "He's the man I told you about," Kevin said, turning to the girl. "The one Mom and me saw at the airport."

"He has nice clothes," the little girl said, talking about Mason as if he weren't there.

To Mason, Kevin said, "My mom's in the kitchen with Aunt Mary. She's making peanut butter cookies. But she can stop for a minute."

"I'm right here, Kevin," Chris said, wiping her hands on a towel as she came up to the door. She gave Mason a frosty look before turning her attention to Kevin. "Why don't you and Tracy play in the backyard while I talk to Mr. Winter?"

"But we were playing with the Legos in the bedroom," he protested.

She put her hand on his shoulder and steered him behind her. "You can finish later."

"Can we take the Legos outside?"

"Are you ever allowed to take them outside?"

"No," he answered.

"Nothing's changed."

"Can we have a cookie?"

"Ask Aunt Mary to give you one."

"Can we have two?"

"*Kevin*," she said, her voice taking on a tone that told him he'd pushed far enough. He yielded, took his friend's hand, and headed for the kitchen. When he was gone, Chris again faced Mason, fire in her eyes. "What are you doing here?"

"I wanted to see Kevin," he answered, deciding for the simplicity of honesty.

"You know how I feel about that."

"I thought you might have given it some more consideration by now," Mason said, trying to sound conciliatory and reasonable, even though the effort was choking him. The profound sense of fair play that cried out for him to take what was rightfully his was the very thing that stopped him from carrying it out. As much as he would have liked to ignore

Chris's claim on Kevin, he couldn't. She was as much Kevin's mother as he was his father—maybe not by right of birth, but certainly by right of time put in.

"I can hardly think of anything else," she said.

"I suppose it would be foolish of me to hope you might have changed your mind."

"That's not the way I would have put it, but that pretty much sums it up."

"I've run across some incredibly stubborn people in my life, but none as—" He stopped. Insulting her would get him nowhere. "Look, I only want what's best for Kevin. He needs a father every bit as much as he needs a mother. I have no intention of trying to take him away from you. I just want to be a part of his life and to make him a part of mine."

"If you really wanted what was best for Kevin, you wouldn't be here now. Having a father suddenly appear in his life isn't going to make it better; it's only going to confuse him. Especially a father like you."

He couldn't keep the anger from his voice any longer. "What in the hell makes you think you know what kind of father I'd make?"

She leaned against the door frame and folded her arms across her chest. "Everyone who lives in this city and reads the newspapers knows what kind of man you are. You live in a glass house, Mr. Winter, and whether by an error in judgment or by design, you leave your blinds open so that everyone can look inside."

He threw his hands up and let out a groan

of disgust. "Terrific. My son is being raised by a card-carrying member of the moral majority. Jesus Christ, woman, do you always let others do your thinking for you? Aren't you capable of forming your own opinion based on what you see instead of what you read?"

She stood unflinching against his tirade. "You stand for everything I'm against," she said evenly, when he had finished.

To control the urge he had to wrap his hands around her throat, he shoved them into his pockets. "Like?" he demanded.

"The Auburn Dam, a new marina on the Sacramento River; tax breaks for the wealthy; buying political influence, and when that doesn't work, using bullying tactics to get what you want; allowing yourself to be auctioned off like a piece of meat—shall I go on?"

"It doesn't count that the auction was for charity, I suppose," he said, unable to resist baiting her.

"To you it might," she shot back. "But try to explain that to a little boy watching his father parade down a runway, bumping and grinding for the benefit of a bunch of stupid women in the audience."

"You've been to one of these things, I take it?"

"I've read about them."

"Oh, I see. We're back to the newspapers again." He dropped his gaze, thinking about what she'd said. "And the bullying tactics you say I use, you've read about those in the paper, too?"

"Yes."

"And my anti-environmental stance."

"Yes."

"Is that it?"

"Isn't it enough?"

When he looked up again, he was careful to keep his expression innocent, free of any trace of the fury he felt. "I just thought you might be saving the best for last. But I guess you missed the article that said I've fucked every woman in the county worth looking at between the ages of twenty-one and fifty."

She stared at him for several seconds before answering. "But we know that isn't true," she said sweetly. "Don't we, Mr. Winter?"

He was so surprised by her answer that he was momentarily speechless. He'd expected her to stand toe to toe with him, but not to best him. "You know as well as I do that you don't have the money for a long court battle. What's it going to take to wake you up to the facts?"

"If you could see beyond your own self-centered world, you'd realize what I'm fighting for has nothing to do with money or facts or righting old wrongs. I love Kevin more than I love my own life. I'll do whatever is necessary to protect him."

He couldn't argue with her anymore. She had created her own little world and her own brand of fanaticism to protect it. She was the guardian angel and he the devil. "I'm sorry I bothered you," he said, admitting defeat. He shot her a final glance and was surprised to see a look of puzzlement cross her face.

Turning, he started back toward his car, listening to the door close and the lock snap into place behind him. "Someday, Kevin," he promised. "Someday soon."

13

Mason nodded in acknowledgment of Walt Bianchi's arrival at the dinner table. Rebecca had insisted that it was far more important for the newest executive of Winter Construction to be at the charity function rubbing elbows with the movers and shakers of Sacramento society than it was for her and had insisted Walt be given her ticket. She'd been right, of course, but she'd also been obnoxiously smug at finally being given an excuse to stay home and curl up with one of the dozens of unread mystery novels she'd been collecting over the years.

Mason held his hand up to stop the waiter from pouring another glass of wine. He'd already had too much that night, in an attempt to soften the edges of his anger at Chris Taylor. When it became evident that alcohol wasn't the answer, and that if he drank any more he would have to let Kelly drive them home or take a cab, he switched to coffee.

At least one aspect of the evening was a pleasant surprise: Walt Bianchi was a master at working a crowd. In three short hours he had charmed everyone from the mayor to Travis Millikin's wife. When Mason asked him what he thought of Linda Ronstadt, who'd been hired as the evening's entertainment, Walt had said he didn't know. His face totally serious, he had gone on to say that if she didn't have anything to do with the construction business, he didn't have time for her.

Were it not for the uneasiness Mason felt over Walt's uncanny resemblance to his brother, he would have been able to enjoy the performance more. As it was, he found himself questioning his newest employee's actions and feeling suspicious of how easily the man ingratiated himself with others. He even wondered how much of Bianchi's skill had been used on him when he'd interviewed Walt for the job.

He hated doubting the man, especially for such questionable reasons. People deserved to be judged on what they did, not how they looked or what others said about them.

Too bad Chris Taylor didn't subscribe to the same theory.

Damn, here he was again, right back to where he'd started the evening. It galled him that she wouldn't stay in the corner of his mind he'd relegated her to. Instead she insinuated herself into every thought, every action.

"Hey, anybody home?" Kelly purred into his ear, slipping her arm through his and pressing her chest against him.

He leaned toward her and smiled. "I'm being neglectful, and to the most beautiful woman here, no less. I apologize."

"Apology accepted." She propped her chin on his shoulder, letting her breath warm his ear. "Why do I get the feeling you're not having a very good time?"

"Because you're not only beautiful, you're intelligent.

"Stop that," she whispered playfully. "You're getting me hot."

There were certainly worse ways to end an evening.

She smiled seductively. "Give me a couple of minutes to say my good-byes and we can leave."

When she was gone, Mason turned to Walt. "Learn anything?" he asked.

Walt laughed. "I'm finding that's one of the things I like most about you, Mason. You cut right to the chase." He angled himself to make their conversation more private. "Interestingly enough, I discovered you're even more feared and hated by certain people than I had anticipated you would be. Which tells me I've made the right choice in deciding where I wanted to work and whom I wanted to work for."

"That's an interesting observation." It was precisely the way he would have responded in the same situation.

"By the way, what is this waterfront project I keep hearing people whispering about? I don't remember you saying anything about it when you hired me. Did I miss something?"

"Which people?" Mason asked, tensing. Up until the past few months, his attempts to buy the land along the Sacramento River had been considered a joke by the other builders in the community: Winter's Wonderland, they called the project, convinced that if he ever got permission to build his miniature city within a city, he would be bankrupt or insane or—better yet as far as they were concerned—both, before he saw any of the buildings occupied.

The problems inherent in trying to build anything on the ecologically fragile ground were monumental. The land incorporated a city's and two counties' building codes and involved getting permission from both a city council and two county boards of supervisors, as well as dealing with the State Flood Control Agency, the Parks and Recreations Department, and the Water Quality Control Board, to name but a few. It wasn't surprising that to everyone but Mason, the project seemed the height of idiocy, something no builder in his right mind would even consider. Certainly no bank or savings and loan would even consider financing the project, unless it wanted the feds breathing down its neck, questioning its loan policies.

Still, Mason had persisted, confident the last laugh would be his, assured he had a free run at the project because he was the only one with the balls to take it on—until six weeks ago, that is, when he began picking up bits and pieces of information that led him to believe someone else had recognized the potential profit to be made by developing the riverfront property Mason had come to think of as his own.

Walt put his hand to his face as if rubbing his chin, but in reality he was blocking his lips

134

from being seen by anyone who might be trying to listen. "I believe two of the people in the group were tied into the city council somehow. I couldn't catch their names, but I can tell you what they look like. I did over-hear one of them refer to the man he was talking to as Al Lowenstein and to another as Bart or Bert, something like that. I tried to give the impression I couldn't hear them, but as soon as Lowenstein recognized me, they changed the subject."

Mason nodded. The grouping didn't sur-prise him, but the subject did. Al and Bart together couldn't come up with the financing to put in a community shopping center; they weren't the threat. But for them to have heard enough about what was going on to be talking about it that night meant the threat was real. "Let me know if you hear anyone else talking about the project," he told Walt. "And pay particular attention to what's being said."

"Anything specific?"

The carefully worded question was a bid for more information, something Mason wasn't ready to give. Why he felt reluctant to take Walt into his confidence, he wasn't sure; he only knew that if the feeling continued, Walt wouldn't. "No," Mason told him after several seconds. "Bring me anything you hear."

Mason caught the scent of Kelly's per-fume a half second before she arrived. "Ready?" he asked, standing.

She touched the tip of her tongue to her lip. "Oh, yes..." she said, so that only he could hear. She smiled as she leaned into him and pressed a quick kiss to his cheek. "And then some," she added in a throaty whisper.

Mason looked down at Walt. "I'll see you in the office on Monday," he said.

"And if the rest of the evening should prove interesting?"

Mason realized that, in order to prove himself, Walt intended to stay until all that were left were drunks and waiters. It was precisely what he would have done in Walt's position; that pleased him. "Call Rebecca. She'll know how to get in touch with me."

He turned his attention back to Kelly, taking her arm as they moved through the banquet hall, nodding to acknowledge those he knew, smiling at familiar faces, stopping twice to pass on bits of information to people he hadn't seen in a while.

Stepping from the air-conditioned lobby into the warm night stripped the last remnants of the party atmosphere from them. The heat settled over them in a subtly sensual way, telling them they were overdressed for the night air. It was a time for opening car windows and letting the wind stir the senses.

"Do you still have that spa?" Mason asked while they waited for his car to be brought around.

"And the perfect cabernet sauvignon to go with it. Hand-carried all the way from France by yours truly."

Kelly owned a travel agency and was out of town as much as she was in. Although he normally preferred California wines, when Kelly took the trouble to bring something home with her, he knew he was in for a treat.

He let his glance slide to the fullness of her breasts where they mounted above the emerald green silk dress. The work Kelly put into keeping her body as fit and lean as it had been when she was a collegiate backstroke champion did more than produce flesh that was taut and firm; it gave a sensuous, athletic grace to the way she moved. He found that kind of confidence incredibly sexy.

But it wasn't the amazing body or the beautiful face alone that attracted Mason to Kelly. It wasn't even the sex, which was the best he'd ever had with a woman he didn't love. It was that being with her was uncomplicated. If tonight was like every other night they had spent together, they would have several hours of uninhibited, sometimes wildly improbable sex and part friends in the morning. It would be all right with both of them if they didn't see each other again for months. There would be no strings and no hurt feelings.

It was exactly the kind of relationship Mason needed, and the only kind he would ever allow himself to get involved in again. He'd had love in marriage and he'd had love outside of it, and he'd had the pain involved when each ended. The highs were great, but the lows had damn near killed him.

He slipped his arm around Kelly's shoulders and pulled her against his side, feeling her heat penetrate his tuxedo. The action created a desire so sudden and intense it almost overwhelmed him. If he hadn't heard the roar of his Porsche coming down the concrete ramp, he would have skipped the ride home and taken her back into the hotel.

She looked up at him and smiled. "Good things come to those who wait, Mason."

"Does nothing get past you?"

She eyed the bulge in his pants. "Some things are more obvious than others."

He grinned. "I've missed you," he said, pressing a kiss to her forehead.

"Not for much longer," she replied, pulling his head down to meet her upturned lips. She thrust her tongue into his mouth in a deep, probing kiss.

Mason congratulated himself on the seemingly unaffected manner in which he helped Kelly into the car, took his keys from the attendant, and left the parking lot. He was surprised to see the teasing look on Kelly's face when they pulled up to the first stoplight.

"I'll bet you believe you got away with it, don't you?" she said.

"That parking attendant never suspected a thing."

"Why do you suppose he thinks he didn't get a tip, because you were in a hurry to get home to watch Johnny Carson?"

Mason thought about it for a minute and then laughed. "I'll catch him next time."

Kelly hiked up her skirt, took Mason's hand, and put it on the inside of her thigh. "Liar," she said. "You don't have the slightest idea what he looked like."

By the time they arrived at Kelly's duplex, they were both on the verge of climax from the prolonged foreplay that had gone on in the car. They dropped their clothes by the front door, sank down on the Persian rug in front of the fireplace, and finished what they had started in the car, stopping only long enough to put on the condom Mason had taken out of his pants pocket.

When the initial storm of passion was spent, Kelly climbed on top to straddle him and ride out the last of her spasms as she moved against his erection. "That was good," she said, splaying her fingers across his chest. "But it was only the appetizer."

"Do you ever have a full meal?" he asked.

"Only with you." She caught his nipples between her fingers and rubbed them in a circular motion. "If I could persuade you to tell me how you manage to stay hard all night, I'd get a patent on it and be set for life."

He ran his hands up her thighs until his thumbs were pressing against her wetness. "You're what keeps me hard," he said.

She laughed. "If it's me, how come my magic doesn't work with anyone else?"

He abruptly sat up, catching her and pulling her against him. "I can't imagine," he said, arching his back to feel the weight of her breasts pressing into him.

"Want to get that wine and soak for a while? I feel like being wet and slippery on the outside, too." She stopped as if a thought had just occurred to her. "You can stay the night, can't you?"

It was on the tip of his tongue to say yes, but when he opened his mouth, "No" came out instead. He was as surprised as she was.

"I'm sorry," she stammered. "I just assumed..."

Since he had no idea why he'd told her he couldn't stay, coming up with a ready and logical reason was damn near impossible. "It's my son," he finally said, again surprising them both.

"What son?" she asked, leaning back so that she could look at him.

He hesitated, reluctant to go into details with her. "It's a long story," he answered at last, a glimmer of comprehension forming that was as illogical as it was obvious. He was a father now, and in his mind, fathers simply didn't go to a woman's house with the express intent of fucking the entire night away. He looked at Kelly and shrugged helplessly. "I don't understand it myself. When I do, I'll tell you about it."

She stared at him. Finally, anger gave way to frustration, and frustration to acceptance. "Well, how about one more for the road?"

He chuckled. "You're not talking about a glass of wine, are you?"

"Hell no."

He pulled her back into his arms. "Good."

"If this is all I'm getting, it had better be," she said, wrapping her legs tighter around his waist.

He kissed her, deep and wet and lingering, looking for the escape he had planned earlier that afternoon. What he got instead was an image of Chris Taylor, standing on her front porch, telling him what a morally bankrupt bastard he was.

So much for a good time.

14

Chris leaned back in her chair and glanced out the window. After an entire morning spent at the computer, she was exhausted, she was bored, and she was out of ideas. There were only so many ways for an accounting firm to announce they'd taken on an "exciting" new partner who in reality was as boring as every other accountant who worked for Norman Johnston and Associates, but it was up to Chris to make it sound as if a new caped crusader had joined the ranks in the company's ongoing battle with the evil IRS. It was an ego thing that the company insisted on every time someone came on board, more for the benefit of the old employees who also had their names and qualifications listed in the pamphlet, Chris suspected, than for the new one.

But no one had asked her for a critique. Her job was to provide the copy. And since this assignment happened to pay better than most, and she was in desperate need of money, it wasn't even appropriate to complain.

Allowing herself a few minutes to clear the cobwebs from her mind before going back to work, she watched as an autumn wind tugged leaves from the elm tree across the street and sprinkled them on the lawn. October was a beautiful month in Sacramento. It hadn't been as pretty when she was a child, but over the years people had planted for the season, and now the streets were lined with trees adorned in brilliant reds and oranges and yellows.

Kevin had a passion for running through the crisp fallen leaves. The sounds of the crack and snap beneath his feet never failed to bring shouts of laughter from him. The neighbors, most of them older couples who rarely got to see their own grandchildren, tolerated Kevin's mischief with good grace, even allowing him to jump in their raked piles on cleanup days, only insisting that he stick around to help bag the leaves afterward.

The neighborhood provided what Chris could not. The people who lived there were as close as Kevin would ever come to an extended family.

Chris flinched. At least that had been the way it was until Mason Winter had happened into their lives. She readjusted herself in the chair and prepared to go back to work. Just as she turned the screen back on, the telephone rang.

"Hello," she said.

"Chris, it's Paul. I'm afraid I've got some bad news."

She tensed. "What is it?"

"Mason has filed an ex parte application and has gotten a temporary order allowing him to see Kevin."

"How?"

"How doesn't matter. If you recall, I told you in the beginning this was likely to happen. We've stalled him by dragging our feet as long as we can, Chris." He paused. "There's something else," he added, reluctantly.

"What?" she asked, feeling an icy fingertip work its way up her spine.

"He isn't just filing for a hearing about visitation rights; he's asking to have the adoption set aside."

"Can he do that?"

"He already has. But that doesn't mean he's going to win," he quickly added.

Chris was too stunned to answer immediately. "I thought he just wanted to see Kevin on weekends. At least that's what he's been claiming all along. Do you know what made him change his mind?"

"My guess is that he's asking for it all in order to get the piece he wants, but I could be wrong. Remember, I've never met the guy. You have. What do you think?"

She considered the question for several seconds before answering. "I think he's used to getting what he wants, and he doesn't give a tinker's dam who gets hurt in the process. Now do you understand why I have to fight him? How can I let a man like that have influence over Kevin? He may have a legal right to see his son, but I have a moral obligation to stop him."

"Chris, I want to talk to you as a friend for a minute," Paul said, his voice hesitant. "I know why you're doing this, and I respect your reasons..."

"But?" she said warily.

"You're beginning to sound a little strident, and that's not going to do your cause any good."

"For Christ's sake, Paul, this is my son we're talking about. How am I supposed to sound?"

"Like it or not, Mason Winter is a highly respected member of this community. If you want to prove him an unfit father, you're going to need a lot more evidence than we've been able to come up with."

"How can you say that? Mason Winter stands for everything—"

"I know, he stands for everything you're against. But you've got to remember that not everyone thinks 'conservative' is a four-letter word, Chris. A lot of judges who might wind up hearing this case would look at you as a throwback to the sixties. And as for the number of women he's reputed to have gone out with, he's single and as far as anyone knows, they are, too. No one's going to get very excited about that."

"What are you trying to tell me?"

"Give in on this one, especially since you don't really have any choice. Let Mason see Kevin for a few hours a week. Let's get something on record showing that you can be reasonable and cooperative. Even though the judge didn't specify it, perhaps I can persuade Mason to let you go along on the visits. That way you can see for yourself whether or not he's as bad as you imagine."

"Imagine?" Chris questioned. "You think I'm imagining the influence someone like Mason could have on a child like Kevin?"

"I'm sorry. That was an unfortunate choice of words, but the point still needs to be made, Chris. Mason is Kevin's father. We both know that eventually he is going to get the legal right to see his son on a regular basis. We can postpone the inevitable for only so long."

"That's the whole point. The longer we can hold off, the older Kevin will be. Right now he's too easily influenced. He's like a sponge. Mason could undermine everything I've done just by letting Kevin be around him. Kids don't do what you say, Paul, they do what you do."

"All I'm suggesting is that this might be the way to make the transition a little easier on both you and Kevin."

"Don't worry about me. I've accepted that I'm going to lose full custody of Kevin in the end."

"If you've accepted that... Never mind."

"Say it, Paul."

"I just hate to see you lose everything else in the process if you don't have to. Where are you going to get the money to fight him, Chris?"

"When the time comes, I'll sell the house."

"Good God, you can't do that. It's all you have."

"Kevin is the only important thing I have. The house is nothing." She was lying. The house was important to her, too, just at the other end of the scale when it came to how she felt about Kevin. Since there wasn't any other way for her to come up with the money she needed for legal fees, the house became dispensable.

She'd thought about a second mortgage but, after checking into the costs, discovered she would never be able to make the payments. The one thing in her favor was that houses in her neighborhood sold almost as quickly as they were listed, frequently at more than the asking price, so the sale wasn't something she had to arrange right away. For a while, at least, she and Kevin could enjoy their home.

"There's something you'd better take into consideration before you put the house up for sale, Chris. It's not going to do much for your case if the judge finds out you intend to make Kevin pay for your day in court by moving him into an apartment or to another house in a less desirable neighborhood. That judge isn't going to give a damn about your feelings. Kevin is the only one who will count. The boy has a father who is ready and willing to give his son the moon if he should ask for it. If you sell the house Kevin considers home just to win a point, you'll look like a self-centered, manipulating shrew who will go to any length to keep a father from seeing his son."

"Thanks for the vote of confidence."

"You came to me because you knew I would be completely honest with you no matter how rough things got or whose feelings were involved. That's the way I operate."

"But I wouldn't fire you if you showed a little compassion and understanding."

"Chris, I couldn't be more caught up in this thing if you were my own daughter and Kevin my grandson," he said softly.

"I know," she said and sighed. "It's just so hard sometimes. I keep thinking I'll wake up from this nightmare someday, but it just keeps going on and on."

"I would suggest you tell Kevin that Mason is his father before they meet each other," Paul said, bringing the conversation back to its original subject.

"They've already met, but you're right. If I don't tell him, Mason will, and I think it would be better for Kevin to hear the truth from me."

"Is there anything I can do to help?"

Chris had been realistic enough to know the time would come when she would have to tell Kevin that his father was alive and wanted to see him, but she'd foolishly hoped she would have years to prepare for that day. "Do you really think you could talk Mason into letting me go along on his visits?"

"It's worth a try."

"How much time do I have?"

"He wants to see Kevin on Saturday."

The words hit like a blow to the stomach. "That's only two days away."

"I'm sure Mason and his lawyer planned to take you by surprise. Keep your opponent off guard. It's classic battle strategy."

"Isn't there also something about possession being nine-tenths of the law?" she asked in a wry tone.

He sighed. "I wish I could do more, Chris."

She leaned back in her chair and closed her eyes. "I do, too, Paul," she said softly. Mary's car horn sounded out front, telling Chris that she was back from picking the kids up at school and was dropping Kevin off out front. "I have to let you go. Kevin's home and the door is still locked."

"I'll get back to you as soon as I've set things up with Mason's attorney. Is twelve o'clock at your house all right for Saturday?"

"Yes, that's fine—if there isn't any way you can delay the visit," she added, knowing full well he would do what he could, but unable to keep from reminding him how important his efforts were to her.

"I'll do what I can, but don't count on anything."

"Thanks, Paul." She hung up and raced for the door, meeting Kevin just as he was preparing to press the doorbell. "I'm here," she said in a rush.

"I know," he said, handing her a still damp picture of a pumpkin patch he'd painted that day.

"Oh? How did you know?" she said, bending down and giving him a quick kiss. She had to keep herself from grabbing him and holding on, knowing that to do so would not only scare him, it would alert him that something was going on.

"Because you're always here when I come home," he said logically.

"Did you have a good day?"

He wiggled past her and dropped his back-pack on a chair. "Uh-huh."

"What did you do?"

"Lots of stuff."

She had worked hard to give Kevin stability. He knew without question that she would always be there for him, that he could count on her to protect him and shelter him from pain, and that her love was unqualified.

"What kind of stuff?" she asked, keeping up her end of their daily ritual.

"Miz Abbott cut up a pumpkin and we cooked it."

Chris picked up his backpack and put it in the closet. "Did you eat any of it after it was cooked?"

He made a face. "It didn't taste very good. Miz Abbott said that tomorrow we're going to put a bunch of other stuff in it and make pies. I told her we should have you do it, 'cause you make the best pies in the world."

Chris laughed. "And what did she say to that?"

"That you could help us with the Thanks-giving party."

Unable to resist touching him any longer, she bent and lifted him up in her arms. "I missed you today," she said, planting a kiss on the end of his nose.

"What did you do while I was in school?"

"I worked all morning."

A nagging inner voice told her that if she was going to tell him, she had to begin as soon as possible. He would have a hundred questions that wouldn't occur to him all at once.

149

It was important that there be time for her to answer them all. She took a deep, steadying breath and plunged in. "Then, just before you came home, Paul Michaels called." She paused. "Do you remember Mr. Michaels?"

"He's the man who helped you adopt me."

"That's right." So, it had begun, but where did she go from here? "He had something very special to tell me, something that concerns you, too," she went on. "It's about Mr. Winter. Do you remember Mr. Winter?"

Kevin shook his head.

"The man we met at the airport a few weeks ago," Chris prompted. "He came here a couple of times, too."

"Oh, yeah."

She put Kevin down and led him into the kitchen, where she took an apple from a wicker basket on the counter, washed it, and cut it into quarters, using the ordinary task to stall for time to collect her thoughts. "Mr. Winter would like to see you," she said at last.

Kevin took a bite of apple, waited until it was half chewed, and asked, "How come?"

"He thinks you're special, and he..." And he what? She was about to yank Kevin's footing out from under him and couldn't find the words to provide a safety net. "Do you ever think about your mama Diane?" she asked, deciding to try coming at it from a different angle.

"Sometimes. Mostly when I look at her picture."

"Do you ever think about the man she loved who was your daddy?"

He stopped chewing and looked at her. "Sometimes I talk to Tracy about him."

"How would you feel if you could see your daddy?" God, how she hated referring to Mason Winter that way. Calling him "daddy" to Kevin gave him a legitimacy he had done nothing to earn.

Kevin thought about her question. "Would he be like Uncle John?"

Chris shook her head sadly. "There's no one else in the world like Uncle John. Just as there's no one else like you," she quickly added, realizing how negative the comparison could sound. "But I'm sure, in his own way, your daddy would be just as nice."

"Is Mr. uh..." he struggled to find the name. "Is the man from the airport my daddy?"

"Yes," she admitted reluctantly. "Mr. Winter is your father."

A slow smile spread across Kevin's face. "When is he going to move in?" he asked.

Chris stared at him open-mouthed. She had anticipated a hundred questions, but that one hadn't even occurred to her.

15

Chris had just stepped from the shower the next morning when Paul Michaels called.

"I'm afraid it's no go, Chris," he said. "Mason's attorney told me that your attitude in the past had destroyed any spirit of cooperation they might have had. There's no way he's going to let you go along on the visit."

Chris propped the phone between her shoulder and ear while she wrapped a towel around herself She was leaving the thermostat at sixty-two to save money, but in a house that desperately needed new insulation, sixty-two felt more like fifty-two. "Those were his exact words—that I had destroyed any spirit of cooperation?"

"Right down to the punctuation."

A flush of irritation warmed Chris's face. "Well, he can just screw his spirit of cooperation," she said. "If he thinks—"

"Calm down, Chris. I said I'd try to get his approval. I tried and he said no. Remember, this was a long shot to begin with."

"How much time does he get to spend with Kevin?"

"Two hours."

"God, anything can happen in two hours."

"Have you told Kevin yet?"

"Yesterday." She rubbed the goose bumps on her arms, trying to create heat with friction.

"How did he take it?"

"Too damn well, as far as I'm concerned." She rethought her statement. "No, I don't mean that. He's excited about having a father and anxious to meet him."

"I hope you have sense enough to realize what a credit that is to the way you've raised him. You've done a hell of a job, Chris. Kevin is about the happiest and most well-adjusted kid I've ever met."

"Now if I can just keep him that way through all of this. I'll do whatever it takes."

"Including letting Mason become a part of his life?" Paul gently prodded.

"It's going to take a lot to convince me that one doesn't automatically preclude the other."

"Call me and let me know how the visit goes."

"I'll do that," she promised. She hung up the phone, ran for the bedroom, and made a dive for the down comforter at the foot of the bed, wrapping it around her trembling body. It took several minutes for her to realize she wasn't shaking from the cold alone. When she did, she got up and dressed, determined not to give in to the urge to curl up in the fetal position and feel sorry for herself.

The next morning, an hour before Mason was due to arrive, Chris turned the thermostat up to seventy-two. She wasn't about to let him notice any of her economies. Kevin was dressed in a new pair of Oshkosh jeans and a red and blue striped shirt. She'd even pulled out the leather bomber jacket she'd found on sale that past summer and had put away for a Christmas present.

The sun had been up only a few hours when she realized she could have saved the jacket. It was going to be one of Sacramento's glorious Indian summer days, shirtsleeve weather.

For what had to be the tenth time in the past twenty minutes, Kevin left the sofa where he had been sitting beside Chris and went to the front window to part and then peer through the curtains. "What kind of car does he have?" he asked again.

She lowered the newspaper and looked at him. "He has a little red sports car and a big yellow truck," she answered indulgently.

"Not a green car with a black top?"

"No—at least not that I've seen."

"Oh," he sighed, disappointment heavy in his voice as he shuffled back across the room.

She untucked her feet from beneath her and lifted him onto her lap. "He'll be here, Kevin," she said, wrapping her arms around him and propping her chin on his shoulder. "It's just not time yet."

"Tell me some more about him," he insisted.

"I've told you everything I know."

"Tell me again."

She closed her eyes and said a silent prayer for patience. Saying nice things about Mason for two days had left a bitter taste in her mouth. Especially after Paul's phone call the day before. "Which part?"

"About how he didn't know I was born."

She settled back into the sofa, pulling Kevin with her. "Your mama Diane wrote him a letter telling him all about you, but somehow the letter never got mailed. So all this time he didn't know he had a little boy—"

"Who looks just like him," Kevin chimed in.

"Who looks a lot like him," Chris corrected.

154

"Then what happened?"

"The letter was delivered five years after it should have been, and when your daddy discovered he had a son, he wanted very much to see him."

"He already saw me."

"He wants to see you more and become your friend."

"Does he want to be your friend, too?"

She couldn't lie to him; she couldn't even stretch the truth about something that important. "I don't think so, Kevin," she said.

He leaned his head back so that he could see her. "Why not?"

"Do you remember when Melissa's mother and father got a divorce?"

He nodded.

"They did that because they stopped liking each other, but they didn't stop liking Melissa." Not getting the immediate understanding she'd hoped for, she tried coming at it from another direction. "You know how much you like David?"

Again he nodded.

"And how much Tracy doesn't like him?"

"She thinks he's a nerd."

"Well, you like him and she doesn't, but that has nothing to do with the way you and Tracy feel about each other. Your father and I don't have to like each other in order to love you."

"Does that mean he won't live here with us?"

Chris rolled her eyes toward the ceiling. He was always doing that to her. She was ten yards down one path and he was twenty yards down another. "That's right," she told him.

"I was thinking maybe—"

"I know what you were thinking." At least now she did. "But that's never going to happen. It was your mama Diane who loved Mason, not me."

"But you could."

Not in a million years, her mind screamed. To Kevin she simply said, "He's not my type." To keep him from pursuing the subject, she changed it. "Have you told Tracy about your new father?"

"She thinks it's bitchin'."

"*Kevin!*" she exclaimed, almost choking on his name. "Where on earth did you pick up a word like that?"

He looked genuinely surprised that she was upset. "From Mark, at school. He says it all the time."

"Well. I don't ever want to hear you say it again." No sooner was the sentence spoken than she realized the opening she'd left him. When it suited him, Kevin could be as literal as a backwoods preacher.

The doorbell rang, startling her. She glanced at the regulator clock on the far wall. Great, she thought, seething, perfect, wonderful. Just when she was in the middle of chewing Kevin out, Mason showed up.

Kevin jumped off her lap and ran for the door.

"Stop," she said as loud as she could without being heard by someone standing on the front porch.

She raced after him, catching him by the arm. "Please don't use that word again around anyone until we have a chance to talk about it." It was on the tip of her to add "especially in front of your father," but she changed her mind. The last thing she wanted to do was burden him with special instructions on how he should or shouldn't act in front of Mason.

Chris gave Kevin a gentle shove toward the door as she let go of his arm. "Go ahead," she said, stepping back. "Now you can answer it."

Mason swallowed to clear his throat. He reached up to adjust his tie and remembered he wasn't wearing one. He hadn't been this nervous in a long, long time, not since that day in court when he had first faced his father and brother in the lawsuit he'd brought against them. If looks could kill, he would have died that day. But he hadn't. He'd gotten through that and he would get through this. After all, it was only a five-year-old boy he was facing this afternoon, not two people who wished he'd drop off the edge of the earth.

He was having a hard time believing that, almost five months after discovering he had a son, he was finally going to get to spend some time with him. Not even the careful instructions Rebecca and Travis had lavished on him had lessened his anxiety about the meeting, however. He didn't have the foggiest idea what five-year-old boys liked to do or what they talked about.

He looked up as the door opened. Kevin

greeted him with a smile that melted his worries. "Hi," Mason said.

"I know who you are," Kevin interrupted excitedly. "You're my dad."

So she'd told him. He was grateful for that and would have to remember to tell her so. He returned Kevin's smile. "I passed a park on the way here and thought maybe we could go there to talk for a while and get to know each other a little better." Rebecca had been adamant that he not take Kevin someplace noisy or crowded or too filled with activity for them to talk to each other.

"Mom didn't fix me any lunch because she said you'd probably take me someplace to eat."

"Lunch sounds good to me, too." Mason glanced up and saw Chris standing in the shadows. "Would you like to come along?" he offered.

The look on her face let him know he'd caught her off guard. "But your attorney said—"

"I know what my attorney said, but in this instance, he wasn't speaking for me." Mason had decided the best way to handle Chris was to keep her off balance. He'd abandoned any hope of dealing with her on a rational level. Besides, it wouldn't hurt to have her along this first time. He might be able to pick up a clue or two on how to communicate with Kevin that would make future visits easier for both of them. "I was out of town when Paul Michaels called with your request and didn't have a chance to answer myself."

"I'm not dressed to go out," she said, obviously flustered. "If you'll give me a few minutes, I can change."

She was wearing blue jeans and a cream-colored cable knit sweater and looked just fine to him, but he'd learned it was useless to argue with women about whether what they were wearing was right or not. It seemed reasonable that Chris would think like Diane, who had been especially fastidious about her appearance, always insisting she wanted to look perfect for him, never believing she could have worn sackcloth and he would have thought her beautiful. "I'll wait," he said.

"Come inside," Kevin insisted. "I can show you my room."

Mason glanced at Chris for confirmation of the invitation. She hesitated a fraction of a second and then nodded. "I'd love to see your room," he told Kevin.

As he followed Kevin through the house, he took time to look around, noting the things he had missed seeing the last time he'd been there, mentally cataloging everything for future reference. The furnishings were nice, but except for a few antiques, which appeared authentic, they were inexpensive. The pictures on the walls, mostly original watercolors with a couple of signed and numbered lithographs, were also nice, but as far as he could tell, there was nothing noteworthy. If Chris Taylor had money, she hadn't spent it on the house.

Kevin led him to a bedroom at the end of

the hall, went inside, and indicated to Mason that he should sit down on the bed. Mason pulled a chair out from the desk instead. He didn't want Chris coming in and chastising him for messing up Kevin's bed as well as his life.

The posters on the walls were of various endangered species: whales, African elephants, wolves, and sea otters. There was a Greenpeace sticker on the mirror and shelves filled with books and stuffed animals. The corner of Mason's mouth lifted in a disbelieving smile. Chris was a 1990s version of a hippie and was raising his son to follow in her footsteps. He'd seen her type all his life. It wasn't that they were losers; it was that they counted for nothing at all. They ran around with their little signs protesting the cause of the week, patting themselves on the back when they saved ten tigers while forgetting the ten thousand people who were left homeless and starving in the process.

"This is where I keep my baseball cards," Kevin said, pulling a box out of the closet. "Mom thinks they're dumb, but she lets me collect them anyway."

"You like baseball?" Mason asked hopefully. It wasn't his sport, but he could learn to like it for Kevin.

"Uh-uh," Kevin answered. "I just like the cards." He laughed. "And the bubble gum."

"What about football?"

"I watch it sometimes with Uncle John. He likes it a lot. Someday he's gonna take me and Tracy to San Francisco to see the Forty-Niners play."

"I didn't know your mother had a brother," Mason said.

Kevin frowned. "She doesn't. She had a sister, though...my mama Diane. But she died."

"His uncle John is a friend," Chris said coolly, coming into the doorway.

Mason shot her a questioning look. "Of yours or his?"

She bristled at the implied suggestion. "Of both of ours."

"I see."

"Do you?"

Kevin moved between them. "He's Tracy's daddy," he offered.

"Perhaps we'd better be going," Mason said, standing up. "We only have a couple of hours," he added, looking pointedly at Chris.

"Yes," Chris agreed. "It's amazing how fast the hours can disappear sometimes."

Mason took them to lunch on the *Delta King*, a converted riverboat docked at a pier in Old Sacramento. Kevin, to Mason's surprise, passed on a hamburger and french fries and ordered prawns. He was doing nothing Mason had been led to believe was normal for a five-year-old. His manners and social graces were honed much finer than Rebecca had told him he had any right to expect; there hadn't been any of the probing questions he had anticipated, nor had there been the awkwardness he had assumed, under the circumstances, would be unavoidable. Plainly,

Chris had spent a lot of time with Kevin and had given him the love and sense of security he needed in order to face the world with confidence.

Mason was intrigued by his son. He was bright and articulate and interested in everything. He'd bubbled with excitement when they drove by the skeleton of the Capital Court Hotel and Mason told him that he owned the building. Inordinately pleased with Kevin's enthusiasm, Mason also told him that he could arrange for them to ride to the top in the construction elevator and that, when they were up there, they would be able to see all of Sacramento. Kevin had been awestruck and ready to go that afternoon.

Later, as the three of them were walking from the parking lot to the restaurant, Chris had quietly informed Mason that she didn't want Kevin on a construction site and that he would have to wait until the hotel was finished before he took his son anywhere near the place.

While they waited for their lunch, Mason asked Kevin if he'd ever gone skiing. He said he hadn't but that a lot of his friends went all the time and that someday he wanted to go with them. When Mason asked if he would like to go with him that winter, Kevin beamed.

Later, when Kevin got up to look out the window at a passing cabin cruiser, Chris told Mason that she didn't want Kevin to go skiing, emphasizing that she considered him too young and the sport too dangerous.

When Kevin lingered over dessert and the two hours they had been gone from home had

162

begun to stretch into three, Chris suggested it was time for them to leave. On the way home, Kevin started talking about a boy at school who tried to get what he wanted by beating up on everyone.

"I used to know a kid just like that," Mason said, not mentioning that the kid had been his brother.

"What did you do?" Kevin asked.

"When I got big enough to hit him back, I gave him a black eye."

Chris gasped. "Violence only creates more violence," she said. "It solves nothing."

"It kept that kid from ever hitting me again," Mason replied.

"It was still wrong," Chris insisted. "It's precisely that kind of attitude—"

"Oh, my God." He groaned. "You're not only out to right all the wrongs in the world, you're one of those people who think you can stop a tank by lying down in front of it. But then, I don't know why that surprises me. It all fits."

Kevin watched their exchange, twisting his head back and forth as if straddling the net in a tennis match. "My mom doesn't like me to hit people," he said to Mason. "She says if somebody wants to be that way, I shouldn't play with them anymore. Then if nobody is their friend, they'll stop hitting people."

"Your mother has beautiful theories, Kevin."

"What does 'beautiful theories' mean, Mama?" Kevin asked, turning to Chris.

Chris shot Mason a withering look. "He means that I'm right, sweetheart."

They turned the corner on Forty-second Street and started down the block. "Look!" Kevin exclaimed. "There's Tracy." He leaned across Chris and waved. As soon as Mason had pulled the truck to a stop, Kevin had his seat belt off and was clamoring to get out. "Can I go to Tracy's, Mama? I want to tell her about our lunch on the boat."

She opened the door, stepped out onto the sidewalk, and reached back to help Kevin down. "All right," she said. "But only for an hour. Tell Aunt Mary to send you home by four."

Kevin took off down the street before Mason had made it around the truck. Chris turned to him. "You can see where his priorities lie," she said.

"I can't say I think much of your fighting style. Don't hurt anyone with your fists, but do as much damage as you can with your mouth. Is that the idea?" he asked, unfazed by Kevin running off without saying good-bye, understanding intuitively a little boy's eagerness to see his friend. Besides, after the three hours he'd just spent with Chris, he was eager and ready to do battle with her, and that was best done in Kevin's absence. "I can't believe you're the same woman Diane used to talk about."

"That's all right, because I can't imagine what she saw in you either."

"It amazes me that Kevin has turned out as unaffected as he has after being raised by—"

She jumped in before he had a chance to

finish. "How do you know what Kevin is or isn't? You've spent a total of three hours with him. You don't have the slightest idea what he's really like."

"No, but that's about to change. I'm not going to let you keep me from seeing him again. And there isn't going to be any more of this two-hour crap. I want Kevin next weekend—all of it." Now he'd done it. He'd put his foot in his mouth, and he was either going to have to chew or spit. He was the one who'd pushed for the ex parte order, which gave him limited visitations right away, rather than waiting until a hearing could be arranged. "Forget next weekend," he said before she had a chance to answer. "I'm going to be out of town on Sunday."

He caught a movement out of the corner of his eye, looked up, and saw Kevin running back toward them, followed closely by Tracy. They veered into a pile of leaves, scattering them by kicking their feet as high as they could, and then ran back onto the sidewalk again.

"I forgot to give you a hug good-bye," he said with joyous spontaneity, holding his arms open.

Mason wasn't prepared to be blindsided by such a powerful emotion. Wordlessly, he lowered himself to his haunches and waited for his son to come to him. Small arms wrapped themselves around Mason's neck and held on tightly for several exquisite seconds.

The embrace was over almost as quickly as it was given, and Kevin and Tracy were on their way back to her house. The feeling that had come over Mason lingered, however, too good to share and too important to ruin with words. It had been a long time since anyone had made him feel that special with just a touch. Guarding the moment, wanting to make it last as long as he could, he went around to the driver's side of the truck without speaking to Chris, then climbed inside and drove away.

Chris watched him leave, filled with a terrible sense of foreboding. It had been wrong to let Kevin see him. What had been started that day would be difficult, if not impossible, to stop. She refused to believe that it was Mason himself who so fascinated Kevin. More likely it was simply the idea of having a father. Like all children, Kevin wanted what everyone else had.

For the first time since she and Kevin had started their life together, she regretted that she hadn't married. Mason would never have been able to gain a hold over Kevin if he already had a father.

But it was stupid to linger on what-ifs. She had enough to think and worry about in the here and now. For instance, how was she going to keep Mason from seeing Kevin next Saturday, even for two hours?

She started up the walkway to her front door, imagined herself inside alone, and decided what she really needed was someone to talk to. Not just someone, but Mary, the person she always turned to when things were bad, or good, or just plain ordinary. Mary was one of those extraordinary once-in-a-lifetime friends, always there, always ready to listen.

Except today.

"I'm sorry, Chris," John said, opening the screen door for her to come inside. "You missed her by five minutes. She waited around as long as she could, but the deli closes early today, so it was either leave or cook."

Chris stepped inside. "I just needed someone to talk to," she said.

"I'm a good listener," he answered. "And no one's ever accused me of slacking off in the talking department, if you want someone to fill in when you stop to take a breath."

"Are you sure you want to get dragged into this?"

He put his arm across her shoulders. "Come on over here and sit down while I get us some coffee." He led her to a chair. "Or would you rather have a beer?"

"Coffee's fine." She wanted every bit of her reasoning power intact.

He fixed hers the way she liked it, with half a packet of sweetener and a splash of milk, then handed it to her and sat in the chair beside her. "Now tell me how it went," he said, propping his feet up. "Is he as bad as you thought?"

"Worse."

"That's too bad. Kevin seems happy as a clam. I was hoping things had worked out for you, too."

"Kevin's on cloud nine. What kid wouldn't be with a rich new father who's promised him the world wrapped up in a nice shiny ribbon?" She blew on her coffee to cool it. "When Mason first came to pick Kevin up, there were a couple of minutes when I actually thought I might have judged him wrong. He didn't have to let me come along today, but he did. And boy, am I glad I went."

She turned to face John. "He has no idea what it takes to be a real parent. In his mind, it's all weekend fun and games. He thinks he can take Kevin on Saturday morning, spoil him rotten for two days, and then give him back to me to discipline the rest of the week. I get the work, he gets the reward."

"Did he say that?" John asked, his tone incredulous.

"In the space of two and a half hours, Mason told Kevin he would teach him to ski, take him boating next summer, let him crawl all over a high-rise construction site, and fly him to Disneyland over Easter break. How in the hell can I compete with that when what I get is mornings he'd rather stay in bed than go to school, evenings when I make him stop whatever he's doing and come inside because it's getting dark, and nights I make him go to bed just when he's finished putting his train set together? I feed him things he's not crazy about because they're good for him, and...and I'm rambling."

"That itinerary Mason set up does seem a little much. But you can't blame him for—"

Chris kicked off her shoes and drew her feet up under her. "That's not the worst of it, John. I could live with the high-flying weekends. I know Kevin loves me, and nothing Mason can do or buy is going to change that. The real rub is that it appears Kevin's new father is an Old Testament man. He believes in all that eye-for-an-eye macho garbage and isn't the least bit hesitant to tell Kevin all about it." She leaned heavily back in the chair. "What am I going to do? Mason Winter is the kind of man I've purposely avoided all my life. Everything I've worked so hard to instill in Kevin, Mason can destroy in a year's worth of weekends."

"Not everything," John said. "Kevin will be a little confused at first, but he'll come around."

"How can he? If he loves us both, how can he not be torn apart by our differences?"

"No two people see eye to eye on everything. Kids are amazingly adaptable, Chris. This is something I see at the firehouse all the time. Half the guys I work with are divorced. They're going through the same thing you are."

"Have they found a way to get through their differences without hurting their children?" For all of her ranting and raving about Mason and what she saw wrong in him, it was Kevin and the effect all of this would have on him that had her sick with worry.

John thought for a minute. "The compromising that's involved works better for some than for others. Kids seem to go through a stage where they're really confused and they take their frustration out on everyone around them no matter how cooperative and well-meaning their parents are. They usually end up hurting themselves the most."

"You see what I mean? I can't let that happen to Kevin. He's already been through enough." Her voice was edged with pain. "He's a wonderful little boy, John. I know all parents think their kids are special, but not many children have gone through what Kevin's been through. He deserves the best life I can give him. If I take the easy way out of this thing, I'll never be able to forgive myself."

"You have to do what you think is right, Chris."

"Even if I think that Kevin should never see his father again?"

John hesitated. "If you believe in what you're doing, it's much easier to forgive yourself if you find out in the end that you were wrong."

"It isn't forgiveness I'm looking for."

"I know, but sometimes that's all we get."

16

Mason swung his feet over the side of the bed and sat there for several seconds. It was six forty-five, and there wasn't a reason in the world for him to get out of bed except that he was tired of lying there.

He hated holidays. They were the only times during the year that he felt at odds with himself. He couldn't go to the office without running into someone from security—someone who felt sorry for him because he had no family to spend the day with. He couldn't visit the job sites for the same reason.

Eating alone at a restaurant drew as much, if not more, attention. In a nutshell, holidays meant he became a prisoner in his own house. This Thanksgiving was no different from any other, except for the added wrinkle of Kevin.

When they'd been together that past weekend, Kevin had insisted Mason tell him where he was going to eat dinner and who would get the drumstick. After using up all of his customary evasive tactics, Mason had finally admitted he didn't have any plans for the day. For once Kevin seemed at a loss for words. He couldn't conceive of anyone not being a part of a celebration that included a big turkey dinner. They'd ended the day with a promise from Kevin to ask his mother if Mason could come over for the day, and a strong, passionate plea from Mason not to say anything.

He could have sidestepped the whole issue by telling one small white lie to Kevin, but somehow the words wouldn't come out. Mason had been raised under a blizzard of white lies and evasions, and no matter how uncomfortable the truth, he refused to do the same to his own son.

Should Chris call to invite him to dinner, either because of pressure from Kevin or out of some bleeding-heart need of her own, he had decided to tell her he'd already been asked. In itself, that wasn't a lie. He had been asked, by at least a dozen people, including Rebecca and Travis, who always invited him and, thank God, were never surprised or hurt when he turned them down.

This year he'd even received an invitation from Walt Bianchi's wife when she'd come by the office earlier that week. Mason had actually spent some time considering her offer. He'd thought spending some social time with Walt might give him a new angle on the man. There was something about Walt that made Mason feel ill at ease around him, nothing he could put his finger on, certainly not his performance at work, which was proficient and at times masterful. Maybe the problem was that he was too good.

Or maybe Mason just couldn't stop seeing his brother every time he looked at Walt.

He went into the living room and turned on the gas log in the fireplace. It was a poor imitation of the fire it was supposed to mimic, but it gave the room a nice glow. After picking up the *Sacramento Bee* from outside his front door, he went into the kitchen and made coffee, noting the set of small fingerprints on the sleek black refrigerator, evidence of Kevin's visit and the housekeeper's week off.

He reached for the dish towel to wipe them off, but stopped short of the action. Everything about his apartment was perfect, almost to the point of sterility—a little like his life. It gave him a perverse pleasure to see something that so obviously didn't belong. But it also saddened him to realize how many fingerprints he'd already missed on the shiny surfaces in his life.

Chris shivered as she threw back the covers and reached for her bathrobe. The automatic set-back thermostat wasn't working, which meant she had to turn the furnace down herself each night and then get up a half-hour early to warm the house for Kevin. She stepped into her slippers and started out of her room, letting out a little cry of surprise when she ran into Kevin.

"What are you doing up already?" she asked, pulling her robe tighter around her.

"I was coming to see if you changed your mind about asking Daddy to dinner. We could call him now if you wanted to. He said he wasn't going anywhere today."

Her heart sank. Why wouldn't Kevin let it go? "I told you, it wouldn't be right for me to invite Mason to someone else's house. If we were having dinner at home, it would be different." Thank heaven she had John and Mary to use as an excuse.

"But Aunt Mary said if you wanted to ask him, you could. I heard her."

The only way he could have heard that particular conversation was by purposely eavesdropping. Chris thought about hauling out lecture 13B about how wrong it was to eavesdrop, but she was tired of being the bad guy. Until Mason happened into their lives, she and Kevin had never argued. Now it seemed they were always going at it about something. No matter how hard she tried to prevent it, Kevin was being torn, caught between his burgeoning love for his father and his loyalty to her.

She tried never to say anything bad about Mason, but she couldn't bring herself to say anything really good about him either. For days after Kevin saw his father, he would work on her to try to bring them together, to make them a family like Tracy's. By default she was turning into the heavy. It was a role she didn't like, one that put her at odds with Kevin and stole moments of happiness that she had once taken for granted.

"Aunt Mary was just being polite. You know as well as I do that their house isn't big enough for the people who do come. It would be wrong for us to make it even more crowded." The excuse sounded lame even to her.

"I could sit on his lap."

She reached for him to give him a hug. He pulled away. "Kevin, *please* try to understand."

He dropped his chin to his chest, refusing to look at her.

"Why don't you come back to bed with me while the house warms up?"

"I don't want to," he said, heading back to his own room.

Her hands curled into fists at her sides. "Damn you, Mason Winter," she swore softly through clenched teeth.

Mason gathered the newspaper and dropped it into the trash. He glanced at the clock and made a face. Only fourteen more hours and he could call it a day. He went to the window and looked outside. Clouds were beginning to gather for what was supposed to be the first big storm of the season. Some of the pricier ski resorts had been dumping artificial snow on their slopes for several weeks already, trying to entice people up for the holiday.

Mason had thought about going skiing, if for no other reason than to get out of the city for a while. Figuring it didn't much matter whether he spent Thanksgiving in his condominium at Lake Tahoe or in Sacramento, he'd been half packed when Rebecca informed him that she'd managed to set up an informal meeting the evening before with several of the increasingly restless property owners on the riverfront project.

It was a meeting he'd been pushing for since the first rumblings of discontent had reached him. He didn't hold much hope of finding out who was actually behind the divide-and-conquer strategy; even if he was able to get a name, he knew it would lead to a dead end. What he really wanted to know was how serious the other prospective buyer's offer was and, with any luck, to come away with a feel for how high he was willing to go.

The problem Mason faced was that the three farmers who'd been the most reluctant to go along with signing the first right of refusal document held the key pieces of property. Without those pieces of land, the deal would fall through. The trouble was, the farmers knew they had him. Essentially the deal rested in their hands. He had no one but himself to blame for his position; he had been blinded by his passion to see the river-front project built. Now all he had to find out was how much that blindness was going to cost and whether or not he could afford it.

He couldn't approach the banks for financing until he had the land in his back pocket. The possibility that he would have to let go of his dream was staring him in the face. If he blinked, it could be gone. What would he do then?

He turned away from the window and headed for the shower. It was time he got started on something productive that day.

Chris gingerly carried the pumpkin pie from the counter to the oven, trying not to spill any of the custard while she maneuvered around Kevin, who was busy making cookies from the leftover piecrust dough.

"Look, Mom, I made one like a fire truck for Uncle John."

She closed the oven door and turned her attention to Kevin's artwork. "What's that one next to Tracy's piano?"

"It's Daddy's new hotel."

Chris grimaced. Would she never learn to leave well enough alone? She'd been jumping through hoops all morning to keep Mason out of their conversation and now, without thinking, she'd provided the ground work for him to barge right back in. "What's that one over there?" she quickly added, hoping to distract Kevin.

"That's his car. I'm making him two cookies, since he can't come to dinner with us."

"How nice," Chris said, gritting her teeth. "I'm sure he'll like that."

"That one's for you," he said softly, pointing to a lopsided heart. "Cause I love you, and I'm sorry I made you mad."

"I love you, too," she said, wrapping her arms around him. "And you didn't make me mad."

When she let him go, he went back to working on his fire truck. Several minutes passed before he spoke again. "After dinner, could we take Daddy his cookies?"

Chris closed her eyes and counted to ten. Tenacity had shown itself to be the driving force of Kevin's personality from the day he was born. In the five and a half months he was in the hospital, other babies with less serious problems had died while Kevin had clung to life, pulling through one potentially fatal crisis after another. Then she'd said daily prayers of thanks for his bullheadedness; now there were times when it drove her nearly crazy.

"You'll be seeing him on Saturday," she offered, without any real hope the answer would satisfy him.

"All right," he said unexpectedly.

The dejection in his voice and in the slump of his shoulders tore at her heart. Damn you, Mason Winter, she swore for the second time that day. Damn you to hell.

Mason rolled up the set of blueprints he'd been studying and stuck them in the box beside the drafting table in the office off his bedroom. He really liked the work being submitted by the new architect he was thinking about hiring for the riverfront project. The man's work managed to look clean and classic at the same time, pulling in a feel for the history of the area without being burdened by it. The open spaces were uncluttered, the parking areas unobtrusive.

For a moment, as he'd studied the plans, he thought he'd come up with a way to pass the rest of the day. It had been several weeks since he'd actually walked along the river, immersing himself in his dream, getting his fix. But then he'd realized that, with someone else suddenly showing an interest in the property, it was better that he not seem too eager.

Not until the idea had come and gone and he was again left with his own aloneness did he acknowledge why this holiday was turning out to be so hard to get through. Feelings he'd thought he no longer possessed had risen to haunt him.

Holidays were for families, a time of wondrous smells, spontaneous hugs, laughter, and love. Only months ago he had been inured to such feelings, believing with a comforting conviction that he was going to live the rest of his life alone in an uncomplicated, dispassionate limbo where no one walked into his life but no one walked out, either.

But then Kevin had arrived and the safety net had disappeared.

Now it hurt to spend Thanksgiving alone.

Mason went to the closet to get his coat, not caring where he was going, only that he was getting away.

Chris stood at the kitchen doorway watching as Kevin folded plastic wrap around the last of his cookies, making sure there was enough left on the top to tie a length of curling ribbon around it. He had been working on the project all morning, mostly in thoughtful silence. What should have been a joyful time for them both had been awkward and guarded as they struggled to find something to talk about that wouldn't somehow lead to Mason.

It was the first time in their five years together that Chris and Kevin had felt uncomfortable with each other. She felt that she was losing Kevin and that what was happening to them now was merely a sampling of things to come. In rational moments—the few she had anymore—she recognized that this wasn't entirely Mason's fault. In his own way, he'd come to love Kevin. Years ago she might have doubted it was possible to feel a real commitment to another person so quickly, but her own experience with Kevin had shown her that love could be sudden and so strong that everything else paled in comparison.

And now that love compelled her to do something she passionately did not want to do. "Kevin," she said, drawing his attention. He looked up at her. "I've changed my mind." She went on quickly, before she had a chance

179

to change it again. "You can call your father and ask him to dinner, if you still want to." The words felt as if they'd been ripped from her.

Kevin sat perfectly still, staring at her. Finally he climbed down from the chair, went to her, and wordlessly wrapped his arms around her legs.

She bent and pressed a kiss to the top of his head. "You'd better hurry," she said, feeling an uncomfortable and completely unanticipated twinge of jealousy at his profound happiness. "Aunt Mary wants to eat at three."

"Should I call Aunt Mary first?"

"I already took care of that."

He smiled. "Thanks, Mom."

"You're welcome. Now get with it. You still have to get dressed."

Kevin raced for the phone, dialed the number he'd had memorized for weeks, and waited. After several seconds he looked up at Chris. "It's not him," he said. "It's his machine."

"Are you going to leave a message?"

He thought about it, then shook his head and reached over to put the receiver back in its cradle.

"I think you should say something," Chris said, her love for Kevin superseding her dislike for Mason. "At least wish him a happy Thanksgiving."

Kevin put the phone back to his ear. "Daddy?" he said. "Me and Mommy wanted you to come to dinner with us, but we didn't find you. Happy Thanksgiving." He started to hang up, thought of something else he wanted to say, and leaned into the phone. "From Mommy, too," he added, carefully avoiding looking at Chris.

17

The doorbell rang, interrupting Chris's train of thought. She hurried to put as much of the sentence into the computer as she could remember before she lost it entirely. Then she scooted back her chair and ran for the door. She'd promised herself years ago that one day she'd have an intercom installed so that she wouldn't have to leave her desk to answer the door, but like most other things that cost a lot of money and weren't an absolute necessity, she'd never gotten around to it.

"Mason," she said, her surprise outweighing her irritation at having him show up in the middle of the week unannounced. With an obviously expensive raincoat over his customary suit, and his dark hair glistening with mist, he looked proper and meticulously put together, as if he'd just walked out of a PBS special about winter in London. "Kevin isn't here," she told him, acutely aware of her baggy sweat suit and naked face. "He doesn't get home from school for another hour."

"I know. I came to see you."

"Why?" she asked, suspicion heavy in her voice. They had settled into an uneasy truce over the past few weeks. Chris wasn't sure why it had happened, whether it was the holiday season or simply a regrouping of forces, but for the time being, she welcomed the lull in their storm.

"I wanted to talk to you about Kevin's Christmas present."

Christmas was a week and a half away, and for the first time in her life, she had finished her shopping early. It wasn't the lack of money that had made her get her act together; it was knowing Kevin would be home from school for the holidays. These days she jealously guarded every moment she could spend with him. She wasn't about to waste time in the malls when they could be together.

Considering how she felt about being alone with Kevin herself, it was even more surprising that, in a flash of goodwill, she'd told Mason he could take Kevin for a couple of hours on Christmas Eve, something neither of their attorneys had dared suggest. Perhaps that was why he'd come today, to thank her again. If so, he should have had sense enough to realize what she'd done wasn't for him; it was for Kevin.

With reluctance, she moved out of the doorway and indicated to Mason that he should come inside. "I don't have much time," she said. "I have a press release to finish and drop by the office before I pick Kevin and Tracy up at school."

"I can get back to you later..."

"You're here now. We might as well get this over with."

He wiped his feet on the mat and stepped inside. "I wonder if this is how a bill collector feels," he mumbled.

She smiled despite herself. "What did you expect?"

The look of sympathy he gave her caught her off guard.

"I know you don't believe this," he said, "but I do understand what you're going through. It must be hell—"

"You couldn't possibly understand what I'm going through," she snapped. "You don't have the foggiest idea—" She stopped herself. Traveling the same territory over and over again was not only a waste of time and energy, it was counterproductive. As fervently as she wished Mason would disappear, it wasn't going to happen.

She'd tried to convince herself her feelings weren't affecting Kevin, but the signs were too clear to deny. He was always trying to play peacemaker, to be the perfect little boy so that his mommy and daddy would want to live together with him. One way or another, for Kevin's sake, she had to learn to tolerate Mason's presence or, failing that, to put up a convincing front.

"Would you like a cup of coffee?" she asked, reeling in her temper as if she had a whale on the end of the line.

Mason blinked. "Uh, yes, I would."

"You can sit in here, and I'll bring it to you." While there was no warmth in her voice, she congratulated herself on at least managing to sound civil.

"Thank you," he told her, slipping out of his raincoat.

She took the coat from him and hung it on a hook in the hallway. "If you're interested, there's a photo album with some of Kevin's baby pictures in it under the end table," she said on her way to the kitchen. "There are also several pictures of Diane in there," she added, almost as an afterthought.

Stunned by her about-face, Mason was reluctant to reply for fear of breaking the spell. For months he'd been trying to come up with a way to ask to see pictures of Kevin as he was growing up, but had all but scrapped the idea as impossible. Moving quickly, before she could change her mind, he went to the end table and pulled out a leather-bound album. After turning on the lamp beside a glide rocker, he sat down and propped the heavy volume on his lap.

The first few pages were covered with pictures of Diane, as a plump, cherubic baby with masses of curly blond hair, as a gangly preteen with impossibly long legs, and then as a breathtakingly beautiful young woman, wearing a prom gown and glowing with life. Memories swirled around him, stealing his composure as they poignantly reminded him of what had once been his and the years wasted in hurtful anger at an abandonment that had not been what it had seemed.

When sadness and loss overwhelmed him, he looked away from the album, focusing on the Christmas tree and the presents beneath it, absently noting that several of them had been wrapped in hand-decorated paper. The patterns reminded him of stamps he'd cut from potatoes as a child to decorate chains of red, white, and blue paper for his family's yearly Fourth of July party. Those had been the good years with his mother, a time when she'd been there for him, before his father had demanded she make a choice and the choice she'd made had been to turn her back on her son.

Forcefully reminding himself that Chris had only gone into the kitchen and would be back shortly, he returned to the album. Already walking an emotional tightrope, he decided to bypass the rest of the section devoted to Diane, hoping that someday he would be able to talk Chris into letting him have copies made.

The first pictures he found of Kevin were faded Polaroids obviously taken shortly after his birth. Mason studied the fuzzy images for long seconds, trying to reconcile them to other pictures he'd seen of premature babies. He saw nothing of the robust boy he now knew in the wrinkled and shrunken baby. It was as if he were looking at a stranger.

Turning the page, he caught his breath in stunned disbelief. The tiny child who had, in the earlier photos, been lying on a table nearly unencumbered now had tubes and wires attached to every part of his body. Mason tried to look away, to protect himself, but no matter how hard he tried, he couldn't take his eyes off the photograph. The longer he stared, the more his horror grew. What he'd originally thought was a shadow on Kevin's stomach, he saw was actually an open wound. His mind skipped to the day he'd first seen the jagged scar on Kevin's abdomen and his automatic assumption that it had been caused by an accident.

Realizing for the first time how close he'd come to never seeing his son at all, Mason broke out in a cold sweat. While the logical part of his mind told him he couldn't have missed what he had never known, the part that had nothing to do with logic was sickened at the mere thought.

Already, in the short six months since he'd learned he had a son, Mason's life had radically changed. There was hardly a waking moment when he didn't think about Kevin. Any plans he made for the future were formulated with Kevin in mind. For years he'd been living in a cave, telling himself he enjoyed the darkness. Kevin had made him face the lie.

Chris came into the room, startling him out of his trancelike state. "Why did you let me see this?" he asked, struggling to pull himself together before she could see how he had been affected.

She put the tray on the coffee table. "It must be the season. I can't think of any other reason I should be nice to you." She handed him a cup. "Can you?"

His immediate reaction to her flippancy was anger. In the second he took to form his answer, he realized she was using words as a shield. She might hate him, but she also feared him. And why not? Even her seeming graciousness at inviting him in and offering him coffee was nothing more than her way of getting to know the enemy.

"I suppose I could come up with several pedestrian reasons why we should be nice to each other," he said. "But there's only one compelling reason—Kevin."

She fixed him with a stare. "Did you mean that to put me in my place or just to point out what a bitch I am?"

"Believe it or not, neither."

"Since you've given me a choice, I'll take 'not.' "

Unwilling to chance glimpsing another of the pictures of Kevin, Mason closed the album. "What happened to him?"

Chris's eyebrows drew together in a puzzled frown. "Who?" A look of understanding appeared before he could answer. "Oh, you mean Kevin. It was a nasty little infection called necrotizing enterocolitis, NEC for short. The disease struck very fast, but it took a couple of years before he was free of the effects."

"Years?" Mason said, trying to grasp the implications of something that devastating.

"He wound up losing half of his intestines to the infection. The half that was left didn't tolerate food very well, so in order for him to grow, he had to be supplementally fed through a broviac line in his chest."

"How long did that go on?"

"Over a year."

"You mean you had to bring him home like that?"

The defensive look left her eyes at the memory. "It was scary, but I would have done anything to get him out of that hospital. He only weighed six pounds when I brought him home. A month later he was up to nine."

"My God," Mason said, leaning back in the chair. "How did you—"

"I'm sorry," she said, putting her coffee cup back on the tray in a movement that was as formal as it was rigid, "but I just noticed what time it is, and since I have to leave pretty soon, maybe you'd better tell me why you came."

Mason's hunger to know more about his son was far from sated. He wondered whether it was the time Chris was concerned about or the potential thawing in their relationship. Either way, his questions would have to wait for another day. "I wanted to get Kevin's sizes. The skis and boots will have to wait until he can go in with me to be fitted, but I want to get him a snowsuit and some gloves to put under the tree."

"What are you talking about?" she asked, obviously confused. "I thought we already discussed this."

"Discussed?" he snapped. "I'd hardly call what passed between us that day a discussion. As I remember it was more an edict." He cringed at the aggressive way he'd jumped on her question. What was it about Chris Taylor that brought out the worst in him? He modified his tone. "Since Kevin and I have a

188

skiing trip planned the week after Christmas," he said, trying to sound reasonable, "I thought it would be a good idea if he—"

Chris's face flushed in anger. "I can't believe you," she said. "No, I take that back. I *can* believe you. I don't even know why I'm surprised. If I'd spent five seconds thinking about it, this is exactly what I would have expected. I told you I didn't want you to take Kevin skiing. Did you listen? No. But then, why should you? You do whatever you want. The hell with what anyone else wants. If you think I've spent five years taking Kevin in and out of hospitals and doctors' offices just to see him wind up wrapped around some tree, you'd better think again."

Mason closed his eyes. When he opened them again, he said, "Obviously Kevin hasn't told you what we've been doing every Saturday."

"Obviously," she snapped.

Mason realized now that Kevin had never actually said he'd talked to Chris. "I've been taking him to dry land ski school—I thought, with your approval."

"And how did you think this magic approval happened? Was I supposed to have seen the error in my judgment and changed my mind overnight? How gullible do you think I am?" She got up and began pacing the small room. "You bastard," she said, a choking sound in her voice. "Until you came along, Kevin was sweet and innocent and open. Now you've taught him how to lie and manipulate."

Mason went to the wall rack to retrieve his coat. It was senseless to stay and listen to her rant. She refused to accept that her compulsive possessiveness could have anything to do with Kevin's confusion. Still, he couldn't resist a parting shot. "When you've calmed down a little," he said, "you might ask yourself how I can be such an influence for bad when I have him only three hours a week and you have him all the rest."

She glared at him. "You can tell him whatever you want to about why you're not taking him skiing," she said. "I don't even care if you blame the whole thing on me."

He couldn't let it go. "Why are you so dead set against my taking him?"

She threw her arms up in disgust. "It doesn't surprise me that you can't get it through that ego-riddled head of yours, so I'll go over it one more time—nice and slow. Skiing...is...dangerous."

"For Christ's sake, look around you. Kids a lot younger than Kevin go skiing all the time—and live to tell about it."

"Give it up," she warned. "You'll never change my mind."

"It isn't me you're hurting, it's Kevin."

"Nice try, but it doesn't wash. A hell of a lot of kids never go near a ski slope, and they're all getting along just fine." She opened the door and stood to one side. "I must have been out of my mind to think this could work. You have the fatherly instincts of a snail."

"Oh, come on, now," he said, walking toward her. "Surely you can do better than that. I thought you made your living thinking up clever new ways to say the same tired old things." Jesus, what was the matter with him? He never talked that way.

"Get out of my house. Get out of my life."

"Your house, gladly. Your life? Perhaps in another two or three years, when Kevin moves in with me."

He left without a backward glance.

18

Chris waited and prepared herself for the day Kevin would insist they ask Mason to Christmas dinner, but he never did. On the surface, their holiday wasn't any different than it had been the year before. She and Kevin got up early to open their presents and had dinner with the Hendricksons at two. Then, as soon as the dishes were cleared and the kitchen cleaned, Kevin and Tracy began their odyssey, going from one house to the other, playing with each other's new toys until it was time for bed and they were too tired to resist.

Through it all Kevin had seemed the same as always—perhaps a little quieter, perhaps a little less enthusiastic about his presents, but there was nothing Chris could put her finger on.

There were no ski clothes under the tree, nor did Kevin ask to call Mason. Chris was tempted to question him about it, but decided to leave well enough alone.

They were halfway into January when Mary called Chris one afternoon and asked her to come over right away, telling her mysteriously that she'd meet her at the front door and to be careful not to make any noise.

"What's up?" Chris asked, shivering from the coatless dash she'd made to her friend's house.

"Come with me," Mary whispered. "There's something I think you should hear." She led Chris down the hallway to within a few feet of Tracy's bedroom.

"I don't want to play house anymore," Tracy said. "I don't like it when you're mean. I want you to be nice."

"Daddies aren't nice to mommies," Kevin protested.

"They are, too."

"Are not."

"My daddy is nice to my mommy," Tracy reasoned.

"I don't care," Kevin shot back. "If you don't do what I say, I'll take your baby on a long, long plane ride, and you won't ever find her."

"I'll tell if you do."

"It won't matter," Kevin said.

"Yes, sir. My daddy can make you give her back."

"Not if I don't want to. Daddies can't make mommies do anything they don't want to do. My daddy can't even make my mommy let me go skiing with him."

Chris had heard enough. "How long has this been going on?" she asked Mary.

"For quite a while." She quietly led Chris

out of the hallway and into the kitchen. "I wasn't going to bother you with it, but then I decided that maybe it was something you should hear after all."

Mary pulled a chair out for Chris and then sat down across the table from her. "I couldn't love Kevin any more if he were my own, Chris. It's tearing me up to see what this bitterness between you and Mason is doing to him."

The pain Chris felt for Kevin was like a wound that would not heal. Lately it had seemed as if each new day brought a fresh sprinkling of salt with it. "I'm afraid it's going to get a lot worse before it gets better."

"What do you mean?"

"Remember when I had you watch Kevin for me last week?"

"Yes," Mary said, encouraging her friend to go on.

"I had an appointment with Paul Michaels."

"Since this is the first time you've brought it up, I assume the meeting didn't go well."

Chris attempted a smile. "He wanted to prepare me for what we are likely to come up against when we get into court."

"The date's been set, then?"

"There's a hearing scheduled to consider Mason's motion to have the adoption set aside."

"That makes me so mad," Mary said. "He knows he's never going to get them to do that. Why is he even trying?"

"I suppose he thinks it shows how much he cares and how deeply he's been wronged. I never contested the claim that Mason is Kevin's father. Why bother? Anyone with eyes can see the genetic link. Obviously his attorney thinks that if I stand up in court and admit that, it will make his case stronger. I'm sure the lawyer also wants a chance to grill me on why I never tried to find Mason in all those years. In the process, he'll cast doubts on my claim that I knew nothing about Diane's letter until Mason showed it to me."

"It just doesn't seem fair that so much can rest on the cleverness of two men who have nothing at stake but their fees."

"Better them than King Solomon." She thought about it a minute. "No, that's not right. It was the real mother who wound up with that baby. Do you suppose there's a modern-day judge as wise?"

"When is the court date?" Mary asked.

Chris let out a sigh. "Three weeks from today."

"There must be a small part of you that's looking forward to getting it over with."

"There was, but after talking to Paul, it's gone." She put her elbows on the table and covered her face with her hands. "I must have been living in some kind of fantasy land to think Kevin could be left out of this thing."

"They're not going to make him testify," Mary said.

"No—at least not in court. Paul said the judge will probably turn everything over to the Probation Department. They will send people to investigate me and Mason. They'll also interview Kevin and most likely recommend he see a psychiatrist."

"That's the dumbest thing I ever heard. Kevin doesn't need to see a psychiatrist."

"Really?" Chris asked, blinking back tears. "You can still say that even after what we just heard in Tracy's room? That was hardly the attitude of a well-adjusted child." She pinched the bridge of her nose in an effort to keep more tears from forming. "I'm so worried about him, Mary. Ms. Abbott called me last week and said that Kevin has been disrupting the class. I know it's probably my imagination, but it seems as if he never smiles anymore." She held out her hands in a pleading gesture. "What am I going to do? I've thought about it until my mind is numb, but I can't come up with an answer."

Mary reached for Chris's hand. "You two have weathered worse storms than this," she said. "Give it time. Something will occur to you."

Chris lost her battle with her tears. Slowly, silently, they slid down her cheeks. "Somehow, watching him fight to heal his body wasn't as hard as seeing him fight to understand and still love parents who obviously hate each other." She slipped her hands from Mary's and wiped the moisture from her face, then rolled her eyes. "Mason once accused me of being histrionic. I'm glad he didn't hear me lapse into that bit of melodrama."

"Don't be so hard on yourself. You've gotten through this a lot better than I would have."

She gave Mary a weary smile. "You have to say things like that. You're my friend."

"A real friend would be able to help you. I can't even find the life preserver to throw overboard to help you save yourself."

Chris ran her finger across a nick on the edge of the oak table. She glanced at the wallpaper on the far wall and listened to the tick of the grandfather clock in the living room. Mary and John's house was as familiar to her as her own. She knew that John had scarred the table when the screwdriver slipped while he was repairing the toaster. She and Mary had put the wallpaper up one day when John had taken Tracy and Kevin fishing; it had taken John three weeks to notice the change, even though he'd complained about the color of the kitchen from the day they'd moved in. Mary had bought the grandfather clock for John with the money her mother had sent her for her birthday. She'd never told him, knowing he would feel guilty at her sacrifice.

The Hendricksons were Kevin's family and hers. Mason didn't belong and never would. Yet another direction for Kevin to be pulled. How many emotional chains could a little boy drag behind him and still grow into a whole, strong man?

"I can't let the Probation Department put Kevin through all those interviews," Chris said. "He would feel like they were asking him to take sides, and that would tear him apart."

"But you don't have any choice."

"There has to be some way," Chris said. "I've reached the point where I'll do whatever it takes."

19

When Chris arrived home from Mary's, she called Paul Michaels and asked him to arrange a meeting between Mason and her before they were to appear in court. He told her he would contact Mason's attorney and try to work something out.

It took Paul three days to nail something down.

"They're suspicious and not inclined to go along with your request, Chris," Paul told her when he called.

"Did you tell them I was doing this for Kevin's sake?"

"Yes, several times. I might as well have been speaking Chinese for all the good it did me. They just don't believe you're ready to negotiate in good faith. And since you wouldn't tell me what you had in mind, there wasn't a whole lot I could do to convince them otherwise.

"Not 'wouldn't' Paul—*couldn't*. I don't know myself what the answer is. All I know is I have to at least try to see if Mason and I can work something out before Kevin is subjected to a bunch of strangers poking into his life and his psyche. He's been hurt enough."

"The intention is noble, Chris."

"But?"

"I'm just afraid you're going to say or do something that will work against you when we finally do end up in court."

"I'll be careful."

There was a long pause before Paul answered. "I don't want to get your hopes up, but I may have an idea how we can pull this off without hurting either your position or Mason's," he said. "I'll get back to you in a couple of days if I can work things out."

"And if you can't?"

"Then we'll do it your way."

"Thanks, Paul."

"I haven't done anything yet.

"You listened."

"We're going to win this thing, Chris. Maybe not the way we had envisioned, but—"

"As long as Kevin's the one who comes out on top, I can live with anything."

"Keep that thought," he said and hung up.

Four days later, after he'd nailed everything down, Paul got back to Chris.

"If you have any plans for next Wednesday, cancel them," he said, catching Chris on her way out to pick up groceries.

She tensed. "What's up?"

"You and Mason have an appointment with judge Harold McCormick in his chambers at ten o'clock."

"To do what?"

"To battle it out, no attorneys, no social workers, no one but you and Mason—with Judge McCormick to act as referee and to answer any legal questions that might come up."

"Mason agreed to this?"

"I know it's hard for you to believe, Chris, but I've become convinced that Mason wants what's best for Kevin every bit as much as you do. All I had to do was find a neutral party who was satisfactory to everyone, and it was a go. I'm assuming Judge McCormick is all right with you?"

"If he's good enough for you, I'm not going to question him."

Paul chuckled. "He was my pick."

Chris felt hopeful for the first time in months. "I should have known," she said.

Chris was still going over her conversation with Paul Michaels the day before the meeting as she tried on clothes. Eventually, she wound up going through everything in her closet that wasn't made out of denim or canvas. She couldn't decide which look she was after, only that nothing she owned provided it. The years she'd spent on the corporate ladder had taught her that dressing for success wasn't a garment industry myth. She was keenly aware of how hard it was to change a first impression.

A man could put on a standard gray suit and be done with it. A woman had to decide if the same standard gray suit would be perceived as threatening if she wore it unadorned, if adding a brightly colored scarf would make her seem flighty, or if, God forbid, she wore a vest with the suit, she would look too sexy.

Being average height helped. A tall woman was invariably perceived as aggressive, no matter how she dressed, and it was almost impossible for a really short woman to be taken seriously.

Luckily Chris was the same size she'd been

when she worked for Wainswright Brewing Company, and the clothes she'd worn then still looked as good today, except that the skirts were a little on the long side and the colors of the blouses were several seasons old.

All she had to do was make a choice. Simple enough. Just figure out what Judge McCormick's mental image of an ideal mother was, and go with it.

She sat on the corner of the bed, stared at the closet, and let out a sigh.

Mason pulled into the parking lot opposite the courthouse, got out of his car, and buttoned the jacket of his gray suit. He'd just left a meeting with Travis, Rebecca, and Walt about the cost overruns on the Capitol Court Hotel. Although he'd only half listened to what was being said, he'd still left upset.

The two subcontractors involved were men he'd never worked with before and probably wouldn't work with again. The jobs they were doing were half-assed, their bills were padded, and someone had to be on them all the time. Usually that someone would have been Mason or Travis or Walt, but because of all Mason had going on in his private life, with Travis trying to cover for him by being in three places at once, and with Walt spending several days each week in Los Angeles, some things had slid by that would normally have been caught.

But none of that mattered, at least not in comparison to what was about to happen.

He'd tried not to get his hopes up about what would transpire in McCormick's chambers. There was no reason to think Chris had suddenly turned into a rational, compassionate woman. His attorney had strongly recommended he reject the proposed meeting, saying it was simply the same old song being sung in another key. At first Mason had agreed. But the more he thought about it, the more promising the idea sounded. In the end, it was the fact that they would meet in Harold McCormick's chambers without their attorneys that had convinced him to go ahead.

Walking up the courthouse steps, Mason wondered if Chris knew that the judge she'd chosen was an old and close friend of his, one of the first he'd made after he moved to Sacramento.

Somehow he doubted it.

Chris looked up as Mason entered. How long, she wondered, would she have to know him before she stopped being surprised at how much he looked like Kevin? Or, more correctly, she supposed, how much Kevin looked like him.

"Good morning," Mason said, taking the seat opposite her in the small waiting room.

She nodded in acknowledgment of his greeting.

"Has Harold's secretary been by?" he asked.

Harold? Mason was on a first-name basis with judge McCormick? No wonder he'd agreed to the meeting. Calm down, an inner voice warned her. Never let them see you sweat. Oh, great, now she was quoting television commercials to herself.

"She came in about five minutes ago and said the jud—" She quickly corrected herself. "She said Harold should be on time."

Mason leaned back in the chair and stretched his legs out in front of him. "How's Kevin?"

"He's at Mary's today," she said stiffly. "He was sick to his stomach last night so I kept him home from school."

"Was he sick this morning?"

"No."

"But you still kept him home from school?" he asked, incredulous.

Chris took a slow, deep breath. Today of all days she couldn't afford to lose her temper. Calm, cool, deliberate, and rational—those were the watchwords. "I did what I thought best," she said evenly, "based on several years' experience with Kevin."

"Wasn't today the day he was supposed to finish the book he's been putting together?"

She felt the muscles in the back of her neck tighten. "If he gets through today all right, he can go back to school tomorrow and finish the book."

"How much school has he missed this year?"

She doubted five minutes had passed since Mason had come into the room and already she wanted to strangle him. She was beginning to think this meeting was a waste of time. They couldn't agree which brand of cola was better; how were they ever going to come to a meeting of minds on something as important as Kevin's future? "I assume you have a purpose behind asking, that it's not just an idle question?"

A woman with short blond hair, dressed in a bright red maternity smock, came into the room before Mason could answer. "The judge is ready to see you now," she said. "If you'll come with me, I'll take you to him."

The room she led them to was small but beautifully appointed. The walls were covered in oak paneling, the floor in a highly detailed Persian carpet. The chairs were upholstered in a lush forest green material. The man sitting behind the desk had a neatly trimmed mustache and a rim of gray and black hair surrounding a bald pate. Chris guessed him to be anywhere between thirty-five and fifty, old enough to have children of his own but not so old that he couldn't see new solutions to old problems. His rounding stomach flattened when he stood to greet them.

"Mason," he called out. "How good to see you again." He came around the desk. "And you must be Christine Taylor," he said warmly to Chris.

After shaking hands with them both, he brought two chairs into the middle of the room, told Mason and Chris to be seated, and then perched on the corner of his desk and looked from one to the other.

"I can't say I've ever come across anything like this before," he said, getting directly to the point. "If nothing else, today should prove interesting. But let's hope it's more than that. Now, who would like to start?"

Mason sat forward in his chair and looked at Chris. "Since Ms. Taylor's attorney is the one who suggested this meeting, perhaps she should."

Chris glanced down to collect her thoughts, saw a piece of lint on her black skirt, and automatically picked it off. The one thing she hadn't taken into consideration when she decided to wear her Chanel suit was the mental baggage that would come along with it. In her mind, she was Kevin's mother—blue jeans and sweaters. When she'd caught a glimpse of herself as she was dressed today, in the store windows she'd passed on her way there, however, what she saw was the up-and-coming executive she had once been. The distraction lasted no more than a fraction of a second, but left her a little off center.

"I, uh, I wanted to see if there wasn't some way to save Kevin...to keep him from going through an investigation by the Probation Department. Not that we wouldn't come through fine; we don't have anything to hide. It's just that lately he hasn't been doing very well in school...and he's even been getting into fights with his best friend, Tracy. I've tried to protect him from my personal feelings about what's happening." She looked over to Mason. "Actually, we both have, but Kevin is a very bright little boy and—"

"And he fills in the blanks for himself," Harold McCormick finished for her.

"Yes," she said softly. "That's why I don't

want him put through anything else. I know my son. It doesn't matter how good the Probation Department psychiatrist is, Kevin is going to feel that he's being asked to take sides. I don't understand why Kevin is so infatuated with his father, but I accept the fact that he is."

"So what you hope to accomplish today is to work out an agreement between you and Mason on the custody of Kevin?"

"Visitation rights," she amended. "Not custody."

Mason broke in. "What kind of visiting arrangements did you have in mind?"

Chris swallowed. She was giving him more than she wanted him to have, but knew she had to be realistic if she was going to get him to agree. "One full weekend a month and two weeks every summer after he turns ten."

"You can't be serious," Mason said.

"If you add up the hours, it's over six times what you have now."

"What I have now stinks."

"How often do you see Kevin?" Harold asked Mason.

"Three hours every Saturday."

"And who arranged that?"

Mason gave Chris a piercing look. "She did. Which should give you some idea how possessive she is about Kevin. She can't bear the idea of him being out of her sight for more than a couple of hours. I'm not sure whether it's the 'dangerous' sports I might introduce him to or the 'dangerous' new ideas, but she's so panicked about the time he spends with me that she's right there at the front door waiting for him when I bring him home."

"How do you feel about what Mason just said?" Harold asked Chris.

"He doesn't know what he's talking about. Kevin goes lots of places without me, and as long as I know and trust the person he's with, I don't worry about him at all."

"But you do worry about him when he's with Mason?"

She considered hedging, but decided honesty would get her farther. "Every minute he's gone."

Mason started to say something, but Harold held his hand up to stop him. "Why is that?" he asked Chris.

"Because Mason doesn't have the foggiest idea what it is to be a real father. He thinks it's all fun and games. He might be able to bandage a cut knee, but he has no idea how to handle hurt feelings or what to look for if Kevin starts to get sick or why it's important to pay attention to an upset stomach."

"How do you know all this?" Mason demanded. "Do you have some crystal ball that tells you who and what I am? Or are you still relying on the newspapers to keep you informed?"

Harold shifted position. "I think we'd better—"

"I know what kinds of things you tell Kevin," Chris said.

"What do you do, quiz him about me?" Mason shot back.

"I don't have to. If you knew anything at all about children, you would know they're prone to repeat things they hear. They don't need to be prompted. All you have to do is listen once in a while."

"Perhaps if I had more opportunity to listen, I'd—"

Harold got up and walked around the desk. "I think I've heard enough," he said. "You two are about as close to an agreement on how to raise your child as Jim Bakker and the IRS are on how to run a charity." He shook his head. "Too bad you aren't married. The lines wouldn't be so fuzzy."

Long seconds passed without anyone saying anything.

A slow smile spread across Harold McCormick's face. "I know it sounds crazy but, actually, that's not such a bad idea. Have either of you ever thought about it?"

Confused, Chris looked from Mason to Harold McCormick, wondering if she'd missed something.

"Thought about what?" Mason asked, looking equally confused.

"Getting married," Harold answered. "It could be the perfect solution to your problem."

20

"Why in God's name would I want to marry Mason Winter?" Chris asked.

Mason started to get up. "I knew today was going to be a waste of time."

"Hear me out," Harold insisted.

Mason hesitated. Not until everything fell apart had he realized how much he'd wanted this meeting to succeed. He wasn't as blind to what was happening with Kevin as Chris seemed to think he was. He saw the subtle and not so subtle changes. Worrying about those changes and trying to figure out what he could do to help had kept him up more nights than he wanted to acknowledge even to himself. It was only at those quiet times, when he was sure there was no chance he would be tempted to unload his worries on someone else and then have to see his own doubt reflected in their eyes, that he admitted, even to himself, how worried he was about whether he could be the father Kevin needed. His bedside table was covered with books on fatherhood by everyone from Benjamin Spock and T. Berry Brazelton to Bill Cosby.

But books weren't enough. If he'd learned nothing else in his time with Kevin, he'd discovered that being a parent wasn't something he could succeed in doing on a part-time basis. Perhaps if he and Kevin had had a background, a few years together to form a foundation for their relationship, things would have been different. As it was now, they were constantly playing catch-up.

The bottom line was that he didn't want to be a weekend father; he wanted to be the real thing. After much frustration, he'd finally accepted that what he wanted was impossible for the foreseeable future. Until Kevin was old enough to make up his own mind about which parent he wanted to live with, Mason could only bide his time and hope for the best at the upcoming trial.

"I'll give you five minutes," Mason said, sitting back down.

"Well, I won't," Chris said.

Mason grabbed her arm as she reached for her purse, forcing her to stay where she was. "Remember what's at stake here," he said. "It's time we stopped thinking about ourselves and started putting Kevin first." His action, his words, surprised even him.

Mason sent Harold a penetrating stare. "I'm giving you the benefit of the doubt and assuming you have some concrete suggestions to follow that ludicrous one."

Harold picked a pencil out of a caddy, held it in the middle, and rocked it back and forth, tapping out a staccato rhythm on the desktop. "What I'm suggesting isn't as off the wall as it might seem," he said, his eyes dancing with excitement. "At least it won't be after you've thought about it for a while. I talked at length with both of your attorneys before we got together today. They filled me in on what's been going on since last August and how it all came about, and they also told me a lot about the two of you—what you're like and what's going on in your private lives."

He focused his attention on Mason. "I already knew you, and there weren't any real surprises." He turned to Chris. "I've never had the pleasure of meeting you before today, Ms. Taylor, but after my talk with Paul, I feel I can confidently say that your life centers around your son—which, as far as I'm concerned, is just as it should be."

The tapping slowed. "Kevin sounds like a kid I'd be proud to call my own." And then it picked up again.

"So where does that leave us?" Harold went on rhetorically. "It leaves us with two good, decent people who are making a third person's life miserable and putting each other through hell in the process."

Mason suddenly realized that his hand was still wrapped around Chris's arm. He let go of her without looking at her.

"The sad and yet promising thing about all of this," Harold went on, "is that both of you want the same thing—Kevin's happiness."

He looked at Chris. "I know you're aware that Mason is convinced he has something to contribute toward that end, and frankly I think he does, too. A boy learns what it is to be a father by having a father to emulate. You may not agree with Mason's philosophy of life, his political party, or the things he does or says, but those things don't necessarily make him a bad person. To tell the truth, I'm not too crazy about Republicans myself, but I've been known to invite one or two into my home on occasion."

"I don't need anyone to champion me to Ms. Taylor," Mason said dryly.

Harold smiled. "Like I don't need a lower golf handicap."

"Could we get on with this?" Chris asked.

Harold turned his attention back to Mason. "I don't think you'll contest the fact that Chris is Kevin's mother in every way but genetically and that she has every right to go on being his mother. You know as well as I do that there isn't a court in this country that would set aside Kevin's adoption. I realize you don't agree with all of her ideas and ideals, but as hard as it is for you to accept, Mason, her way of thinking is what's going to save this planet for Kevin and Kevin's children."

Mason groaned.

"All right," Harold conceded. "Enough said about that. Back to finding a way to make sure you both get what you want and Kevin still comes out the winner. I'm not fool enough to suggest marriage because I think there's any love between you. Quite the contrary. Actually, the way you feel about each other is the reason this could be a logical, if not the perfect, solution.

"Mason, you want to see more of Kevin so that you can get to know him well enough to become a real father to him—something you probably couldn't accomplish even if you were awarded visitation every weekend, which I can assure you isn't likely to happen. Chris, you don't want Mason to take Kevin for long periods because you're not sure what kind of influence he's going to have on an impressionable five-year-old. I can assure you that, while it's unlikely Mason will get every weekend, he has a very good chance of getting every other weekend and every other holiday and at least two consecutive months in the summer."

Harold leaned forward, his enthusiasm evident in his body language. "But what if you could be a part of their interaction, Chris? And, Mason, what if you could have Kevin sitting across the breakfast table from you every morning?"

He held out his arms, coaxing them to become involved in a dialogue. "All you'd need is a house with two wings and a common living area. Think of it as a small, exclusive dormitory, with Kevin as the graduate student. When he's older and better able to cope with parents who live apart, the two of you can get a divorce."

Mason shook his head. "I can't believe you have the guts to suggest something like this." He looked at Chris to see if she was as disgusted as he was. She had a thoughtful, almost resigned expression on her face.

"I can't believe I'm saying this, and a voice in the back of my head is telling me I'm going to regret admitting it, but the whole thing makes a crazy kind of sense to me," she said to Mason. "I've finally accepted that, one way or another, whether I like it or not, you are going to be a part of our life, Kevin's and mine. I've spent the past month trying to reconcile myself to that fact and with the fact that there's nothing I can do about it."

She glanced at her hands, folded into fists on her lap. "You and I may be stubborn, Mason, but neither of us is stupid. It isn't as if by getting married we'd be entering into something blindly or with any expectation other than giving Kevin some normality in his life."

Mason tried to shake the feeling that he'd stumbled into a Rod Serling script. "What kind of normality comes from living a farce, for God's sake? Do you really want Kevin growing up thinking marriage means a house with separate wings with a demilitarized zone in the middle? The life he has now is a hell of a lot closer to the norm than this harebrained scheme Harold's suggesting. Lots of kids come from single-parent households and do just fine."

"And lots of them don't," Harold interrupted. "I see the results of broken homes every day, Mason, and I'm sick to death of the waste. I'll deny it if you ever tell anyone I said this, but at times I think our society would be a hell of a lot better off if parents went back to staying together for their children's sake."

A long silence followed.

"Why do we have to get married?" Mason asked. The question surprised him even more than it did Harold or Chris. To ask such a thing meant that he was actually considering what only seconds ago he had thought of as lunacy.

"Forget I said that." He stood up and prepared to leave. He had to get out of there. He needed time to think, to mull things over, to come up with a better plan.

"It would be to everyone's advantage to make the arrangement legal," Harold said, "but most of all it would help to protect Kevin. And Kevin's the reason we all came here today, isn't he?" he added pointedly.

"Please stay, Mason," Chris said with a sigh. "I don't like the idea of getting married any more than you do, but we don't count in this any longer. If you have a better idea than Harold's tell me about it. I promise I'll listen. Just don't walk away. I can't stand seeing Kevin hurt anymore."

"I'll think about it," Mason said. "That's all I can give right now."

"You don't have much time," Harold said.

"I'm aware of the court date." Mason turned his attention to Chris. In the same tone he might have used in addressing someone about to jump off a building, he asked, "Are you sure this is something you'd seriously consider?"

Chris stood up, plainly wanting to be on equal footing when she answered him. "Five years ago, I made a commitment to Kevin to give him the best life I could, even if in the process it meant sacrificing my own."

Mason met her gaze; one corner of his mouth turned up in an ironic grin. "And that's what you think marrying me would mean?" To his surprise, she responded with an embarrassed smile.

"I didn't mean to sound so melodramatic.

It was an emotional time for me back then—even more so than now. I didn't know from one day to the next whether Kevin was going to live. I made some pretty heavy-duty promises to myself and to him."

A flash of understanding shook him. So this was what it was like to be a real parent—commitment so complete that in all cases the child came first. How could he hope to compete with her? What could he possibly do to top Chris's offer? "You realize, of course, that your willingness to go along with this scheme puts me in an untenable position."

"I only want what's best for Kevin. I can't worry about the position it puts either of us in."

"How can you be so sure this is the answer?"

"I'm not. But as I already told you, I've accepted that you're in this for the long haul, that you're not going to back down someday and let Kevin and me slip quietly into the night. I know now that one way or another I have to deal with having you in my life for the next ten or fifteen years. It's only a matter of how, to what degree, and which way would be best for Kevin."

"I can see you have no illusions about the arrangement."

"None."

Over a lifetime of making decisions, he'd discovered that he could take days to think about something but invariably he wound up coming full circle and going with his first basic instinct. This time there was a difference —his head was telling him no, his heart was

215

saying yes. Kevin wanted a family as much as he needed what a family could give him. The only problem was the kind of family he and Chris would be providing. "I can't get past the idea that Kevin is going to grow up with a warped idea of what marriage is all about."

"That falls pretty far down on the list of things I'm worried about right now."

"What about—"

Chris tilted her head back and looked up at the ceiling. *"What about Kevin?"* She asked in a strained voice.

Mason stared at her. He tried to imagine the two of them living in the same house. Their life would be one ongoing argument. But then he remembered what Harold had said about sitting across the breakfast table from Kevin every morning.

Was the joy of having Kevin with him worth the grief of living with Chris?

Christ, yes! an inner voice shouted. It was time that empty spot inside of him stopped aching.

"All right," Mason said.

Chris caught her breath and gave Mason a frightened look.

"All right?" Harold echoed. "Does that mean you'll do it?"

Mason continued to stare at Chris, sensing in her an almost frantic desire to leap past him and run for the door. "Just tell me the time and the place."

Harold came around the desk. "Next Wednesday, same time, same place." He glanced at Chris. "I assume that's all right with you? The sooner the better?"

"Does it have to be *that* soon?" she asked, swallowing.

"Getting cold feet already?" Mason asked her, enjoying having the focus taken off of himself for the moment, all the while knowing the same feelings would hit him as soon as he left Harold's office.

Chris reached for her purse. "Don't worry, I'll be here."

When she tried to pass him, he caught her elbow. "There are a couple of things that need to be done before next week. Since we're already here, we might as well take care of them today."

"Like?"

"The license for one. A prenuptial agreement for another."

She opened her mouth to answer him, but no words came out.

"Cat got your tongue?" Mason prodded. He thought a minute. "Or is it possible I've called your bluff?"

Chris pulled her elbow from his grasp. "I don't play games where Kevin is concerned. I said I'd marry you and I will." She walked to the door. "Now, let's get on with it. I have some errands to run."

He doubted she had anything pressing that afternoon, but it was a damn good exit line. He held out his hand to Harold McCormick. "I feel a little funny thanking you for what you've done."

Harold laughed. "You can thank me

later—when Kevin is the contented little boy we all want him to be."

"I hope to God you're right," Chris said.

Mason echoed her prayer in his mind, even though he doubted that even divine intervention would be enough to pull this off.

21

"You're doing *what*?" Mary choked.

Chris got up to close the door between the kitchen and the back of the house where Kevin and Tracy were playing. "I know at first hearing it sounds crazy, but if you give it enough time, the idea will grow on you."

"And if you give green beans enough time in the refrigerator, mold will grow on them. You and Mason can't stand the sight of each other. How in the world are you ever going—"

Chris sat back down at the table opposite Mary. "We're going to take it one day at a time. It's the only way we can."

"Have you really thought about this? I mean *really* thought about it? What if it doesn't work? Where will Kevin be then?"

"Right back to where he is now. Only I'll know I gave it my best shot, and I can get through anything if I know that."

"If Kevin were old enough to know what you had in mind, he'd never let you do it."

"It would be a moot point then, wouldn't it?"

Mary threw her hands up in the air. "Wait until John hears about this."

"There isn't anything either of you can say that I haven't already thought of. You're just going to have to trust that I know what I'm doing on this one, Mary."

"Didn't Amelia Earhart say something like that before she took off around the world?"

"Maybe, but I like to think it was also what Chris Evert said when she first picked up a tennis racket." She tried to prop up a drooping daisy in the arrangement she'd put on the table earlier that morning. Her plan to wait until the last minute to tell Mary about the wedding had lasted about twenty-two seconds into their conversation. It wasn't that she needed Mary's approval, which was about as likely as a healthful doughnut; what she needed was someone to talk to. Sometimes saying things aloud put a different slant on them—not better or worse, necessarily, just different. Right now the only slant she had scared the hell out of her.

"Have you told Kevin?"

"Not yet." Chris watched the daisy drop its head and tilt to one side. She tried shoving it between two pieces of leatherleaf fern. It stayed upright long enough for her to pick up her coffee cup again.

"Then there's still time to change your mind with no harm done." Mary leaned across the table, took the wilted daisy out of the arrangement, and tossed it into the sink. "I'm sure Mason would understand. He's probably having second thoughts, too."

"Would you cut that out? The reason I told you about this was to get some positive rein-forcement," she said, lying but feeling no guilt, "not a rehash of my own thoughts."

Mary sat back in her chair and folded her arms across her chest. "Where are you going to live?" Her body language could have been interpreted by a not-very-bright two-year-old.

"In a mutually-agreed-upon house that has separate wings for privacy and a common living area."

"What will happen to your house?"

"I'm going to rent it out until Mason and I are divorced, and then I'll move back in."

The fight left Mary. Her shoulders sagged. "God, I'm going to miss you."

It was the same thought that had earlier plunged Chris into her depression. "It's not like we'll be leaving the state," she said without much conviction.

"Tracy will be lost."

"So will Kevin, once the newness of having his mother and father living together wears off." Chris refused to think about what the move would do to her. Whether it was a quick wave from the doorway, a whole afternoon spent rehashing some bit of news that had caught their eye in the morning paper, or just a leisurely jog around the park, one way or another she and Mary saw each other every day. Mary and John were like the air she breathed, vital to her existence, yet taken for granted until it was gone.

"You know John thinks of Kevin as one of his own."

"That's something I made a point of telling Mason after we left Judge McCormick's office. I wanted him to know how John and Kevin feel about each other. He's promised not to interfere in their relationship." Chris had been prepared to do battle with Mason over how important a role the Hendricksons would play in their lives. He'd surprised her by agreeing with her before she had a chance to complete her argument.

"What else did you two talk about?" Mary asked.

"We agreed that, except where Kevin is concerned, Mason and I will continue to lead separate lives. As much as possible, everything will go on as it does now. I'm keeping my job and my own circle of friends, and he's doing the same. We'll continue to go out with other people, but we're to make every effort to keep our 'liaisons' discreet. Which, of course, will be a piece of cake for me, but should prove to be an interesting problem for Mason. I'm sure the kind of women he's used to going out with don't know the meaning of 'discreet.' "

"That's it?" Mary prodded. "You didn't set up guidelines for dealing with Kevin? Or decide how you're going to handle it when Mason tells him he can do something that you don't want him doing? Like skiing?"

Mary's concerns were an echo of Chris's own. Until six months ago Chris had never had to compromise where Kevin was concerned. "We went over a few things," Chris said. "We're both aware that we might have a problem—" She grinned sheepishly. " 'Problem' may be too mild a word," she admitted. "But I came away feeling that Mason is going to be more cooperative now that he doesn't have to fight to see Kevin."

"Actually, what took up most of the time was the prenuptial agreement he wanted me to sign."

Mary came on point, her attention sharply focused. "I wish that surprised me more. What did the bastard want you to do, promise you'd give him half of everything you owned when you got divorced?"

"That's what I went in expecting, too."

"And that's not what you got?"

"He tried to talk me into a settlement that would equal half of what he earned while we were married but not payable in one lump sum. He said he didn't want to be forced to sell at the wrong time."

"Wait a minute. Are you sure you were talking to the real Mason Winter?"

"It doesn't matter. I told him the only thing I would agree to was that we both walk away with exactly what we brought, no more, no less. I can take care of myself. I always have. I don't want anything he has and I sure as hell don't need it."

"And he said?"

"That I would change my mind."

"He could be right."

Chris recoiled at the thought. "You know me better than that."

"All I'm saying is that it's pretty hard to go back to a life of pinching pennies after you've stopped bending over to pick them up off the sidewalk."

Mary wasn't just speaking hypothetically. She'd grown up in luxury, with someone poised to attend to her every need. She'd been even more catered to when her father was governor. It was nothing short of amazing that she'd turned out to be as down-to-earth as she was. "Is that how you felt when you married John?"

Mary smiled. "In the beginning, living on a budget was a new and fascinating game. Thank God I was mature enough to realize the emotional wealth John gave me when the game got old."

"I'm sure I'll get the same kind of emotional wealth when the marriage is over and I can move back into my house."

"So that's how you ended it?"

Chris nodded. "Mason is going to have his lawyer draw up the papers and send them to me to sign."

Mary got up and went to the window to check on Kevin and Tracy. "Boy, wait until the newspapers get hold of this. They're going to have a field day."

"That's one of the reasons we're keeping it small and getting it over with as quickly as possible."

"How quick is quickly?"

Chris made a face. "Next week."

Mary let out a snort. "I don't know why I should be surprised. That makes about as much sense as any of the rest of it."

"Why put it off?"

"Because you might come to your senses."

"I'd like you and John to be there. It may not be a real marriage, but I have a feeling it's the only one I'll ever have and I don't want it to be witnessed by strangers."

Mary groaned. "Just don't ask me to be happy for you."

"I won't."

"Do you realize how much you sound like a condemned woman inviting her friends to the execution?"

"You're not helping matters," Chris said. "I could use some support on this, especially since I'm not going to change my mind."

"I'm sorry." Mary covered her face with her hands and let out a sigh. After several seconds she curled her fingers into fists and propped her chin on her knuckles. "I'll try harder from now on. You certainly don't need another anchor to drag you down."

Chris knew that no matter how much or how long she talked, she would never convince Mary that the marriage wasn't a horrendous mistake. But she also knew that in a couple of hours, after the news had had a chance to settle, Mary would come around, if for no other reason than that Chris needed her to. Reaching across the table, she squeezed Mary's hand. "Thank you. I suppose I could get through this without you and John, but I'd rather not have to try."

"John's not going to be the pushover I am."

"With both of us working on him, he won't

be able to hold out long," Chris said, wishing she felt as confident as she sounded.

The following week was surprisingly uneventful. Chris waited until the morning of the day she and Mason were to be married to tell Kevin. The only secrets he could keep were the ones he forgot about ten minutes after he was told. To tell him that his biggest wish was coming true and then ask him not to tell anyone about it was tantamount to her going on a diet the same day she got a job in a chocolate factory.

While the days passed relatively quietly, she spent the nights tossing and turning, seeking sleep that became increasingly more elusive the closer she got to the day of the wedding. When she did manage to fall asleep, she woke up feeling drained, with a recurring dream playing in her mind.

She dreamed she and Kevin were at Disneyland, alone and having a wonderful time. They went on his favorite rides—the Pirates of the Caribbean, the submarine, and Alice in Wonderland's Teacups—ate lunch in Frontierland, and then went in to see the singing bears. When they came out, Mason was waiting for them.

Where Kevin had been only pleasantly happy about their vacation before, he came alive with excitement when he saw his father. The whole tone of the day changed. They abandoned the gentle rides for those that were no more than thinly disguised roller coasters. Before each one, Chris told Mason that Kevin hated violence, even in his entertainment, and then was forced to stand at the bottom and listen to his squeals of laughter, watching as father and son got off the ride hand in hand, eager to go again.

Chris didn't need a psychiatrist to interpret the dream for her. What she really needed was someone to tell her whether it was a warning or a prophecy.

22

Fighting an almost overwhelming fatigue, Mason closed the file folder in front of him, put his elbows on his desk, and pinched the bridge of his nose, not even looking up when he heard the door to his office open and someone come inside.

"You must have gotten the report," Rebecca said, obviously zeroing in on his appearance and drawing the right conclusion.

"Last night."

"And?"

At last Mason looked up. He was a little taken aback to see Rebecca wearing a dress rather than her usual business suit. Instead of commenting, however, he filed the fact in the part of his brain reserved for bits and pieces of information that had flags attached to them for easy retrieval. "It seems our competition for the riverfront project is coming from the south."

"Well, I'll be damned," she said softly. "So Walt was right after all. Is it L.A.?"

He wished it was that simple, another contractor heading north, trying to make his fortune in the twenty-first century's version of a gold rush. "Not quite that far," Mason said enigmatically, wearily leaning back in his chair.

Rebecca's puzzled frown changed to one of dawning understanding and then stunned surprise. "Santa Barbara?" she gasped.

"Bingo," he said, taking his usual pleasure in watching how quickly she grasped the situation and filled in the blanks.

As if afraid her legs were about to give out, Rebecca crossed the office and sat down on the leather sofa. "I never would have guessed it, not in a million years, especially after all this time. What could your father and brother possibly hope to gain? This is your territory. They'll never unseat you."

"It took me a while to figure it out, but then it was like a light bulb going on in my head. Think of it, Rebecca. Stealing the riverfront project from me will gain my father and brother an entrance into Sacramento construction they couldn't buy with a ten-million-dollar advertising budget. When you want the kingdom, you don't do battle with the serfs. You go to the top and try to carve out your piece of the pie from there."

"Are you sure it's the kingdom they're after? Maybe it's the king."

He ignored her question, not because he didn't think it had merit, but because he wasn't ready to deal with something that was beginning to make more and more sense. He'd thought himself free of his father and brother, free of the fighting and the anger and the pain. After all this time, why come after him now? Why dredge up the past when it was so unnecessary? Hadn't he left them the greater part of southern California? They weren't big enough to take on more. "No one cares about family feuds anymore, especially one that's over a decade old. So how could they hope to get press with that?" he asked unconvincingly.

"You're wrong about that. Remember the Mondavis? People read everything they could get their hands on about that family feud."

"Only because the Mondavis make wine, and people associated with the wine industry have a mystique about them. As far as the general public knows or cares, construction people drop out of school in the eighth grade, scratch their butts in public, and drink beer for breakfast. Nobody gives a damn about them."

"Maybe you've hit on something with that publicity idea," she said, making no attempt to hide her sarcasm. "The riverfront project is considered a little off center by most of the citizens of our fair city to begin with. If you gathered up the people who think you can pull it off and put them in this office, we'd still have room for a small dance floor in the middle. Now, what's going to happen when the nay-sayers find out that your own father and brother are rushing in to tilt at what everyone considers Mason Winter's private windmill? I'll tell you what they're going to do. They're going to shake their heads and cluck their tongues and say how unfortunate it is that insanity runs in families."

"I think you're—"

"I'm not through talking yet," she said. "You can't afford to get so caught up in how you feel about the project and how you feel about your family that you miss the obvious."

"*What* obvious?" he nearly shouted.

"I don't know yet," she admitted. "All I know for sure is that things aren't what they seem—a long way from it. There isn't a banker in this country who's offered to stick his neck out on this one, even with you doing it. What makes your father and brother think they'll get backing?"

"Maybe they already have it," he said, feeling a tightness in his throat. It would tear his heart out to see a friend take over and build what Mason had come to think of as his private dream; to watch Southwest Construction do it would kill him.

Rebecca pressed her fingertips to her temples. "I need time to think about this," she said, then with a sardonic smile added, "Maybe they're just pissed off because you didn't invite them to the wedding."

He blinked. All of a sudden it dawned on him why Rebecca was dressed differently today. "Jesus, I forgot that thing was today."

"I'm sure Chris would be thrilled to hear you refer to your wedding as 'that thing.' "

He laid a piercing look on her. "If you don't have anything constructive to say—"

"Shut up," she finished for him, smiling.

"Precisely." He lifted his cuff from his watch and groaned. "I'm supposed to be there in an hour."

"If you hurry, you still have time for a quick shower and a fresh suit."

He thought for a minute. "You're a woman," he said, stating the obvious in his attempt to make a point. "Do you suppose Chris would mind very much if we put this off until next week?"

Rebecca got up from the couch and crossed the room. She put her hands on the desk and leaned forward, staring down at Mason. "Under the circumstances," she said evenly, "putting it off could very well mean calling it off. Is that what you want?"

"You know as well as I do that what I want doesn't figure into it." He stood up and reached for his jacket.

"Don't whine, Mason. It isn't macho."

For the first time that day, he smiled. "I'm going upstairs," he said. "Do what needs to be done while I'm out of town."

She made a face. "You couldn't possibly mean what I think you mean, could you? You're not really planning to get married and then immediately take off for Santa Barbara? Not today of all—"

"No editorials," he said, interrupting her. He reached for the door and then as an afterthought added, "Just make the arrangements for me so that no one else knows what I'm doing, and that includes Janet. I don't want her to have to lie about my whereabouts or possibly to slip up." He gave her a mischievous look and a wink. "You can consider your silence on the subject a wedding present."

"You can't afford to have me give you such an expensive gift. You know as well as I do that I'm the string on your balloon. Without me..." She shrugged expressively.

"Someday the last word is going to be mine," he muttered as he headed out the door.

Chris drew her coat closer around her, refusing to acknowledge that the chill she felt had nothing to do with the overcast February sky. She grabbed Kevin's hand to keep him from charging up the rain-slick courthouse steps ahead of her. From the instant she'd told him what they were going to do that day, he'd been as excited as she was nervous, as eager as she was hesitant, and as confident as she was unsure of herself.

Earlier that morning, as she was getting dressed, she'd purposely thrust all of her insecurities into a mental box and tried to shove it to the back of her mind. Only it wouldn't stay there. The box kept coming back, wrapped in a bright, shiny bow.

Chris couldn't shake the thought that she was going kicking and screaming to a place Diane would have given anything to attain. Two of the players in the day's drama had been brilliantly cast; Kevin was the perfect child and Mason was obviously the father. Only the

231

role of mother had a stand-in. Too bad, but at the last minute the lead couldn't make it, something about dying on the way to the rest of her life.

Every hour that passed marked a battle won in her fight to keep Mary and John, who were following close behind, from discovering the extent of her doubts. The slightest hint and they would have her out of there and on her way back home.

"There he is," Kevin said, jumping up and down, pointing to a man dressed in a beautifully tailored Burberry raincoat about to enter the building through a heavy glass door. "There's my daddy," he called as he turned to the Hendricksons, bubbling with pleasure. He turned back to Chris. "Hurry, Mom. If we go faster, we can catch him."

"We'll see him in the judge's chambers, Kevin," she said, reluctant to face Mason one minute before she had to. The disappointment in Kevin's eyes sent a stab of guilt through her. This morning was proving to be even harder than she had imagined. No matter how many times she reminded herself why she was doing this, she couldn't seem to take satisfaction in Kevin's happiness. "All right," she said without enthusiasm. "We'll see if we can catch up."

"I love you, Mom," he said, taking her completely unaware.

The sharp edge of her doubts rounded. "I love you, too, Kevin."

They went inside and discovered Mason had waited for them. He was with a tall, thin woman in an expensively tailored raw silk dress, and a short, stocky man wearing a blue pin-striped suit that made him took even shorter and wider than he was.

Kevin let go of Chris's hand, sprinted across the marble floor of the lobby, and threw his arms around Mason's legs. The twinge of jealousy that started to surface disappeared almost before Chris could acknowledge its existence when she saw the look that came into Mason's eyes. His love for his son was like a beacon, drawing others with its purity and guilelessness, making anyone less fortunate want to bask in the glow and take away with them a sense of all being right with the world.

"Come here, Mom," Kevin said, holding out his free hand.

Chris exchanged a quick look with John and Mary, took a deep breath, and went with them to join the others.

"This is Miz Rebecca, Mom," Kevin said, indicating the tall woman. "I told you about her, 'member? She's the one who gived me the big box of colors."

Smiling warmly, Rebecca held out her hand. "I'm so very pleased to finally meet you, Ms. Taylor."

"And this is Travis," Kevin continued before Chris had a chance to reply to Rebecca. "He's Daddy's friend, and now he's my friend, too."

A thick, callused hand engulfed Chris's. She could feel the restraint in the handshake as clearly as the strength. When she and Diane were growing up, Harriet had insisted they choose their friends with care, saying a lady was judged by the company she kept. In theory, Chris agreed. She did judge people by their friends, but not in the way Harriet had intended. Whom a person chose to spend time with gave a strong clue to that person's own personality. On first meeting, Chris liked Mason's friends. A glimmer of hope surfaced; perhaps one day she would find something to like about Mason, too.

"I'm pleased to meet you," Chris said. "Both of you." She stepped back and introduced John and Mary to Mason and his friends. An awkward moment of silence followed.

Mason glanced at his watch. "It's time," he announced.

Chris witnessed a quick chastising look pass from Rebecca to Mason. "Perhaps Chris would like to freshen up first," she said.

"No," Chris interjected. "I'm fine." She wanted to get the wedding over with as quickly as possible. Once it was in the past she could stop thinking about it and get back to a semblance of routine. It was the wait that was driving her crazy.

Mary slipped her arm around Chris's shoulder. Chris was taken aback at the profound look of compassion on her face. She quickly glanced at the others. With the exception of Kevin, they looked as if they'd gathered to hear the sentencing on a felony conviction.

For the first time in a long while, Chris's

funny bone was tickled. She started thinking about what kind of picture the seven of them presented to passersby. No one would ever guess why they were really there. The more she thought about it, the funnier it became. She put her hand over her mouth, feigning a cough, to cover the giggle that bubbled up from her chest. She was busy congratulating herself on her successful ruse when she glanced up and caught a man in a plaid shirt and quilted vest sending a commiserating look her way. It was too much to keep locked inside. She burst into laughter.

Mason eyed her. "Are you all right?"

She tried to answer him, but couldn't string three words together without breaking into peals of hiccuping laughter.

"She's just nervous," Mary said, an apologetic smile playing around her mouth.

"I'm sure that's it," Rebecca agreed. "I know that's how I would feel under the circumstances."

"Nervous hell," John muttered. "Scared shitless is more like it. Not that I blame her."

"Mom?" Kevin questioned hesitantly.

They were gathering a crowd now. "I'm okay, Kevin," she managed to say seconds before breaking into laughter all over again. She dug through her purse, hunting for a Kleenex to wipe the streams of tears from her cheeks and eyes.

"Maybe you should go to the ladies' room," Mary suggested.

Chris waved her off. "No..." she gasped, "I'll be...all right. Just—" She stopped to bite her lip and let a wave of laughter pass. After a minute she took a deep breath and finished. "Just give me...a couple more seconds." She took another deep breath and then another. Finally she was calm again.

"See?" she said brightly. "I'm fine."

"Then let's get on with it," Mason answered in a tone that implied he thought she was a long way from being "fine."

Judge McCormick's very pregnant secretary came out to the hallway to greet them. "So you're Kevin," she said, taking his hand and walking with him into the judge's chambers. "This is a pretty big day for you."

"Yep," he answered, skipping along beside her. "Me and my mom and dad are gettin' married. We're going to live together like Tracy and Aunt Mary and Uncle John."

Before Chris could fall in behind the others, Mason pulled her aside. "Are you still sure you want to go through with this?"

She frowned. "Why do you ask?"

"After what happened downstairs I thought—" He shrugged. "Quite honestly, I don't know what to think."

Her answering smile was tinged with embarrassment. She decided she owed him an explanation, if for no other reason than to keep him from trying to have her certified. "I just started thinking how off-the-wall this whole thing is. One thing led to another..."

"Go on," he prompted.

She shrugged. "It just occurred to me that

no one who saw us could ever have guessed the real reason we were here. Once that thought entered my head and I started imagining what other people were probably thinking, I was too far over the edge not to fall."

"Does this happen to you often?" he asked.

She grinned. "Two or three times a year, tops. Funerals, car wrecks, sad movies—things like that are usually what sets me off."

Responding to her smile, he said wryly, "In other words, I'd better think twice before asking you to go anywhere with me."

"If those are the places you had in mind, that would probably be a very good idea."

She couldn't help but notice that he, too, had stopped fighting the idea of getting married. A calm acceptance seemed to have claimed them both, almost as if they'd been given something to numb them. Chris was too much of a realist to think it would last but enough of a dreamer to hope so. Getting through the next ten years would be a lot easier if they weren't at each other's throats all the time. That they might be friends was too much to ask. Right now she'd settle for neutrality.

"Shall we go inside?" he asked, offering her his arm.

"I'm as ready as I'll ever be," she said, lightly resting her hand on his coat sleeve.

Twenty minutes later, she walked back out of the office as Mrs. Mason Rourke Winter.

23

Kevin left Harold McCormick's chambers in Mason's arms, as happy as Chris had ever seen him. He'd stood between her and Mason during the brief ceremony, holding their hands, establishing both symbolically and physically the link between them.

Chris had expected to feel something—if nothing else, relief that the pressure she'd been under the past week was over. All she felt was a mind-boggling numbness. Old problems hadn't been solved so much as new ones had been created.

She and Mason had a lot to settle between them, issues they had mutually and wisely agreed to put off discussing until after the wedding. They'd both recognized that trying to hammer out even the simplest things, like where they would live, was one way to make sure the marriage never took place.

She stood to one side and watched the interaction between Mason and Kevin for several more seconds, seeking confirmation that what they'd all gone through that day would not be in vain. John came over to help her with her coat.

"They look good together," he reluctantly admitted.

"I was just thinking the same thing," she said, taking comfort in the warmth and protectiveness of his friendship. One of her greatest fears was that somehow, in gaining Mason,

Kevin would lose John. She knew there was only so much she could do to keep that from happening.

"The two of you are in my prayers, kiddo," he said, playfully tugging on a lock of her hair.

Chris hugged him. "So what else is new?"

"I'm not ready to admit this to anyone else yet, but I'm starting to think maybe the three of you have got a shot at working this thing out."

She gave him a disbelieving look. "Oh? And what has brought you to this startling conclusion?"

"Looking at the two of them together. You can't fake the way they obviously feel about each other. I understand now why you agreed to this marriage. You saw it, too. I've got to tell you, Chris, I've never admired anyone more than I admire you right now for what you're doing for Kevin. I doubt he'll ever understand the sacrifice you made, and maybe that's the way it should be, but I understand, and I want you to know that I think you're one hell of a woman."

"Me too," Mary said, coming up to them.

"This is quite a mutual admiration society we've got going here." Chris was embarrassed by their praise.

"How about if we take Kevin home with us and give you and Mason some time alone to work out where you go from here?" Mary said.

"Thanks," Chris said. "I was just about to suggest the same thing."

When they reached the lobby, Mary and John

and Kevin said good-bye and went off in one direction, and Rebecca and Travis, saying they had to get back to work, took off in the other, leaving Chris and Mason alone.

"I don't have much time," Mason said. "My plane takes off in an hour."

"You're leaving?" Chris said, taken off guard. "Where are you going? And why now?"

He looked startled, as if she'd hit him. "I beg your pardon?"

"Why didn't you say something earlier? We have—"

"My God, I can't believe I'm hearing this. You don't really think I'm going to report my comings and goings to you."

"Whenever they concern me, I sure as hell do."

"Just how does today concern you?" he asked, his voice dripping sarcasm. "Surely you weren't expecting a honeymoon."

She felt the muscles in her jaw tighten. "Not even in my worst nightmares."

"Then what is it?"

"There's the little matter of finding a house. Correct me if I'm mistaken, but I thought that was what today was all about."

"Oh, yeah, I forgot." He pulled his raincoat open and dug into his pants pocket, bringing out a key. He handed it to her. "Call Rebecca. She's got all the information."

Chris stared at the shiny bit of brass resting on her palm. "What's this?"

A look of impatience crossed his face. "Precisely what it looks like."

Before answering, she reminded herself of

the only wise thing her high school tennis coach had ever told her: "If an opponent can get you to lose your temper, he's halfway to a win."

"What is it for?" she asked evenly.

"The house I bought for us last week."

"You bought a house without letting me see it first?"

"Not to put too fine a point on things, but I thought it best for us to stay away from each other last week."

"It never occurred to you to wait so that I might have some input into the decision?"

"For Christ's sake, it's just a house."

It flashed through her mind to tell him why she cared—the big reasons, like keeping Kevin close to his old neighborhood, and the small ones, like having a room she could work in where she could keep the curtains open and not worry about glare on her computer screen—but she knew she would have to reveal too much of herself in the process and likely would gain nothing. She'd look at the house first, and then present her argument in a clear, businesslike manner—something a man like Mason was capable of understanding.

"You're right," she said. "It is just a house. I'll look at it and get back to you."

"You don't have to do that. Rebecca can handle any questions you might have. Give her a call when you're ready to move and she'll have my secretary arrange everything." He pulled his sleeve back to look at his watch. "I'm sorry to run out on you," he said, softening his earlier attitude. "But this trip isn't something I can put off. Tell Kevin I'll bring him a surprise."

He turned to go and she caught his arm to stop him. "Don't bring him anything," she said.

"Why not?" he asked with a tinge of impatience.

"Kevin should look forward to seeing you, not to what you bring him." Watching him as he thought about what she'd said, she picked up a questioning, hesitant look in his eyes. She understood his reluctance to trust her. She didn't trust him either.

"Thank you," he said at last, plainly deciding that she wasn't trying to mislead him. "I realize I have a lot to learn about being a parent. I appreciate your help, especially under the circumstances."

"Don't you think it would be a little stupid of me to go through all of this for Kevin and not do everything I could to see that it worked?"

"Not everyone would react in the same way. I just want you to know I appreciate your cooperation," he said.

He'd spoken the words in much the same way she imagined he would close a business letter to a recalcitrant subcontractor. "Any time I can be of help, please don't hesitate to call," she said, slipping into a matching formality.

"Well, thanks again."

"No problem."

"I'll see you in a couple of days."

"Take your time," she said, pasting on

what she hoped would pass for a smile. "We'll be here."

She watched him leave.

Because she was afraid he would get the wrong idea if she followed him, she remained where she was for several minutes, standing in the middle of the courthouse lobby, surrounded by strangers less than a half hour after what should have been one of the biggest days of her life.

Somehow she didn't feel like laughing now.

24

Chris caught her breath as the elevator doors swung open on the twenty-seventh floor of the Winter Construction Company Tower. For the first time, Mason's prestige and power hit her on a personal level. It was one thing to read about who and what he was in newspapers and magazines, quite another to see the quiet opulence of the head office firsthand. The paintings on the paneled walls were originals, and although Chris's art education had not extended past a few college courses and a love of museums, she was convinced that the eighteenth-century portrait of a child was a Henry Raeburn and the landscape a Bonington.

It was turning out to be quite a day. She'd been married and abandoned and nearly overwhelmed by a reception area, all in the space of an hour.

"May I help you?" a black woman in a red and white cashmere sweater asked from behind the reception desk.

"I'm looking for Rebecca Kirkpatrick's office."

"Is Ms. Kirkpatrick expecting you?"

"Yes. At least I think so."

"Let me call her for you," she said pleasantly. "May I give her your name?"

Again Chris was impressed. She wondered if Mason was clever enough to have hired such a personable receptionist or if he'd just lucked into her, the way he seemed to luck into everything else—including the way he'd found out about Kevin.

"Chris...uh, Chris Taylor," she finished awkwardly. Even though she'd decided it would be expedient to use Mason's name, she couldn't bring herself to say it out loud.

The receptionist punched a button and then spoke into her headset so softly Chris couldn't make out the words. When she had finished, she looked up, smiled, and said, "Ms. Kirkpatrick is delighted that you could make it, Ms. Taylor. Her assistant will be right here to take you to her."

A buzzer sounded, an oak door swung open, and a man, dressed in a blue blazer, red tie, and gray slacks, whom Chris judged to be on the light side of twenty-five, greeted her. "Ms. Taylor," he said enthusiastically, extending his hand. "Randy Padilla. I can't tell you how glad I am to meet you." He held the door for her to go inside. "That's really one terrific kid you have. He reminds me a lot of my sister's boy, always asking questions and always on the go."

"You've met Kevin?" Chris asked, following him down a long hallway.

"Several times. I come in on Saturdays two or three times a month to catch up on my homework. It's quieter here than at my apartment."

"Mr. Winter lets you use the office for homework?"

He chuckled. "When it involves anything to do with school, 'let' isn't the operative word around here, it's more like 'insist.' Mason's really big on education. He even ties our bonuses to how well we do in school."

Something didn't seem right. And it was more than the egalitarian use of Mason's first name by someone who was obviously on a lower rung of the office ladder. It sounded as if Kevin was a regular visitor, and yet he'd never told her a thing about it. Why not?

Why indeed, she thought sadly, remembering how quiet he had become after she lost her temper one time when Mason took him to San Francisco without asking her first.

What else had Kevin kept from her?

"Well, here we are," he said, opening an office door and stepping aside to let Chris enter.

"Thank you," she told him.

Rebecca got up from behind her desk and came across the room to greet Chris. "Even though the circumstances could be better," she said, "I'm really glad we'll have this chance to get to know each other."

She took Chris's coat and hung it in a closet beside the bookshelf.

"Mason said you have some information for me about the house?" Although Chris's first instinct was to accept Rebecca for the warm, outgoing person she seemed, an insistent inner voice told her to watch herself, that Rebecca was Mason's friend, not hers. Too many unexpected things had happened that day for her to let her guard down now. No one was turning out to be the way she'd thought they would be.

"Before we talk about the house, how about if we have a cup of coffee and I tell you a little bit about myself and how I fit into the grand scheme of things around here? Do you have time?"

"A cup of coffee would be nice."

"Great, I held off having any myself, thinking you might be as chilled to the bone as I was when I got back. Why don't you have a seat on the couch while I get it ready?" She went to a sideboard, opened an accordion door that revealed a compact kitchen area, and measured coffee into a drip machine.

While Rebecca was occupied, Chris looked around the office. It was decorated in shades of green, maroon, and brown, all brought together by a splashy pattern on the couch and chairs, separated out again in the carpet, drapes, and wallpaper. The furniture had been made out of a tightly grained reddish wood Chris couldn't identify. Each piece was elegant and understated, obviously hand-crafted, and obviously expensive.

The view from the corner windows was spectacular. They were high enough to over-look the gold-leafed dome of the State Capitol, the spires of the Cathedral of the Blessed Sacrament, and an undulating sea of treetops in a city that prided itself on its trees.

"Have you been with Winter Construction long?" Chris asked.

"Since the beginning. Only Travis and Mason have been here longer."

A peculiar feeling came over Chris. She was the outsider and she wanted in, but for the life of her she couldn't figure out why. "Then you must have met Diane."

"Met her and liked her very much," Rebecca said, her voice soft and thoughtful. "I never believed she just got up one morning and decided to walk out on Mason. Not the way they felt about each other."

"Mason must have believed her. If he hadn't, it seems to me he would have looked for her."

Rebecca transferred the coffee into an antique silver coffee server, placed two del-icate china cups on the tray, and brought it across the room. "He had his reasons for believing what he did," she said. "I'm sure he'll explain them to you someday."

"Reasons?" she questioned, not asking for an explanation, only expressing her doubts.

"They aren't what you think," Rebecca said as she settled into a chair and poured their coffee. "But that's all in the past. Let's talk about what's happening now. Has Mason told you how crazy we all are about Kevin?

He's like a breath of fresh air in a smoke-filled room. I can't tell you how happy I am that he's become a part of all of our lives, especially Mason's, and especially now."

Chris felt as if it were autumn and she was the last leaf clinging to the tree. For the past several months, Kevin had been existing in a world she knew little about. And what did Rebecca mean by 'especially now'? "No, Mason didn't even tell me he'd brought Kevin to the office. We don't talk to each other any more than is absolutely necessary," she admitted, surprised at the feeling of regret.

"Oh...I'm sorry if I've made you uncomfortable. I knew communication between you and Mason wasn't always the best; I just didn't know it was that bad."

"You must be aware of the real reason we got married." She couldn't believe Mason wouldn't have confided in the two people he'd brought to witness his wedding.

"To give Kevin some stability in his life," Rebecca volunteered. "But that doesn't mean you and Mason can't be...friends."

Chris almost choked on her coffee. "Did he say that?"

"God, no. He'd have my hide if he knew I'd even suggested such a thing. Mason protects his independence better than the Forty-Niner front line protects Joe Montana." She shrugged. "I just thought that if the two of you find you really can live together without killing each other, you might as well make the best of it. You may not be aware of this, but there's a lot of socializing involved with Mason's business.

It isn't the kind of thing he can skip and still hope to keep up with what's going on."

"Meaning?"

"Meaning people attend these things in pairs."

"Mason and I have agreed to go on with our own lives. He doesn't expect me to become a part of his any more than I expect him to become a part of mine."

"I'm not surprised he told you that."

Chris was becoming progressively more uneasy. "Is there some reason I should doubt him?"

"No," she insisted. "It's just so like him not to tell you how awkward it will be for him to show up at functions without you, particularly in the beginning. Everyone is going to be curious. Remember, all anyone knows for sure is that you caught one of the city's most eligible bachelors."

Before Chris could protest, Rebecca quickly added, "I know that kind of thinking is enough to make you gag, but it happens to be the way things are. A lot of women out there are going to be wondering what you have that they don't, and they aren't going to give Mason a minute's rest until they find out."

Chris let out a disparaging laugh. "That's easy—I have Mason's son. Once the word gets out, they'll back off."

"How is the word going to get out?"

"I'm sure Mason will tell them."

"Have you seen or heard one word about Kevin from anyone outside Mason's immediate circle since the day Mason found out he had a son?"

With a start, Chris realized Rebecca was right. The news that Mason Winter had discovered he had a son five years after the fact should have been the hottest gossip to hit town since Senator Montoya's video debut showing him selling political favors to the highest bidder. It wasn't as if the secret had been kept solely because no one but Mason knew. If what she'd seen today was any indication, everyone remotely close to him knew about Kevin. The implication was sobering and thought-provoking. What was it about Mason that inspired such loyalty in his friends and employees?

"No, I haven't," Chris admitted. "But there really isn't any reason for Mason to keep Kevin a secret any longer."

Rebecca pulled back in surprise. "You've got to be kidding. If this got out now, the press would be camped on your doorstep. They would make Kevin's life a living hell. Mason's not about to let that happen."

"Then just how does he plan to explain me and Kevin?"

"You'll have to ask him that one." She picked up the silver pot and poured them both more coffee. "I hate to belabor the point, but I wanted to be sure you understood why it was important for you to put up a good front about this marriage."

When Chris started to answer, Rebecca held up her hand to stop her. "I've gone this far," she said with a self-deprecating laugh. "I might as well go all the way and tell you about the upcoming Valentine's Day dance at the Crocker Art Museum. It's a benefit for a fairly new charity in town, which happens to be desperately needed. The main goal of the organization is to set up long-term care programs for babies born to drug-addicted mothers."

Chris sensed Rebecca's interest in the charity went beyond getting dressed up once a year and writing a tax-deductible check. "You seem to know quite a bit about them."

"I should," she admitted, smiling. "I'm on the board. Mason encourages those of us who can to become involved with the community in any way we choose. This just happens to be my way. Travis goes into disadvantaged neighborhoods and helps establish parks and playgrounds for the kids."

Chris considered telling Rebecca about the time she'd spent teaching inner city women about prenatal care and nutrition and how frustrating it had been to watch the drug-addicted mothers and know what was happening to the babies. But she discarded the idea as being too much of an overture. If they were to be friends, they would have time later on for such confidences; if they weren't, Chris preferred Rebecca to know as little about her as possible. "What does Mason do?" Chris asked, interested in spite of herself.

"Too much. I've been after him for years about being such a soft touch. All anybody has to do is ask, and he's there." Rebecca put her cup on the table and leaned forward toward Chris. "Getting back to the dance for a minute, I know Mason will never ask, especially not after the two of you already agreed you wouldn't step on each other's toes socially, but it would mean a lot to him if you'd—"

"I really don't want to talk about that now," Chris said. She refused to be backed into a corner in a room she hadn't even known existed. Just the thought of spending an evening with Mason clones was enough to make her shudder; ten years' worth of such evenings would leave her a blithering idiot. "This is something Mason and I are going to have to discuss. I didn't get into this thing to be his companion."

"You're right," Rebecca said. "You and Mason should work this kind of thing out between you. I only brought it up because I knew he wouldn't and I felt it was important for you to have all the information you need to make an informed decision." She sat back in her chair. "To be honest, I have a tendency to try to protect Mason—at times even from himself."

Chris eyed her. "And you feel he needs protecting from me?"

"Only until you get to know him," she admitted. "When that happens, he won't need me anymore."

"I appreciate your honesty."

"Just because I'm Mason's friend doesn't mean I can't be yours."

"I'm sure you'll understand if it takes me a while to accept that," Chris said.

"Fair enough. Now why don't we get on to the business of the house? I'm sure you have a hundred things you'd like to get done today."

Chris returned the translucent china cup and saucer to the tray. "Not the least of which is getting a look at this house while it's still daylight." Instantly the anger she felt over Mason's preemptive behavior returned.

"Great idea," Rebecca said enthusiastically, ignoring Chris's mood swing. "You're going to love it." She got up and went to her desk. "Kevin will, too."

She pulled a manila envelope out of the top drawer, then came back and handed it to Chris. "Everything you need is in here, including the names of a couple of movers and decorators. Most of the house is in really good shape, but I have a feeling you're going to want to do something with the kitchen and the sun room."

Chris swallowed her anger. Jumping all over Rebecca because of Mason's arrogant behavior was not only counterproductive, it was unfair. "Now all I need to know is where it is."

Rebecca laughed. "I'm sorry, I just assumed Mason would have told you. He was so excited about finding the house, I'm surprised he didn't shout it from the rooftop."

Chris was beginning to think there were two Masons, the one Rebecca knew and the one she'd been dealing with. In Chris's most imaginative dreams she couldn't picture Mason getting excited about a new house. "What makes this place so special?" she asked warily.

"It's only a block and a half from where you live now."

Chris was speechless. When finally she'd gathered her wits about her again, she was still unable to believe the obvious and asked, "Why was that important to Mason?"

Rebecca frowned, as if confused by the question. "He didn't want you and Kevin to be uprooted any more than was absolutely necessary."

"But I thought..." Chris shook her head. "Never mind what I thought."

An understanding look took the place of the frown. "You have a lot to learn about Mason," she said softly.

"I can see that," Chris answered, her equilibrium shaken.

Before going to the house that would hold her next decade of memories, Chris drove around Sacramento, visiting the places of her own childhood, trying to connect with who and what she was.

She stopped for her seventh cup of coffee of the day at Java City, switching to decaffeinated while she took refuge in the isolation of the constantly changing crowd. Opening the envelope Rebecca had given her, she discovered it held few surprises. There was a short, businesslike note from Mason, instructing her to charge whatever she needed for the new house to his accounts, followed by a list of stores in and around Sacramento, just one of which she was even vaguely familiar with, and only because of the twice-a-year clearance sale.

She felt as if she'd shifted into the fast

lane while driving a Volkswagen. How was she going to keep up? Her insistence that she would take care of half of the household bills echoed in her mind, seeming as ludicrous to her now as it must have seemed to Mason after their first meeting in Harold McCormick's chambers a week ago. After all, houses with separate wings were bound to have enormous overhead.

What had she been thinking of? Into what cloud had she stuck her head?

More importantly, what was she going to do about it now?

Realizing she was only putting off the inevitable, she shoved the papers back into the envelope and left the coffee shop.

A peculiar mix of emotions passed through Chris as she drove down J Street and then cut over to M. Only one did she try to deny.

Somewhere under all her fear and anger and anxiety there was a bud of excitement. She'd recognized the house Mason had bought the instant Rebecca had given her the address. She'd passed it a hundred times on her evening walks, and when she allowed herself to dream of such things, that was the house she dreamed about living in one day.

Built in the Colonial style with a brick facade, white shutters, and a slate roof, the house bespoke a quiet elegance that said "welcome." There was a perfectly shaped twenty-five-foot blue spruce in the side yard and a fifty-year-old elm in the front. Banks of azaleas bordered the driveway, creating solid rows of color in March and April.

Chris had never been inside. While only a block and a half from her own home, the houses here were four and five times as large, and the people who owned them were the social elite of the city.

She hadn't even known the house was for sale.

And now she was going to live there.

She pulled up in front of the house and parked on the street. The wind whipped her coat open as she climbed out of the car, sending a chill through her that left her teeth chattering. For long minutes she stood on the sidewalk in the cold, staring at the house.

How did that old expression go? Be careful what you wish for. You just might get it.

25

Mason leaned his head back against the seat, closed his eyes, and tried to concentrate on the hum of the jetliner's engine. The six days he'd spent in Santa Barbara had left him drained, sucking so much energy from him that it had taken a real effort to get up each morning.

He could have hired someone to do what he'd done—to talk to the people at the chamber of commerce, to visit construction sites and pick up on gossip, to get a feel for the mood of a city under the siege of a water shortage—but no matter how detailed the report, it wouldn't have contained the nuances of conversations that at times were even more important than what was being said.

Any contractor based in a city determined to limit future growth was bound to be feeling the effect. But Mason wasn't so naive as to think that might be the sole reason for his father and brother making their move against his riverfront project. If Southwest Construction needed to expand to stay healthy, there were far easier places to go in Sacramento.

Mason had discovered that, while the drought had caused some serious problems, it hadn't affected the building business as much as he'd anticipated. To cover the losses in other areas, Southwest had moved into remodeling, taking three-hundred-thousand-dollar bungalows and turning them into slightly larger three-million-dollar bungalows.

His biggest surprise had come to him one night when he was having dinner alone at his hotel. It was one of those revelations that, when it hit, was so obvious he was left feeling like an idiot for not having noticed it long before. His father and brother were not the construction giants he remembered. Actually, when compared to Winter Construction, they were pretty ordinary, even small-time.

Which made their move on the riverfront project even more confusing and, in a way, more threatening. Were his father and brother simply acting as a front for someone else? Was there another contractor behind the scenes, waiting to throw in with them as soon as they secured the property?

Whatever it was, Mason now realized that his theory about using the project for publicity to make a big splash when Southwest moved to Sacramento didn't hold up under the facts.

Mason left Santa Barbara feeling like a kid assembling a puzzle without having access to the picture on the lid. He'd found and put together all the pieces with straight sides, giving him a frame, but he still had no idea what was supposed to go inside.

The plane began its final descent, drawing his attention to the window. He looked outside and caught a glimpse of his office tower. A feeling of homecoming came over him. He loved his adopted city, loved the excitement of watching it grow, the strutting pride of its developing skyline, its determination to keep a community feel about it, no matter how big it became.

Even though it still scared him a little, he didn't try to deny that there was another reason he was excited to be home. He was only hours away from seeing Kevin. Hell, he chided himself as he turned from the window, he might as well be honest: his emotional tie to Kevin scared him a lot. Just being in the same city with his father and brother had made him realize just how vulnerable he'd made himself by letting Kevin into his life. After Diane left, he'd made a promise to himself that he would never let anyone get that close again.

And now look at him.

The one thing in his favor was that Kevin wasn't going to walk out on him. One day he'd leave—all kids did—but that wouldn't be for years yet. Mason had time to prepare, to cushion himself against the loneliness.

Mason wasn't foolish enough to hope that Kevin would stick around after he grew up. That kind of thing didn't happen anymore. He'd heard the men and women who worked for him complain often enough that when their kids went away to college, they went away for good. Well, he'd be prepared when the time came. Forewarned was forearmed.

Mason slipped out of his seat belt when the plane stopped rolling, grabbed his carry-on bag, threw his raincoat over his arm and joined the crush of exiting passengers. As he neared the end of the departure tunnel, he glanced up and saw Travis waiting for him.

Although he'd told Rebecca to send a car, he was pleased that Travis had shown up instead. They had a lot of catching up to do.

"I take it you didn't have much time for the beach while you were down there," Travis said. "You're as lily white now as you were a week ago."

Mason smiled in greeting. "It's good to see you, too."

"So, how was it?" Travis asked, running his hand over his day's growth of beard. "Bad as you thought it would be?"

"I went down angry and came back confused." He shifted his bag to his other hand and started walking through the terminal toward the escalators. "Something just doesn't make sense about this. The one thing none of us figured is that Southwest isn't big enough to handle the riverfront project by themselves. They couldn't put together the financing or the manpower. They've got to be fronting for someone."

"Who?" Travis asked. "Better yet, why? Your dad's never been one to let anybody in on anything if he didn't have to. You of all people should know that."

"That's not what's eating me. Every time I head down a new road, it leads right back to the idea that this is personal, that Southwest—" He stepped aside to let a woman in a wheelchair pass. "Hell, I don't know why I'm afraid to say it—that my father and brother are out to get me." He grinned self-consciously. "Sounds a little paranoid, doesn't it?"

"Maybe the lump you put in their throats finally got too big to swallow."

"But why now, after all this time?"

"Who knows with them two? They never did do things the regular way. And no one ever accused them of belonging to Mensa."

They'd reached the street entrance. Mason glanced outside, saw the sheets of rain whipping past the lights, and stopped to put on his raincoat.

"I hate this," he said. "There are a dozen things I should be doing, and here I am, all wrapped up with a couple of small-time contractors who want to move up in the world."

Travis chuckled. "I never thought the day would come when I'd hear you talk about those two like that. It sure sounds good."

Mason opened the door for his friend and then followed him through. A blast of frigid air slammed into them, forcing them to lean into the storm to make their way across the street. "Holy shit," Mason muttered. "Has it been like this the whole time I was gone?"

"Pretty much."

"Which means the blocks didn't get set on the Watt Avenue job."

Travis hunched his shoulders and drew his head into his coat, turtle fashion. "If you think I'm going to freeze my ass off, standing out here jawing with you when there's a car with a heater in it waiting for me in that parking lot, you're crazy."

"You're getting old, Travis."

"Maybe, but I can still work circles around the likes of you."

Mason smiled to himself as he lowered his head and silently followed Travis. God, it felt good to be home.

Chris opened the screen on the fireplace and added another piece of wood. The cord she'd had delivered that morning was as seasoned as promised, and the oak logs burned with a beautifully dancing flame.

Curled up in front of a crackling fire on a stormy night with Kevin at her side in the house of her dreams—what more could she ask?

What more indeed? Perhaps that it not be an illusion?

Illusion or not, tonight was hers. After five days of backbreaking work to get the house in order, she was going to take one evening just to sit back and enjoy the fruits of her labor. Tomorrow she'd be at the computer again, trying to catch up with the assignments she'd been ignoring all week.

At least there was evidence of her hard work. The house looked terrific, if a bit eclectic. When she'd first seen Mason's apartment, she'd thought it would be impossible to combine his furnishings with hers and come up with any kind of harmony. But after the movers dumped everything off and she and Mary spent two days trying out different combinations and arrangements, she was pleasantly surprised to discover that her furnishings were picking up a touch of class while Mason's were taking on a little warmth.

Rebecca had stopped by twice, once to drop off some mail for Mason and the other time just to see how Chris and Kevin were getting along. The first time, they'd eaten tuna fish sandwiches while sitting on cardboard boxes; the second time, Chris had served tea and some of Mary's fresh-baked cookies in the living room. In each case, Rebecca had been appropriately surprised and complimentary at how much Chris had accomplished in the house.

Several times during both visits it had been on the tip of Chris's tongue to confess that she'd been reconsidering going to the charity dance with Mason. She felt she owed him more than a simple thank-you for finding a house that allowed Kevin to stay in his neighborhood, and attending the dance with him might be a good way to show her gratitude.

When she finally decided she would go, she told herself it was as much because she approved of the organization sponsoring the event as it was a way to thank Mason. During Kevin's hospital stay a little girl who weighed only a pound and a half had been put into the isolette next to Kevin's. Because the mother had been on heroin, the baby had suffered the pain and trauma of withdrawal. She died two weeks later, untouched by anyone outside the hospital staff. Her short life and tragic death were indelibly stamped in Chris's mind. While she didn't believe a dance was what was needed to help drug-addicted babies, a little attention to the problem couldn't hurt.

As always, whenever something triggered a memory of the time Chris had spent in the hospital with Kevin, she looked for him, seeking reassurance. She found him where he'd been for the past hour, sprawled on the floor, working on a picture for Mason's office.

A feeling of contentment settled through her as she closed the fireplace screen and went into the kitchen to start dinner.

By the time Travis dropped Mason off at the office, it was nearing six o'clock. As Mason stepped off the elevator, the night watchman greeted him and then informed him that because several streets around town were flooded, Rebecca had insisted all of the employees take off for home as soon as they could wrap up their work. Disappointed that he had missed her, Mason let himself in to check his messages.

Walking down the hallway to his office, he considered calling Rebecca and having her meet him for dinner. They'd already talked briefly on the phone about what he'd learned in Santa Barbara, but he was anxious to find out if, after mulling it over, she'd reached any new conclusions.

His dinner plans disintegrated when he flipped on the light over his desk and saw the note she'd left him stating she had a date and not to bother trying to get in touch with her that night because she wasn't sure what time she'd be in.

He quickly sorted through the mail and then went through his engagement calendar to get a fix on the upcoming week. When he hit Thursday and saw the heart Janet had drawn with the word "Dance" in the middle, he groaned. Of all the functions he attended, he looked forward to this one the least. Hearts and cupids weren't his style. At least not anymore. That part of him had died with Susan, flickered momentarily to life again with Diane, and then had disappeared forever.

But more than the hearts and cupids, it was the day itself that disturbed him. With all of the days of the year to pick from, Susan had chosen February 14 to get married. After she died, just getting through the day had been a big part of his self-prescribed therapy. When at last he was able to think of Valentine's

Day as more of a nuisance than an anniversary, he knew he was on the road to recovery.

Finding a way to maintain his sanity through the loss of Susan and then Diane had carried a high price tag, one he never intended to have to pay again.

Fatigue nudging him toward depression, Mason pushed himself away from his desk, left the office, and went upstairs to his apartment. His first thought when he opened the door and saw the empty living room was that he'd been robbed. And then it came to him.

Chris.

Somehow she must have gotten it into her head that his moving in with Kevin meant he intended to give up his apartment. Now, what in the hell was he going to do with an unfurnished apartment?

It didn't take long for the irony to hit him. This was exactly what he'd been looking for—a chance to get rid of that god-awful furniture. He'd have to remember to thank Chris.

But before he did that, he had to take care of one more thing. He went into the bedroom to use the phone, grateful to see she had lacked either the foresight or the time to have it disconnected.

Sitting on the floor cross-legged, he dialed Kelly Whitefield's number and waited. "Kelly, it's Mason," he said in reply to her husky hello.

"Mason who?" she answered playfully.

"I know, it's been too long. But I'm calling to take care of that. There's this dance at the Crocker next Thursday..."

"That's Valentine's Day."

He hesitated, as if looking it up. "Well, I'll be damned, you're right."

"You can't possibly believe I don't already have a date for Valentine's Day."

"I was hoping I might be able to offer something you couldn't possibly refuse."

"Hmmm...and what might that be?"

"Name it."

There was a long pause. "As soon as it's reasonably possible, we'll leave the dance, and the rest of the night it'll just be you and me."

Her suggestion should have aroused him, but he felt nothing. He decided he must be even more tired than he'd thought. "You got it."

"I have to be downtown that day, so I'll meet you at the museum."

"Sure you don't want to go out for something to eat first? It could be a long night."

Her voice dropped to a low purr. "I'll have something waiting for us here. Strawberries and champagne. How does that sound?"

He knew she was expecting some kind of response, but he couldn't come up with one. "I can hardly wait," he said lamely. He started to hang up and then, in what he hoped was a seductive voice, added, "If you won't let me feed you, at least be sure to get plenty of sleep the night before."

Her quick intake of breath let him know he'd pulled it off. He said good night and hung up while he was still ahead.

With the last of his business taken care of, there wasn't any reason to stay in his apartment, and yet he couldn't summon the energy to leave.

Which, when he thought about it, didn't make any sense.

All the way home he'd been chomping at the bit to see Kevin. Mason leaned back against the cold wall and stared at the empty room.

After months of beating his head against Chris's brick wall, he had exactly what he'd been insisting he wanted. Now it was time to put up or shut up. No more hiding behind the excuse that he couldn't be a real father on a part-time basis.

But once the initial greeting at the door was over, what exactly was it that a real father did when he came home after being away for a week? And after that, what was he supposed to do on a day-to-day basis?

Why was it so easy for Chris? How had she walked away from a career and slipped into motherhood, apparently with no more effort than it would take to change from a suit to a pair of jeans?

Or had she? Was he missing something? Were there hidden seams in the fabric that held Chris and Kevin together? He'd sure like to think so. It would help to know if she'd gone through just a little of what he was feeling.

Too bad he couldn't ask her.

26

Chris was spooning the potatoes into a serving bowl when the front doorbell sounded.

"Want me to answer it?" Kevin asked, putting the finishing touches on the picture for his father, which he'd brought into the kitchen in order to be with Chris while she set the table for dinner.

"That's okay, I'll go." She grabbed a towel and wiped her hands as she headed for the door. Peeking through the beveled glass sidelight, she was taken aback to see Mason standing on the front porch.

"Why didn't you use your key?" she questioned, opening the door. "You kept one, didn't you?"

"I wanted to give you some warning that I was here."

What could he possibly have thought she was doing? "Why?" she snapped. "So that I could stash the dope?" Only Harriet had been able to push Chris's buttons quicker, but she'd had years of practice.

He ignored her sarcasm and stepped into the living room. "Where's Kevin?" he asked, looking around.

She took a deep breath to calm herself. They had a lot of years ahead of them. If they could find a way to get through this first night amicably, maybe it would set a precedent. "In the kitchen. We were just about to sit down to dinner."

She took his coat and hung it up in the closet. "I cooked a roast big enough for leftovers. Would you like to join us?"

"I ate on the plane," he answered too quickly.

"What? Peanuts and coffee?"

"Look, we need to get something straight between us. I agreed to *share* a house, not to play house."

She had to remind herself how much she hated violence, that it never solved anything, and that it represented the basest human instincts. Still, a part of her ached to punch him in the nose. "For once in your life, try thinking with the head on your shoulders, not the one between your legs. I was offering you a meal, not a key to my bedroom."

Mason ran his hand across his forehead and then through his damp hair, paused, and gazed across the room. "I'm sorry. I was out of line. It won't happen again."

"Which is about as likely as the sun not coming up in the morning," she retorted.

He caught her off guard when he looked at her and smiled. "Not very original," he said in a low, coaxing voice. "I've come to expect better of you."

Despite herself, she returned his smile. "Give me a minute or two. I'll come up with something better."

Several uncomfortable seconds passed, and then Mason said, "Actually, I am kind of hungry."

If he could try, so could she. "It isn't anything fancy, just plain old-fashioned comfort food—meat, carrots, potatoes, and gravy."

"Sounds wonderful. It's good for me to take a break from lobster and caviar once in a while."

She cocked her head as if to listen more closely. "Was that an attempt at humor I just heard?"

"Not from me. I have an image to maintain."

In hopes of prolonging their fragile truce, Chris decided to try to make another overture. "Why don't you come into the kitchen with me? Kevin is dying to see you."

"God, I've really missed him."

"He has a surprise for you," she said, leading the way.

"Oh? Not a present, I hope. Especially since I followed your advice and didn't bring him anything."

Kevin looked up from his drawing as Chris stepped through the doorway. "Look who's here," she said.

The second Kevin saw Mason, he let out a squeal, jumped up and came running across the room.

Mason scooped him up in his arms and held him close.

Strangely, Chris felt none of the embarrassing resentment that usually hit her when Kevin rushed to Mason. As she watched their reunion, she saw Mason close his eyes, as if trying to keep her from seeing how deeply moved he was. She wondered about his reaction, but not as much as she wondered about the fear she'd seen before he had a chance to close her out. What could he possibly be afraid of now? He'd won.

A buzzer sounded behind her, drawing her attention. She grabbed a potholder and opened the oven door.

"Biscuits, too?" Mason said. "Reminds me of the meals my mother used to make when I was a kid." He pulled out a chair and sat down, Kevin on his lap.

Chris slid the biscuits off the cookie sheet and into a straw basket lined with a checkered napkin. "Do you come from a big family?"

He paused as if trying to figure out how to answer her. "Average."

The look he gave her warned her not to ask any more questions about his family. She busied herself with another place setting while she tried to think of something else to say. "How was your trip?" she asked at last, thinking it the safest possible subject.

"Fine," he answered curtly, closing that door, too.

She glanced at him and attempted to figure out if he was reacting to her or to her questions.

"How come you went to Santa Barbara?" Kevin chimed in, temporarily relieving Chris of the responsibility for keeping the conversation going.

"There were some people I had to see," Mason told him. His tone was gentler, but his answer was every bit as evasive.

"How come?" Kevin pressed.

"Business."

Kevin reached across the table for his picture. "What kind of business?"

Chris watched Mason struggle with his

271

answer. Obviously he didn't want to talk about his trip and what he'd done, but he didn't want to cut Kevin off or lie to him either.

"I wanted to see...if I could find out why...uh, why another construction company is trying to buy a piece of property I want to buy for myself."

"And did you?" Chris asked, as she tried to cover her intense curiosity with a veneer of nonchalance.

"Not to my satisfaction."

"See what I made for you?" Kevin interjected. He held the drawing up for close inspection. "It's for your office. Like the one by the table."

"So it is," Mason said, admiring Kevin's artwork. "I don't think John Baldessari could have done better himself."

Chris finished carving the roast. "Let's eat," she suggested.

When they were all settled around the table, Mason looked at Chris and said, "If I came across sounding a little close-mouthed about the trip, it's because I'm not used to answering questions about where I go and what I do. If and when it concerns you and Kevin, I'll try to be more open from now on."

Her fork stopped midway to her mouth. He had an amazing ability to imply that he was yielding when in reality he was slamming a door. "In other words," she said evenly, not wanting Kevin to pick up on the tension between her and Mason, "stay out of your business?"

"Perhaps if you could tell me why you

should be there," he answered in the same conversational tone, "I might be persuaded to change my mind."

He had her. What possible reason could she give for wanting to know what he did outside the artificial environment they'd set up for themselves? Idle curiosity? She didn't believe that herself. How was she going to convince him? And why did she want to?

"More potatoes?" she asked, letting go for the moment.

After dinner Mason helped clear the table, then wiped the stove and counters while Chris loaded the dishwasher. It didn't take long for a cloying feeling of domesticity to settle in, making him want to run. He excused himself, saying he had to make some phone calls. The look Chris tossed in his direction left him no illusion that she'd believed his excuse.

Mason was halfway to the room he'd already mentally selected for himself when it occurred to him that Chris might have chosen that part of the house for herself. He hadn't left his mark anywhere, or laid claim to any set of rooms, so how would she have known? And yet he discovered when he opened the bedroom door and saw the outline of his furniture in the shadows, that somehow she'd intuitively made the same decision.

He shook his head in wonderment. Could it be that once in a while they shared the same wavelength after all?

Not likely.

He flipped the light switch. Same old furniture, all right. She'd even brought the drapes that had been on the bedroom window in his apartment. Would he never escape them?

Unlike the rest of the house, there was no feeling of warmth here. At first he couldn't figure out why, and then it hit him. This was the only room that hadn't benefited from the merger of his and Chris's household belongings.

He chuckled, wondering how the decorator he'd hired to do his apartment would react if he could see how Chris had combined things. As he remembered Mr. Roberts's final statement—that the entire apartment had been put together with "purity of design" in mind and that each piece of furniture must remain where it was because it relied on the one next to it to make the proper statement—Mason decided that the living room Chris had assembled would probably be enough to put the decorator in the hospital. He would have to make sure Mr. Roberts was scratched off the list of people who were to be invited to his new home. Having one of the guests die of heart failure tended to put a damper on a party.

He froze. What was he thinking of? He wasn't going to be throwing any parties at this house, at least none that he'd invite his friends to.

Mason had his jacket off and was working on the tie when Kevin came bounding into the room and jumped on the bed, destroying the tautly stretched geometric lines on the custom-made spread. After being lectured by good old Mr. Roberts about the incredible quality of the silk that had gone into making the bedspread and what an enormous effort it had been to find just the right seamstress to work on the material, Mason had never so much as sat down on his own bed to tie his shoes.

And now here was Kevin, shoes and all, rolling around on the bed as if he were on the front lawn.

"Mom said you could read me a story if you wanted to," he said, bringing a dog-eared book out from underneath his T-shirt.

Mason stared at his son, at his eager upturned face, his sparkling eyes, and finally, inevitably, at his scruffy tennis shoes. "I'd love to," he said.

He felt like a condemned man suddenly set free when he went over to the bed and sat down beside Kevin. As he let out a contented sigh he basked in the warmth that this small being had brought into the room and into his life.

Every doubt that had assailed him during the past week disappeared as he propped pillows against the headboard, nestled snugly into the silk with Kevin at his side, opened the book, and read aloud how Winnie-the-Pooh went visiting, ate too much honey, and got stuck in Rabbit's front door.

27

Chris spent the next day shopping for a dress to wear to the dance. She started at Nordstrom's, enjoying the assistance of a wonderfully solicitous salesclerk, who helped her choose several appropriate gowns to try on, each more beautiful than the one before.

A problem arose in the dressing room when Chris realized that, by allowing herself to be caught up in the moment, she had neglected to look at the price tags. When she'd set out on her quest, her only goal had been to find the most spectacular dress in Sacramento. In this one instance, the cost was secondary. She'd dip into her savings if necessary, spend up to five hundred dollars, if that was what it took. This was to be her first and last excursion into Mason's world, and she wanted to do it right.

As it turned out, five hundred dollars wouldn't have made a decent down payment on the sequined number she finally decided she had to have. In an embarrassing moment for both her and the salesclerk, Chris walked away from Nordstrom's empty-handed.

After working her way through the Pavilions shopping center, Sacramento's answer to Rodeo Drive, and then I. Magnin and Macy's and several small specialty shops in selected shopping centers around town, Chris gave up and called Mary for advice.

After telling her that she would explain her reason for wanting the dress another time, Chris managed to get information from Mary without giving any—a first in their relationship. It wasn't that Chris was trying to keep what she was doing a secret so much as it was knowing that Mary would question her judgment in accompanying Mason to a social event.

With the lectures Mary had already given Chris about not allowing herself to be put into the limelight unless she intended to stay there, Chris knew it would be useless to try to convince her friend that her debut into Sacramento society would also be her swan song.

Chris understood Mary's hesitancy and the reasons for her being publicity-shy. As the governor's daughter, she'd been on display constantly and had grown sick of the attention. But Chris was merely the wife of a local contractor. As soon as the dance was over, any curiosity Mason's friends might have about her would end, too. She could go back to her own life, and Mason could go on with his.

Chris shuddered at the thought of telling Mary the truth: that she'd decided to go to the dance with Mason because she felt she owed him a favor and this was the best way to repay him.

Sometimes a little secret or two was a good thing. Now was one of those times. Chris certainly didn't need any more friction in her life.

That evening, at Mary's suggestion, Chris tried Loehmann's, a clearinghouse for designer-label clothing. She found her dress there. It was floor length, completely covered with red and white sequins that started in a starburst pattern at one shoulder and went all the way to the hem, and it fit like a second skin. It had been years since she'd worn anything so beautiful. Staring at her reflection in the three-way mirror, she had to admit, albeit reluctantly, that it felt kind of good to slip into something besides jeans and sweat suits once in a while. Best of all, her foray into elegance wound up costing her only two hundred fifty dollars—well below the maximum she'd set.

Now all she had to do was figure out a way to tell Mason she was going with him without making it sound as if she intended to make attending social functions with him a permanent thing.

That evening when it became obvious Mason wasn't going to come home until long after Chris and Kevin had gone to bed, Chris wrote him a note telling him that she had decided to accompany him to the dance the next night. She had Kevin put it on Mason's nightstand after agreeing that he could add his own message first.

By the time she got up in the morning, he'd already gone to work. She tried reaching him at the office to find out when they would be leaving for the dance, but Janet told her he was spending the day in the field and was not expected back until late afternoon. Chris felt awkward about leaving a personal message with Janet and was too embarrassed to admit she didn't have her own husband's car phone number. She hung up after saying the call wasn't important and she'd catch up with him later.

But she never did.

Then it was a half-hour before Chris had decided was a realistic hour for a dance to start, and Mason still wasn't home. She was ready and waiting, more nervous than she'd been before any of her high school proms, put out with herself for caring, all the while trying to deny that she did.

She'd finally broken down and decided to call the office again when she heard the key in the front door, glanced up, and saw Mason coming inside. Plainly in a hurry, he shrugged out of his coat, hung it up, and then started across the living room. When he finally caught sight of her, he stopped in mid-stride and stared at her, much the way she imagined he would have if she'd sprouted another head in his absence.

"What's with the dress?" he said, regaining his composure.

"It's for the dance tonight. I should think that would be obvious," she said.

"What dance?" he asked.

"The Valentine's Day dance at the Crocker Art Museum," she offered, beginning to feel more than a little uncomfortable. "You know, the one I mentioned in the note."

"What note?"

"The one I left in your bedroom last night."

He frowned. "The only note I found was one from Kevin."

It took a minute for her to figure out what had happened. "I don't suppose you bothered to turn the paper over and look on the other side?"

"Why should I have?"

"Because that's where I told you I would go to the dance with you tonight. The note wasn't supposed to be from Kevin; it was from me."

"How did you know about the dance?"

Chris had a sick feeling in the pit of her stomach. "Rebecca told me."

He His shoved his hands in his pants pockets and let out a sigh. "She had no business doing that."

Now it was her turn to ask the questions. "Why not?"

"Because you have no business at that dance."

The one sure way to stiffen Chris's spine was to tell her she couldn't do something, "Oh? And why is that?"

"For one thing, you weren't invited. For another, you wouldn't fit in."

"Is that right? That must be a first. An invitation that purposely excludes spouses." *Spouse?* Good grief, could she really have said that?

He eyed her. "What kind of game are you playing, Chris? You no more want to spend an evening with me than I want to spend one with you."

It wasn't just her dignity he wanted to grind under his boot, it was her pride. She stood taller, squaring her shoulders. "Sooner or

280

later people are going to find out about this marriage. I happen to prefer sooner. That way, once it's out in the open, I can put the anticipation of it happening behind me and get on with my life."

He started to say something, then decided against it. The clock on the mantel ticked loudly in the silence as he stood and stared at her.

"Suit yourself," he finally said, walking past her and into his bedroom.

Not another word passed between them afterward, not even when they went outside to get into the car. Although it was only a fifteen-minute ride to the museum, it seemed to Chris like an hour. Once the car was moving, she thought of a hundred reasons why she should have stayed home, not the least of which was her tendency to cry when she was really mad. She vowed to bite a hole through her lip before she'd ever let Mason see her shed a tear.

How had she let herself be drawn into such a mess? And why did she keep digging the hole she was in deeper and deeper? If she hadn't let her stupid pride get in the way, she would have bailed out when Mason gave her the chance. But no, she was too stubborn for that. She had a point to make.

Only now she couldn't remember what it was.

Mason pulled the Porsche into the line of cars waiting for valet parking. Determined to look anywhere but at him, Chris stared out the window and watched the people walking up the sidewalk and getting out of their cars.

At first what she saw seemed a little strange.

Then she began to wonder if it was some kind of bizarre coincidence.

And then the truth hit her with all the subtlety of a baseball bat.

Everyone was dressed in the same two colors because the annual Valentine dance was Sacramento society's version of a black and white ball. She turned to Mason.

"You bastard," she seethed. "You could have told me."

"As I recall, I did. I said you wouldn't fit in, but you didn't want to listen." He turned off the car engine and held out the keys. "I'll see you at home," he said, dismissing her as casually as he would a bellhop. "But please don't wait up. I'm going to be late. Very, very late."

When she didn't take the keys from him right away, he dropped them in her lap. "I assume you know how to drive a stick shift? If not, the doorman would be happy to call a cab for you."

"Why?" was all she could think to ask.

He reached for the door handle. "I meant it when I said I wasn't signing on to play house. I've had all the domesticity I want in this lifetime. Our living together is a means to an end, nothing more."

"So you thought you'd teach me a lesson by driving me down here and letting me see what a fool I've made of myself? Well, fuck you, Mason Winter. I'm here and I'm going to stay." She flung the keys at him, opened the door, and got out.

Mason caught up with her at the foot of the stairs. "Come back to the car with me," he said, keeping his voice low so that only she could hear.

"I'd rather drink lighter fluid."

He grabbed her arm. "You don't know what you're doing. The people inside will—"

"Will what?" she shot back at him. "Treat me like a leper? An outcast? Or, God forbid, make me feel that I don't belong?" She wrenched her arm from his grasp. "I've been immunized, Mason. No one in there could do anything to me you haven't already done in spades." She picked up her skirt and ran up the stairs.

Mason stood on the sidewalk and watched her disappear into the beautiful old Victorian house that was the main building of the museum complex. He felt like a heel. What was it about Chris that brought out the worst in him? Every time it looked as if they might have a chance to become friends, he wound up acting like the bastard she'd accused him of being.

Tossing his keys to the parking attendant and nodding absently to those who called out a greeting to him, Mason climbed the stairs to look for Chris. He spotted Rebecca with Walt Bianchi and his wife in the main ballroom, and ducked into one of the side rooms to avoid them. Rebecca would be all over his case if she caught the slightest hint about what had happened between him and Chris, and he only wanted to deal with one furious, infuriating female at a time. He and Rebecca would talk about this—oh, were they ever going to have a talk about how she had gotten him into this mess—but not tonight.

Mason went from one room to the next, stopping periodically to say a quick hello to people who insisted he join them and then moving on. Dressed as she was, Chris should have stood out like a rosebush in a wheat field, but he saw no sign of her.

After he'd been through each room twice and then once more for good measure, he decided she must have followed his advice and taken a taxi home. A strange feeling of disappointment passed through him and then was gone.

He checked his watch, took a glass of wine from the tray of a passing waiter, and went into the main ballroom to wait for Kelly.

A half-hour later he was standing on the platform that had been brought in for the band, talking to Travis and Walt, when a pair of white-gloved hands slipped lightly over his eyes.

"Guess who?" a lilting female voice queried.

He hesitated, as if considering her question. "Barbara Bush?"

Kelly laughed. She dropped her hands to his shoulders and turned him toward her, then gave him a kiss. "Sorry I was late," she said. "Miss me?"

Out of the corner of his eye he saw Travis and Walt staring at him, looking decidedly uncomfortable. "I was beginning to think I was going to be stood up," he told Kelly.

"You've got to be kidding." She leaned into him and lowered her voice to a whisper. "I found the most delicious-looking strawberries at David Berkley's today. The champagne is on ice.... I wouldn't have missed tonight for the world."

Mason was only half listening. Standing on the platform had given him the height advantage to see a flash of red in the field of black and white across the room.

So she hadn't left after all. His heart quickened its beat. He passed it off as anger even though it wasn't anger he was feeling.

Once he'd spotted Chris, he couldn't take his eyes off her. As he watched, he saw her closed out of one group after another, never blatantly—the people who attended these parties didn't operate that way—but with chilling precision. First one person would turn his back to her, as if to talk to someone else, and then another would do the same. Soon she was left standing outside the circle, alone.

It made him ill to think of how many times she'd undoubtedly been shut out in the hour and a half she'd already been at the party.

His heart went out to her. He knew what it was like to be on the outside, only he hadn't handled the experience with Chris's grace and determination. Even though, to the casual observer, there was nothing humble or crestfallen about the way Chris looked or acted, she reminded him of a lonely child who was convinced there was someone, somewhere, who would be nice to her because to think any other way was to give up a part of herself.

How did she do it?

Better yet, why did she do it?

"Mason?" Kelly said, drawing his attention. "Is something wrong?"

He glanced at her and saw the concern in her face, letting him know he'd been lost in his own world for a long time. "There's a lot wrong with tonight," he reluctantly admitted. "But nothing I want to talk about now."

She put her arm through his. "Then if it's not conversation you want," she said, "how about a dance?"

"I can't, Kelly, not tonight. Please forgive me." He turned to Walt. "Would you mind filling in for me on this one?"

Walt's mouth dropped open and then snapped shut. "Mind?" he said with precisely the right amount of gallantry. "It would be the highlight of my evening."

Travis folded his arms across his chest. "I wouldn't let Denise hear you talking like that," he said, looking pointedly at Mason. "Wives have a funny way of thinking you should save that kind of thing for them."

When Walt and Kelly were out of earshot, Mason turned to Travis. "So you saw her, too."

"Dressed like that in this crowd, it'd be pretty hard not to. What the hell's going on, Mason? There's no way you couldn't have known what would happen to her if you brought her here in that outfit."

"It's a long story," he said wearily. "One I'm not very proud of." He looked over to where he'd last seen Chris, but she was gone. Frantically, he searched the crowd, his need to find her sudden and urgent. At last he spotted her, standing beside a potted palm, a solitary island in a sea of people.

"Somehow that doesn't surprise me," Travis said with unrestrained anger. "You act like a real son of a bitch where that gal is concerned. How about you letting me in on what she did to deserve this kind of treatment?"

As if Chris could feel him looking at her, she turned her head and met his gaze. For long seconds, they stared at each other. "She didn't do anything," Mason said softly.

"Then why—"

"Let it go, Travis."

"I can't. Not this time. I've watched you shut away the best part of who you are for nigh onto six years now, and it's high time I did something about it."

"There's nothing you can do," Mason told him. "The best part of me isn't shut away, Travis; it's dead."

"The hell you say."

"The marriage was a mistake. If it weren't for Kevin, I'd get out of it tomorrow."

"Mistake or not, there's no reason you should let these people get away with what they're doing to—"

"I know." Mason put his hand on Travis's shoulder. "I intend to take care of that right now."

28

Mason went over to where the eight-piece orchestra was playing, talked a minute with the man who was leading them, took the microphone from its stand, and waited for the music to stop.

"Ladies and gentlemen," he said. "If I may have your attention, please. I hope you will forgive this moment of self-indulgence on my part, but I would like to make an announcement." He waited for the last hum of conversation to disappear.

"This is a very special night for me, one I wanted to share with you, my friends." Pragmatism allowed him to swallow the hypocrisy.

"Two weeks ago, in a quiet, intimate ceremony, I was married." He almost laughed aloud at the gasps of surprise. The reaction he saw on Kelly's face wasn't so funny. He deserved whatever she was thinking, and more.

"And because this is the perfect day as well as the perfect setting, I've waited until tonight to formally introduce my beautiful bride to all of you." Heads swung back and forth, searching for an unfamiliar face. Mason stared at Chris, silently pleading with her to stand her ground. He was giving her the ammunition to thumb her nose at those who had turned their backs on her. Now it was up to her.

"At my request, she agreed to forgo the traditional black and white of the evening in favor of red." Slowly, dramatically, the spotlight that had been focused on Mason and the orchestra swung across the room and shone on Chris.

"Ladies and gentlemen—friends—I am pleased and honored to introduce my wife, Mrs. Christine Winter."

He watched with growing admiration as Chris not only stood her ground but squared her shoulders and raised her chin, ready and willing to take anything he threw at her. He could feel the intensity of her gaze even though he knew it was impossible for her to see him through the glare of the light.

He waited until the applause had died down to add, "Now, if I haven't embarrassed you too much already, Chris," he said, dropping his voice to an intimate murmur as he spoke directly to her, "I have one more favor to ask. Would you lead off this next dance with me?"

Again the crowd burst into applause.

Mason waited.

The applause grew louder.

Still he waited for some sign from her.

Finally she dipped her head in acquiescence. Mason stepped down from the platform and started toward her.

He smiled when he saw she had no intention of meeting him halfway; he would have to go to her.

So be it. She deserved that, and a hell of a lot more.

The crowd on the dance floor parted to let him through. He took his time, letting her remain in the spotlight, forcing those who had ignored her to give her their time after all.

When at last he was standing in front of her, he purposely kept his arms at his sides, making no move to take her onto the dance floor. In this, he would let the final decision be hers.

For an instant she let down her guard and he could see the fear behind the bravado. He sent her a look that begged her to trust him. She responded by holding out her hand to him.

He took her hand in his own, turned it palm up, and raised it to his lips. All around them, people sighed as if they had been collectively holding their breath.

Wordlessly Mason led Chris to the middle of the dance floor. As he took her into his arms, the orchestra began to play. The song was "Lady in Red."

When he was sure they couldn't be overheard, Mason bent his head and spoke softly into Chris's ear, letting the softness of her hair caress his cheek, the heady floral scent of her perfume wash over him. "I'm so sorry," he said.

Her spine lost its stiffness. She leaned back and looked up at him, her eyes brimming with unshed tears. "I can't live like this, Mason," she said. "I want an annulment."

29

The music played on, inexorable. Seeing the pained confusion in Chris's eyes and knowing he had put it there gave Mason pause. He could cope with her anger—at times he thought he actually took a perverse pleasure in doing battle with her—but this was different. He'd hurt her, and there was no justification for that, not even the anger and resentment he'd felt toward her almost from the day they'd met.

Although he didn't really understand his anger, he knew it was caused by more than the day-to-day annoyances and the differences of opinion between them. Those things he forgot almost as quickly as they happened. If he could find a way to get along with people who meant nothing to him—sleazy contractors on the job and women at parties who wore their IQs in their bras—why couldn't he find a way to get along with Chris, the mother of his son? It was as if he'd embarked on a campaign to drive her away.

"Can we talk about this later?" he asked, stalling for time. He might not know what he wanted from her, but he knew he didn't want an annulment.

Chris closed her eyes and leaned her head into his shoulder. He thought for a moment that she was going to pass out, but then realized it was only the fight that had left her. As they silently moved to the music, their bodies touching in mock intimacy, he said, "You have these people in the palm of your hand. Now all you have to do is decide what you want to do with them. You could close your hand into a fist, or you could hold your hand up and let the wind sweep them away."

"And what about you?" she asked.

"You'll give me another chance. Not because I deserve it, but because that's just the way you are."

She looked up at him. "How do you know that?"

"I'm not sure. I just do."

The music stopped. There wasn't much he understood about this night, but he knew he wanted her to forgive him as much as he'd ever wanted anything in life. He cupped her face with his hands, holding her still, forcing her to look at him.

"Please..." he said. "We can work things out."

A lone tear escaped the corner of her eye. "You don't know what you're asking."

He became acutely aware of the warmth of her body against his, the feel of skin beneath his hands, the smell of her perfume. An overwhelming urge to kiss her came over him, to have the softness of her lips touching his, the taste of her on his tongue, the feel of her breath on his cheek. Stunned by the impulse, he took a step backward.

Someone tapped him on the shoulder. "I didn't think it was possible to keep a secret in this town," a man's voice boomed. "What other little surprises have you got in store for us?"

The spell was broken. Mason felt his public

mask slip back into place. "You don't try to top perfection," he said, smiling as he turned to Felix Schrager, CEO of the largest bank in the Sacramento Valley.

"I just wanted to get a personal introduction to the woman who managed to accomplish what this town was betting would never happen."

Mason looked at Chris. The decision was hers. She could tell Felix to go to hell, turn on her heel and walk away, or stay and join the game. He would do nothing to prejudice her.

She took a moment to think about it, her face a reflection of her warring emotions. Finally she offered Felix a gracious, if hard-won, smile and extended her hand. "Christine Taylor," she said and then corrected herself. "Winter."

"Oh, one of those hyphenated names. I understand that's becoming quite popular again. Well, I'm pleased to meet you, Christine Taylor-Winter," he said, putting his own interpretation on what she had said. "The name's Felix Schrager. I trust we'll be running into each other a lot from now on. Can't tell you how pleased I am at the prospect. I get real tired of the same old faces."

A small crowd had formed around them. The same people who had shunned Chris as an outsider were now eager to meet her and welcome her into the inner circle.

Mason slipped a protective, platonic arm across her shoulders. "Are you up to this?" he asked softly.

She glanced up at him, a pasted-on smile making it to her lips, but not her eyes. "Is there a graceful way out?"

"Give it fifteen minutes and we can leave."

She nodded. The crowd pressed forward.

The fifteen minutes stretched into an hour. If Mason hadn't called a halt, it would have gone on all night.

On the way home, Chris said, "We should have told them we had to get back to Kevin. No one would have questioned our leaving then."

"I don't want them to know about him."

"You plan to keep him hidden?" she asked, dumbfounded.

"I want to keep him as far away from what you saw tonight as I possibly can. He shouldn't ever have to doubt why someone wants to be his friend."

"How are you going to keep him from telling everyone himself? He's proud of you and wants the whole world to know he finally has a daddy, just like all his friends."

"As long as that's all I am to him, there shouldn't be a problem."

"But that's not all you are. I discovered that for myself tonight—the hard way." She turned to look out the window. The rain that had been threatening all day had finally come, leaving the streets sparkling with jewels of reflected light. "Not one person I approached at that dance wanted to have anything to do with me until they found out I was your appendage."

"You're no one's appendage," he said angrily. "And most especially not mine."

She still hadn't settled in her own mind how she felt about the rejection and, later, the acceptance she'd experienced that night, and until she did, she didn't want to talk about it anymore.

"Who was that woman?" Chris asked to change the subject, not realizing until she'd said the words aloud how easily they could be misinterpreted.

"Kelly Whitefield," he answered without asking her to elaborate, even though there had been more than two hundred women at the party. "We've been friends for a long time."

"You should have told me you were planning to meet her there. It would have saved all three of us a lot of grief—and you a lot of explaining to her later."

"I don't have to explain anything to Kelly."

Chris laughed mirthlessly. "I wouldn't be that understanding if I were in her position."

"She doesn't have anything to be understanding about. We're friends, nothing more."

One of the red sequins on her dress was coming loose; she made a mental note to sew it back on when she got home and then discarded the idea. She'd never wear the dress again. "That's a rather cavalier way to refer to a lover," she said expressionlessly.

He cast a sidelong glance at her. "What makes you think we're lovers?"

Not only wasn't it any of her business, if she wasn't careful, he'd get the impression she cared. "Are you denying it?" she asked, plunging ahead despite herself.

"No, just asking how you knew."

"By the way she looked at you...and at me." Damn it, she might be able to fool him, but not herself. She did care, and she hated herself for it. She turned her head to look outside again. "She's beautiful," she said, her breath fogging the window.

"Kelly isn't like any other woman I've ever known. She's—" He shrugged. "She's different, that's all."

Wonderful, just what she needed, to sit there and listen to Mason sing the praises of another woman. "You were foolish to marry me and take a chance on losing her."

"I'm not going to lose her."

"Oh, I see." She forced herself to look at him. With any luck, what she saw would hit her hard enough so that she would be able to walk away. But it wasn't a smug or triumphant Mason she saw; instead he seemed troubled, confused.

"You can't lose what you've never had," he said. "Kelly and I really are just friends...even though there are times when our friendship becomes intimate," he added with brutal honesty.

She didn't trust herself to say anything more. They rode the rest of the way home in silence, but when they were inside the house, Mason turned to Chris and said, "Before I forget to tell you, I want you to know how proud of you I was tonight."

A spark of her earlier resentment reignited.

"What makes you think you have the right to take pride in anything I do?"

Instead of responding to her anger with his own, he backed off. "I didn't mean that the way it sounded. I just wanted you to know that I was impressed with... No, let me put it another way: I *admired* your courage."

Realizing he hadn't meant to be condescending any more than she had meant to climb on a soapbox and spout feminist rhetoric, she offered him a quick smile of apology. "What would you say if I told you my courage came from never having learned to drive a stick shift?"

He eyed her. "I'd say you were lying."

The clock on the mantel chimed twice. "It's late," she said, beginning to feel as if the room was closing in on her. She needed to be alone, to think about what had happened that night, and to decide what she was going to do about it. "And I have to get up early tomorrow morning."

"Don't go yet," he said.

Something in his voice stopped her. "I don't have anything else to say to you tonight, Mason. Besides, don't you think the person you should be talking to now is Kelly, not me?"

He dropped his gaze to the floor. "You're right," he said. "Even though she isn't expecting one, she deserves an explanation." Wearily he reached for his coat and moved toward the door. "I'll see you in the morning."

Chris fought a disappointment that threatened to crush her. "If I'm not here when you get back," she said cheerfully, determined not

297

to let him see that she cared, "I'll be at Mary's picking up Kevin."

He turned around, a puzzled frown on his face. "You're going to pick him up tonight?"

"No, in the morning."

Understanding dawned. "I'll be back long before then," he told her.

A swell of relief washed over her. "You don't have to. Not on my account. The deal was that both of us would lead our own lives, no questions asked."

"I won't go if—"

She couldn't take any more. What if she did tell him she didn't want him to go? What then? What possible difference would it make? "Would you please just get out of here? I'm tired and I want to go to bed."

He reached for the doorknob. "Chris—" he said, his back to her.

"Yes?"

"About the annulment..."

"What about it?"

"Would you give it another month? If we can't work things out to your satisfaction by then, I won't stand in your way." A long time passed before he added, "I really don't want to lose Kevin."

"A month of good behavior and then what?" Even though Mason had seldom been home in the past two weeks, when he was there, he and Kevin were inseparable. If she broke them up now, Kevin would never forgive her.

"I'll leave that up to you," he said, still not turning around.

Her footing had been taken from her. She

felt like a cartoon character who had stepped off the edge of a cliff and just gotten around to looking down. In seconds she would be falling. And it would do her no good to know how far she would fall or how long it would take; she was too far from any handhold for it to make a difference. "All right," she said. "But don't expect me to go to any more parties."

When he opened the door and left, she wasn't sure whether it was his sigh of relief she heard or the wind.

30

Unable to sleep, Mason got up early the day after the dance and headed for work, his car windows down, his thoughts a million miles in another direction. His hunger—he'd eaten a skimpy lunch and missed dinner the day before—didn't hit him until he passed the New Roma Bakery where the smell of freshly baked bread permeated the air.

Smell had always been the most evocative of his senses, summoning memories more quickly than sound or even sight. Diane had been the one to introduce him to the pleasures of bread still hot from the oven. She would work all morning, mixing and kneading and forming the dough. After it was in the oven, she would allow herself one early peek at the bread's progress. Standing at the oven door, her eyes closed, a rapturous smile on her lips, she'd take in a dizzyingly deep breath. She'd once turned to him and said, "If heaven is all it's cracked up to be, it will smell just this way."

Were you right, Diane?

As soon as the bread was finished and had been coaxed out of its pan to cool on a wire rack, she would grab a knife and slice the ends from the loaf, taking infinite care to avoid crushing those first, delicate pieces. Next came the butter, not the small pats that restaurants put on the plates, but generous slatherings that melted into the bread and occasionally dripped down the sides and onto a finger.

Then came the tasting of the results of Diane's four hours of loving labor. She would hold the bread for him while he took a bite, her eyes intently watching him, as always receiving her greatest pleasure from pleasing him.

It had taken Mason several tries to appreciate Diane's almost obsessive passion for freshly baked bread, but once he was hooked, the hook was deeply embedded. Because their schedules were full, they rarely performed the time-consuming process more than once a week, Sundays usually, but with an occasional Saturday thrown in for experimenting with cinnamon rolls or whole wheat hamburger buns.

Afterward, invariably, there would be traces of melted butter at the corners of Diane's mouth. Before she could wipe it off, he would stake a claim, touching his tongue to the sensitive skin and then slipping it between her lips to taste the bread as she herself had tasted it. Sometimes the kiss would deepen and they would make love, sometimes they would just sit and hold each other and talk about the week past and the one to come, and sometimes, if need be, they would go their separate ways. Whatever happened the rest of the day, it would be better for the morning they had spent together in the kitchen.

Now there were only memories, and what had once brought such pleasure brought nothing but pain. Even his love for Kevin was clouded. How could he abandon himself to that joy knowing it was his only because of Diane's sacrifice? But when that had been her intent, how could he not?

He pulled up at a stoplight, slipped the car into neutral, and wearily rubbed his eyes. Even loving, benign ghosts could become burdensome at times.

As always, the thought brought waves of guilt. If he didn't keep Susan's and Diane's memories alive, who would?

What right did he have to complain if his mind and his life got a little crowded with the effort? He was still here, wasn't he?

But at what price? He'd been hurt, but that didn't give him the right to hurt others. Especially not Chris. She'd done nothing to deserve the way he'd treated her last night—nothing except get a little too close, maybe. He had to make her understand that the way he felt, the man he was, had nothing to do with her.

The least he could do was be civil to her and perhaps, in the process, stop making her day-to-day life miserable. It wouldn't hurt to show a modicum of appreciation for what she'd done, what she was still doing for his son. He had been friends with Rebecca all these years and still maintained an emotional distance. Why not with Chris?

Once he'd made the decision, he felt an almost overwhelming urge to do something about it as soon as possible. When the light changed, instead of going straight ahead, Mason circled the block and drove back to the bakery. He went inside and ordered an assortment of freshly baked pastries, moving quickly to eliminate any possible second thoughts about what he was doing.

Arriving back at the house fifteen minutes later, he wasn't surprised to find that Chris was still in bed. She didn't have to pick Kevin and Tracy up to take them to school for another hour yet. Why not sleep in, when the only things you had to get up for were an empty house and bad memories of the night before?

He started the coffee, put the pastries on a plate, and then, on impulse, pulled a tray out of the cupboard. Suddenly, serving Chris breakfast in bed seemed a fitting gesture, one he hoped she would recognize for what it was, conciliatory rather than self-serving. As much as he wanted to keep her from filing for an annulment, he also wanted to say he was sorry.

While he waited for the coffee to finish

dripping, he glanced out the kitchen window and saw that the first of the daffodils had opened. He was smiling when he opened the drawer and took out a knife. Diane had loved daffodils; perhaps Chris did, too.

He couldn't find a vase, so he used a glass. The overall effect wasn't as elegant as it might have been, but all in all, he liked what he saw. He felt good when he picked up the tray and started out of the kitchen.

Too good.

Standing at Chris's bedroom door, hand poised to knock, he stopped and looked down at the tray, at the carefully folded napkins, the rainbow mugs, the rolls and butter, and the bright yellow daffodil sitting at a jaunty angle in its jelly glass. The hair on the back of his neck stood on end. What in the hell was he doing?

He looked at the paneled door. What was really on the other side? What did he want to be there?

Not again, a voice inside him cried out. Protect yourself. Get away while you still can.

But from Chris? It didn't make sense. He tried to analyze his fear. What he felt for Chris was a crazy combination of embarrassment over the way he had treated her and gratitude for the love and care she'd given Kevin, nothing more.

So why the hesitancy?

Because she might get the wrong idea, and then where would they be?

He quietly returned to the kitchen, cleaned up after himself, and put the pastries back in their pink box. Janet would look at him a little funny when he gave them to her to put in the break room, but she'd never question him or suspect why he'd bought them.

Climbing back into his car, Mason felt his protective mantle slip into place again, even while he wondered briefly at the sharp feeling of loss that had accompanied it. As he drove downtown, a thought kept resurfacing. What would he have found on the other side of Chris's door? Would she have welcomed him?

More likely, she would have thrown something at him.

But what if she hadn't?

Not one to dwell on what-ifs and if-onlys, Mason ordered himself to think about the work ahead of him that day. But, as he soon discovered, that was easier said than done.

When Chris heard Mason get in his car and leave, she rolled over to look at her alarm clock. He was getting a late start, probably because he'd stayed longer at Kelly's house than he had planned.

Furious with herself for caring enough even to speculate on the matter, she swung her legs over the side of the bed and got up. Why should she care whether he had stayed the whole night?

Because she didn't want Kevin to see his father behaving like a randy teenager, she reasoned, reaching for her robe.

She went into the bathroom to brush her teeth. Looking at her reflection in the mirror, seeing the haunted eyes that stared back out at her, she couldn't hide from the truth any longer.

How she felt had nothing to do with Kevin.

She leaned against the sink and dropped her chin to her chest. Dear God, what was she going to do? How could she be falling for a man who looked at her as if she were something that grew on the dark side of a tree? Hadn't she already had enough grief in her life?

Where had this perverse aspect of her personality been hiding? Since when did she go for the chest-thumping, ego-centered Mason Winter type?

Since the moment she'd allowed herself to acknowledge that the glimpses she'd seen behind the facade were the real Mason, she answered herself truthfully. From a purely factual standpoint, Mason was rich and powerful and, without question, the most handsome man she'd seen outside of the movies. What was more impressive was that he appeared to be totally oblivious of his looks and to the women who did double takes when they met him and the ones who turned to take a second look when he passed them on the street.

All of which meant nothing to Chris. She could have gone a lifetime and never been persuaded to give him a moment's notice, if not for Kevin. And in the process of watching father and son together, she'd discovered a startling truth. There was something fundamentally appealing about a man who forgot himself in his love for a child. Mason became a different person when he was with Kevin.

He came alive, opened up, gave of himself without thought of return. He smiled, and he laughed, and when he thought no one could see, he looked at his son with a hunger that took Chris's breath away.

Then there was the house. Chris had always believed it wasn't what people said but what they did that was their true measure. While Mason's buying the house without even consulting her had rankled at first, the sensitivity and thoughtfulness behind his choice had more than made up for it.

And the way he'd come to her rescue last night, providing the means for her to restore her dignity when, in truth, it was she who had broken their pact to lead separate lives.

She'd fought seeing the good and gentle side of Mason. She supposed now that she had simply been protecting herself. The reason didn't matter. What she was going to do about this new insight did.

After putting her toothbrush back into the medicine cabinet, she rinsed out the sink and headed for the kitchen. The smell of freshly brewed coffee hit her as soon as she rounded the corner. But the pot was empty, seemingly undisturbed. She looked around. Everything appeared precisely as she'd left it the night before, and yet she sensed Mason had been there.

She went to the sink to fill the coffee pot, letting the water run several seconds to clear any lead residue from the pipes. When she stuck the pot under the faucet, she noticed a speck of yellow peeking out from the guard on the garbage disposal. She investigated and discovered that it was a daffodil.

What in the hell was a daffodil doing in the garbage disposal?

On his way out to lunch, Mason looked up just as the elevator doors started to close, and saw Rebecca coming toward him. He blocked the doors with his hand and waited for her. "We missed you at the meeting this morning," he said conversationally.

She stepped inside and cast him a sidelong glance. "Since you didn't need me there, I decided to stay away."

"For any reason in particular?" he asked, knowing that Rebecca rarely sidestepped anything.

"I figured it was best if we didn't see each other any more than necessary today."

So that was it. She thought he was still upset about the dance. "I'm not mad at you," he told her. "At least not anymore."

"How nice," she said icily.

His eyes widened with interest at her tone. "I take it there's something else eating you?"

"Nothing an apology and a little groveling won't take care of. At least I hope that's all it's going to take."

"I don't expect an apology," he said magnanimously.

She turned on him. "Good thing, because that's just about the farthest thing from my mind right now."

"Then would you mind telling me what it is you're talking about?" he said, his patience wearing thin.

"I'm meeting Chris for lunch," she said, her voice heavy with meaning.

Now he really was confused. "Why?"

"To try to convince her I had nothing to do with what happened last night."

Mason shoved his hands into his pants pockets and looked up to watch the floor numbers as they grew steadily smaller. "She doesn't blame you," he said with finality.

"Did she say that?"

"No. But there isn't any reason—"

"That's what I thought."

"Look, you're going to have to trust me on this, because I'm not going to go into it with you." He took a deep breath before adding, "What happened last night was completely my fault."

The elevator stopped to pick up another passenger, effectively ending their conversation. When they reached the ground floor, Rebecca pulled Mason aside. "I know it really isn't any of my business, but why have you made it your current goal in life to convince Chris that you're pond scum?"

He thought of a dozen different ways to answer her and finally settled on the truth. "I don't know," he admitted reluctantly.

A slow smile spread across Rebecca's face. "Want some help figuring it out?"

He cocked an eyebrow at her. "Do I have a choice?"

"You're falling for her."

"Not in a million years," he said, too quickly to convince either one of them.

"Tell me again six months from now and I'll believe you."

"I won't have to," he said. "Something tells me my marriage will be past history by then."

"Not if you don't want it to be," Rebecca insisted.

"I'm beginning to think that's exactly what I want," he said. When she started to answer, he waved her off. He didn't have the time or energy or inclination to continue their conversation. "Give my regards to Chris," he said. "And tell her I won't be home tonight."

"If that's true," Rebecca said, her anger barely restrained, "you're going to have to give her that message yourself." She turned on her heel and left him.

Mason watched her go, wondering how much deeper he could dig the hole he'd put himself in before the sides collapsed.

31

Chris woke up on Saturday morning feeling restless, not knowing what she wanted to do, only that she needed to get away for a while. Nine days had passed since the Valentine's Day dance, each one a little more tense than the one before. When Kevin came wandering into the kitchen half an hour later, she looked at him and thought about how easily and spontaneously they had once lived.

She bent to plant a quick kiss on his cheek as he passed. "Let's do something today," she said. "Something fun."

"What?" he asked, not responding with as much enthusiasm as she would have liked, but not dismissing the idea either.

"Oh, I don't know...." Then the idea hit. "Let's go on a picnic. You pick the place and I'll pick the food."

He thought a minute, a spark of interest lighting his eyes. "Let's go to the ocean," he suggested, excited at least. "We could take my kite. And some bread for the sea gulls." He became more animated with each new idea. "And my bucket and shovel. And a sack for the shells we find."

Chris leaned over the sink to look out the window, checking the sky for clouds. "I think that's a great idea," she announced. "It's a beautiful day. If we get started right away, we'll have all afternoon."

"I'll get Daddy." He hopped off the stool and headed for Mason's bedroom.

"No, Kevin—stop," she said.

He turned, a puzzled frown on his face. "How come?"

"I thought maybe today it could just be the two of us," she said, her forced cheerfulness sounding a little phony even to herself. She grabbed a dish rag and began wiping an already clean counter. "You know, like it used to be. That way, Mason could have some time for himself. I'm sure there are lots of things he'd like to get done without us underfoot."

"He doesn't have nothing to do today," Kevin announced with confidence. "I asked him last night."

Frantically Chris searched for another reason to leave Mason behind, but none sprang to mind. "Then I suppose we should invite him to go with us," she said, feeling her previous joy dim to a grim acceptance.

When Kevin was gone, she got the picnic basket out of the pantry and started filling it with cups and plates and napkins. She was wrapping leftover chicken from the night before in plastic wrap when Kevin came back.

"Dad doesn't want to go," he announced, hiking one leg over a chair.

"That's a shame," she said, commiserating while trying to hide her pleasure. "He's going to miss out on a real good time."

"I don't want to go anymore, either."

"Sure you do," she coaxed. "We'll stop at the Nut Tree on the way and you can get a new toy to play with in the car." She almost choked when she realized what she'd just done. Bribery? Could she really have sunk so low that she would try bribing her own son into going on a picnic with her?

"I don't want a new toy."

"All right," she said, accepting defeat and resisting the impulse to scream. "Maybe we can go next week." She plunked the chicken back into the bowl and put the bowl back into the refrigerator. "How about some breakfast?"

"I'm not hungry. I'm going to go back to bed and read my book."

She reached over and ruffled his hair as he passed. "How about the two of us going over to the park and feeding the ducks this afternoon? Not too many people remember to visit them this time of year, so they're probably hungry."

"Okay," he said, his slippered feet making soft scuffing noises on the tile as he moved toward the door.

Chris counted to ten, waiting until Kevin was out of earshot before she flung open the basket and started shoving silverware back into the drawer. She was mentally running through the collection of obscenities she considered too offensive to say aloud, when Mason came into the room.

"What are you doing?" he asked, stopping to watch her.

"Precisely what it looks like," she snapped.

"But I thought you and Kevin were going somewhere today."

She glared at him. "Kevin changed his mind."

"Because of me?"

"No, because he found out I was planning to make him eat chicken again." She shoved the plates back up in the cupboard. "Of course because of you. Why else?"

"I'm sorry. I was only trying to help. I thought if I told him I didn't want to go, the two of you would have a chance to be alone together."

She eyed him suspiciously. "Why would you do that?"

He opened the refrigerator, took out the orange juice, and poured himself a glass, all the while keeping an eye on her. "You really don't like me, do you?"

Growing uncomfortable under his scrutiny, she swept past him and put the basket back in the pantry. "Whether I like you or not has nothing to do with how I feel right now."

"What is it, then?"

"I'm frustrated," she exploded. "And there isn't anything I can do about it. I want things to go back to the way they were, but they can't. You're here, and even if you disappeared tomorrow, there's no way Kevin and I can go backwards. One way or another, you're a part of us now."

She could have added that there'd been a couple of times when she'd wondered if she would change things even if she had the opportunity. For all the negative disruption Kevin had had in his life in the past seven months, she couldn't deny that he had gained more than he'd lost. He loved having a father. No—she had to be honest, if only with herself—it was far more than the idea of having a father that Kevin loved, it was Mason himself.

"You make it sound as if you're trapped."

"In a way, I am."

The air became charged between them. "Would it help if I left?" he asked.

She was stunned. It wasn't like Mason to drop his defenses that way. He'd said the words as if they were being pulled from him, and there was no doubt in her mind that he meant them. All she had to do was ask and he would be gone. "No," she said.

"No, it wouldn't help, or no, don't leave?" he asked softly.

"Kevin would never forgive me."

"Forget Kevin for a minute. How do you feel?"

What did he want from her, a confession that she cared? She could just imagine what he'd do with that, how he would hold it over her. "I promised you another month," she said, evading a direct answer. "I don't back down on my promises."

He nodded, as if acknowledging that he'd gotten as much from her as he was going to get. After several seconds he went to the pantry, took the basket back out, and put it on the counter. "I feel like a picnic," he said. "Want to come along?"

What in the hell was that all about? Was he trying to make amends for ruining her own picnic plans? Or was he making an overture of friendship? While the rug hadn't been yanked out from underneath her, Chris couldn't help feeling Mason had given it a good tug. She swallowed the sudden bubble of pleasure that had filled her chest. "Where did you have in mind?" she asked, playing along.

"Oh, I was thinking the ocean might be nice. We would probably have the beach all to ourselves this time of year."

"Strange you should say that. Not too long ago, I was thinking along those lines myself. Do you suppose we might be able to talk Kevin into coming with us?"

"Can I tell him we'll leave last night's chicken here and stop somewhere for sandwiches?"

She smiled despite herself. "I'm a little tired of chicken myself," she admitted.

"I guess it's a go, then." He gave her a little bow of acknowledgment and started toward Kevin's room. He was through the doorway when he paused, turned, and came back. "Chris?"

She stopped what she was doing and gave him her full attention. "Yes?"

From the look on his face, what he was about to tell her wasn't easy. He shrugged. "I guess I just wanted to say a long overdue thanks."

"What for?"

"Making it easier than you had to."

Embarrassed, she made a dismissive gesture. "I'm the one who wanted to go on a picnic in the first place, remember?"

"I'm not talking about the picnic." He reached up to rub the back of his neck. "You haven't tried to interfere or influence the way Kevin felt about me, not from that first day you let me take him. It took me a while to understand why you waited until you and I were alone to tell me what a jerk you thought I was."

She didn't know how to answer him because until then she'd had no idea that he'd noticed, let alone appreciated, her efforts to help him connect with Kevin. "What did you expect, Mason?"

"In the beginning, I was afraid you would

315

try to turn Kevin against me. But all I had to do was take the time to really listen to Kevin when he talked about you to figure out that you never said anything bad about me when you and Kevin were alone, not even when you were sure I was the worst thing that could have happened to him."

"Why would I want Kevin to think badly of his own father?" she asked, honestly confused by his gratitude over something which, to her, was a fundamental part of being a parent. "What good would that do?"

He stared at her long and hard, as if trying to figure out whether or not she was being coy. "Without me in the picture, you could go back to having him all to yourself."

So that was it. How could she have been so dense that she hadn't seen it before? There had been more than the obvious reasons for Mason wanting to spend as much time with Kevin as he could. He had wanted to prove he wasn't the man in the portrait he believed Chris was painting.

"I couldn't do that to him, Mason. He has to make those kinds of judgments, for himself." An embarrassed smile lifted the corner of her mouth. "There really wasn't any reason for me to keep Kevin from knowing you, once I figured out you weren't the complete ogre I originally thought you were."

"When did you figure that out?"

Her smile turned into a self-deprecating chuckle. "The knowledge was slowly building all along, but I finally gave in to the facts a couple of weeks ago."

"Want to clue me in on what I did that changed your mind? I know it wasn't the wedding."

"It was the house."

Now it was his turn to look confused. "The house? I don't understand."

"There were a hundred other places you could have picked for us to—"

"What sense would that have made?" he interrupted. "Why uproot you and Kevin unnecessarily?"

"Precisely," she said. "Without even consciously thinking about it, you put us first."

"It wouldn't have been logical to do it any other way," he said, obviously struggling to understand her reasoning. He grimaced. "God, I sound like Mr. Spock."

"If we don't get a move on," she said, taken aback to realize what she really wanted was to go on talking to him, "it's going to be dark by the time we get to the beach."

A slow smile lighted his face. "Which beach did you have in mind?"

"Stinson? Is that all right?"

"It's my favorite."

She laughed. "Liar. I'll bet you've never been there. I'll go farther than that. I'll bet you haven't taken a day off since you moved to Sacramento."

"All right, so I haven't been there, but I've at least heard about it. And you're wrong about the days off." He made a face. "I really hate to bring this up now, but if you recall, I like to ski."

"You're right. I did forget." What was going on between them? They were actually holding an ordinary conversation. Almost as if they liked each other. "Which just goes to show I'm not the kind who carries a grudge."

With a wonderful spontaneity, she took his arm and guided him out of the room, not considering the familiarity of her action until after she had touched him. She expected him to pull away as he had done in the past, if not physically then emotionally. She breathed a mental sigh of relief when it didn't happen. "You were on your way to get Kevin, remember?"

"Don't worry about us. We'll be ready to walk out the door in fifteen minutes," he said, a note of challenge in his voice.

With her heart feeling lighter than it had in months, Chris called out to his retreating back, "I'll be ready in ten."

"I'll bet you dessert on the way home that you're not."

"You're on," she said, grabbing a box of crackers from the cupboard and flinging it into the basket.

Ten minutes and an odd assortment of seconds later, she was loading the day's supplies into the back of Mason's truck. "Dessert's on you," she said with a self-satisfied grin.

"Will I never learn not to underestimate you?"

It was the best compliment he could have given her. Perhaps the magic would last a little longer after all.

That night Mason couldn't sleep. He kept going over and over the day he'd just spent with Chris and Kevin, unable to allow himself to take pleasure in the good time he'd had. He couldn't help worrying that he and Chris had started down a dead-end street and that sooner or later they were going to have to pay a higher toll than either of them could afford.

He didn't want to mislead her, to let her think what they'd shared that day could ever develop into anything more. Their situation was too pat. From all outward appearances, they were the perfect triangle—mother and father and child. But two of the lines would never—no, could never—meet; the triangle would never be complete. Someday soon they would have to talk about it. He had to make sure she understood how things were with him, and that, above all else, he didn't want to hurt her.

Finally he grew tired of trying to sleep and decided to get up. He slipped on his robe and headed for the kitchen, thinking maybe a beer would help relax him. As he rounded the corner, he discovered Chris had beaten him there. She was standing at the stove, a carton of milk in her hand, a tin of cocoa on the counter beside her. The flannel nightshirt she was wearing clung softly to her hips and buttocks and stopped at mid-thigh. Technically, it was no more revealing than anything else he'd ever seen her wear, even less so than the dress she'd worn to the dance, but something about seeing her in the clothes she wore to bed caused an intense and unwelcome stirring in his groin.

Chris wasn't beautiful in the classic sense,

319

not the way Susan and Diane had been. There was nothing fragile or ethereal about her. The spark in her eye was more mischievous than come-hither; the tilt of her head was challenging, never compliant. Her body was as hard and lean as his own, and he had no doubt that she could hike as far as he could, ski as long, and make love with as much energy. She looked more like a Joan of Arc than a Rafael madonna, someone who typically insisted on carrying the picnic basket, not just the blanket.

Because he could more easily picture her slaying a dragon than allowing herself to be swept away by a Prince Charming, he wasn't surprised that she'd never married. The only reason she would allow a man in her life was that she loved him to distraction—or that he happened to be the father of her child—never that she needed him. By watching Rebecca and the men she'd become involved with over the years, Mason had learned that few males could accept that kind of independence in a woman. The reasoning was something he had never been able to fathom, but he'd seen it happen too often not to believe it was true.

"How long are you planning to stand there and stare at me without saying anything?" Chris asked, not turning around.

"How did you know I was here?" he asked, avoiding answering her question by asking one of his own.

She faced him. "I heard your bedroom door open, and I listened for you to come down the hall."

"I couldn't sleep."

She held up the milk carton. "As you can see, couldn't either." She set it on the counter, reached for a spoon, and pried open the cocoa tin. "Want some?"

"No, thanks," he said automatically, and then, "What the hell, a cup of chocolate sounds better than a beer. It's been a long time..." It was on the tip of his tongue to add, "not since Diane and I were together," but he thought better of it.

She tried to lower the flame under the pan, but it went out. Grumbling, she turned the burner on again and then bent over to check it. The action brought her nightshirt up high on her legs, exposing a thin strip of silky lavender underwear. He told himself to look away, but the message got lost somewhere between the telling and the doing. Caught up in watching her, he was stunned to realize how compelling his desire was to go to her and run his hand up the length of her thigh, to feel the smoothness of her skin under his caress, the yielding scrap of lavender, to have her sigh at his touch and turn to him....

He mentally shook himself and searched for something to say that would break the spell. "Diane used to make hot chocolate when she couldn't sleep."

"I know," Chris answered. "She learned that particular trick from me." She measured another cup of milk and added it to the pot, along with two more heaping spoonfuls of cocoa.

"You're nothing alike," he blurted out,

still not free of the disquieting image of what it would feel like to have Chris respond to him.

"So you've said."

"I don't mean that in a comparative sense," he added quickly, realizing how easily she could misinterpret his comment.

She took another mug from the cupboard. "Don't worry. You're not the first person who's made that observation. I'm used to it." She held the mug between her hands and added softly, "Or at least I was once."

Her tone touched a responsive chord. "You still miss her, don't you?"

"With Kevin as a reminder, it's hard not to. At least it doesn't hurt so much anymore. Now when I think about her, I can even laugh at some of the memories of the things we used to do together."

With Diane as a buffer between them, he was able to cross the room and stand next to Chris. He had wondered what might happen should he remember too clearly what it felt like to have Chris in his arms. He had held her only for the length of a dance and she hadn't wanted to be there, but still the memory of the feel of her lingered. "Getting that letter was like losing Diane all over again."

"Only this time you had to deal with guilt, too," she said astutely. "It couldn't have been easy to find out that she didn't deserve the horrible things you'd been thinking about her all those years."

"How did you know?"

She sighed. "I suppose because it's the way I would have reacted."

"You think we're so much alike?" he asked, keenly interested in her answer.

She kept her gaze focused on the stove. "Probably more than either of us would care to admit."

"Maybe that's our problem. It's opposites that attract."

After dipping her little finger into the chocolate, she turned off the burner and poured the steaming cocoa into the mugs. When she'd rinsed the pot and left it to soak, she reached overhead and took down a package of miniature marshmallows.

Anticipating what the stretch would do to her nightshirt, Mason busied himself with taking the mugs to the table. He needn't have bothered. In his mind's eye, he saw her as clearly as if he'd stood and watched.

He was as confused by his own feelings as by the way Chris was acting. Until today he'd done nothing to deserve her thawing attitude; if anything, his behavior at the dance should have given her enough fresh ammunition to last another month or two. What had happened to make her willing to put her trust in him again, as if the dance had never happened, to give him a mile when he hadn't earned an inch?

Then she dropped a bomb without even a whistle of warning to mark its approach. "Why is it more comfortable for you when we aren't getting along?"

His jaw dropped. "You're imagining—"

"No, I'm not," she said evenly as she sprinkled a handful of marshmallows into each cup.

"You'd like me to think I am. I suppose it would be easier if I did, but I have a perverse tendency to avoid taking the easy way out of anything."

To stall for time, he sat down and reached for the mugs, sliding one across the table to where Chris would sit and then wrapping his hands tightly around the other one, as if to warm them. "Is that why you decided to raise Kevin yourself instead of putting him up for adoption?" he asked, evading her question with something he knew she would feel compelled to answer.

She put the twister back on the bag of marshmallows, tossed it on the counter, and sat down. "Actually, I did arrange for him to be adopted, but the decision was a long way from taking the easy way out."

This was the first Mason had heard about anyone else being involved in Kevin's life. He was intensely curious. "What happened?"

"The people who were to take him decided they didn't want to deal with a sick baby," she said. After several more seconds, she added, "It was almost as if Kevin knew the only way I'd give myself permission to keep him was if no one else would."

"Jesus." He shook his head. "There's so much I don't know about what happened back then."

"You know everything you need to know." She took a drink, then licked the film of marshmallow from her lips.

Mason's gaze fixed itself on her mouth. A powerful urge to kiss her came over him. He wanted to taste her, to feel her lips yield at his touch, to feel her warmth. He tried passing the impulse off to the thwarted evening he had planned to spend with Kelly, but couldn't quite convince himself. Especially when he admitted that what he was feeling went beyond understandable lust. What he really ached for, what had been missing from his life for far too long, was the feeling that he had the right to touch a woman with simple intimacy and know that his touch would be welcomed.

The recognition of his need made it stronger, forcing every other thought from his mind until it became so powerful he felt as if he would suffocate if he couldn't find a release. He struggled to take a breath.

"It's getting late," he said, amazed that words could find voice through the turmoil of his mind. "If it's all right with you, I think I'll take my hot chocolate back to my room and finish it there."

Her disappointment was evident in the confused look she gave him. "Of course it's all right with me," she said too quickly. "I was just thinking the same thing myself. The only time I get to sleep in is when Kevin happens to be spending the night at the Hendricksons." She stood up and tugged on the bottom of her nightshirt.

Even though his statement had precipitated her leaving, Mason felt disquieted at the prospect of losing her company. As he watched her pick up her mug and head for the door, it became critically important to him to make her understand that she'd done nothing to cause his abrupt about-face. "I had a wonderful time today," he said, unable to keep a stiffness out of his voice.

"Me, too," she said, rewarding his effort with a smile.

"Maybe we could do it again sometime," he said, the effort sounding lame even to himself.

"I'm sure Kevin would like that."

He nodded and raised his mug to her. "I'll see you in the morning."

Her hand covered the light switch. It became apparent she was waiting for him to leave first. For a brief moment he allowed himself to wonder what it would be like to follow her instead of turning his back and walking away.

Heading for his room, he made a promise to himself. The next time he couldn't sleep, he would count sheep. There would be no more late night encounters between the two of them. It wasn't fair to Chris, and it sure as hell wasn't something he ever wanted to put himself through again.

32

Chris pulled a hooded sweatshirt on, zipped it up, and sat on the edge of the bed to tie her running shoes, taking a second to rub the goose bumps on her bare legs. She glanced at the clock. Ten minutes before she was to meet Mary and begin their jog from hell. They'd promised each other that this was the morning they would get back into their five-mile routine instead of the quick two miles they'd been running for the past month. With less than three hours of sleep behind her, Chris was betting Mary would be calling the paramedics for her long before they'd made it to the park.

She was as bewildered this morning about the day she'd spent with Mason as she had been when she'd crawled into bed last night. On the one hand, there was Kevin, who'd been an absolute delight to be around yesterday, his happiness creating a glow to rival that of a fireplace. On the other, there was the strange way Mason had reacted to the lessening of tension between them.

Lessening of tension? Who was she trying to kid? There had actually been a couple of times when it seemed they were the family they purported to be, when Mason had looked at her with eyes hungry for the affection she lavished so easily on their son. Yet always there was the reserve that told her if she dared to respond to him, he wouldn't just turn and flee, he would attack before running.

Why did he feel the need to protect himself from her? What did he think she wanted to do, lull him into a relationship? Couldn't he tell that she no more wanted to muck up a potential friendship with something physical than he did? Just the thought of it terrified her.

She finished tying her shoes and started for

Kevin's bedroom. Her hand was on the doorknob before she realized she didn't have to wake him up and take him over to the Hendricksons. Today was Sunday. Mason could watch him while she and Mary ran.

She started to leave a note and then heard Mason stirring in his room. After it became obvious he wasn't going to come out right away, she went to his door and lightly tapped on the wooden frame.

He answered her knock wearing a pair of jeans with only the top button buttoned. Plainly she'd caught him just getting out of bed. His near nakedness disconcerted Chris and she momentarily forgot why she had come.

"Is something wrong?" Mason asked, obviously as surprised by her visit to his room as she was by the way she had found him.

"No," she told him, regaining her composure. "I just wanted to make sure you were going to be home for a while. I didn't want to wake Kevin and take him with me if I didn't have to."

He glanced at her feet, his gaze taking in her bare legs before settling on her face again. "Going jogging?"

"Against my better judgment."

"I wondered how you kept in such good shape."

She smiled. "I never know how to answer that kind of statement."

"It was just an observation."

She was tempted to ask him what he did that made him look as if his second home was a gym. There wasn't a spare ounce of fat on his body. Knowing his schedule, she found it difficult to believe he had the time to work out, but the definition of muscle on his arms and shoulders could hardly be natural.

Kevin had inherited his father's basic build. Did that mean eventually he would develop Mason's broad chest and light matting of hair? Uncomfortable with where her thoughts were leading, she nervously ran her hands down her shorts and then stuffed them into the pockets of her sweatshirt. "Well?" she prodded.

"Well what?"

"Are you going to be here?"

"Oh...yes, I am."

"Good." She took a step backward. "I shouldn't be gone too long."

He stepped into the doorway and leaned one shoulder against the frame. "Take your time."

On impulse she asked, "Would you like to come? John could watch Kevin."

He chuckled and shook his head. "On my list of favorite things to do, running ranks right below having a tooth pulled."

She blinked in feigned surprise. "Boy, that's a lot higher than it is on my list." Knowing Mary would be waiting for her gave Chris the nudge she needed to get going. "Tell Kevin I'll fix him blueberry pancakes when I get back," she said, turning to leave.

She was almost to the front door when she heard him call her. She started back across the living room just as he appeared at the end of the hallway.

"Do you think Kevin would like to go out

to brunch this morning?" He quickly added, "You, too, of course."

"That sounds nice," she said, inordinately pleased at his suggestion, even if his extension of the invitation to include her did seem like an afterthought.

"I'll make the arrangements."

Not knowing what else to say, she nodded and left. Her feet seemed inches off the pavement as she ran to Mary's house.

Mason stood at the window and watched Chris until she was out of sight. He then went back to his room to finish dressing, wondering at how easily he had abandoned his resolve, only hours old, to put distance between himself and Chris again and reestablish the reserve in their relationship. While it might be to Kevin's advantage to have his parents playing house, it was a long way from what Mason wanted. He had a feeling it wasn't what Chris wanted either.

Still, he reasoned, an occasional outing couldn't hurt. As long as both of them were aware that what they were doing was for Kevin's sake, there really wasn't any reason they couldn't attempt some normality in their relationship once in a while. It was always easier to navigate in calm waters.

Even if it turned out that Kevin could handle the eventual divorce earlier than either he or Chris expected, that time was years away. One way or another, they had to find a means of communicating with each other.

This weekend had been a decent beginning. Now if they could just go on that way, perhaps someday they might even grow to like and respect each other, much as he and Rebecca had.

That was it—the perfect solution. From now on, whenever he thought about Chris, he would liken her to Rebecca.

He groaned at the thought. Did he really want two Rebeccas in his life?

More to the point, a small, persistent voice needled him, not once in all the years he'd known Rebecca had his heart skipped a beat when she'd come into a room the way it invariably did when he caught sight of Chris.

"Wow," Mary gasped, catching up to Chris as they made their third pass by the tennis courts in McKinley Park. "If I didn't...know better...I'd suspect you took...something this morning. I've never seen you...this hyper."

Chris laughed. "I probably won't be able to get out of bed tomorrow."

"I've got to stop a minute," Mary insisted. She pulled up, bent at the waist, and put her hands on her knees. Several deep breaths later, she stood up again. "Could we walk for a while?"

"Why don't we just head back instead? I told Mason I wouldn't be gone too long."

"Doesn't that guy ever take a day off?"

Chris hesitated. She'd been trying to find a way to bring up what had happened between herself and Mason over the past two days, but couldn't find the words—most likely, she reasoned, because she wasn't sure what had happened. The week before, Mary had been uncharacteristically quiet when Chris told her about the dance, her only comment being a completely unexpected "Who would have thought Mason Winter could play the knight-in-shining-armor role."

"Actually," Chris said, "he took all day yesterday off. We went to Stinson's Beach for a picnic." She cast a glance in Mary's direction to see what kind of response she was getting to the news.

The anguish of fatigue was replaced with wide-eyed curiosity. "Oh?" Mary said, drawing the word out for maximum effect.

"And the three of us are going out to breakfast this morning—Mason's suggestion, not mine."

Mary stopped and pulled the headband from her hair. "Have I missed something? Is this the same man who made a date with another woman two weeks after he married you?"

Chris shrugged. "I don't understand it either."

"Maybe this is his way of apologizing for being such an asshole."

"I thought of that, too."

"But?"

"He's already playing to a captive audience. Why spend time on props when you don't have to?"

Mary cocked an eyebrow in speculation. "Something tells me he's finally taken a good look at what's been handed to him on a silver platter and discovered he might be interested after all."

Chris let out a derisive snort. "Fat chance."

"Well, it sure would be nice if I'm right," Mary said, a wistfulness in her voice.

"Why?" Chris asked, her curiosity piqued.

"Because you've already fallen for him, and I don't want to see you get your heart broken."

Chris sucked in a surprised breath. "Where in the world did you get a crazy idea like that?"

"When you spent two whole days looking for a dress to wear to the dance, you tossed out a mighty big clue."

"I had to do that. I was on a budget."

"Is that why you tried to hide what you were doing from me?"

"I didn't tell you because I knew you would tell me I was making a mistake."

Mary eyed her. "And that was the last thing you wanted to hear. What you were after was a chance to knock Mason Winter's socks off, and you didn't want the voice of reason getting in your way."

Good God, could Mary be right? Could her actions have been that calculated without her even being aware of it? "Why would I want to do that?"

"If you set aside the fact that Mason is Kevin's father and that it would make your lives a lot easier if you could stop living a lie, what you're left with is pretty basic stuff. Pure and simple, Mason is a hunk. You may live in California, but that doesn't mean your bed can't get damn cold on a lonely winter night."

Chris cut across the grass to sit on one of the park benches. Nothing Mary had said was new to her. In one form or another, the same thoughts had been floating around in her own mind for a couple of weeks. But hearing them said out loud gave them a validity she wasn't sure she was ready to face. "I'm too old for this," she groaned.

Mary sat down beside Chris. "It's those damn hormones," she said, a smile playing around her mouth. "They'll get you every time."

"That's it? No words of wisdom? No offer to help me dig an escape tunnel?"

"Give him a chance," Mary said, serious again.

Several seconds passed before she answered Mary, and when she did, it was in a choked whisper. "The thought petrifies me."

They remained on the bench, watching the tide of joggers reach its peak and then slowly diminish. Finally the cold got to them and they set off for home.

While Mason was waiting for Chris to return and Kevin to wake up, he made a pot of coffee, started a fire, and sat in the living room to read the morning paper. When he finished the paper, he gathered it together again and was in the process of putting it under the coffee table when he noticed the photograph album Chris had shown him that tumultuous day in December.

He stared at the album, aware of the Pandora's box of emotions it contained and caught off guard by how forcefully he was drawn to it and repelled by it at the same time. He'd finally admitted to himself that Chris had been dead-on with her analysis: he was still in the throes of dealing with his feelings about Diane. The eight months since he'd discovered the real reason she'd left him wasn't enough time to have worked through his guilt. There were so many unanswered questions. Why had he been so eager to accept her abandonment at face value? Had his ego been so fragile that he'd not only believed her story that she no longer loved him but anticipated it?

He was consumed with a desperate need to tell Diane how sorry he was—for believing her reason for leaving, for being so caught up in his own concerns that he hadn't noticed what was going on with her, and for not being there when she had finally reached out to him. He couldn't even remember why he had been out of the country.

Realizing the guilt would never lessen if he refused to face it, Mason picked up the album and opened it, starting at the beginning again, forcing himself to go over pictures he'd already seen in the hopes that familiarity would make this second time easier.

Again he saw Diane as a baby, and again he noted there was nothing in the way she looked that tied her to Kevin. He touched the tip of his finger to her image and stroked the child she had been, telling her over and over again how sorry he was. It seemed so wrong somehow that Kevin should carry his stamp and not hers.

What had he ever done that was good enough to deserve such a gift?

The room faded to a soft blur as tears clouded his eyes. It was the first time since Diane had left him that he'd allowed himself the luxury of admitting how much he had hurt and how deeply he had missed her. A band wrapped itself around his chest, cutting him with every breath.

Behind him came the sound of Kevin bounding through the kitchen. Mason quickly wiped his eyes and closed the album.

But not before Kevin had come into the room and seen what he was doing. "What's wrong, Daddy?" he asked. He stopped several feet away and stared.

A dozen lies popped into Mason's mind, none of them worthy of Kevin. He settled on the truth "I was looking at pictures of your mama Diane when she was a little girl, and they made me very sad."

"How come?" Kevin asked, coming closer.

"Because I loved her and I need to tell her something and I can't."

Kevin climbed onto the couch and sat close to Mason. "You can tell me," he said with a child's perfect logic.

Mason put his arm around his son and drew him close to his side. "I'm afraid it wouldn't be the same."

"How come?" Kevin said again. With some children it was "why," with Kevin it was always "how come?"

"Because—" What the hell? Why not just tell him? "I want to tell your mama Diane that I'm sorry for being mad at her all those years when I didn't know about you.

Kevin thought a minute and then announced with supreme confidence, "She would say it was okay."

Mason's answering smile was filled with sadness. "How do you know?" he asked, bemused at how desperately he wanted to believe what Kevin had told him.

"Mom says that my mama Diane was the kind of person who loved everybody. Tracy's like that, too," he reasoned. "When I do something that makes her mad, she never makes me say I'm sorry two times."

How did the old saying go? Out of the mouths of babes? Mason bent and pressed a kiss to the top of Kevin's head. "Thank you," he said.

Kevin began to squirm. "Where's Mom? I'm getting hungry."

At the mention of Chris, Mason felt the band slip back into place around his chest. His defenses down, he had been on the verge of making a terrible mistake with her. Thank God he'd caught himself in time. "She should be back any time now," he said. "She and Aunt Mary went running."

Chris slowed her pace as she rounded the corner and caught sight of her house. Still reeling from her talk with Mary, she was hesitant about seeing Mason again so soon. Now that she'd faced her feelings, how was she going to walk through the door and take up where the two of them had left off, as if nothing had happened?

That was the rub. Nothing had happened—and yet nothing was the same.

Damn it. She didn't want to fall in love with Mason Winter. He'd made it plain that he wanted nothing more from her than that she be a mother to his child. His actions spoke even louder than his words. She wasn't foolish enough to think what they'd shared the day before was anything more than a polite apology for the way he'd acted about the dance.

And that hadn't even been his fault. Oh, he could have been less of a jerk about the whole thing, but, bottom line, he hadn't done anything to encourage her or to give her the smallest indication that she would be welcome in that part of his life.

So why had she gone to the dance?

She was standing on the front porch, out of reasons not to go inside. Pasting a noncommittal smile on her face, she opened the door. Immediately she was hit with the smell of French toast.

"Hi, Mom," Kevin called out to her. "We're in the kitchen."

Chris paused, confused. Hadn't Mason said he wanted to take them out to breakfast? She glanced at the clock on the mantel. She hadn't been gone long enough for them to have given up on her.

She walked toward the kitchen, pulling her hood off and then unzipping her sweatshirt as she went. Mason and Kevin were at the table, finishing their breakfast. He looked up when she entered. "I thought—"

"I'm sorry about going ahead without you," Mason said breezily. "There are some things I wanted to get done at the office today, and I decided to get an early start."

"But we saved you some," Kevin chimed in.

Her disappointment threatened to crush her. Not until then had she realized how much she was looking forward to their morning together. "I thought you said you didn't have anything to do today," she said, furious with herself for not being able to keep a telltale catch from her voice.

Mason took his and Kevin's plates over to the sink. "Something came up."

She refused to let him see how much she cared. "Gee, I guess some things work out for the best, after all," she said, slipping out of her sweatshirt and draping it over the back of the chair. "Mary wanted me to go shopping with her this morning. I hated to tell her I couldn't go, and now I don't have to."

Mason eyed her. She had a sinking feeling he didn't believe a word of what she'd said. But he didn't pursue it. Instead he nodded and told her, "You're right. Sometimes things do work out for the best."

She had to get out of there before she made a fool of herself. "I'm going to take a shower," she announced, apropos of nothing.

"I'll probably be gone when you get out."

God, what she wouldn't have given for a good exit line. Lacking one, she simply left, afraid if she stayed any longer, her heart would fall off her sleeve.

Mason arrived at his office an hour later, waved away the security guard, and let himself in with his key. For the first time in recent memory, he wasn't looking forward to spending a day in the office by himself. Instead of taking the direct route, he decided to wander the halls for a while. He was startled to find Rebecca working at her desk, but welcomed the prospect of company for his misery.

She looked up as he entered. "I thought you said you were going to take the weekend off," she said.

"Seems to me I remember you saying something like that yourself."

"Yeah, but I don't have a son who thinks I walk on water waiting for me at home." She pushed her chair back and propped her feet up on the desk. "What's your excuse?"

"I guess I just don't feel like getting my feet wet today."

"My, my, humor," she said, making a disparaging face.

"Did you get up on the wrong side of the bed this morning, or have you been this way all weekend?"

She rocked back and brought her feet to the floor with a loud thud. "This isn't a good day for us to be talking about things, Mason. I came here to be by myself because I'm not fit to be around anyone else in the mood I'm in."

He knew Rebecca well enough to pay attention to her warning—she didn't say such things idly. But he cared about her too much not to see if there was something he could do to help. He shoved his thumbs in the pockets of his jeans, his hands fanning out over his hips. "Want to talk about it?"

"You don't want to hear what I have to say."

"I thought this was about you."

"It is, but what I'm feeling about me is all tied up with what I'm feeling about you."

He drew in a deep breath, preparing himself. "You might as well lay it on me. I'd just as soon hear what you have to say as imagine it."

"You know that guy I told you I've been going out with the last couple of months?"

"The one you met in San Francisco?"

She nodded. "He's married."

"And you just found out?"

She turned away from him and stared out the window. "No," she said, her voice emotionless. "I've known all along."

Mason tried hard not to let her see how surprised he was. Rebecca had an iron-clad rule about dating married men. Or at least she'd had one up until then. "And now he's backing out of leaving his wife?" He couldn't come up with any other reason she would be so upset.

"He never intended to leave her." She swung back around to face Mason. "Shocked?"

He was, but that wasn't what she needed or wanted to hear from him. "Should I be?"

"I'm lonely, Mason. And, it seems, willing

341

to settle for whatever I can get. Or at least I was until today. I realized this morning my pride was too high a price to pay." She shrugged. "So I go back to being lonely."

"How do I fit into all of this?"

"I'm so mad at you I can hardly stand to look you in the face. You've been handed everything I was willing to trade my integrity for, and you're too damn stubborn to appreciate it."

He understood her anger. What he didn't understand was her reasoning. "Stubbornness has nothing to do with it."

"Oh? Then what is it?"

He started to answer, but couldn't say the words out loud. "It doesn't matter."

"She isn't going to die on you, Mason."

"How in the hell do you know that?" he snapped, as angered by her accusation as he was by his own transparency. "Can you give me some kind of guarantee it's not going to happen again?"

"Nobody gets a guarantee like that. Dying is a part of living, Mason. It happens to all of us eventually. Crawling into a hole and letting life pass you by isn't the answer."

"And you think you know what is?"

"You have to take a chance—"

"Goddammit, I took a chance. Look what it got me."

"Where did this sudden streak of cowardice come from, Mason?"

He had never been so angry with her. What right did she have to question him? "From watching one woman die and imagining the other one doing the same. From knowing there wasn't a damn thing I could do to stop Susan's death and that Diane would probably be alive today if I hadn't insisted we make love when she forgot to bring her diaphragm on that stupid weekend cruise.

"Don't try to convince me lightning can't strike the same place twice, Rebecca. I've been there. I've seen it happen." He turned away from her and walked over to the window.

Moments later, Rebecca came up to him and stood silently by his side. Not looking at her, Mason added, "I won't go through it a third time. I can't."

33

The next two weeks passed in a stifling formality. Mason made a point of coming home every night in time to spend at least an hour with Kevin before he had to go to bed. Twice they went to a Sacramento Kings basketball game together; the third time they invited Tracy and John to go with them. Mary and Chris spent the evening at the Tower Theater watching a subtitled movie.

Mason developed a reserved, standoffish attitude with Chris, polite to the point of stiffness, painfully careful with any questions he had about the household or Kevin. It was as if they had never touched or fought or exchanged anything but inanities. Instead of their time together becoming something they could build on, it became a void, empty and meaningless. After a while, Chris began to doubt her own memories of the dance and the picnic on the beach.

The times the three of them were together, she became the outsider. Knowing the exclusion wasn't intentional, that it was merely another manifestation of Mason's remoteness, did nothing to lessen the hurt. She didn't understand why he continued to shut her out of even the most ordinary aspects of his life, but she didn't question him about it, afraid he would misinterpret her caring. He was doing precisely what he had promised. So what did it matter that he was aloof and withdrawn with her? What had given her the impression she had the right to expect anything else?

While the artificial calm between herself and Mason was distressing at times, it gave Chris the opportunity to catch up with the assignments she'd let slide during the move and its aftermath. Her insistence that it be her responsibility to assume the normal household bills while Mason took care of the mortgage payments had seemed reasonable and equitable at the time. She hadn't taken into consideration that adding another person and doubling the size of the house meant more than doubling the gas and electric bill. There was even another mouth to feed, on occasion. Once her old house was rented, she would be all right. Until then she would have to scramble to make ends meet.

It was a beautiful, sunny March morning, and instead of going for a walk with Mary to admire the beds of tulips in the neighborhood, Chris had to force herself to stay inside to put the finishing touches on an incredibly boring press release for a tire company. She was removing the last page from the printer when the doorbell rang.

She dropped the paper on her desk and ran for the door. One of the things she liked best about Mary was that she rarely took no for an answer.

But it wasn't Mary standing on the front porch; it was a woman Chris had never seen before. She was wearing a designer suit and a hesitant smile and looked as if she owned and used every Jane Fonda exercise tape ever made. Chris judged her to be in her early sixties. On the street behind her was a taxi, its driver standing on the sidewalk, leaning against the front fender.

"Can I help you?" Chris asked.

"I'm looking for Mason Winter's house."

Chris became instantly wary. This woman looked nothing like the reporters who had been after her for interviews ever since the Valentine's Day dance, but appearances could be deceiving. "Is he expecting you?"

"Then this is his house?" the woman asked, answering a question with a question.

"Yes..." Chris admitted hesitantly.

The woman waved the driver on, then turned back. "I'm Mason's mother," she said. "Am I to assume you're his wife?"

Chris was too stunned to answer. How had

she gotten the impression Mason had no family?

"I'm sorry to arrive unannounced," she said. "But, quite honestly, I was afraid that if I didn't, Mason wouldn't see me."

"He...he's not here now."

"Yes, I know. I called his office before I came. I wanted some time alone with you so that we could get acquainted."

"Mason didn't tell me—" Chris stopped, suddenly realizing what she was about to say. She put herself in this woman's position and tried to imagine how awful it would feel to know ~~Kevin~~ Mason had never mentioned her to his wife.

"You don't have to explain," the woman said. "I didn't expect that Mason would have told you about me, or about his father and brother."

Chris couldn't have been more astonished if Mason's mother had knocked on the front door dressed like the Easter Rabbit. Abruptly realizing they were still standing outside, Chris said, "Would you like to come in, Mrs. Winter?"

"Please, call me Iris. And, yes, I would like to come in."

Iris stopped in the middle of the living room and looked around. "You can't imagine the number of times I've wondered about the kind of house Mason was living in. I pictured him surrounded by glass and brass, with leather furniture and white carpeting. That's not the real him, of course, but it would be easy to hide who he really was in that kind of surrounding. I'm pleased to see I was wrong."

346

Chris hesitated. Since Mason was obviously not on the best of terms with his family, it seemed to her that any details about his private life should come from him. "We combined households when we got married," Chris said, sidestepping the issue.

Directing her gaze at Chris, Iris revealed ocean-blue eyes filled with a poignant sorrow. "I haven't come here to pump you for information," she said. "I wanted to meet you...and my grandson. You probably don't know this, but he's the first of his generation in our family. Robert and Claudia, that's Mason's brother and his wife, decided not to have children."

"You know about Kevin?"

"Yes," she said, her voice tinged with excitement. "For months now I've been trying to think of a way to see him without my sudden appearance causing a problem. But there never seemed to be an opportune time, so I stopped trying to find one and just hopped on a plane. I understand he looks just like his father."

Now Chris was really confused. "Mason told you about Kevin?"

She shook her head sadly. "Mason and I haven't spoken in years."

"Then how—"

"It's a long story." She pressed the tips of her fingers to her temples as if trying to hold off a headache.

"Would you like some aspirin?" Chris asked.

"No, but a cup of coffee would be nice." She

smiled. "I'm addicted to caffeine, I'm afraid. If I don't get my morning quota, I start to get one of these damnable headaches."

"I was just about to make a fresh pot," Chris said. "Make yourself comfortable, I'll be right back."

"Would you mind if I came with you?"

The mystery of where Mason had picked up his aloof politeness was a mystery no longer. Most women Chris knew would have simply tagged along. "Not if you don't mind looking at a sink full of breakfast dishes," Chris said, leading the way into the kitchen. She had a feeling it would be a first for Iris. Mason's mother looked like the kind of woman who vacuumed under the bed every day.

"I'll bet you think I starched Mason's underwear when he was growing up," Iris said, following.

Chris pulled up short, nearly causing a collision. She turned to look at Iris and saw a mischievous twinkle in her eye. "That's quite an icebreaker."

"Well, one of us had to do it."

Chris smiled. "I think I'm going to like you, Iris."

"I can assure you, Chris, the feeling is mutual."

When they were settled at the kitchen table with their coffee, Iris asked, "How much has Mason told you about himself?"

It was one of those "Have you stopped beating your wife" questions. No matter how Chris answered, it would sound wrong. If she admitted he hadn't told her anything, she might as well reveal to Iris the whole story behind the marriage. If she said he'd told her everything, she'd end up tripping all over herself, trying to keep up her end of the conversation. "I think what you're really asking is how much Mason has told me about you."

"I suppose that's part of it. I am curious about what kinds of things he would tell his new wife about his family, but what I really want to know is whether or not he's told you about Susan."

"Susan?" Chris blurted out, instantly realizing she'd given the answer away.

"I was afraid of that," Iris said, reaching for her coffee. "I know why you and Mason got married, Chris. And I know there's every reason to believe it will never be more than a marriage of convenience unless you understand what happened to Mason that made him the man he is today."

Chris became guarded. "I'm confused. The impression I'm getting is that there hasn't been any contact between you and your son for a long time, and now you want me to believe you've developed this sudden interest in the success of his marriage?"

Iris put her coffee back on the table, untouched. "Our estrangement was Mason's doing, not mine. He never understood the position he put me in when he asked me to choose between him and his father." She sent Chris a beseeching look. "How could I side with him and lose the man I had been with my entire adult life, the man who would grow old with me while my son was busy making his way on his own?"

"Who was Susan?" As long as she'd blundered into admitting she didn't know, she decided she might as well go all the way.

"Mason's wife."

Chris almost choked on her coffee. "Where is she now?"

"She died."

"How?"

"Cancer."

Bits and pieces of information that had been floating in Chris's mind settled and began to form a whole. Now she had some insight into why Mason might have wanted Diane to have an abortion, and why Diane would have left without telling him where or why she was going. Trapped by the past, they had been unable to do anything but what they had.

"Susan was an amazing and brave woman," Iris went on. "She fought the cancer for almost three years...tried everything...went to clinics here and in Europe. And she kept on going to them long after she'd accepted the inevitable, just to ease Mason's mind that they had left no stone unturned. Mason was inconsolable when she died. I didn't think he would ever let himself love anyone else."

"And then Diane came along," Chris said, her heart breaking all over again for her sister, only this time the sorrow she felt was for Mason, too. Twice he had lost a woman he loved, one through death, the other by abandonment—or what he had believed at the time to be abandonment. Which had been crueler?

And who had been braver—Susan, who had gone through her pain with Mason at her side, or Diane, who had suffered alone?

Did it matter?

"I was so sure Diane and Mason would make it," Iris said. "They were so much in love...at least that was what I heard."

"Who told you?" Despite their estrangement, Iris seemed to know an amazing amount about Mason's private life.

"That isn't important."

Chris couldn't help feeling that it was important, but pressing Iris for an answer she obviously wasn't willing to give would only alienate her.

"You said Mason forced you to choose between him and his father," Chris said. "Why? What happened?" Lost in her own world and her own problems, Chris had been ready, even eager, to accept Mason at face value. She'd been unable or unwilling to look behind the facade Mason presented to her. In her own way, had she been as self-centered and self-absorbed as she'd accused him of being?

"I think that's something he should tell you about himself."

"He hasn't, up to now, and I somehow doubt that he ever will. Mason and I don't talk about things like that."

"I'm not a neutral observer. My version would naturally be weighted toward Stuart—Mason's father. In this instance, I think what you hear should prejudice you toward Mason."

Her reasoning sounded logical, even compelling, but Iris's refusal to tell Chris what had caused the rift in the Winter family struck an odd note. "I think there's more to it than that," Chris said, refusing to let it drop. Then it hit her. "Could it be you don't want to tell me because of the part you played?"

The question hit home. Iris looked as if the heat had been turned up twenty degrees. "I hope you and Mason work things out between you," she said. "You're just the kind of woman he needs."

"What kind is that?"

"You have the tenacity of a bloodhound...and you care."

"I hope you haven't gotten the wrong impression about why I care," Chris felt compelled to say. "Mason is Kevin's father. I've accepted their relationship and the fact that it's ongoing. If I can help Kevin by understanding Mason, I'll make the effort."

"You really believe that's all there is, don't you?" Iris said, sounding genuinely surprised.

"I know that's all it is."

Iris nodded sagely.

Chris got up to put her coffee cup in the sink. After several seconds she turned and looked at Iris. "I'm sorry to disappoint you," she said, carefully choosing the words she would use. "I realize you came here today hoping to discover that Mason had finally found someone to make him happy and that you could go home and stop worrying about whatever wrongs you think you did him. But I'm not that someone, Iris." It wasn't that she didn't want to be, she could have added, but didn't. When Mary had forced her to recognize her true feelings about Mason, she hadn't done Chris any favors.

"Perhaps Kevin will be that person for Mason," Chris went on. "But that's an awfully big burden to put on some very small shoulders."

Iris looked down at her hands. "It wasn't what I did," she said. "It was what I didn't do. I stood by while Mason's father and brother systematically shut him out of a company that was rightfully one-third his." She began to rub her temples again.

"Before my own father died, he told Stuart that even though, for legal reasons, he had willed Southwest Construction to him alone, his intent was that it be divided between Stuart and Robert and Mason equally."

Chris dumped Iris's now cold coffee into the sink and refilled the cup.

"Thank you," Iris said, picking up the cup and taking a sip.

"So the company originally belonged to your father?" Chris asked.

"My grandfather," Iris answered. "Mason was in high school when my father died. He'd been accepted to Stanford, and I talked him into getting his degree before he joined the company. That was a mistake. While Mason was gone, Stuart and Robert grew very close. Inevitably, when Mason came back four years later, he was the outsider.

"Stuart and Robert indulged him for a while, even allowing him to try out a few of his ideas when it didn't get in their way. They were sure he would fall on his face and they would have the excuse they needed to get rid of him. Only Mason didn't fall on his face; he found a cement contractor going out of business, bought the lot and inventory, and started building tilt-up warehouses. He succeeded beyond even his own expectations." She ran her index finger around the rim of the cup, removing all traces of lipstick.

"I foolishly believed that Stuart and Robert would come around once they saw how capable Mason was. Instead, they closed ranks against him. Because there was nothing in writing to prove my father had given Mason a third of the company, Stuart and Robert figured they could just fire him and be rid of him."

"Knowing Mason, I would say they figured wrong," Chris said.

"He took them to court and won. Southwest almost didn't survive the settlement."

Chris let out a low whistle. No wonder Mason didn't talk about his family.

Iris's voice dropped to a husky whisper. "Mason asked me to testify for him, but I just couldn't. In hindsight, I realize now that I did Mason a terrible injustice. I put my head in the sand and tried to make the whole thing go away by pretending it wasn't happening."

The suffering on Iris's face looked as fresh as if it had all happened the day before. The men in her life had put her in an impossible situation, damned by her husband and older son if she did as Mason asked, damned by Mason if she didn't. There had been no escape route for her, no way to come through unscathed. Whichever direction she chose, she wound up losing.

Chris couldn't do anything to change what had happened, but she sure as hell didn't have to become a part of it. She went over to the built-in desk at the far corner of the kitchen, opened the top drawer, and pulled out an envelope. Coming back to the table, she slid the envelope in front of Iris.

Iris looked up questioningly.

"They're pictures of Kevin," Chris said, smiling. "He really does look like his father."

With trembling hands, Iris reached inside and pulled out the photographs. Slowly she moved from one picture to the next, studying them as if trying to memorize every detail. When she had finished, she turned to Chris. "Thank you," she said simply. "That was the nicest thing anyone has done for me in a long time."

The look on Iris's face was all the thanks Chris needed.

34

Iris's visit left Chris with much to think about. Another week passed with little to distinguish it from the two weeks before. Mason kept his emotional distance from her, but grew constantly closer to Kevin. The two of them were busy building a history. Now and then, their conversations even contained a "remember when."

Chris became an observer and discovered she was looking at Mason differently than she ever had before. She found herself wondering how much of his behavior toward her was a reflection of who she was, and how much of it was defensive. It was possible—and more likely than she cared to admit—that he just didn't like her and that they would never become real friends.

She'd decided not to tell him about the visit from Iris, at least not right away. To keep Kevin from becoming a part of the subterfuge, she and Iris had agreed to meet "accidentally" in the park later that day. When they found each other in the rose garden, Chris told Kevin she was a friend, not a lie exactly, but closer to one than she liked.

Because Iris thought it important to get back to Santa Barbara before anyone noticed she was gone, she only had an hour with her grandson. When she left, the look she gave Kevin was filled with such longing and regret that it haunted Chris for days afterward.

After her talk with Iris, Chris frequently found herself ruminating on the unhappy family backgrounds she and Mason had in common. A niggling worry began to set in that they might be in the process of passing that questionable legacy on to yet another generation. If they were, would Kevin then pass it on to his own children?

Where would the cycle end?

It was her week to drive Kevin and Tracy

to and from school, and as she waited outside the stucco building for the bell to ring, her thoughts drifted back to Iris's visit and the mental upheaval those few hours had created. Chris felt as if she'd been racing down an expressway in her attitude toward Mason and had suddenly been given the option of taking a series of off-ramps. Not only was she faced with the decision of whether or not she wanted to take any of those exits, but she also had to determine where they might lead her and whether, if once she got off, there would be any way back.

Understanding why Mason behaved the way he did had a tendency to soften her perceptions of what he'd done. She no longer wondered if his driving need to become a part of Kevin's life was centered around his own male ego, or if he'd been acting out a compulsion to lay claim to what was his and damn the consequences to everyone else. She saw now that Kevin was a safe harbor for Mason, a place where he was wanted and needed and would not be abandoned. Mason could reach out to hands eager to hold him; he could give the gift of himself without worrying that it would be rejected.

The door to Mason's own family had been closed to him, leaving him nowhere to go.

Until Kevin happened into his life.

Now Mason had an emotional home, and he'd been given the opportunity to show his own father what a father should be.

And Chris was being hauled along for the ride, not because she was needed or wanted, but simply because she and Kevin were a package deal.

After what had gone on between them the past two weeks, Chris no longer held any illusions that Mason would ever see her in another light; even friendship seemed to be out of the question. He wasn't the kind of man who could hold a friend at arm's length; Rebecca and Travis were proof of that. It was painfully obvious that Mason wasn't about to let her come any closer than she already had.

She could hurt him simply by learning where his vulnerabilities were, and he wasn't about to let that happen.

Too bad she didn't have the same ability to protect herself. Somehow, when she wasn't looking, Mason had slipped past her own barriers and gotten inside. Now all she had to do was decide what she was going to do about it—cut her losses or allow herself to buy into the fantasy that, if she waited long enough, someday Mason would stop being the oak, become a willow, and allow himself, occasionally, to bend in her direction.

If he did, what then? What was it she wanted from him? If Mason never bent, when Kevin was grown and she and Mason were divorced, to whose home would Kevin and his wife and their children go on holidays? Would it be she or Mason who spent Christmas alone?

Was it really only seven months ago that her life had seemed as simple and straightforward and predictable as summer following spring?

The bell rang, snapping her out of her troubling thoughts.

Tracy came bounding out of Ms. Abbott's class, skipping across the asphalt playground, consuming pent-up energy. As Chris's gaze scanned the remaining children pouring through the doorway, a tiny warning flag raised itself and began to wave.

Kevin and Tracy should have come out together.

Finally she saw him. He was walking instead of running, and carrying his backpack instead of wearing it slung over his shoulders, but otherwise at first glance he seemed the same child she had dropped off four hours earlier. It wasn't until he was climbing into the car that she saw the glazed look in his eyes.

"What's up, Kevin?" she asked, her heart in her throat. "Not feeling good?"

"He threw up his snack," Tracy offered in reply.

Chris's heart skipped a beat. She'd read in the morning paper that a new strain of flu was making its way through Sacramento. She put her hand on Kevin's forehead. He was damp but not hot. "How do you feel now?" she asked him.

"Okay."

"No, he doesn't," Tracy said. "I heard him tell Miz Abbott his tummy hurt."

"Is that right, Kevin?"

"I'm okay now," he said, glaring at Tracy.

"Maybe we'd better stop by Dr. Caplan's just to be sure," Chris said, keeping her voice steady and matter-of-fact. Would she forever be tied to the past where Kevin's health was concerned? All it took was a stomachache and she was right back where she'd been five years ago, her heart racing, her mind set on panic.

"I'm okay," he said with a show of impatience.

"Still—" Chris began.

"Ah, Mom," he wailed, her name drawn out in a singsong. "Stop treating me like a baby."

She gritted her teeth. *Something else I have to thank you for, Mason—Kevin's rush to grow up.*

"All right," she conceded. "We'll wait. But you have to promise me you'll say something if you start feeling bad again. If we get to it right away—"

"Uh-huh," he said, pulling the door closed with a metallic thud.

"So tell me what you did today," Chris tossed out, making a show of letting the subject of Kevin's health drop.

"We pressed flowers," Tracy answered. "But we can't tell you why, 'cause it's supposed to be a surprise."

Chris smiled. With Mother's Day less than two months away, it didn't take a lot of gray matter to figure out what the secrecy was all about.

The rest of the way home, Tracy gave a running commentary on the intricacies of selecting and pressing flowers while Kevin stared out the window.

Mason knocked on the open door to Rebecca's office to get her attention. "Have you seen the report Walt sent over on the hotel?" he asked.

"I had Randy give it to Janet this morning. Have you checked with her?"

"She's at lunch," he said, already turning to leave. "I'll look on her desk."

"Mason?" she called to his retreating back.

"Yeah?" he said, more impatiently than he'd intended. He had a meeting with Travis in fifteen minutes and wanted the report behind him.

"I've been getting some strange vibrations. I think there's something funny going on with Oscar Donaldson."

The sandwich Mason had eaten only minutes before suddenly felt like a bowling ball in his stomach. Rebecca didn't say things like that on a whim. He went into her office, not bothering to close the door behind him. "I thought Oscar told Walt that if we got the commitment to sell mailed out to him this week, he would sign."

"He did. But that was yesterday. He called me this morning and said he wants some more time to think it over."

While Oscar Donaldson's land wasn't pivotal to the riverfront project, without it there would be a crown but no jewel. It included a section that had once been a natural marsh, not remarkable in itself but important because Mason had intended to restore it to its former state, both for the aesthetics and to try to gain some support from the environmentalists.

"Are you sure he isn't just jockeying for a better position?"

"He hasn't played that game with us before. Why start now?"

"So you think someone from Southwest might have been talking to him again?" Mason asked evenly. He had already gone through his own private hell, running around like Chicken Little, covering his head while he waited for the sky to fall, positive that any and every blink by the property owners meant they were being swayed by the "evil forces" of Southwest. He didn't relish going through it again with Rebecca if she had caught his paranoia.

"Why else would Oscar be getting cold feet?"

"Maybe someone from the Sierra Club got to him."

"Get real, Mason. This man has been cited for using banned chemicals."

"How about going over there this afternoon and seeing what you can pick up on? Pretend you went to see Ferguson and, since you were already there, decided to stop by to see Oscar, too."

She sat forward in her chair, resting her elbows on the desk, her chin on her folded hands. "Because Oscar specifically asked me to stay away. He said he'd call me when he was ready to talk again."

"Son of a bitch," Mason said, no longer able to deny the obvious. "They've gotten to him and he doesn't want us to know he's considering their offer."

"That's what I think, too. Now what are we going to do about it?"

"Up the ante—buy it outright if we have to."

"You can't be serious. The bank—"

"I'll cover the cost myself."

Rebecca came out of her chair. "That's just about the dumbest thing I've ever heard you say. There's no way I'm going to let you commit your own funds to—"

"Let me?" Mason exploded.

Unfazed by Mason's anger, Rebecca came around the desk with a determined stride. "I've been with you every step of the way on this thing, but you're going to lose me, too, if you aren't careful. Buying that property with your own money would be crazy and you know it. At least I hope to hell you're not so besotted with this project that you can't recognize—"

"Since when is owning a piece of land crazy?" he asked, outshouting her.

"If that's all this was about, it wouldn't be. But you know as well as I do that the outlay won't stop there. The instant the rest of those people smell cold hard cash, they're going to be on you like fleas on a dog. What are you going to do then? Buy them all out? They're going to have you by the balls, and they're going to squeeze until you scream. Go along with it, Mason, and you'll end up a eunuch."

"Nice analogy," he said sarcastically.

"You don't like it because you know I'm right." Her attention was drawn to someone behind Mason. "Travis—come in here and back me up on this thing."

"What thing?" he asked, stepping into Rebecca's office.

"Mason thinks he can bankroll the riverfront project with his own money. He wants to buy Oscar Donaldson's property out-right—today."

The color drained from Travis's face. He turned to Mason. "Jesus Christ, what've you been putting in your coffee? You pay one of them people, you're going to have to pay them all. The only way you're going to come up with that kind of money is if—"

"I sell something," Mason finished for him.

"The minute you do that," Rebecca jumped in, "everyone's going to think you're in trouble."

"And it won't matter whether or not the trouble's real," Travis added in their verbal Ping-Pong match. "No bank will let you get within ten feet to explain, once the word gets out." Travis jammed his hands in his pockets. "Goddammit, Mason, when are you going to get your head out of your ass on this thing? You're not ready for something like this project yet. If you don't let it go, you're going to go down with it."

Mason had hoped that, eventually, given enough time, Travis would come around and that, even if he couldn't give his whole-hearted support, he would at least stop being the voice of doom. Until this project, the two of them had been a near perfect combination. When Mason's reach had overshot his grasp, Travis had been there both to modify the reach and to find ways to make the grasp larger. But without Mason's need to keep reaching, the company would still be the small-time outfit it had been in Los Angeles.

Not until the riverfront project had Travis stood dead set against something Mason had proposed.

Whether because the effort was too great or because the spirit of adventure was diminishing, Travis had grown wary, occasionally saying things that gave Mason the impression he thought Winter Construction should be content with the niche it had already carved for itself.

"This isn't a stockholders' meeting," Mason said, frustrated with the anchors Travis kept throwing out behind them. "Last time I looked, it was still my name out there on the front door."

"Thanks for straightening me out on that," Travis said. "I'll be sure to keep it in mind from now on." He stormed out of the room.

"Now you've done it," Rebecca railed. "What in the hell did you hope to gain by that crack?"

"There wasn't any other way to get him off my back long enough to do what has to be done. When it's over, I'll apologize."

"And you think that's going to cut it?"

"You're pushing too hard, Rebecca," Mason warned.

"I just have one more thing to say."

"Then say it and get on the road. I want to know what's going on with Donaldson by tonight."

She stabbed him with a piercing look. "The smart rats are the first ones to jump off the sinking ship, Mason. If it turns out that Travis was right about this and you go down with the weight of it, do you really want to go alone?"

He pulled up short under the impact of her words. "They've never jumped before," he said carefully, reluctantly heeding her warning. "And as I recall, this isn't the first time we've been listing."

"Because up until now the respect given has engendered loyalty. But you better believe that without one you don't get the other."

As usual she was right on target and with soft-nosed ammunition. "I'll look for Travis," he said, acknowledging the need to do so.

She nodded. "And I'll find out what I can about Donaldson."

He was halfway out the door when he turned and looked back at her. "Rebecca."

"I know," she said.

This time he couldn't let himself off so easily. "You didn't fool me, you know," he said. "No matter what happens, if I go down, I won't be standing on the deck alone. I could throw you overboard and you'd climb back on." Embarrassed by the words and his need to say them aloud, he glanced away and then, feeling the action somehow diminished the meaning, forced himself to look back at her.

For an instant, as they stood and stared at each other, he thought he saw a glimmer of tears in her eyes; then she blinked and was as clear-eyed as always.

"I just wanted you to know that," he said, relieved to see the corner of her mouth twitching toward a smile. He could handle anything she dished out, except tears.

"You just want me around because I know where the life preservers are."

"Hell, you're not even close. If I'm going to be floating around in that great big ocean, I want someone interesting to talk to," he said, and walked out with a lighter heart than he felt he deserved.

35

Mason was in his office when Rebecca called him from her car phone four hours later.

"Are you sitting down?" she asked.

"Just give it to me," Mason said, leaning back in his chair, drained from the tension of waiting for her call.

"Oscar Donaldson sold his property outright to Southwest an hour before I got there."

"Son of a bitch," Mason breathed. "Why?" he demanded. "Never mind that—how?"

"They were willing to pay him twenty-five percent over what we were offering, but only if he signed today and only if he didn't get in touch with you to give you the opportunity to counter. Donaldson's wife told me that the lawyers for Southwest swept in like a plague of locusts as soon as they heard he had told us he wanted more time."

"What? Say that again."

"Which part?"

"The part about them hearing Oscar was vacillating."

"Oh," she said. "I see what you mean."

"Didn't you say Oscar called you this morning? How could anyone outside this office have known about that?"

"Mason, I don't like what you're thinking."

"Then come up with another explanation."

There was a long silence on the line. "I can't," she admitted. "But who would do such a thing?"

Mason shielded his eyes with his hand, blocking out everything but his thoughts. "I have a pretty good idea."

"You do?" she asked, clearly taken off guard. "Tell me."

"When you get back." He needed time to recover and gather his wits about him, and he needed to do it alone.

"I'll get there as soon as I can, but it's going to be another half hour or so. The traffic is starting to get heavy."

"Don't tell anyone else about this, Rebecca," Mason added as an afterthought.

"Not even—"

"No one."

"Mason, you can't think—"

"I'm afraid I can," he said. "Meet me in my office as soon as you get back and we'll talk about it."

After he hung up, he sat perfectly still at his desk, his anger growing in direct proportion to his self-admonishment for not following his instincts. Physically ill from a fury that had no immediate outlet, he picked up a sheaf of papers and threw them at the wall. The small bundle ruptured on impact, scattering the large white pieces of paper like giant confetti.

Several minutes later, there was a light tapping at his door. Before Mason could answer, Travis peered inside. While they had made their peace, there were still lingering wounds from the battle.

"I'm going to stop by the hotel and then head for home. Is there anything you want to go over before I leave?" He caught sight of the paper littering the floor. "Hey, what happened here?"

"Come inside," Mason said, ignoring both of Travis's questions. "And close the door behind you."

"Sounds ominous," Travis said, only half joking.

"I want to talk to you about Walt."

Travis came inside. "What about him?"

"When you saw him earlier, did you happen to tell him that Oscar Donaldson was getting cold feet about signing?"

Travis shifted his weight from one foot to the other and then back again. "Why?"

"Because I think he's been passing inside information to Southwest."

For the second time that day, the color drained from Travis's face. "What happened?"

"Oscar sold his land to my father not two hours after he talked to Rebecca this morning and told her that he wanted another week to consider our offer."

"I don't understand how that—"

"There's no way my father could have known Oscar was getting cold feet unless someone in this office told him."

Travis swallowed. "You may be right about

that, Mason, but you're way off base thinking Walt's responsible. He wouldn't do something like that. He's not the type."

Mason got up and started to pace, crossing the distance between his desk and the couch in six long, agitated strides. "I've been going over and over it in my mind and it's the only thing that makes sense. Right from the start there was something about him that bothered me. I should have paid more attention to my feelings."

"Screw that notion," Travis insisted. "You're blaming this on Walt because he looks like your brother, pure and simple. You haven't got one shred of proof he had anything to do with what happened this afternoon."

"How can you be so sure I'm wrong?" Mason said evenly.

"I just am. You're going to have to trust me on this one."

Mason stopped his pacing and stared out the window, focusing on the land he'd lost that day. He turned to Travis. "If not Walt, then who?" he asked.

Travis pressed his hand to his forehead, as if trying to hold something in or, failing that, force something out. "How the hell should I know? But the damage is done. There's no good going to come from starting a witchhunt."

Several minutes passed before either of them spoke again. Finally it was Travis who broke the strained silence. "Maybe it's for the best, Mason. You went too far when you let yourself get personally involved in this thing. Now that it's over, you can get on with your life, move on to something else."

"It's not over," Mason said, his voice low and menacing. "Not by a long shot."

"What are you going to do?"

"I'm going to find out who's been leaking the information."

"How are you going to do that?" Travis asked, his face drawn, anxious.

"I'm going to pay my father a visit. It's something I should have done a long time ago. But before I go, there are a few things I have to take care of right here."

"You want me to—"

"No thanks, Travis. I appreciate the offer, but this is something I have to do myself."

"If that's the way you want it," Travis said, turning to leave. He turned back again. "You know, Mason, some things in life are better left alone."

"This isn't one of them, Travis."

He nodded sadly and then left.

For the first time since the idea for the riverfront project had come to Mason, he was concerned about what it would end up costing. Only, unlike Travis, it wasn't the money Mason was worried about.

36

Mason climbed out of the cab, paid the driver, and started up the walkway to his father's house. Fourteen years was a long time for so little to have changed. There was a new palm tree in one corner of the yard and green pebbles where there had once been grass; otherwise, nothing seemed to have marked the passage of time.

The house itself meandered expansively around a courtyard and was built in the traditional Spanish style, with whitewashed walls and a red tile roof. Depending on their mood, observers could look to the west and watch the waves rolling across the ocean or to the east and try to count the city lights that swept up the hillside.

Growing up in this house, he'd taken the beauty for granted. Not until he was into his teens did he realize he led a privileged existence, that not everyone woke up to the sound of surf and sea gulls coming through the bedroom window, and that maids and gardeners didn't automatically come with houses.

His memories should have been good ones. There had been happiness here, at least that was what he told himself the few times he thought about his childhood home anymore. Surely he and Bobby must have been friends once; after all, they were brothers.

And even if his father hadn't liked his younger son, there must have been a time when he didn't actively hate him, either.

Why couldn't he remember the birthday parties and Christmas mornings and laughter over the Sunday comics that must have taken place in this house? Did his father or brother ever think of the good times? And, if they did, was he a part of their memories, or did they blank him out, like cutting an image from a photograph?

How would Kevin remember his childhood? Would he have to struggle to summon memories of the good times? Which corner of his mind would hold the day he and Mason and Chris had spent at the beach? Would the day come when Kevin challenged the way he had been raised, as Mason himself now did?

Mason stepped onto the porch and pressed the doorbell. He listened to the familiar chime, its melody longer than most, and wondered if it still drove his father crazy on Halloween.

Just as the last note was dying, the door swung open.

Iris stood in the doorway wearing an electric blue dress. There were pearls at her throat and a glass of wine in her hand. "My God," she said, her voice an awe-filled whisper. "Is it really you, Mason?"

"I haven't been gone that long, Mother."

She put her glass on the marble-topped table that stood beside the door and opened her arms to him. "I hoped and I prayed, but I never really believed this would happen."

Mason took a step backward. "I haven't come for a family reunion," he said. "I want to see Dad."

Disappointment erased the spark of excitement from her eyes. Her arms fell limply to her sides. "Of course," she said, hiding behind her country club voice. "It was foolish of me to think otherwise."

Mason winced. He hadn't meant to be

cruel. "Is he here?" he asked, softening his own voice.

"I expect him any minute. Would you like to wait for him inside?"

"Are you sure Dad would permit it?"

"It doesn't matter whether he would or not. This is my home, too, you know."

The years might not have changed the house, but they had done something to the woman who lived there. Iris Winter wouldn't have had the temerity to lay claim to the roses that grew in her garden when Mason left home, let alone half of the house. "Since when?" he asked.

"Since the day it finally occurred to me that I've paid for it time and time again with the hours I've spent taking care of it. This house represents the wages I've never collected. Now are you going to come inside or would you like me to bring a couple of the lawn chairs from around back so that we can sit out here while we wait for your father?"

"I'll come in," he said, enjoying the idea both because it would be a thorn in his father's side to come home and find Mason there and because his mother had had the guts to invite him.

When they were in the living room and Iris had offered Mason wine and he had refused, she directed him to a sectional sofa and then sat down beside him, careful not to risk a rebuke by coming too close. "I assume this isn't a social call."

"It's personal."

She folded her hands tightly together and

placed them in her lap, as if seeking a way to keep them still. "Is that why you came here instead of going to the office?"

It was painful to see how hard she was trying. "I got a late flight out of Sacramento. What I have to say can't wait until tomorrow."

"Are you sure it needs to be said at all?" she asked evenly, her tone belying the pleading look in her eyes.

"Still trying to play peacemaker, I see."

She reached for his hand; he moved away before she could touch him. "Do you still hate me so much?"

She was an innocent bystander and he was treating her like an accomplice. "No, Mother, I don't hate you," he said, bending a little. "I just don't trust you. Your loyalties—"

"Are divided?" she finished for him. "How could they not be, Mason?" She sighed in frustration. "Now that you have a son of your own, I pray that someday you'll understand the position that you and your father put me in. But I guess it's too soon for that to have happened."

"How do you know I have a son?" he asked, fighting to keep his voice steady. The look on Iris's face told Mason that she had realized her mistake. The air crackled with the tension between them.

"I can't tell you," she said. "It would mean breaking a confidence."

She had only confirmed what Mason had figured out for himself on the plane coming down. Only his need to deny the truth had kept him from seeing the obvious sooner.

To give himself something to do, he got up

and walked over to the fireplace. He put an elbow on the mantel and stared, unseeing, at the painting on the wall above. "It's fascinating when you think about it," he said. "The person who betrays me is the one who engenders loyalty from my mother."

"You haven't been betrayed."

"Oh, no? What would you call it?"

"The person who told me about Kevin is someone who cares deeply for both of us."

Footsteps sounded in the tile hallway. Seconds later, Stuart Winter walked into the room.

Mason stared at his father. Age hadn't diminished him; if anything, it had made him appear even more portentous. The last of the black had faded from his hair, leaving a leonine crown of gray to frame a face weathered and toughened by years of working outdoors. His body was as lean and unbending as ever, his smirk as denigrating.

Stuart unbuttoned his jacket and propped his hands on his hips. "You're not buying into that crap, are you, kid?" he asked, a self-satisfied grin pasted on his face.

"How long have you been out there listening?" Iris asked.

He ignored her, continuing to focus his attention on Mason. "You know I've never been big on giving advice, but tonight's kind of special—what with you coming all this way and taking the time to stop in to say hello—so I'm going to make an exception. If I were you, I'd be real careful of any man who told me he was stabbing me in the back for my own good."

He chuckled. "Those are the kind of people who bear close watching."

"Stop it, Stuart," Iris said sharply, leaping to her feet. "I've had enough of your hatefulness."

Both Mason and Stuart turned to her, astonished looks on their faces. The mouse hadn't just roared, she'd attacked.

"I won't have you talking to Mason that way," she went on before either man had regained enough composure to comment on her outburst. "You've hurt him enough. It's time to end this feud between the two of you, once and for all."

Stuart's eyes narrowed as he glared at his wife. "I haven't even begun the battle," he said menacingly. "This son of yours is about to learn a lesson at his daddy's knee—one he'll be a long, long time forgetting."

"Why are you doing this to me?" Mason asked, seeing his chance to begin what he'd come there to do. "After all this time, why now?"

Stuart threw his head back and laughed, plainly enjoying what he perceived to be a pleading tone in Mason's voice. "Because the opportunity presented itself, Mr. Hotshot."

"You won't win," Mason warned, making sure there was no shading of doubt in his proclamation.

" I'm warning you, Stuart," Iris said. "Keep this up and there will—"

"Found a nice little stone for your slingshot, did you, Mason?" Stuart asked, dismissing Iris by drowning her out. "Well, I wouldn't put too much faith in that working twice. You may look like a little bit of a man standing beside your daddy, but you're no David."

"And you're Goliath?" Mason asked. "Is that how you see yourself?" He came across the room. "What does that make Bobby? Your shield-bearer?"

"You're running scared."

Mason grinned but was careful to keep it from looking too self-confident. It was important that Stuart see him as stupidly brave, not cunning. "What makes you think so?"

"Why else would you be here?"

"To warn you to back off. Sacramento is mine. Move Southwest up there and I'll crush you." From somewhere in the back of the house came the sound of a telephone ringing.

"How are you going to crush me when you can't even manage your own business?" Stuart tapped Mason's chest with the tip of his finger, driving home the point in the most humiliating way possible, putting himself in the position of a father disciplining his recalcitrant son. "Not to mention the people who work for you."

"Who did you get to do your dirty work?" Mason asked, his heartbeat thundering in his ears. Although the scenario was unfolding precisely as he had planned, he found that he was being caught up in the drama. If he wasn't careful, he would lose the control he needed to pull it off. Just because his father was a pompous ass didn't mean he was stupid.

The phone continued to ring, unheeded.

Stuart's triumphant smile exposed teeth

stained by fifty years of cigarette smoking. "That would be too easy. Why should I tell you who the snitch is when you can drive yourself crazy wondering?"

"Because if you don't, you'll miss seeing the look on my face when I find out."

Mason's logic gave Stuart pause. He appeared confused. Instead of addressing the issue, he turned on Iris. "Would you answer that goddamned phone?"

She looked at her son. "Mason..."

"I'll be all right, Mother," he assured her, acknowledging the gift she'd given him. She could no more protect him against Stuart than she could change the course of what was about to happen. It was enough that she had stood with him, no matter how ineffectual her effort.

"Well?" Mason asked when she had left the room. "Are you going to tell me?"

"I have to admit, it's tempting. But cutting off my source of information now would be premature."

Forcing the issue was the only way Mason had to make his father believe he hadn't already figured out who'd been feeding him information. "You can't possibly think I'm going to confide anything of importance to anyone on my staff until I do find out."

"Even better," Stuart gloated. "It will be interesting to see how long you can last, trying to run the whole company by yourself." He chuckled. "Not to mention what your devotion to duty will do to your private life. This is turning out even better than I had hoped."

He'd hit a soft spot. "I'd sell Winter Construction before I let anything that happened there touch my son...or my wife."

Stuart's mouth opened in surprise. The seconds it took him to regain his composure spoke volumes to Mason. His father knew nothing of Chris and Kevin. And yet, seemingly, he knew everything about the riverfront project. What had appeared straightforward only minutes ago had suddenly become convoluted.

Before Stuart could say anything in reply to Mason's inadvertent slip, Iris came back into the room, a stricken look on her face. "Mason, that phone call was for you. A woman named Rebecca told me to tell you that Kevin is in the hospital."

A sick feeling of déjà vu came over Mason. He struggled to breathe through the crushing weight on his chest. "What happened?" he asked, as terrified of her answer as he was desperate to hear it.

"She said he has the flu. She's going to the hospital now to be with Chris."

"The flu?" he repeated blankly. Why would Kevin be in the hospital because of something that simple? It didn't make sense. And then it came to him: the times Chris had seemed to overreact to one of Kevin's stomachaches, his demand to take Kevin skiing and her countering with a refusal to see him in the hospital again, her fear of taking him into crowds... Jesus, he'd come to know Chris too well to go on thinking of her as simply paranoid and overprotective. Why had it taken him so long to realize his son wasn't immortal?

"I suppose this Kevin character is your son," Stuart said. He snorted. "Somehow it doesn't surprise me that you'd produce a weakling kid."

Mason turned on his father. "Be careful what you say, old man," he warned, his voice a low growl.

"Mason," Iris shouted. She ran across the room and placed herself between the two men. "Don't do anything stupid," she said to Mason, a pleading look on her face. "He isn't worth it."

She faced Stuart. "Get out of here," she demanded.

"No one tells me what to do in my own house," Stuart immediately countered.

Iris turned back to Mason and reached up to cup her hands around his face, forcing him to look at her. "My purse is in the hall closet," she said, talking to him slowly and clearly, as she might to someone who was in shock. "The keys to my Mercedes are inside. Take them and back the car out of the garage. I'll be waiting for you on the sidewalk."

Mason nodded. He looked at his father, not realizing until he found his answering look empty of all compassion that, for one foolish moment, he'd hoped to find a spark of understanding, perhaps even a momentary flash of concern in his eyes. Numbly Mason did what his mother had instructed, unmindful that he had not finished what he'd come there to do.

He found Iris's brown Coach purse on the same hook she'd used since he was a child. Opening the zipper on his way out to the garage, he fumbled through the contents, searching for the keys. When he was standing beside the car and still hadn't found them, he went to the workbench and dumped everything out on the counter. A photograph fell out and drifted to the floor. Mason bent to pick it up and was stunned to see Kevin's image smiling back at him.

Only one person could have given Iris that picture.

He closed his eyes against the pain of knowing. Not Chris, a voice inside him cried out. Please...not Chris. He needed her to be there for him.

Was there no one left whom he could trust?

37

Chris heard rapidly approaching footsteps in the hallway and glanced up from the book she was reading just as Mason pushed open the door to Kevin's hospital room. There was a desperate panic in his eyes that Chris recognized from the countless times she'd seen the same look reflected back to her in a mirror.

Mason had been out of the office when she'd called earlier that day. Chris had left the message that Kevin was in the hospital with

Rebecca rather than Janet, thinking it would be better for him to hear the news from someone who was close to him. Only somehow the information that it wasn't serious, and that Kevin was being admitted more as a precautionary measure than because he was critically ill had gotten lost in the shuffle.

When a frantic Rebecca had appeared less than an hour later and announced she had tracked Mason down in Santa Barbara at his parents' home, Chris had instinctively known the torture Mason would be putting himself through. She'd insisted they try to locate him en route and tell him what was really going on.

After dozens of phone calls, they finally learned that he had hired a private plane to fly him home and that it would be impossible to contact him until he landed. Rebecca had driven to the airport to meet his flight. She'd called a short time ago to tell Chris that she had missed him by minutes.

Now, seeing Mason walk through the fires of his own personal hell, Chris felt her heart going out to him. She got up to intercept him. "He's all right, Mason," she said, making a point of keeping her voice steady and calm.

He ignored her attempt to reassure him, stepped around her, and went to Kevin's bedside. His gaze swept the monitors, the I.V. lines, and finally his son's sleeping face. "What happened?" he demanded.

Chris came up to him. She lowered her voice to a whisper. "He has the flu."

"And?"

"Some diarrhea and vomiting."

"And?" Mason insisted, implying she was keeping something from him.

"And nothing."

He turned on her, anger seething from every pore. "They don't put people in the hospital because they have diarrhea and vomiting."

"If the people are anything like Kevin, they do." She took his arm and made him come with her across the room, where they would be less likely to be overheard. Kevin might not be critical, but he was sick and needed all the sleep he could get.

"What in the hell is that supposed to mean?"

"Kevin dehydrates faster than someone who has all of his intestines," she explained patiently. "He can get very sick very fast and go into shock. Because it's happened twice before, Dr. Caplan doesn't take chances anymore. He starts treatment as soon as Kevin shows symptoms."

He grabbed her by the arms, his voice more a growl than a whisper. "You've known this all along and you didn't bother telling me?"

She wrenched herself free, her patience wearing thin. Mason was carrying his worry about Kevin too far. "During which of the long-drawn-out conversations we've had recently should I have brought it up?"

The angry look on his face turned contemptuous. "You might at least have mentioned it to my mother," he said, pausing to let the words sink in. "I'm sure, under the circumstances, she would have been happy to pass the information along."

Chris felt as if a cold hand had been laid across her back. Why had Iris told him about the visit when she'd been the one who had insisted on secrecy? It wasn't fair. With all she and Mason had already gone through, with all they still had ahead of them, why this? And, sweet Jesus, why now? "This isn't the time or place for us to go into that, Mason."

"Since there isn't going to be any other time or place for us, if you have something to say, you'd better say it now." When she didn't immediately answer, he pushed her aside, dismissing her from his sight as easily as he'd just dismissed her from his life. He picked up the plastic chair Chris had been sitting in and took it with him to Kevin's bedside. He sat down and, with infinite care, reached for the small hand lying on top of the green bedspread.

Drained from all that had already happened that day and in the months that had led up to it, Chris stood and stared at Mason, trying to decide what she should do. It would be so easy to let this be the end of it, to stop fighting, pick up the pieces, and go on with her life.

She flinched at the thought. She wasn't the type to take the easy way out of anything. If there was a bumpy road somewhere, she would find it, all the time trying to convince herself that the unspoiled scenery was sure to make the trip worthwhile.

Whether it made sense or not, she couldn't walk away. She wouldn't give up on Mason, even though he'd obviously given up on her.

Right or wrong, she loved him.

Soundlessly, she slipped from the room and went to the lobby to make a phone call.

Twenty minutes later Mary arrived.

"Why didn't you let me know sooner?" she scolded as she met Chris in the waiting room.

"Everything happened so fast, and he's doing fine. Dr. Caplan said he can probably go home in a couple of days." Anxious to get on with what she'd decided had to be done, Chris turned and started back toward the pediatric wing. "I wouldn't have called you at all tonight, but if Kevin wakes up, I don't want him to be alone."

"I assume this mysterious errand has something to do with Mason?"

"Yes," she admitted. "We have to get some things settled between us. I have a feeling if I put it off any longer, it might be too late."

Mary let out a snort. "It's about time one of you made a move."

They came to Kevin's room. "Give me a minute," Chris said.

Mary nodded in understanding. "I'll wait at the nurses' station."

Chris took a deep breath and went inside. Mason was still sitting where she'd left him, his arms propped on the bed, his hand clutching Kevin's. She went to him and said in a soft but insistent voice, "I want to talk to you."

He didn't look up. "We've already said everything there is to say to each other."

He wasn't going to make it easy. The only

way she was going to get him out of there was to make him angrier than he already was. "For Christ's sake, Mason, stop acting like the little boy who's just discovered there isn't any Santa Claus. If you insist, I can say what I have to say right here, but it will probably wake Kevin up, and I'm sure you don't want that any more than I do."

He hesitated before gently laying Kevin's hand back on the bedspread. When he turned to Chris, there was a fury in his eyes that gave her pause. "I'll come with you, but only because you have something I want."

Telling herself that she didn't care why he came, only that he did, she swallowed a retort and led the way out of the room.

"What is she doing here?" Mason asked, spotting Mary as soon as they were in the hallway.

"She's going to stay with Kevin while you and I talk."

He folded his arms across his chest and leaned against the wall. "Give it up, Chris." Propping one foot up behind him, he stared at the yellow line running down the middle of the floor. After several seconds he looked up at her again. "I told you, I'm not interested in anything you have to say. What's it going to take to convince you?"

Mary left the nurses' station and came toward them. She nodded to Mason, made quick eye contact with Chris, and then went into Kevin's room without saying anything to either of them.

"Let's go," Chris said.

Mason threw his hands up in the air. "I should have known. Nothing is simple or straightforward with you. Well, you can forget it. I'm not going anywhere."

"The hell you aren't," she said. "You owe me tonight, and by God I'm going to collect." She took his arm.

He pulled himself free. "How do you figure?"

There were a hundred ways she could have answered, but they all involved how she felt about him, and to tell him that now would leave her exposed and vulnerable. She settled for the absurd. "Because I let you talk me out of taking the chicken on the picnic."

His answering look cut her with its hostility. "Is this your idea of a joke?"

She decided to ignore the question. "My car is outside. We can take it or we can walk home. Which would you prefer?" It would take less than ten minutes for them to get there, either way, but if they walked, the exercise might work off some of the tension between them.

Mason glanced at the door to Kevin's room. "Are you sure it's all right to leave him?" he asked. It was his first civil question.

"Mary has stayed overnight with Kevin every time he's been in the hospital. I'd trust her with his life. Besides, if anything happens—and it isn't going to—we'll only be a phone call away."

Mason let out a disparaging laugh. "Trust?" he mocked. "It must be nice to feel that way about someone."

She moved in front of him, forcing him to look at her. "I don't deserve that."

He opened his mouth to answer her, then clearly thought better of it. "This isn't the place."

A lump formed in her throat. Now that he'd agreed to leave, she wasn't as convinced as she had been that it was such a good idea. The hospital was neutral ground. At home there would be no reason to whisper or to be as cautious with the words they used.

Realizing she was scared, scared her all the more. It was mind-boggling to think that less than four months ago she had been frantically looking for a way to keep Mason out of her life; now here she was, desperate to find a way to keep him.

"No, you're right—this isn't the place," she finally answered him. She turned to go, letting out a sigh of relief when she heard him following.

Because Mason insisted he didn't want to be out of phone contact any longer than absolutely necessary, they took Chris's car, forgoing the exercise and therefore any possible easing of tension it might have brought to them.

"I'm sorry I didn't have a chance to tell you about your mother before you found out yourself," Chris said, unlocking the front door. Once inside the living room, she tossed her purse and sweater on the closest chair. "I tried several times, but you haven't exactly been the easiest person to talk to lately."

" 'Sorry' doesn't cut it, Chris," he said, moving past her to turn on a lamp. "Not any more than trying to lay the blame on me does. You had plenty of chances to tell me that my mother was here, and yet you chose not to." He turned on her, an accusing look on his face. "For Christ's sake, we live in the same house."

"Why isn't simply believing me an option?"

"Why should it be?"

"Because I've never done anything to give you reason to doubt me."

"That I know of."

"Hold on just a minute." She was glad for the opportunity to bolster herself with some righteous indignation. With little else to support her, she'd take whatever help she could get. "You have no right to say something like that to me, and you know it. I admit I probably should have told you that your mother was here, but at the time I couldn't see anything wrong with giving her a couple of months to find a way to tell you herself."

"Is this why you brought me here, to try to convince me that you're really on my side and that you'd never do anything that wasn't for my own good?"

As if suddenly overcome with exhaustion, he sat down heavily in the armchair beside the lamp, let out a frustrated sigh, and covered his face with his hands. Several seconds later, when he looked up at her again, the mask was back on, his voice flat, defeated. "I already have enough people like that in my life, Chris. There isn't room for any more."

She suddenly realized there was something going on with Mason that she knew nothing about. Somehow, even though she wasn't involved in whatever was happening, it was affecting her. The cold hand that had been pressing itself against her back slithered up her spine and closed around her neck, making her feel as if she were choking. How was she going to fight an unknown enemy?

"Why are you so determined to push me away?" she asked, blindly searching for something that would give her a clue to what was going on.

"I should think it would be obvious. I don't want you. And I sure as hell don't need you. If you weren't Kevin's mother, we would never have had anything to do with each other."

Her options were all gone. He wasn't going to give her the time or the opportunity to slowly lead up to what she had to say. "You're lying."

He sat back in the chair and shook his head in wonder. "Good God, don't tell me you've managed to delude yourself into thinking I care about you."

She watched his face more than she listened to his words. All she needed to know she saw in the haunted, lonely way he looked at her, like a child trying to convince everyone around him that he really didn't care if he was the last one picked to play on a team. His almost frantic need to deny what he was feeling was bound to make her own declaration sound threatening. Still, she played her trump card. "I love you, Mason."

He moaned as if she'd hit him, then looked away. "Don't do this to me, Chris."

"It took me a long time to realize it was happening," she added, her courage faltering at the intensity of his reaction. "So long, in fact," she added softly, "that once I knew, there was nothing I could do about it."

He looked at her, a frightened, hunted-animal expression on his face. "I don't want you to love me."

"I'm not Susan," she said, plunging ahead. She'd come too far not to say it all. "And I'm not Diane. I'm me. I can't promise you I won't get hit by a car someday or that I won't be standing under the wrong building if we have an earthquake, but I've already made it through thirty-seven years. There really isn't any reason to think I won't make it through another thirty-seven."

Unable to keep from touching him any longer, she crossed the room and knelt in front of him, insinuating herself between his open legs. "I won't leave you, Mason. Please don't leave me."

He tried to stand. She gently touched his arms, and the fight drained from him. Slowly he sat back down. When he turned away, she reached up and placed her hands on the sides of his face, turning him to look at her. Somehow she had to find a way to make him understand. "I love you," she repeated.

At last he met her gaze. "I'm sorry, Chris, but I can't love you back." He took her hands from his face.

For the first time it occurred to her that she

might be wrong, that he really didn't love her. "Why not?" she asked, leading with her chin because there was nothing left for her to do.

"It has nothing to do with you," he said. "It's me. You were right. Loving Susan and then Diane changed me. But you're wrong to think knowing you can make it right again. The part of me that might have loved you is gone, Chris. It died a long time ago. There's nothing left."

"I don't believe that." She couldn't.

He grabbed her arms and held her out in front of him. "What is it going to take to convince you?" he asked, a note of desperation in his voice.

Chris felt as if her heart had stopped beating. What had seemed so simple at the hospital—the idea that all she had do was break down and admit to Mason how she felt and everything would fall into place—had turned into a Gordian knot. She could get up and brush herself off and still walk away with dignity—but to what point? She would feel the loss forever.

"Make love to me," she said on impulse. "If you still tell me afterward that you could never love me, I'll accept it."

"Why are you doing this to yourself?" His hands dug painfully into her arms. "Jesus Christ, where's your pride?"

She shrugged. Tears stung her eyes. "I don't know," she admitted.

Long, tension-filled seconds passed. For an instant it seemed he would release her, get up, and walk away. But then he raised his hands and threaded them through her hair, cupping the back of her head and bringing her to him. He opened his mouth and covered hers, kissing her as if he meant to devour her in his hunger.

She let out a cry of pent-up longing and pressed herself against him, fighting to meld herself to him, unable to feel she was close enough.

His tongue sought hers as it tasted, then caressed, then probed. He kissed her eyes, her temples, the base of her throat. She was scorched by his burning need and pulled into the fire storm that his abrupt abandonment of his fight to resist her had ignited.

The clothing between them became an intolerable barrier. With trembling hands, she reached up to take off his tie. It became knotted. She fumbled with the buttons on his shirt, but no matter how she maneuvered them, they would not yield. She didn't understand how his belt buckle worked and couldn't get it to open.

"Help me," she said, her voice shaky with wanting him.

With quick, lithe movements, he stood and rid himself of his clothing. She had started to do the same when he took her hands. He ran his tongue across one palm and then the other and pressed them to his bare chest.

"Let me," he told her. Reaching for the hem of her knit shirt, he pulled it over her head, then unhooked her bra and slid the straps down her arms. When the straps reached her elbows, he paused to cup the weight of her breasts in his hands and let his thumbs pass over the nipples until they were taut and thrusting.

Circling her waist with his hands, he lifted her, bringing first one breast and then the other to his lips, capturing the nipple and sucking it into his mouth, stroking it with his tongue.

Chris wrapped her legs around him and leaned her head back, releasing a cry from a pleasure that was so intense it bordered on pain. Fire raced from her breast through her midsection and then to the aching place between her legs. "Mason," she said. "I can't wait."

She clung to him as he carried her into his bedroom. When they were beside the bed, he set her on the floor and reached out to turn on the light. "I want to see you," he said in answer to her questioning look.

Unerringly, his hands maneuvered the zipper downward on her jeans. He slipped the denim over her hips, catching the elastic of her bikini pants with his thumbs and stripping the filmy material from her in the same fluid motion. Caught in a maelstrom of need, she almost climaxed when he slid his hand back up the inside of her thigh, cupped the dark triangle of hair at the apex, and dipped a finger into her moistness.

As they sank onto the bed, the silk spread yielded sensuously beneath them. There wasn't the time or tolerance for gentle or lingering lovemaking. A desperate, long-denied, and driving need guided Mason as he entered her.

Chris welcomed him, raising her hips to meet his thrusts, opening her mouth to his searching tongue. She entwined her legs with his and then wrapped them around him, urging him to go deeper, to merge himself with her, unable to get enough of him.

Mason called her name and tensed; she could feel him nearing climax. It was a moment she wanted to savor, to witness and remember, but only a second later she, too, was swept into that same torrent, and all rational thought was lost.

She gasped in stunned surprise at the strength of the waves of pleasure that swept through her.

Mason eased her descent with delicate, loving strokes, murmuring softly in her ear, "Thank you for loving me...and for staying with me...and for being strong...and for listening to me...and for caring."

When her breathing had returned to normal, Mason propped himself up on his elbow and stared at her, his look all-encompassing. "God, you are so beautiful, Chris—even more beautiful than I had imagined."

Her eyes opened wide. "How long has that been going on?"

A slow, seductive smile preceded his answer. "Truthfully?"

"Of course," she answered, arching her back to lightly press her breasts to the mat of hair that circled his nipples, needing to touch him, to feel his warmth.

"Almost from the beginning."

She lay back against the softly rustling silk spread and made a face. "In plain words, wanting me had nothing to do with liking me."

He chuckled as he rolled over, taking her with him. "Obviously some parts of me are smarter than others."

For an instant the thought hit her that she was dreaming, that what had just happened between them was too perfect, too wonderful, to be real. The panic must have reached her eyes, because Mason took her hand, put it on his chest where his heart was thundering, and said, "I'm real, and I'm here—and I intend to stay here forever."

"I love you," she said.

He kissed her. "After the way I've treated you, I don't understand what you found to love about me."

She moved so that she could snuggle deeper into his side. "Hmm," she murmured thoughtfully, "now that I think about it, I don't either."

But he refused to be baited. "On the flight home tonight I decided we should call it quits."

"Because I didn't tell you about your mother coming here?"

"No. Because it scared me that I cared so much." He drew her closer and pressed a kiss to her temple. "I'm a coward when it comes to how I feel about you, Chris. Thank God you wouldn't let me run away."

"If you had, I would have gone after you."

He cupped her face with his hands and kissed her. "Ask me for something," he insisted. "I want to give you the world."

"I already have everything I want."

"Then make something up."

She smiled at his eagerness to please her. How had she managed to convince herself that her life was complete, that it was everything she wanted, without him? "I want to know you," she said at last. "To really know you. Things like what kind of little boy you were and what schools you went to and whether or not you played any sports. I don't even know if you like eggplant or whole wheat bread or pumpkin pie—I make terrific pumpkin pies, by the way. Just ask Kevin."

And she wanted him to tell her about Susan and about the year he had spent with Diane, but not now. That would come in time, when the past was made easier by the future they would share.

He picked up her left hand and examined it. "If I promise to answer all of your questions, will you let me buy you a wedding ring?"

"As long as it isn't ostentatious." She grinned. "Nothing over five carats."

He laughed. "I was thinking along the lines of a nice gold band."

They were going to make it. They really were. Chris felt a wave of happiness wash over her that stole her breath. "You said you wanted something from me," she said, suddenly remembering.

"I don't—"

"At the hospital you told me you would go with me because I had something that you wanted."

He hesitated. "It's about Kevin."

"What about him?"

"I was angry, Chris."

"I remember."

Again he hesitated. "I wanted you to give me the years I missed with him."

Even though it was obvious he didn't want to hurt her, his voice was filled with such sadness and loss that it was impossible not to feel his pain. For a long time she thought about what he had asked and then, after telling him she would be right back, she got up, took his robe out of the closet, and left. Less than a minute later, she returned and handed him a thick leather-bound notebook.

"What's this?" he asked, taking it from her.

"The diary I started the day after Kevin was born." She sat down on the bed and tucked her legs beneath her. "You're going to find some things you won't like in there. I'm afraid my thoughts about you back then weren't too charitable."

He set the diary on the nightstand and reached for her. "I love you," he said before his mouth closed over hers.

This time they made love with an exquisite leisureliness that was both a promise and a commitment. Chris couldn't help thinking that, for someone who had never so much as bought a lottery ticket on a whim, she had somehow won the grand prize.

38

Mason quietly laid Chris's diary back on the nightstand and slipped out of bed. So that she wouldn't wake up at the loss of his body heat, he carefully tucked the blanket around her. She'd insisted she wasn't really sleepy and only wanted to close her eyes for a couple of minutes before they got dressed again and went back to the hospital, but that had been an hour ago.

While listening to the soft sound of her breathing, Mason had been reading, experiencing Kevin's first year through Chris's eyes. The view had been sobering, giving him insight into the day-to-day victories and defeats the two of them had faced together.

For over six months, the yardstick Chris had used to measure her happiness was Kevin's success or failure to gain weight. Even ten grams, a third of an ounce, had been enough to give her hope. And then had come the time, after Kevin's second surgery when he was four months old and weighed less than five pounds, when he had lost weight every day. Chris's despair was evident on every page.

When her agony became too much for Mason to bear, he had started skimming, looking ahead for the time when there would again be joy at Kevin's progress. As soon as he realized what he was doing, he made himself go back and read every word she had written. How could he do less? If she had lived through it, he sure as hell could read about it.

The brightest spots were the landmark days when, seemingly overnight, tiny, pea-sized pockets of fat had appeared in his cheeks, when he smiled for the first time, when he made his first cooing sounds.

The diary covered Thanksgiving and told about the pictures of Pilgrims and plump turkeys Chris had taped to Kevin's isolette. Then came Christmas, and the tiny Christmas tree with battery-operated lights that Chris set on top of Kevin's heart monitor. One of the nurses hung a stocking with Kevin's name on it below the tree. On Christmas Eve the stocking grew more and more weighted with presents as each new nursing shift came on duty. On New Year's Eve the intensive care unit broke out bottles of sparkling cider and took a minute to raise paper cups to one another before turning back to their fragile charges. Chris spent the last day of the old year and the first of the new in the same way—sitting in a rocking chair with Kevin in her arms.

Nowhere in the diary did Mason find a place where Chris had allowed herself the emotional release of expressing what must have been her deepest fear—that Kevin might not live. It was almost as if writing it down might somehow have made it come true. But the fear was there, hidden between the lines.

What Chris had experienced with Kevin was an echo of what Mason had gone through with Susan. He knew what it was to live with hope and despair as different sides of the same coin.

A chilling, discomforting thought occurred to him. What if Diane's letter hadn't been waylaid? What if he'd been the one called on to sit at Kevin's bedside? Would he have been able to stick it out, to go through what Chris had gone through?

Thank God those were questions he would never have to answer.

What a bastard he'd been, so easily and arrogantly to think of Chris as having stolen Kevin's wondrous childhood from him.

Suddenly overwhelmed by his need to see his son, Mason dressed quickly. Before leaving, he wrote Chris a note, telling her that since he couldn't sleep and she could, it made more sense for him to go in alone to relieve Mary. The "I love you" that he put on the bottom sent a shiver of pleasure down his spine.

After he placed the note on the pillow next to Chris, he took a moment to gaze quietly at her. It was as if he'd spent the past six years standing on the outside of a fence, his hands clasping the steel bars, staring at the people inside. As much as he ached to join them, he couldn't let himself open the gate and become a part of the world they inhabited because, for all the happiness he saw there, he also saw the chance for more sorrow.

And then Chris had come into his life. Without listening to his protests, she'd flung open the gate and pulled him through. It wasn't until he was past the entrance that he realized he hadn't been standing on the outside looking in; he'd been on the inside of a prison of his own making.

And now he was free.

Mason opened the door to Kevin's room and peeked inside, expecting to see Mary. He was taken aback to find a pretty dark-haired woman with alabaster skin talking companionably to the bright-eyed little boy in the bed.

"Daddy," Kevin cried excitedly when he glanced up and saw Mason.

"It's the middle of the night," he gently chided. "You're supposed to be asleep."

The woman stood and extended her hand. "Hi, I'm Heather Landry. You must be—"

"Mason Winter," he supplied for her.

"He's my dad," Kevin chimed in proudly.

Heather smiled and ruffled Kevin's hair. "I kinda figured."

"Where's Mary?" Mason asked.

"She went down to the cafeteria to get a cup of coffee. She should be back any time now."

"Heather Landry..." Mason mused aloud.

"I was one of Kevin's primary nurses when he was a baby," she supplied. "I was getting off shift when I heard he had been admitted. Wild horses couldn't have kept me away."

"Of course." No wonder her name seemed so familiar. Less than an hour ago he'd seen it in Chris's diary. "I know it's a little late, but I've just come to realize how big a thank-you I owe you and all the other nurses who took care of Kevin. Chris is convinced it was the special care you gave him that pulled him through."

She smiled. "Seeing the bright little boy he's become is all the thanks any of us need. We like success stories, Mr. Winter. They're what keep us going." Her voice grew softer as her gaze went from Mason to Kevin. "Besides, I personally think it was the hours Chris spent at Kevin's beside, telling him about the things that were waiting for him when he got home—the butterflies and rainbows and hot fudge sundaes—that did the trick."

Chris had written in the diary about the promises she'd made to Kevin to show him clouds and snowflakes and all the wonders of the world that were outside his isolette.

"Call me Mason, please," he said to the nurse.

"Look what Heather brought me," Kevin said, holding up several books.

Heather shrugged away the look of gratitude Mason gave her. "There hasn't been a time I've seen Kevin in the past three years that he hasn't had a book in hand, so I went to an all-night market before I came to see him."

She opened the bedside stand and took out her purse. "I'd better be leaving. If my husband wakes up before I get home, he's going to wonder what happened to me."

"Will you come back tomorrow?" Kevin asked.

She bent and kissed the top of his head. "You betcha."

"Thank you," Mason told her, inordinately

pleased to have arrived in time to meet Heather and be given yet another glimpse of his son's earlier life.

"My pleasure." She gave a little wave to Kevin as she walked out the door.

Mary came in five minutes after Heather left. She caught sight of Mason, then let her gaze sweep the rest of the room. "Where's Chris?"

"I left her home—sleeping."

She came across the room. "Coffee?" she offered, holding out a Styrofoam cup.

"No, thanks," Mason said.

"Heather leave?" Mary asked conversationally as she pried the lid off the cup.

Mason smiled at the arm's-length dance he and Mary were doing. They didn't know each other well enough for her to just come right out and ask what had happened between him and Chris, but she was obviously dying to know. "She wanted to get home before her husband got worried."

Mary took a sip of her coffee. Frowning at the taste, she walked over to the sink and dumped the rest of the liquid out. After rinsing the residue away, she sauntered back over to Kevin's bed. Several seconds passed in silence; she fidgeted, Mason watched her, Kevin read his book.

Finally Mary took in a deep breath and let it out as a sigh. "So, did you and Chris finally get it on or am I going to have to lock you two up together until you do?"

After Mason got over his initial shock at her bluntness, he laughed out loud. "Let's just say you won't be needing a padlock."

"Whew, it's about time."

"I take it that means you approve?"

She cocked an eyebrow at him. "You care?"

It wasn't something he'd considered before. "I guess I do," he admitted. "You and John are Chris and Kevin's family. It would make things a lot easier on them to have you accept me."

"Aunt Mary likes you, Dad," Kevin said, looking up from his book. "So does Uncle John. Tracy told me so."

Mary smiled. "There you have it." She grabbed her jacket off the empty bed opposite Kevin's and bent to give him a kiss. "I'm out of here."

She was halfway to the door when Mason stopped her. "Mary?"

"Yes?"

"Thanks." It seemed he'd been saying that a lot lately. "For everything."

She made a breezily dismissive gesture. "What else is family for?"

When she was gone, Mason sat on the corner of Kevin's bed and wrapped his hand around the jauntily protruding foot. "It's the middle of the night. Shouldn't you be sleeping?"

"The nurse woke me up to give me a pill."

"How are you feeling?"

He closed his book and laid it on the bed beside him. "Okay."

"Still throwing up?"

"Huh-uh. They gave me some stuff so I wouldn't."

Several seconds passed in silence. "There's something I want to say that I should have told you months ago, Kevin," Mason said. He stopped to clear his throat. Although he didn't know for sure why it was so hard for him to say the words out loud, he supposed it was because of the relationship he'd had with his own father. All the more reason for overcoming whatever barriers had kept him from telling Kevin how he felt. "I love you."

"I know," Kevin said easily. "I love you, too."

Mason smiled and shook his head in wonder. It pleased him immeasurably to have Kevin receive love as easily as he gave it. "How do you know?"

Kevin looked at him, a puzzled frown on his face. "Cause that's what dads are supposed to do."

Mason gave Kevin's foot a squeeze. "You're absolutely right. You know something else dads do?"

"What?"

"They make their little boys get lots of sleep so they can get well faster."

"Aww, Dad."

"All right," he said, easily yielding. "One story and then it's lights out." He shrugged out of his jacket and draped it over the back of the chair.

"Mary said she would read me two."

Mason eyed Kevin and motioned for him to scoot over so that he could sit beside him. In reality, two stories weren't a lot. He would have given Kevin his own amusement park, if he'd asked. "All right," he said, trying but failing to sound stern. "Two stories it is, but not a page more."

Mason settled himself on the bed and Kevin snuggled into his side. Noting that it was the same side Chris had been snuggling against only an hour before, Mason let himself fantasize about the day when the three of them would prop pillows against the headboard and read the Sunday paper together.

A wondrous feeling of contentment came over him. There had been a few isolated times in the past six years when he had secretly allowed himself to dream again of what it might be like to have a family of his own. Not once had the dream come close to the real thing.

39

A strange feeling of being watched came over Mason, rousing him from the depths of sleep. Reluctant to leave the comfort of a dream in which Chris touched him and held him and told him she loved him, he fought against opening his eyes and ending it. But then, as consciousness took over more and more of his mind, he remembered that it wasn't a dream.

Chris had told him she loved him.

His eyes flew open, and he discovered it was Chris who was staring at him, a smile lighting her face.

"How lucky for you that you picked the one person to sleep with—besides me, of course—that I actually approve of." She spoke softly to keep from waking Kevin.

Mason gingerly untangled himself from his son, stood, and took Chris in his arms. "Good morning," he said, giving her a kiss that left no doubt he believed what he'd said.

She wrapped her arms around his neck. "Oh, it certainly is," she murmured and returned his kiss. "Thank you for letting me sleep."

Mason tensed. "What time is it?"

Chris leaned back in his arms and looked up at him. "Seven-thirty," she said suspiciously. "Why?"

"I've got to get to the office," he said in a rush, grabbing his jacket from the back of a chair. He gave her another kiss, only this time it was hurried. "I'm sorry to run out on you, but I have some things to do this morning that can't wait."

"It's all right, Mason," she told him. "I understand."

Obviously she didn't. How could she? Still, amazingly, she seemed willing to give him the benefit of the doubt. "As soon as this particular bit of business is over, I'll be here for you," he said. He'd waited too long for the gift she and Kevin had given him. He sure as hell wasn't going to screw it up. "I'll explain later—I promise."

Chris caught him to her and cradled his face between her hands. "You don't have to explain anything to me, I know if what you have to do wasn't something compelling, you would be here with us today."

He held her tightly to him. "I love you," he whispered into her ear, wishing the words were

409

theirs alone and that they were as fresh and unique as the way he felt about her.

"Call me if you get a chance. I'll be here all day."

"Tell Kevin I'll be back as soon as I can." Reluctantly he let go of her, feeling a sharp loss the instant she stepped away. He slipped into his jacket, made a move to leave, then turned. "Chris, I'm really sorry. I wouldn't go if—"

"Don't say it, Mason," she insisted. "When you explain or apologize, you take away my opportunity to show you how much I believe in you. Just do what you have to—and come back to us as soon as you can."

She'd just given him the best present he'd ever had. Not trusting his voice, he nodded and left. By the time he reached the parking lot, he was whistling. Realizing the sound was actually coming from his own mouth, he pulled up short.

He hadn't whistled since he was a child— when he'd still believed in happy endings.

As soon as he was behind his desk, he called Rebecca's assistant and left word for her to come to his office the minute she arrived. Less than half an hour later she was standing at his door.

"How is Kevin?" she asked.

"He's fine. The doctor came in early this morning and said if he keeps improving the way he has been, he'll probably let him come home tomorrow."

"I really owe you an apology for scaring the hell out of you the way I did, Mason. I should have checked with Chris before I called you in Santa Barbara, but I went a little crazy myself when I found out Kevin was in the hospital."

"Forget it." Thinking about the end result of her phone call, he chuckled. "You never know, it just might have been the blustery entrance I made that pushed Chris over the edge."

Rebecca cocked an eyebrow at him. "What's this?"

He slid his chair back from his desk and smiled. "Let's just say your lectures on my being the world's biggest asshole won't be needed anymore."

"Hot damn," she said appreciatively. "It's about time."

"I'm loath to admit it, but once again you were right."

She studied him. "As much as I like hearing you sing my praises, my antenna is picking up a signal that says there's another reason you wanted to see me this morning."

He gave her an appreciative look and jumped in. "I want you to find a way to leak the information to Ferguson and Pendry that Donaldson has sold out to Southwest. Be sure you mention the twenty-five percent premium he was paid, and make damn sure no one suspects we're the ones behind the leak."

Her jaw dropped. "I don't get it. You want Ferguson and Pendry to contact Southwest?"

"The sooner the better."

"But if Southwest offers them the same

411

deal, they're going to sell. They'd be crazy not to."

"Precisely. It's what I'm counting on."

She shook her head as if to clear it. "I'm sorry, Mason, but you're going to have to explain. I pride myself on being able to keep up with you, but you've left me in the dust with this one. Yesterday you were ready to tie up your own assets, to buy that property outright, and now you're doing everything you can to make sure it goes to Southwest."

"It took me a long time to see it myself," he admitted, motioning for her to sit down in the chair on the other side of the desk. "When I forced myself to look at this thing unemotionally, I realized you and Travis were right. My plan to tie up operating capital in that property was insanity. I was ready to sink millions into land nobody else wanted, just because my father was breathing down my neck." He chuckled. "That was when it hit me. If it was a liability for me to own the river-front property, then—"

"It would be every bit as big a liability for Southwest," she finished for him, her eyes filled with dawning understanding.

"Winter Construction could still function, albeit not as well, with that kind of outlay."

"But Southwest can't. At least not for long." Enthusiasm sparked her words. "With the majority of their operating capital tied up in land that no bank is willing to take a chance on, they won't be able to put up a condo on spec."

"My father has the impression—which I did

nothing to change, I might add—that I'm so besotted with seeing my dream project built I'll pay any price to get the land back from him."

"And he's wrong?" Rebecca asked hesitantly.

"I may be besotted, but I'm not stupid. I never would have gone through with an outright purchase." Mason smiled. "Especially when there's a better way to get what I want."

"Oh?"

"Think about it a minute. It's so obvious it's laughable. All I have to do is sit back and wait for my father and brother to come to me. Once they realize I'm not going to dangle on the end of their string, they are going to try to get rid of the land some other way. They'll never be able to sell it for anywhere near what they paid for it—no one but me is even remotely interested, and it was ludicrously overpriced even before I got into it."

He leaned against his chair and stretched lazily, as if he didn't have a care in the world. "The way I see it, either Southwest comes to me and sells the land on my terms or they go under because of cash flow problems."

"It's beautiful, a perfect case of poetic justice."

Coming forward and clasping his hands together, he said, "But it will only work if we can get them to bite on the Ferguson and Pendry parcels."

She stood up, a mischievous smile playing around her eyes. "Leave that to me." She was halfway out the door when she suddenly remembered something. When she turned, her smile was gone. She started to say something, hesitated, then finally, reluctantly, went ahead. "Have you talked to Travis yet?"

He should have known she'd only be a step behind him in figuring out who had been providing information to Southwest. "No, not yet."

"Go easy on him, Mason. I know he has an explanation."

His earlier enthusiasm about the day ahead was gone. "I wish I felt as sure," he murmured.

An hour later, uncharacteristically, Mason was still postponing the inevitable. He had yet to leave a message that he wanted Travis to see him. He had, however, called Kelly Whitefield and arranged to have an early lunch with her that day.

Finally he couldn't put off calling any longer. He had the receiver in his hand when Travis appeared in the doorway.

"We have to talk," Travis said, his head low as he stepped inside and closed the door behind him.

Mason glanced up and sucked in a stunned breath. Travis looked a good ten years older than he had the day before. The cutting edge of Mason's anger disappeared on a wave of concern. "Yes," he said. "I think so, too."

"I have something to tell you, and I don't want you interrupting or trying to stop me before I'm through."

Mason dropped the pen he'd been using and folded his hands in front of him. "All right. I guess I owe you that."

Travis nervously ran a hand through his hair. "It was me," he began, not picking up on Mason's statement. "I was the one who told your dad about the riverfront project."

Even though Mason had already figured it out, hearing Travis admit what he'd done was like being hit with it all over again. Why, after Travis had risked everything by abandoning his job with Southwest all those years ago to throw his lot in with a green college kid, had he wound up turning on him in the end? Mason had asked himself the question a hundred times and was no closer to an answer than he'd ever been.

"You really scared me on this one, Mason. No matter how much I talked or how many figures I worked up, you just wouldn't see the hard facts about building the riverfront project. The more involved you got, the bigger it grew, until you came up with the crazy idea you were going to build a city in a city. Every time you added some new building or recreation area, the better the chances became that you were going to get yourself buried under the weight of it." He shoved his hands in his pockets and shrugged helplessly. "There wasn't a thing I could say or do that would even slow you down.

"I couldn't just stand by and watch you destroy yourself. Especially not when I thought about how your dad would gloat."

God, could the answer be that simple? Had

Travis only thought to save Mason from himself? "So you went to him?" Mason asked, still muddy on the reasoning.

"Who else could I go to? The builders around here would have laughed me out of their office or tried to have me certified." His eyes glazed with a deep-seated anger. "I found out through a friend of mine that Southwest was looking to expand their operation. Since Sacramento is the hottest market in the country, it seemed logical they'd be coming here. I knew your old man would jump at a chance to best you in your own backyard, and if he could find a way to play the spoiler while doing it, all the better."

Travis had been right on the mark with that one. The memory of Stuart Winter's triumphant smirk would be with Mason the rest of his life.

"Only I never for a minute believed he wouldn't want to take it all the way and put his own stamp on what you had planned so he could rub your nose in it. But he was too smart for me. He never wanted to build the riverfront project. All he was looking for was a way to make you come crawling to him, and he thought that having something you wanted was the way to do it."

"How long did it take you to figure all of this out?" Mason asked.

"He as much as told me so himself, last night."

Mason felt his heartbeat quicken. He was almost afraid to ask the next question. "Did you say anything to him about coming to me with the information?"

"No. He wouldn't have believed me if I had. He thinks he's got me by the balls and that I won't make a move he doesn't approve first."

Mason let out a mental sigh. There was still a chance his plan would work. Southwest needed more parcels to effectively stop him from building. All he could do now was wait to see if they took the bait. "Whatever you do, don't give him any reason to change his mind."

It took a second for the statement to sink in. When it did, Travis studied Mason through narrowed eyes. "You already knew, didn't you?"

"Not all of it."

"Which part were you waiting for me to fill in for you?"

"The 'why.' "

Travis lowered his gaze to the floor, as if what he was about to tell Mason was too painful for eye contact. His voice caught when he said, "You must have felt pretty bad when it came to you."

"Let's just say I've felt better."

"And now?"

Mason couldn't put a finger on what he was feeling. There was anger and sadness and a terrible sense of loss, but there was also hope. "I don't know," he finally said. "I need some time to think about it."

Travis nodded. "If you decide you don't want me around anymore, I'll understand."

"I wish I could say that's not a possibility."

"It's okay, Mason."

For the past fourteen years the world had been black or white for Mason. Something was either right or it was wrong. Then Chris and Kevin had come into his life and opened his eyes to the beauty of gray. While yes and no were still good answers, "maybe" had taken on an importance he'd never thought possible. How could he dismiss all that he and Travis had gone through together, because of the other man's misguided sense of protectiveness? But would they ever be able to recapture what they'd once had? Wouldn't it be better to make the break clean so that both of them could get on with their lives?

"I just don't know, Travis," Mason said, wishing to God he had another answer.

Travis nodded. "I guess I don't really have any right to expect you to feel otherwise."

Mason clasped his hands, stared at them for several seconds, and then said, "There's something else, Travis." Because he didn't know a gentle way to ask, he just said it straight out. "How long have you been giving the details of my private life to my mother?"

Travis jerked upright, his backbone as rigid as the steel beams he strode with such ease. "That's between her and me."

"Not when I'm the one being discussed, it's not."

Travis thought about it and then, reluctantly, yielded. "We've been in regular contact since the day she showed up at the construction trailer twelve years ago and you gave her the cold shoulder," he said defensively. "She's a fine lady and didn't deserve what you and

Stuart did to her. Maybe now that you've got Kevin, you'll be a little more understanding about what it must have felt like for her to lose her child, and you'll see your way clear to calling her once in a while."

"You could have said something."

"Yeah? And have you tell me I pick her or you. What good would that have done?"

In a perverse way it pleased Mason to know how far Iris had gone to maintain even a tenuous contact with her son. "How often did she call?"

Travis blinked in surprise at the question. "Once, maybe twice a month," he answered, his confusion evident. "She would have called more often, but I could never convince her she wasn't bothering me."

"What kind of questions did she ask?"

"How you were feeling, if you were going out with any nice women, what kind of—" He stopped; his eyes narrowed in anger. "You're not thinking she's been feeding Stuart information all this time, are you?"

What was it about him that made him look for a reason to distrust her? "It's a possibility."

"Not in a million years, and you're a sorry bastard for thinking it." Travis's shoulders sagged in defeat. "There's no talking to you about this. You're going to put clouds in a sunny sky just because you want them there." He turned to leave. "Call me when you decide what you want to do about the other thing. I'll be at the hotel."

Mason sat back in his chair and watched

Travis go, feeling a profound sense of loss but unable to do anything about it. Pretending everything was going to be fine and that they could go on as if nothing had happened was not only foolish, it was counterproductive. Mason couldn't tolerate the idea of having someone around him he couldn't trust.

Even if that someone had become the father Mason had never had.

40

"Daddy's home," Kevin shouted as he ran across the livingroom and into Mason's arms.

Chris followed, wiping her hands on a dishtowel. "I tried to reach you at the office to tell you Kevin was being released early, but you'd already left," she said.

Mason gave Kevin a quick kiss. "I didn't know what to think when I opened the door of your hospital room and you weren't there," he said.

"I'm all better."

"Obviously. But shouldn't you take it easy for a while longer anyway?" He looked at Chris. "Just in case?"

"He's fine, Mason. The doctor said there isn't any reason to keep him from doing whatever he wants."

"Are you sure they know what they're talking about?"

She nodded patiently. "His blood work

all came back normal, and he's over the flu." A smile tugged at her mouth. "The only thing left is a mild case of parental paranoia, but I think we can handle that without Kevin's help."

A car horn sounded outside. "That's Tracy," Kevin said, squirming out of Mason's arms and skipping toward the door. "See you later, Mom and Dad."

Mason watched him go. "I told myself the day was going to dawn when a woman would come between us, but I never thought it would be this soon."

Chris laughed as she took Kevin's place in Mason's arms. "Speaking of women," she said, her voice menacing, "how's Kelly?"

"Mmm, I like that," he answered, capturing her mouth in a deep kiss. Janet had obviously told Chris that he'd gone to lunch with Kelly. "Green is such a pretty color on you."

"Well?"

Needing a physical release for the pent-up happiness that had been building since the day before, he picked Chris up and swung her around exuberantly, glorying in the feel of her and taking pleasure in her wholehearted response. "If I tell you anything, it will ruin the surprise."

"Oh, I love surprises," she said, her eyes sparkling. "But I hate waiting. Tell me."

He slowly lowered her so that she moved along the length of him. "Tonight," he said, his voice a husky whisper. "After Kevin goes to bed."

"How about a hint to tide me over?"

He laughed out loud. God, it felt good. "Hints are always followed by guesses."

"And more hints," she said slyly.

He thought a minute, then reached into his breast pocket and handed her an envelope. "You can see what it is, but you can't look inside to see where it is until tonight."

Chris looked at the envelope and then at Mason, plainly confused. "Airline tickets? What does Kelly Whitefield have to do with these?"

"She owns a travel agency."

She shrugged expressively. "And here I thought..."

He buried his face in her hair and murmured in her ear, "No, you didn't. Not for a minute."

"How can you be so sure?"

"Because you know I love you and I'm exactly where I want to be."

"If this is where you want to be, then what's with the tickets?"

"You've got something against a honeymoon?"

She pressed the envelope against her chest. "No, nothing," she said quickly. "But I thought you had all these things you had to get done at work."

"I called your agency to see when and for how long they could clear your schedule, and then I told Janet to clear my schedule for the same time—three weeks next month. As much as I like to think I'm indispensable, there isn't anything Rebecca or Travis—" He stopped and caught his breath at the sharp sense of loss that followed the automatic mention of Travis's name. "Anyway, there isn't anything the office can't handle."

She pulled back to look at him. "What's wrong?"

It was on the tip of his tongue to deny that there was anything wrong when he realized how much he wanted her to know what had happened. She was intuitive and kind, not one to carry grudges—thank God—and, except when it came to protecting Kevin from someone she perceived to be a womanizing conservative, quick to look for the good in people. "I found out Travis was leaking information to my father and brother about some land I wanted to buy."

"Are you sure?" she asked, stunned.

"He told me himself."

"Why would he do something like that?" She thought a minute, then held her hand up. "No, wait, let me guess. He did it because somehow he got it in his head that he was helping you."

"How did you know?"

"You don't even have to spend five minutes with the guy to figure out that he thinks you walk on water. I know it's a cliché, but what he did probably hurt him more than it did you."

Mason ran his hand through his hair, then stopped to rub his neck. "You're right, but that doesn't change what he did."

"Nothing's going to do that," she said, a sadness in her voice. "If it could, don't you think Travis would be the first one standing in line?"

"What you're saying is that you think I

should forget about it and go on as if nothing happened?"

"Can you?"

"No."

"Then build on it. Talk to him about it until it's not so important anymore." She reached up and tenderly touched the side of his face, comforting him the way she might have Kevin. "You can't throw away fourteen years because of one mistake."

Intellectually he knew she was right, but he couldn't shake the feeling that Travis had betrayed his trust. If you couldn't trust someone, what was left? "I have to think about it."

"Don't make it too complicated, Mason. And don't throw away what you have now for what you think you might feel five months from now. Wait the five months first."

He pulled her to him and held her close, saying nothing for several seconds. "I just need a little more time to think about it."

She wrapped her arms around his waist. "I'm sorry," she said. "I know how this must hurt you."

His automatic reflex was to deny that Travis had hurt him, for all the good it would have done. Chris would never have believed him. Already she knew him too well for him to get away with anything like that. Needing the comfort and security of their earlier easy bantering, he said, "Still want a hint about where we're going?"

The look she gave him let him know she understood what he was doing. "You know I do," she said, playing along.

"It's someplace warm but not tropical."

"Not the desert," she groaned. "I can't take heat. I get all blotchy and sweaty and bad-tempered. You'd be filing for divorce before we ever finished the honeymoon."

If he could stay the rest of his life exactly as he was at that moment, he would die a happy man. "Darn it all—now you tell me."

"You don't fool me for—" The phone rang, interrupting her. She put a hand on his chest. "Don't you go anywhere," she said. "I'm not finished with you."

He brought her to him for a quick kiss. When she met his lips with an open mouth and touched her tongue to his, it was everything he could do to let her go.

"I'll be right back," she promised, wiggling free and heading for the kitchen. "Hold that thought."

The call was for Mason. His eyebrows rose in question as he took the receiver from Chris. She mouthed the name Rebecca.

"You've heard something?" he said into the mouthpiece, barely able to contain his eagerness.

"They bit," she said gleefully. "Your brother is flying up to close the deal tonight."

Mason let out a sigh. "I'm very pleased for them," he said, a smile forming.

Rebecca chuckled. "I'll just bet you are."

Mason's next thought hit him like a bull-dozer: naturally, almost compulsively, he wanted to share the news with Travis. The joy, the feeling of accomplishment, wouldn't be complete without him. Not until that moment had he truly understood what it would mean to lose his friend.

"Have you seen Travis?" Mason asked.

There was a telling pause on the line. "No, but I could find him for you."

"Why don't you do that?" he said, feeling his world right itself. "Ask him to meet me..." Where? Not in the office. That was Mason's territory. And then it came to him. "He said he was going to be at the hotel this afternoon. Tell him I'll meet him there in an hour."

"Anything else?"

"Yeah, tell bookkeeping to give Walt Bianchi a raise."

"Okay..." she answered, obviously waiting for him to comment further.

"I owe Walt an apology, but I'd just as soon not say why. I don't want him to know I ever doubted him. Just tell him I said he's doing a hell of a job."

"Anything else?" she asked for the second time.

"No. Is there something I'm forgetting?"

"I don't know, unless you can think of some reason you wanted to apologize to me, too."

Mason chuckled. "I'll bring you back something from my honeymoon."

"Can I put in a few requests?"

"Call Travis, Rebecca."

This time it was her turn to laugh. "Consider it done."

Mason hung up and turned to Chris. He ran his hand through his hair, then shuffled from one foot to the other. He didn't know how to approach her with the idea that had been fermenting at the back of his mind since he'd talked to Travis earlier. Finally he stopped looking for the right words and just spit it out. "I was thinking about asking my mother to watch Kevin while we're gone," he said, and then quickly added, "If anything should happen, Mary and John are right down the street and it's not like we'll be going on a safari where we can't be reached."

Chris caught her breath in surprise. "Oh, Mason, I think that's a wonderful idea. What made you think of it?"

"It's a long, complicated story."

She tenderly brushed her lips against his. "I have lots of time. And there's nothing I would rather do than listen to you. I want to know everything about you, from the time you were a little boy building sand castles on the beach right up to whatever it was you and Rebecca were just talking about. There isn't anything you could tell me that I wouldn't find fascinating." She stopped and made a face. "Maybe I should amend that just a little bit. You can save the details of your friendship with Kelly for a couple of years down the road."

The truly wondrous thing was that he believed her. He thought about all the meals he'd eaten alone, the newspaper articles he'd read and wished for someone to share them with, the glorious sunsets he'd watched by himself. No more. No longer did he have to live his life in solitary confinement. "I'll tell you what, why don't we save those fascinating tidbits of my life for boring moments on the cruise?"

"Cruise?" she said, her voice high pitched with excitement. "We're going on a cruise?"

He groaned. "Damn it. I didn't want to tell you about it until Kelly had everything confirmed. She still has to find out if the yacht is available."

"We're going on a yacht? I thought people took cruises on great big ships."

"Not this time," he said, taking her into his arms again, unable to get enough of her warmth. "I want you all to myself. Kelly is arranging for a yacht and crew to take us through the Greek islands."

"Uh, I hate to bring this up, but are you sure she isn't going to stick us on a freighter headed for the Antarctic? She's certainly been given plenty of provocation." She grinned mischievously. "It's something I would do."

"I keep telling you Kelly and I are friends." He cocked an eyebrow. "Besides, I understand the food on freighters is fantastic." He gave her a kiss filled with a promise of things to come.

"And to be quite honest about it," he murmured against her lips, "I can think of worse things than spending two weeks under the covers with you trying to keep you warm."

"I thought you said you were taking three weeks off."

"Two for you and me, and one for the three of us. I was hoping that if we invited you to come along, you'd break down and let me take Kevin to Disneyland."

She put her head against his chest. "I think

I'm going to like being married to you, Mason Winter."

"Think?" he questioned, resting his chin on the top of her head.

"All right, I know I am. Now, don't go getting cocky on me."

Mason held her, so overwhelmed with the love he felt that he was incapable of speech.

It was Chris who broke the silence. Snuggling close, she said, "Why don't we celebrate Kevin's homecoming with some Original Pete's pizza after you get back?"

"Sounds like a great idea. Why don't you ask the Hendricksons if they'd like to come along?"

When she looked up at him, there were tears of happiness glistening in her eyes. "Welcome to the family, Mr. Winter."

He kissed the tip of her nose. "I can't tell you how glad I am that you invited me, Mrs. Winter. Especially since there's no place on earth I'd rather be."

A half-hour later, Chris stood at the living room window watching Mason's truck turn the corner as he left to meet Travis. When he was out of sight, her gaze drifted to the sky and fixed itself on a solitary high-floating cloud. She stared at the puff of white for a long time, thinking about the good and the bad that had come into her life in the past six years and how many times she'd stepped from one moving train to another, heading in the opposite direction.

And she thought about the sister she'd lost in Diane, who at one time had been the positive, for-sure, never-going-to-change constant in her life and who, it had turned out, was the most ephemeral.

When they were growing up, it had been Chris who'd taken care of Diane, as was the right and role of all big sisters. Not once had it occurred to Chris that someday, in her sister's own indomitable way, Diane would be the one taking care of her—first with a son and then with the man Diane had loved more than her own life.

For the second time that day, there were tears in Chris's eyes as she whispered, "Thank you, Diane. I promise I'll take good care of them."